VICTIMS OF

"Please don't kill me," Julia Stern pleaded. "Please—"

Her voice rose in the beginning of a scream, then was abruptly choked off.

In the silence, a new voice. The voice of the Gryphon.

"I hope you enjoyed that performance, Detective. I found it exquisite. Mrs. Stern conveyed real emotion, don't you think?"

Delgado shut his eyes. He wanted to turn off the tape, throw it in the garbage. He went on listening. He had to hear.

"You may wonder what I'm up to, Detective. I'm playing a game. A wonderful game I invented. The object is to take living women and turn them into dead ones. . . . Let's see you try to catch me before I kill again. . . ."

SHIVER

New from the #1 bestselling author of *Communion*—
a novel of psychological terror and demonic possession. . . .
"A triumph."—Peter Straub

UNHOLY
FIRE
Whitley Strieber

Father John Rafferty is a dedicated priest with only one temptation—the beautiful young woman he has been counseling, and who is found brutally murdered in his Greenwich Village church. He is forced to face his greatest test of faith when the NYPD uncovers her sexually twisted hidden life, and the church becomes the site for increasingly violent acts. Father Rafferty knows he must overcome his personal horror to unmask a murderer who wears an angel's face. This chilling novel will hold you in thrall as it explores the powerful forces of evil lurking where we least expect them. "Gyrates with evil energy . . . fascinating church intrigue."—*Kirkus Reviews*

SHIVER

A NOVEL BY

Brian Harper

A SIGNET BOOK

SIGNET
Published by the Penguin Group
Penguin Books USA Inc., 375 Hudson Street,
New York, New York 10014, U.S.A.
Penguin Books Ltd, 27 Wrights Lane,
London W8 5TZ, England
Penguin Books Australia Ltd, Ringwood,
Victoria, Australia
Penguin Books Canada Ltd, 10 Alcorn Avenue,
Toronto, Ontario, Canada M4V 3B2
Penguin Books (N.Z.) Ltd, 182–190 Wairau Road,
Auckland 10, New Zealand

Penguin Books Ltd, Registered Offices:
Harmondsworth, Middlesex, England

First published by Signet, an imprint of New American Library,
a division of Penguin Books USA Inc.

First Printing, December, 1992
10 9 8 7 6 5 4 3 2 1

PUBLISHER'S NOTE
This is a work of fiction. Names, characters, places, and incidents either
are the product of the author's imagination or are used fictitiously, and
any resemblance to actual persons, living or dead, events, or locales is
entirely coincidental.

Author's Note

This book benefited immeasurably from the contributions of many people. To all of them I offer my sincere gratitude.

My editor, Kevin Mulroy, carefully guided the novel through several revisions, shaping and focusing the story. His perceptive comments and continuing enthusiasm were truly invaluable.

John Paine, Michaela Hamilton, and Elaine Koster provided additional editorial assistance and kept the revisions moving forward smoothly.

Spencer Marks of the Los Angeles Police Department reviewed the manuscript with painstaking care, pinpointing errors in my depiction of LAPD procedures and suggesting more authentic ways of handling the material. Thanks to his efforts, the police scenes have a ring of truth they otherwise would have lacked.

My agent, Jane Dystel, diligently looked after my interests at every step of the publishing process. Her professionalism, courtesy, and continuing belief in the merits of the project made my work much easier.

Finally, a few words of thanks to my friends in L.A. for tolerating my newfound interest in serial killers; to mystery writer Ed Gorman, who kept my spirits up with good advice and positive feedback; and to my parents for their support, encouragement, and love.

Prologue

For two weeks he'd been watching her. Every day, when he came in for lunch, he sat in the front of the restaurant, near the window, so she would be the one to take his order. Sometimes he hesitated over his selection of dessert, just so he could look at her a little longer.

Today he'd decided to make his move. Almost decided. The truth was, he couldn't decide. He wasn't sure what to say. He'd rehearsed a hundred possible approaches, but none was quite right.

She stepped up to the table, her apron rustling prettily, its lace frill catching bars of mote-dusted sun. Terror surged through him and receded, leaving the calm certainty that he would not do it today. Tomorrow, maybe. Yes. He would do it tomorrow.

" 'Afternoon," she said with a smile as she flipped open her notepad.

"Hello," he answered, then instantly regretted it. "Hello" was all wrong—too formal—"hi" was what he'd meant to say. Dammit, he'd practiced saying "hi," and now he'd blown it. She must think he was some kind of jerk. She must think—

"You come in here a lot, don't you?" she asked.

His heart sped up. She was talking to him.

7

Making conversation. She'd never done that before. He didn't know how to respond. He gave it his best shot.

"Uh-huh." That wasn't enough. "A lot," he added.

He was making a fool of himself. She would start laughing at him in a minute, and then the other patrons would stare. Maybe they would laugh too. Laugh and point. He fought the urge to bolt from his chair and escape into the crisp winter sunlight.

"My name's Kathy, by the way."

He'd known her name, of course; it was embossed on the blouse of her uniform. He'd passed many hours late at night hugging his pillow and whispering that one word—"Kathy, Kathy, Kathy"—his voice husky with longing. But even so, he was stunned to hear it from her mouth, offered to him as a gift.

He knew he had to answer. What would a person say?

"That's a very nice name," he tried.

She giggled.

Her laughter cut him like glass. He was sure he'd messed up. And he knew why. He should have offered his own name in exchange for hers. That was what people did. They told one another their names.

"I like it," she said.

"Huh?"

"My name. You said it was nice, and I said I like it. You know."

"Oh. Yes." He was trying to concentrate, but the images kept getting in his way—soundless heat-lightning flashes of her body entwined with his.

"Although I always liked my sister's name better. Eleanor. Isn't it nice, the way that just sort of flows?"

"Yes," he said again.

Suddenly he wanted her to stop talking. He wanted her to go away. It was too hard, sitting here and fighting for calm with her breasts inches from his face, the smooth skin of her cleavage exposed in the vee of her blouse, the smell of her hair invading his nostrils and making it difficult to breathe.

"There's a poem with that name in it," she said. "I remember it from school. This guy who's dreaming about his lost Eleanor."

He blinked. She was thinking of "The Raven," wasn't she? Poe's lost Lenore. Not Eleanor. Lenore.

Suddenly he felt superior. She was the one making mistakes now. He could laugh now, if he wanted to. Laugh at her ignorance.

He decided to do it today after all. To take the opportunity she'd provided him, while he was feeling strong.

"Listen," he said quickly, rushing the words out before his confidence could evaporate, "I've been thinking of seeing that Robert Redford movie, *Out of Africa*, the one that's up for all the Oscars. It's playing at the Rivoli. And I . . ."

This was no good. He'd rehearsed these words, but they sounded wrong here, in front of her. False. Inept. His momentary illusion of superiority had vanished. So what if she didn't know Edgar Allan Poe? She knew plenty of other things. She knew what it was like to be naked with another person. She knew how it felt to kiss open-mouthed, to share tongues. She knew about all the wet secret things that went on in the dark.

"Well, I thought . . . I thought if you wanted to . . ."

His fear was escalating. He felt sick. He could imagine himself throwing up right here in the middle of the restaurant—the bright splash of vomit on the floor—screams, then laughter—Kathy backing away with disgust in her eyes.

No. Come on. Stay in control.

". . . on Saturday night . . . maybe we . . ." His voice trailed off. In his ears it was a whipped dog's whimper.

She frowned. "This Saturday? Oh, jeez, I wish I could, but I can't."

Fear fisted over his heart. She was turning him down. Rejecting him. He'd known it was possible, but now it was real. She didn't want him.

"Okay," he said tersely, wanting only to end this conversation immediately.

"It's just that I've got something planned."

"Sure."

"Look, maybe some other time . . ."

His chair scraped back. He was on his feet. He had to get out.

"You're taking this all wrong," she said.

"Just forget it, all right?"

She spread her hands. "I'm . . . I'm sorry."

Oh, she was sorry for him now. Poor little baby—that was what she was thinking. Pathetic little half-man. How sad that such a miserable loser had deluded himself into believing that he could ever take her out on a date. How pitiful he must be in his lonely apartment with his face pressed to the pillow whispering her name.

He brushed past her, then turned.

"It's lost Lenore," he told her. "Not Eleanor. You stupid cunt."

He slapped her hard across the face, and she fell to the floor in a graceless tangle of limbs, and then he was running out of the restaurant into the cold clear daylight before anyone could stop him.

At first it was only a fantasy. A pleasant daydream, unusually vivid. He would stop whatever he was doing and run the images like a filmstrip in his mind, filling in details one at a time, revising as he went.

Her eyes would be very wide, bright with fear—no, he couldn't let her see him. A blindfold, then. Yes. He would sneak up on her from behind and knock her unconscious, then quickly blindfold her and bind her wrists with rope. Uh-uh. With tape. Heavy strapping tape. Better. Then he would put her in the front seat of his car . . . no, in the rear. Not seated, but stretched lengthwise. Perhaps her ankles ought to be taped too.

All right, start over. First knock her out, then blindfold her, then tape her wrists *and* ankles, and next . . .

The fantasy occupied his mind for months. Winter yielded to spring, and spring to summer. He changed jobs several times. He did not return to the restaurant. He kept expecting his daydreams to fade away, as other, similar reveries had gradually lost their power to move him in the past. But even when dry leaves scraped the sidewalks and Halloween pumpkins began grinning at him from shop windows, he remained haunted by the vivid pictures in his mind, as clear as movie close-ups, and by the sounds, soft and secret and erotic.

Her body slumped in a chair, tied down with clothesline, in the musty, cavernous basement of the abandoned factory. Her shoulders jerking as she came to. The sudden flush of panic in her cheeks, the squeals of protest muffled by the gag in her mouth. Her head whipsawing in a futile effort to shake off the blindfold. Her taped wrists twisting helplessly behind her back. The pop-pop-pop of bursting buttons as he peeled open her blouse. His hand on her breast, massaging gently, gently.

He wasn't sure exactly when it occurred to him that he could actually do it, make it happen, make it real. In time with the idea he felt a thrill of dark pleasure, a slow, prickling current that started in his groin and radiated outward to set his body tingling.

Yes, he thought, *I could do it. But I won't. Too risky.*

He was sure he would be the obvious suspect. After all, many people had seen him slap her.

But as time passed, he began to wonder. Who would connect an incident from last year with a kidnapping today? Besides, even if he were suspected, the police would have no proof; he would see to that. Nor would they have any means of tracking him down. He'd never told Kathy his name—how clever he'd been to avoid giving himself away like that—and the restaurant had no record of him that could be traced; he'd paid for all his meals in cash.

He really could pull it off. Kidnap her, take her to the old factory, and then . . . touch her body. Nothing more than that. He wouldn't hurt her, that was for sure. Not much anyway. Maybe a little bit. But not like the animals. The animals were entirely different. The animals had nothing to do with this at all.

No, he would have his fun with her, and then he would let her go. And because she had been blindfolded the whole time, she would never know who had been with her in the dark.

It could work. It definitely could work.

He went over the same line of argument many times, and always concluded angrily that there was no point in considering the idea. Because even if he could get away with it—and he was pretty certain he could—even so, he wouldn't try. The whole thing was crazy. Sure it was.

The jack-o'-lanterns vanished from the windows, replaced by papier-mâché Pilgrims, then by Christmas trees. A full year had run its course since she'd humiliated him, and still he lay awake at night while in his thoughts she whimpered and squirmed.

A week before Christmas he found himself in an office-supplies store looking at rolls of strapping tape. In that moment he knew he really meant to do it. He bought a ten-yard roll and stashed it in the dark recesses of his closet like a guilty secret.

The next day he drove to the restaurant. He wondered if she still worked there. He almost hoped she didn't. If she'd moved on to a new job, he would never be able to find her, and he would have to let go of the idea for good.

But when he studied the restaurant from across the street, he saw her at once, gliding past one of the front windows. She wore her hair differently now, but otherwise she was unchanged. Still an ignorant bitch who thought herself superior to him.

He watched the restaurant for several days, till he knew her schedule. Her shift began at seven in the morning and ended at four in the afternoon, when the early winter dusk was settling over the streets. She always left alone via a side door that opened on the parking lot where her car was kept. The lot was screened off from the street by a high brick wall. If he struck quickly, nobody would see.

He decided to do it next Tuesday. Over the weekend, while Christmas carolers went from door to door and street-corner Santas rang Salvation Army bells, he made his final preparations.

Monday night was hard. Fear cheated him of sleep. He paced his apartment, his thoughts confused. Did he honestly intend to go through with this plan of his? He'd never acted on any of his previous fantasies. Not the ones involving women, anyway. The animals . . . Why did he keep thinking about the animals? The animals were irrelevant.

The thing was, he wanted to do it so very badly. He could feel desire burning inside him like acid. Somehow he had to relieve that urge. He supposed he could masturbate—that might release the tension at least temporarily—or get hold of a cat and pretend it was her.

But he kept thinking of how she'd said she was sorry. The pity in her voice. The contempt in her eyes. The smile playing at the corners of her mouth.

Abruptly he stopped pacing. "I'll do it," he said aloud. The words sounded unreal, and he wasn't sure he'd actually spoken. "I'll do it," he said again, defiantly this time. "I will."

He knew he was serious this time. He had

made his choice. And in making it, he saw that he had reached a turning point in his life. From this point on, he would not be an ordinary man.

Fresh-fallen snow glazed the asphalt, shining wetly in the twilight. He crouched in a pool of shadow near the side door of the restaurant, exhaling frost, waiting. In one gloved hand he held a length of steel pipe sheathed in foam rubber, a homemade blackjack. He rapped it slowly, rhythmically, against his open palm.

Though he intended to strike from behind, he'd taken precautions to ensure that she would not glimpse his face. He wore a black wool hat, pulled down over his forehead, and a black scarf, raised to cover his nose and mouth.

In the pockets of his coat he carried the roll of tape for her wrists and ankles, the wadded rag that would serve as a gag, and the strip of black velvet he would use as a blindfold.

He was ready.

One thought beat in his brain: *It's real this time.*

Without warning the door creaked open and clanged shut, and there she was, a yard from him, her slim body tucked into a fur-collar coat, her feet clad in squishy rubber boots.

Don't think. Do it. Now.

He sprang up behind her and brought the blackjack down on the back of her head. She staggered, lurching away from him, but didn't fall.

No. That was wrong, all wrong. She was supposed to crumple on the ground at the first blow; that was how he'd always pictured it when he ran this scene over and over in his mind.

He tried to hit her again, but she spun out of

his grasp and whirled on him, the first warbling note of a scream rising in her throat.

He smacked her in the mouth with the padded pipe. She went down. He fell on her. Her hands flew at his face, stripping off the scarf, and suddenly she was looking at him with recognition in her eyes.

She sees me, he thought in escalating terror. *She can identify me now. It won't do any good to blindfold her—*

Sharp nails raked his cheeks. Blood, his blood, spattered the snow.

Fury seized him. She wasn't supposed to fight back. In all his hundreds of fantasies, never once had she fought back. God damn her, she was ruining *everything*.

He slammed the blackjack down on her face. Bone cracked. The sound made him shiver. He remembered the kitten he'd put in the vise, the snap of its leg.

No, don't think of that. Not the animals. This isn't supposed to be like the animals.

But why shouldn't he think of it? What made her better than an animal anyway? What gave her any greater right to live, after the way she'd treated him? The strays he'd collected and taken to the old factory—they'd never done anything to him at all, while this bitch had humiliated him and hurt him and made him bleed. And if he let her go, she would send him to jail.

She clawed him again. The pipe rose and fell. Her nose crunched wetly, like a snail. She writhed on her back, a child making a snow angel.

She didn't look so smugly superior now, did she? She wasn't laughing at him now. And she would never laugh again.

He delivered blow after blow with the pipe while she struggled under him, her head rolling, her back arching, her fingers moving blindly over his body. It felt like sex, like those secret things people did in the dark. Dimly he knew he was being intimate with her in a way he'd never expected.

Finally she lay still. He scrambled off her body, looking down at the crumpled shape on the ground. He almost fled, then hesitated. Slowly he unbuttoned her blouse and cupped her breast with a gloved hand. He squeezed, his fingers kneading the soft flesh still warm as if with life. He had never felt a woman's body before, except in dreams.

"Sweet," he breathed. "So sweet."

He brushed a stray hair from her bloodied face. His mouth found hers. He planted a light kiss on her lips, then shyly pulled away.

"I love you, Kathy. Love you. Love you."

It occurred to him that he could do whatever he liked with her, and she couldn't stop him. He wanted to; he really did. But he was afraid to linger. At any moment someone else might enter the parking lot.

Reluctantly he abandoned her body and ran to his car. He pulled out of the lot and drove aimlessly till he was sure nobody was following him. Then he parked on a side street and sat behind the wheel, letting out long slow breaths till the windshield was filmed with fog.

He'd killed a woman. Not a fantasy creation, and not one of the animals either, but an actual human being. She'd been named Kathy, and she'd worked at a restaurant, and she'd had a sister named Eleanor, and she'd misquoted Edgar

Allan Poe. Now she was a huddle of bloodied meat. And *he* had done it with his own hands.

Yes. He'd done it, all right.

And it had felt good.

Slowly he smiled. A year ago he'd been afraid of that woman. He'd been terrified to ask her out on a date, terrified that she would reject him, as indeed she had. He'd thought she had some sort of power over him.

Now he knew what true power was and who had it.

And he knew that he need never be afraid again.

1

Sebastián Delgado put down the psychological profile from the Behavioral Science Unit and massaged his burning eyes with his fingertips. He'd read the paper at least a hundred times, and it had told him nothing. He wondered if the experts knew any more about this case than he did, or if any rational person could be considered an expert in such matters.

He checked his watch. Five-thirty A.M. His gaze drifted to the cot in the corner of his office, where he'd been stealing rare, restless cat naps for the past four weeks, ever since the investigation had shifted into high gear. The cot was inviting, but he was too tired for sleep, and he didn't want to dream again.

Abruptly he stood up, scraping his chair away from his desk. He needed air. As much air as he could find in the windowless labyrinth of the Butler Avenue station.

He left his office and wandered the hallways. Drunken shouts rose like the wails of alley cats from the lock-up area in the rear of the building. Phones rang and went unanswered.

He entered the Detective Unit squad room, the walls covered with collages of mug shots and departmental memoranda, and crossed to the basin in the corner. He splashed cold water on his face, then dried himself with a paper towel from a dispenser.

On the way back to his office, he saw Detective Tony Sachetti standing outside the closed door of an interrogation room, pouring himself a cup of coffee and muttering irritably.

"Something wrong, Tony?"

Sachetti looked up, startled. His heavy eyebrows lifted in mild surprise. "Don't you ever go home?"

"Not recently. What have you got?"

The smaller man released a grandiloquent sigh. "Real piece-of-shit case. The thing of it is, it should be open and shut, but it's not. Something's screwy."

"Let's hear it."

"Haven't you got enough to worry about?"

Delgado chuckled. "More than enough. Let's hear it anyway."

"Guy named Ruiz is coming out of a bar in Mar Vista, near Palms and Centinela, about four hours ago, at one-fifteen. His car is parked on the street. He's fumbling with the keys when somebody decides it's payday. Either Ruiz puts up resistance or the robber gets nervous; one way or the other, Ruiz winds up being knifed in the neck. Just then, a black-and-white swings by. Suspect takes off on foot and ducks into an alley. Another unit cuts him off at the opposite end. He's collared. Paramedics declare Ruiz dead at the scene, so it's a homicide, and we've got our man. Nice and neat, huh?"

"Sounds like it."

"Except for one problem. The knife. He didn't leave it in the body, so he must've still been carrying it when he started running. But when he got nabbed, he didn't have it on him. Only place he could have ditched it was the alley. But I've got ten guys pawing through garbage and looking under parked cars, and they can't find diddly. That knife has done some kind of disappearing act."

"Can't you make him anyway?"

"We can make him, yeah. But without the murder weapon, I don't know if the D.A. will file."

Delgado frowned. "Let me talk to him. What's his name?"

"Leon Crowell."

Delgado pushed open the door and entered the interrogation room. A young black man, his head shaved bald, sat in a straight-backed chair, his left wrist handcuffed to a steel ring bolted to the wall. He wore a leather jacket emblazoned with the silver and black logo of the Los Angeles Raiders, an outfit favored by youthful offenders in L.A. Delgado had never been sure whether it was the team's rebel image or simply the bold color scheme that attracted the interest of streetwise criminals; but he'd caught himself thinking, at times, that the city's crime rate might not be rising quite so fast if the Raiders had stayed in Oakland.

"Hello, Leon," he said, making no effort to sound friendly.

Leon pursed his lips like a pouting child. "I got nothing to say."

"My friend here"—Delgado indicated Sachetti—"seems to think you killed a man tonight. Want to tell me why he's wrong?"

A shrug. "Man, I don't know nothing about that. I was just out for a walk, you know?"

"At one-fifteen in the morning?"

"I get sort of restless sometimes."

"Why were you running?"

"I like to run, is all. Exercise."

He scratched his nose with his right hand. Delgado studied that hand. A ring of dirt, a perfect circle an inch and a half in diameter, was printed faintly on the palm.

"It's a public street, man," Leon was saying. "Public property. I can run on it if I want to. Says so in the Constitution."

Delgado smiled. "You're a smart fellow, aren't you, Leon?"

"Smart enough."

"I'll bet. But I'm smart too. Do you want to see how smart I am?"

"I don't want to see nothing."

Delgado turned to Sachetti. "You said there are cars in that alley?"

"Yeah. It's right behind the bar, and some of the staff park there. But we searched the cars, Seb. Nothing underneath, and nothing inside."

"No," Delgado said. "Leon's too smart for that. Leon, show Detective Sachetti your hand. Your right hand."

"Say what?"

"Do it."

Slowly, suspiciously, Leon raised his hand. Delgado twisted his wrist, angling the dirty palm at the overhead fluorescents.

"Hey, man," Leon whined, "let go of me."

Delgado ignored him. "See that, Tony?"

Sachetti leaned closed. "I see it. Now tell me what it means."

"It means Mr. Crowell is a quick thinker. He sprinted into that alley, and he knew he had no more than two or three seconds to dispose of the knife."

"There never was no knife," Leon said, his voice reedy with the first piping note of desperation.

"So he ran to the nearest available hiding place," Delgado continued. "One of those cars. He crouched down and shoved the knife into the exhaust pipe. When he did so, his palm made contact with the end of the pipe, which left the circle of dirt marked there."

"I'll be damned," Sachetti muttered.

Delgado released Leon's hand. "Tell your people to check the exhaust pipes, Tony. One of them will contain a surprise. A surprise with Mr. Crowell's fingerprints on it, not to mention Mr. Ruiz's blood."

Leon shifted in his seat and knocked his sneakers together. "Shit."

"I'll tell you something, Seb," Sachetti said with a smile. "That fucking birdman you're looking for doesn't stand a chance."

Delgado sighed. "I hope you're right."

As he returned to his office, Delgado found himself envying Tony Sachetti. The man was out there working the streets, hauling in punks like Leon Crowell, accomplishing something. Yes, that must be nice.

He remembered the quiet excitement he'd felt when he'd been assigned to lead the task force a month ago, after the second victim was found. He hadn't even minded seeing the rest of his caseload transferred to other officers. He was intoxicated with the luxury of devoting twenty-four hours a day to a single case, supervising seventy-five detectives, uniformed cops, and plainclothes officers all working with equal single-mindedness.

It was the kind of massive, resource-intensive investigation that could be launched only when a case was sizzling with media heat, heat that had made it the top priority of the political heavy-hitters downtown.

But after four weeks spent killing himself with work and worry, his excitement had faded, replaced by frustration. He was no closer to a solution than he'd been at the beginning.

Out-thinking Leon Crowell was easy. But the man Delgado was hunting, the man who held the city in the cold clutch of fear, was no small-time street punk. That man would not make the easy, obvious mistakes.

Delgado closed the door of his office and sat at his desk. He picked up the BSU profile and, for no particular reason, began reading it again. He was still on the first page when the telephone rang.

Slowly he lowered the report, looking at the phone, while a chill fluttered briefly in his gut.

He knew. Even before he lifted the handset from the cradle, he knew.

Four minutes later he was guiding his unmarked Chevrolet Caprice south on Sawtelle Boulevard, then east on Pico. He drove fast, whipping around slower traffic, grateful that the streets were still largely empty; rush hour would not begin till seven.

From the crosstalk crackling over the radio, Delgado gathered that Detectives Nason and Gray were already on the scene. Apparently they'd been heading home after a nightlong stakeout when the 187 came in; although not part of the task force, they'd volunteered to secure the crime scene and supervise the uniforms until Delgado arrived.

At six-fifteen he turned onto a narrow residential street lined with thick-boled date palms and leafless elms. Yellow evidence tape had been strung between trees and hydrants to cordon off half the block. Delgado was pleased to see that Nason and Gray had protected a wide area; it was possible, however unlikely, that tire tracks or a discarded object might be found in the street.

The TV crews and print reporters had yet to arrive. A few neighbors in tossed-on street clothes or robes and nightgowns stood well back from the ribbon, their staring faces flashing red, blue, red, blue in the stroboscopic light of patrol-car beacons. The dawn sky, cloud-wrapped, was the color of bone. The air was thick and clinging, like fog.

Delgado parked alongside the cordon, got out of the car, and approached the nearest of the uniformed cops guarding the scene. He flipped his badge at the man, more out of habit than necessity; most of the beat cops knew his face.

"Good morning, Detective."

"I wish it were."

He stepped over a sagging stretch of ribbon, his long legs clearing it easily, and walked swiftly down the street, trailing plumes of breath.

The house was a stucco bungalow indistinguishable from the others lining this street, one sad little box among hundreds of thousands of boxes checkerboarding Los Angeles. Its ordinariness was redeemed only by a garden in the front yard, splashed with waves of silver-blue juniper, spiky yuccas, and snow-flurry dwarf asters.

On the street outside, Nason and Gray were waiting. Delgado shook hands with each in turn.

Frank Nason was a large loutish man, as tall as Delgado and twice as wide, with a battered nose squashed sideways across his face. He made a sharp contrast with Chet Gray, small, soft-spoken, sad-faced. Together they gave the impression of an ex-prizefighter in the company of an unusually somber funeral director. Despite their differences, the two cops had been partners a long time, and, like an old married couple, they had grown to resemble each other, not physically, but in their mannerisms, thought processes, and patterns of speech. Delgado had seen the same phenomenon many times, and it always secretly amused him.

"You got here in a hurry," Gray said.

"I broke some laws."

"Good thing, too. Gonna be a circus. Channel Four is on their way over, so you know pretty soon all the other TV assholes will be doing stand-ups, getting video of the body bag on the stretcher."

"If it bleeds, it leads," Nason said, quoting the alleged motto of all local news teams.

Delgado surveyed the area. He saw perhaps a dozen uniforms; nobody else. The only sounds were low, uneasy conversation and the intermittent crackle of the beat cops' radio handsets.

"Under the circumstances," he said, "I would have expected a greater display of political firepower. Where are our friends from City Hall?" He spoke slowly, his diction impeccable as always, his words edged with the trace of an accent from the Guadalajara *barrio* of his childhood.

"Those pretty boys are still curling their hair to

look nice for the cameras," Nason replied with a snort. "They'll be here when the tape rolls, not before. The mayor's office is sending somebody, ditto the D.A. And you can bet the chief will want to pose for his picture."

Delgado shrugged, having already lost interest in the subject. "What was his means of entry?"

Nason picked at something green in his teeth, working his thumbnail like a dental tool. "Kitchen window. Want to take a look?"

"Later. First give me the rest of what you know."

"This place is owned by Elizabeth Osborn," Gray said. He spelled the last name. "Real-estate agent. Thirty-four. Divorced. She goes jogging every morning with a friend of hers from down the street."

Gray paused, and Nason picked up the story smoothly. Delgado thought of the '88 Lakers, of Magic passing the ball to Kareem.

"Friend's name is Lucille Carlton," Nason said. "So today, at five-thirty, Carlton jogs over here as usual. Sees the door is open. Lights are on. She takes a peek, has herself a coronary, and scrams."

"She runs back to her house," Gray said, "and nine-elevens it."

"Where is she now?"

"At the station, I think. Unless maybe they took her to the hospital. She's in bad shape. In shock, almost."

"I take it Ms. Carlton believes the deceased is Elizabeth Osborn."

"She thinks so." Nason finally succeeded in dislodging the green thing in his teeth. He flicked it away and watched its arc. "Almost sure. But . . ."

"But she can't make a positive I.D.," Delgado finished for him.

"Can you blame her?"

"No. I can't." Delgado sighed. "Who was the First Officer?" The first officer present at the scene, he meant.

"Stanton. Over there."

"I'll get his report. In the meantime, I want a modified grid search of the crime-scene perimeter. The gawkers and loiterers—we need their pictures taken. Surreptitiously, of course. Have the SID shutterbug do it. And send a couple of uniforms to record the plates of every car parked within a radius of three blocks. My people will track down the owners and conduct interviews later."

"You think the scumbag would hang around?" Nason asked doubtfully.

"With this one," Delgado said softly, "anything is possible."

Stanton was standing near a palm tree, one hand holding fast to the rough diamond-textured trunk. The patrolman was young, maybe twenty-two, still starchy with Academy training. He looked green in both senses of the word. His eyes kept wandering toward the house, then away. His lips wore a wet sheen.

Delgado identified himself, flipped open his memo pad, and requested the First Officer's report. Stanton provided essentially the same information Delgado had obtained from Nason and Gray, though in greater detail. Referring to his own notes, he recounted the exact time when he'd been dispatched to the crime scene, the time of his arrival, the time when he called in his report of a 187-PC. PC was the California Penal Code, Section 187 of which covered the crime of homicide. Once the dispatcher had been alerted, Stanton had waited outside the house till Nason and Gray arrived.

Delgado wrote it all down in his neat, elegant script. "Did you touch anything?" he asked finally.

"The door, sir. It was open already, but I pushed on it, just a little, to look in."

"Nothing else?"

"No, sir."

"Not the body?"

"No, sir. I know it's standard procedure to check for a heartbeat. But in this case, it didn't seem necessary. Sir."

Delgado allowed himself a smile. "No," he said mildly. "Not necessary at all." He snapped his memo pad shut. "Thank you, Stanton. Excellent work."

The patrolman tried to smile, but his mouth wouldn't work. His lips seemed wetter than before.

Delgado left him. Then, because he could delay no longer, he walked up the slate path toward the front door of Elizabeth Osborn's house. From his pocket he removed a small vial containing cotton balls soaked in shaving lotion. He tamped one ball into each nostril.

The door was open, the lights inside still burning. No surprises there. In both previous cases, the killer had left the lights on and the door ajar, inviting the unwary to step inside and inspect his handiwork. One of those who had accepted the invitation was now undergoing psychological therapy; the other was making arrangements to move out of state.

Three brick steps lifted Delgado to the doorway. A tiled foyer carried him into a clean upscale living room. The room was empty, the house vacated until the arrival of the forensics unit.

Breathing through his mouth, Delgado approached the middle of the room, where a woman's naked body was sprawled supine on the richly stained, mirror-lustrous oak floor in a tangle of limbs. Near it lay a torn and crumpled nightgown.

A yard from the corpse, Delgado stopped. He studied the body. At the corner of his sight wavered a displaced strand of hair, bobbing over his temple. Unconsciously he smoothed it back, blending it with the jet-black skullcap of hair pasted to his scalp. He let his hand slide over the curve of his head to the nape of his neck, where he felt the hard bony knobs of spinal vertebrae. He massaged them slowly.

With a small start he became aware of what he was doing. Irritated, he thrust both hands into his jacket pockets, then briskly closed the distance between himself and death. He squatted, leaning over the corpse. His stomach twisted.

No doubt a youngster like Stanton thought the veteran cops took this kind of thing with equanimity. They did not. Nobody could. Nor did Delgado want to. A man who could look at this horror and feel nothing was a man capable of murder himself.

He steadied himself, then set to work on an examination of the body. Strictly visual. Hands off.

The victim, he estimated, had stood five-four. She was trim, her muscles well-toned. Age? Thirty-four would be a reasonable guess.

Elizabeth Osborn. Had to be.

He looked at her bare feet, the white beds of

her toenails. Settled blood bruised the knobs of her ankles. Her naked legs were twisted and splayed. Vaginal swabs, Delgado knew, would reveal traces of semen. This man had his fun with the women he killed.

Slowly his gaze traveled up Elizabeth Osborn's groin, her belly, her chest. Her skin was darkly livid, mottled in purple. All visible signs of hypostasis indicated that the body had not been moved. Osborn either had fallen or had been dropped on this spot.

With his index finger Delgado touched the skin between her collarbones; it was cool, but not yet stone-cold. Her left forearm had fallen across one of her breasts, as if in a futile gesture of modesty. A Band-Aid encircled her thumb. Perhaps she had cut herself with a kitchen knife. The small detail seemed poignant, the Band-Aid incongruous on this body.

The woman's right arm lay outstretched on the floor. In that hand, pressed between her fingers, was a small clay statuette.

Delgado had hoped never to see one of those statues again.

Drawing a quick shallow breath, he looked away from the corpse. Suddenly he was tired. He rubbed his eyes, then pressed his fingertips to his high unlined forehead, feeling the hard bone beneath the yielding flesh. He let his hand drop to his cheekbones, high and saturnine, then to his narrow angular chin. He thought of the bony architecture of his face—the zygomatic arch, the maxilla and mandible, the eye sockets and occipitals—terms he'd often used in his analysis of bullet tracks and knife punctures and shattering hammer blows, but which he'd rarely imagined applying to himself. If the skull was the symbol of leering death, he thought randomly, then mortality could be glimpsed in any mirror.

With effort he shook loose of those thoughts. He focused his attention on Elizabeth Osborn's home, trying to get a feel for the woman's lifestyle and financial circumstances. Though the house was modest enough—only a single story, perhaps twelve hundred square feet, and hardly new—Delgado knew it had been expensive; in this part of town, even a stucco box like this one would run three hundred thousand dollars and up. Mortgage payments of two grand a month, easily. Either Osborn had been doing well in her real-estate sales or she'd been heavily in debt, living on her credit cards and charge accounts; these days the latter was more likely.

Delgado's gaze ticked restlessly across the living room. A white oval throw rug, creamy as a puddle of spilled milk, lay on the hardwood floor under a glass cocktail table with chrome-plated legs. Other glass tables were scattered around in an artful illusion of disorder. Glass surfaces, Delgado knew, were unusually receptive to latent prints. There would be plenty of tented arches and radial loops to occupy the Scientific Investigation Division. But whatever prints the evidence technicians found would belong to Elizabeth Osborn, whose fingers would be printed for comparison, or to her boyfriend, if she'd had one, or to a cleaning woman. Somebody. Anybody.

Not the Gryphon.

Pages of a newspaper, probably the L.A. *Times*, were scattered on a futon flanked by chrome torchères. Against one wall stood an entertainment center with mirrored doors, holding a twenty-six–inch Magnavox and a Pioneer stereo system. A reproduction of an *emakimono*, a Japanese watercolor on a horizontal scroll, hung over the fireplace.

The painting and the white walls were spotted with blood. Long slanted splashes like bugs on a windshield.

The stains could have been made when the saw was used, but Delgado didn't think so. The height and trajectory of the marks looked wrong. No, Osborn had still been upright, struggling wildly, releasing an arterial spray like a hellish lawn sprinkler. A dying person could spasm and convulse as frantically as an epileptic in a *grand mal* seizure.

Death was everywhere in this room. Delgado could not escape from it. Sighing, he returned his attention to the statue.

It was a small brown figure, unpainted, four inches long, modeled by hand out of self-hardening clay. The work was unsophisticated but far from inept; there had been speculation that the Gryphon might be an art instructor or a professional sculptor, but it was equally likely that he was a talented amateur.

The sculpture he had made was a representation of his namesake, the raptorial bird-beast of Arabian and Greek mythology, a gargoyle-like monster featuring the head and wings of an eagle joined incongruously with the body of a lion. The clay gryphon was posed rearing upright, forelimbs extended, wings folded, beak jutting dangerously forward. It was a pose often given to the heraldic gryphons on medieval shields.

The dead woman's hands had both fisted in a cadaveric spasm. If Osborn had been holding the statuette when she died, the clay figure would have been crushed. It was intact. That meant the killer had pried open her dead, rigid fingers to insert the figurine. Peering closely, Delgado detected no tool marks on the skin, no grooves cut by pliers or a screwdriver. Tools had not been needed. The Gryphon had done the job by hand. He was strong, then, with a powerful grip. But Delgado had already known that. It would take a strong man to sever muscle and bone with only a hacksaw. Ordinarily a surgeon's electric saw would have been needed to do a job of that kind.

The hacksaw, however, was unlikely to have been the murder weapon. Too unwieldy. No, something else had released the spray of blood that measled the walls. Most likely the same weapon that had been used in the other cases. But what?

There was no way to know. Not now.

Delgado stared down at the dark mushroom of blood sprouting between Elizabeth Osborn's shoulders, crusted brown, soaking into the gaps between the floorboards. It looked eerily like the distorted shadow of the head that was not there. The head that had been sawed off at the base of the neck and taken away.

He sighed, feeling older, much older, than his thirty-six years.

Detective Sebastián Júarez Delgado had spent his entire adult life in the LAPD, and he knew about cops, all cops—plainclothes and uniformed, raw recruits and tarnished brass. He knew how they liked to grouse about their jobs, about the long hours, the bureaucratic paper shuffle, the stretches of enervating boredom interrupted by flashes of electric danger. And he knew, perhaps better than most of them, that such talk was only misdirection, a magician's sleight of hand.

Overtime, red tape, fatigue, risk—none of that was the bad part of the job, the part that made a young man old. The bad part was facing things like this. Not the physical reality as such, not the lake of blood that had gushed from a severed neck, but the implications to be drawn from the sight. Had Elizabeth Osborn been decapitated in a freeway accident, the condition of her body would have been much the same, but its emotional meaning utterly different.

A man had done this. A member of the human species. A man had hacked through gristle and bone to take the prize he wanted. Had he carried it under his arm, or in a zippered bag, like a bowling ball? Had he whistled cheerfully as he left the house, his night's work done?

After what seemed like many long minutes, Delgado looked up from the body again and saw that the SID technicians had entered the living room. He nodded to Frommer, the leader of the team; the thin, bespectacled, constantly agitated man had supervised evidence recording and collection on both of the previous cases. He was infuriated by the Gryphon, who so far had refused to leave anything interesting.

"Hello, Eric," Delgado said, getting to his feet.

"Detective." Frommer nodded in a distracted way. "Christ, I hate the smell of blood."

"You should try these." Delgado tapped his nostrils. "Cotton balls moistened with Aqua Velva. I can't smell a thing."

"I experimented with something like that once. Only I used Mennen Skin Bracer. And I've tried cigarette filters and swimmers' nose plugs too.

Problem is, when I stick anything up my nose, I feel I can't breathe. I know it's irrational—just breathe through your mouth, right?—but I can't help it. The only thing that works for me is coffee grounds on the stove. Handful of fresh grounds in a saucepan, no water, on a hot burner. In five minutes it masks every other smell in the place."

"I'll keep that in mind."

Frommer stared down at the body. "Jesus, look at her. Just look at her. First thing to do is bag the hands and that goddamned statue. You know, I used to like knickknacks."

Delgado nodded. "So did I."

Two of the evidence techs in Frommer's team were busily unpacking their kit bags, removing canister vacuum cleaners, compasses and calipers, four-by-five cameras and video equipment, fiberglass brushes and vials of gray and white fingerprint powder. The cartographer was already plotting the coordinates of the room on graph paper, prior to marking down the exact location of every item of furniture, every ashtray, every bloodstain. The other three would set to work momentarily, snapping photos and bagging evidence. Delgado figured he'd better get out of their way.

Carefully he retraced his steps, backing away from the corpse. On the steps outside, Nason and Gray stood waiting.

"Let's see the window," Delgado said tersely.

The two men nodded. Wordlessly they led him down a hallway adjacent to the living room, into a large and well-kept kitchen.

The lights were off, and Delgado left them that way. The wall switch would not be touched until it had been dusted. Wan daylight, filtering through the window curtains, provided some feeble illumination.

Looking around intently, Delgado saw a linoleum floor of indeterminate color, perhaps blue or gray—a built-in electric range—a stainless steel sink piled with last night's dinner dishes—white steel wall cabinets, charmlessly functional. In one corner a black-paneled side-by-side refrigerator hummed tunelessly to itself; a grocery list was pinned to the door by a magnet in the shape of a saguaro cactus. The saguaro grew almost exclusively in Arizona's Sonoran Desert, and Delgado was willing to bet that Elizabeth Osborn either had recently visited Arizona or had grown up there.

He stepped up to the kitchen window and carefully parted the curtains. The glass had been removed, leaving only a few jagged shards clinging to the frame.

Directly beneath the window there was a dining nook; a three-sided upholstered bench bracketed a small oak-veneer table. A scatter of shining glass fragments dusted the table, the bench, and the floor, but not enough glass to have filled the frame. Delgado turned inquiringly to Nason and Gray.

"Used tape," Gray said, answering the unspoken question. "Love tap with a blunt instrument. Neatly done."

Delgado nodded. With strips of tape covering the window, the glass would not have spilled noisily out of the frame even after a soft blow had shattered it.

"Did you find the tape and the glass?" he asked.

"Yeah. He dropped it right outside the window. In a flower bed."

Delgado nodded. "It's the first time he's tried this method."

"He keeps it interesting," Nason said.

"Too interesting."

The Gryphon's single break-in prior to tonight's job had been accomplished by picking the lock. He'd sprung a standard latch bolt, apparently by using a loid of some kind—perhaps a credit card or a homemade tool.

Delgado returned his attention to the bench. He saw a few crumbs of dark soil scattered on the tan vinyl upholstery. The killer must have planted his foot on the bench after climbing through the window. Lowering his gaze, Delgado spotted similar specks of dirt on the floor near the table. Perhaps two feet away, there were another few crumbs.

For the first time since entering the house, he smiled.

"I think he's given us some help this time," Delgado said softly, speaking more to himself than to the others.

"What do you mean?" Nason asked.

"He tracked dirt into the room. See it? There . . . and there . . . and there."

"Yeah. From the flower bed. But he didn't leave any footprints as far as I can see."

"True. But if we measure the distance between tracks, we'll know the approximate length of his step. From that, we can arrive at an estimate of his height."

"Shit," Nason said. "That might work."

"Retrace your steps carefully," Delgado ordered.

Walking backward, the three men returned to the kitchen doorway.

"No one enters this room again until SID has photographed and measured those tracks," Delgado said. "Tell Frommer to make it his first priority once the living room is taken care of."

"Right." Gray hurried off to convey the orders.

Delgado was still smiling. "He can make mistakes, it seems. Small ones. But those are the ones that will do him in."

From outside the house rose a loud male voice shouting questions at the beat cops positioned around the cordon. A reporter, Delgado assumed. Soon dozens of them would swarm over this neighborhood like flies crusting a garbage pail. This afternoon every local newscast would lead with the story, and the city's panic, already high, would be ratcheted up another notch. Gun stores and home-security outfits would report a new wave of record sales. Not since the Night Stalker case had one killer generated a wave of paranoia of such frightening intensity. People acted as if the phenomenon of serial murder were new to L.A. It was not.

The Gryphon, as Delgado and every other cop in the LAPD knew only too well, was far from the only repeat killer loose in Los Angeles on this chill March morning. No one in the department cared to speculate on how many unsolved homicides were the work of men who killed capriciously, not for gain but for the satisfaction of an anti-life impulse so primal it could scarcely be understood by a normal mind. L.A. had dozens of them, and they were rarely caught.

The Gryphon had garnered more publicity than any of the others, in part because of the sensational aspects of the case, but in greater part because his first two victims, like his third, had been not prostitutes or runaways, not the faceless shadow figures who slept in alleys and turned tricks for a hit of crack, but "decent people," in the cops' own parlance. Julia Stern had been a young housewife; Rebecca Morris had been an upwardly mobile junior executive. So far the Gryphon had worked exclusively in L.A.'s Westside, a patchwork of middle- and upper-class neighborhoods, where attractive young women were not supposed to die random, senseless deaths.

But then, nobody was supposed to die a death like that. Life, any life, was not meant to end that way.

Delgado sighed, his brief smile fading.

A moment later Gray returned with the news that Frommer was eager to get a look at the tracked dirt. "He'll probably put it through microscopic analysis," Gray remarked.

Delgado was barely listening. "Let's check out the rest of the house."

A narrow hallway led past a bathroom, a utility closet, and a guest room that Elizabeth Osborn had turned into a messy, but comfortable, study. At the far end of the hall was the bedroom. The table lamp on the nightstand was unlit. A piano concerto played from a clock radio; apparently the alarm had been set to awaken the woman with soft music. The bed was unmade, the quilted spread flung back hastily. The walls were bare save for an *Arizona Highways* calendar; the photo showed a grove of golden paloverde trees against a wall of striated purple.

Definitely a relocated Arizonan, Delgado concluded.

A stack of mail had been left on the bureau. Delgado looked it over and saw a Century Cable bill, a mailing from the Sierra Club, a Great Western Bank statement, and a catalog from Crane's Department Store. The catalog's cover featured a smiling woman in a straw hat and the cheerful announcement: "Summer's On the Way!" It was a summer Elizabeth Osborn would never see.

"Seb?" The voice was Gray's. "You okay?"

"Just . . . thinking."

"It gets to you," Nason said sympathetically. "You start seeing them in your sleep."

"And hearing them," Delgado said. "Their voices."

Nason blinked. "I forgot about that. You kept that out of the papers, didn't you?"

"So far."

"Good."

The tapes, like many other details of the case, had been withheld from the press, partly to protect the victims' privacy and partly to provide a means of debunking the endless phony confessions that came in over the task-force hotline. If necessary, such information also could be used to distinguish a copycat killer from the original. As yet, thank God, there had been no imitators. In time there would be. In time . . .

"So how do you figure it?" Nason asked abruptly. "You think maybe he woke her up, hustled her out of bed, cooled her in the other room?"

"No. That's not his M.O. He doesn't move them around like pieces on a chessboard."

"Then what's the story?"

"Something like this." Eyes closed, Delgado

watched the scene unroll in his mind. "The Gryphon breaks in while Osborn is asleep. He makes some noise that awakens her. She's not certain if she heard anything or not, so she slips out of bed and looks into the living room to see if anyone is there. The Gryphon strikes from behind. He kills her. Strips the body, tosses her nightgown aside. Rapes the corpse. Takes the head. And leaves the lights on and the door open, as always, when he departs."

Nason grunted. "Sounds reasonable."

"Reasonable?" Delgado shook his head wearily. "Oh, no. There is nothing reasonable about it." He moved toward the doorway, his shoulders sagging. "Let's get out of here. That goddamn music is giving me a headache."

The three men returned to the foyer, making a detour around the living room, where Frommer was aiming a video camcorder at the body as he narrated a running commentary on the crime scene. Outside, several news vans were parked around the cordon; cameras were being mounted on tripods; snarled snakes of microphone cable slithered everywhere.

The coroner's assistant, Ralston, was waiting for Delgado near the front door. He had handled the Gryphon case from the beginning, and he looked very tired of it now.

"Not much I can tell you yet, Seb," Ralston said in answer to Delgado's unvoiced question. "So far Frommer has hardly let me touch the deceased. He's rather protective of his crime scene, as you know."

"You'll get your chance. Have you taken the temperature readings?" That part of the pathologist's examination had to be done as soon as possible.

Ralston nodded. "Rectum and liver. Body temp is ninety-two point three. That puts the time of death at roughly midnight."

Delgado scribbled in his notepad. "The body wasn't moved." It was not a question.

"Uh-uh. Definitely not. That arterial spray makes it pretty obvious she died right here. Standing up, I'd say. The evidence techs will have to chart the trajectories of the spatters in order to fix her exact location."

"Anything else I ought to know?"

"Nothing you didn't notice for yourself. There are no apparent abrasions, contusions, incisions, or ligature marks on the limbs or trunk, not even any defense cuts. The damage must have been inflicted exclusively on the head and neck."

"Just like the others. Did you smell sulfur?"

"No. I don't think it was a gunshot. We've never found any traces of powder on the previous victims."

"And there's no sound of a shot on the tapes. More like . . . cutting or strangling . . . a combination of the two." Delgado shook his head.

"Knife or a straight razor," Ralston suggested. "With a sideways jerk of a sharp blade"—he demonstrated with a slash of his hand across his own throat—"he could tear out the carotid arteries. Plenty of blood then."

"Yes," Delgado said, looking at the living-room walls. "Plenty of blood." He sighed. "Okay. Thanks, Rally. See you at the autopsy."

He rejoined Nason and Gray, standing a few yards away.

"We were just saying the interval's shorter this time," Gray remarked.

Delgado had been thinking of that too. He nodded. "Julia Stern was killed on December first. After that, the Gryphon was dormant for more than two months. Rebecca Morris died on February eighth. Now this one, on March sixth."

"He's going faster," Nason said. "The high doesn't last as long as it did."

Gray nodded. "He's lost it, all right. Out of control."

"Perhaps." Delgado was thoughtful. "Or he may simply be gaining confidence."

"Is that what you think?" Gray asked.

"Yes. This is a man consumed by grandiosity. He sees himself as more than human—as a god. He believes he is without weaknesses or blind spots. He teases us, certain he cannot be stopped. You know, of course, how he ended both tapes."

" 'Catch me before I kill again,' " Nason quoted. "Like that guy in Chicago in the Forties. What the hell was his name?"

"William Heirens."

"Yeah. Didn't Heirens write something similar at one of his crime scenes?"

"In lipstick. On a wall."

"So what's the significance, do you think?"

"The psychiatrists call it a cry for help. A desperate plea to be apprehended, treated, rescued from the irresistible compulsions that drive him."

Nason had caught the skepticism lacing Delgado's voice. "But you don't agree?"

"No. I don't." Delgado looked at him. "Those words are not a plea. They are a taunt. A mocking challenge. He is not asking to be caught. He is defying the very possibility of capture."

"I guess you could look at it either way," Nason said. "How can you be sure?"

Delgado's voice was iron. "Because I know him."

A beat of silence pulsed among them. Gray broke it.

"Well, whether he's losing it or just getting cocky, he's heading for a fall. He's got to make a mistake soon."

"Got to," Nason echoed.

"Oh, yes," Delgado said quietly. "He will. Every man has a weakness, and this man has his. Some flaw in his character—hubris, perhaps, or something else, something we have not yet seen—will trip him up and bring him down. But . . ."

He looked away, not to let them see his face.

"But even so, his fall will not come soon enough."

He stared at the body on the living-room floor, not seeing it, seeing only the future he could not prevent.

If the next interval was shorter still, as Delgado believed it would be, then soon, much too soon, another clay gryphon would roost in a dead woman's hand.

2

The alarm clock shrilled, dragging Wendy Alden out of sleep.

Numb fingers groped for the alarm. Found it. Switched it off. She did not lift her head from the pillow. She couldn't get up today. Too tired. Groggily she pulled her mind into focus, trying to figure out why she was so sleepy, so utterly exhausted. Something had kept her up late last night, much too late. But what?

"Jennifer," she mumbled, remembering. "Right."

Wendy stared at the ceiling, lost in the dreamy twilight of half-sleep, thinking of Jennifer.

Last night, at quarter to eleven, Jennifer Kutzlow had cranked up the volume on her stereo to fill the night with the tuneful strains of Guns N' Roses and contemplate the band's mellow reflections on life. Since Wendy's apartment was directly above Jennifer's, she was able to savor every subtle nuance of the racket, which continued until well after midnight. On a Monday night, yet, when people had to get up for work the next morning.

Wendy had paced her living room, fuming and muttering and fantasizing Jennifer's violent demise, while the floorboards trembled with bass shockwaves that registered 6.5 on the Richter scale. Even after the noise finally stopped, fury and frustration kept her awake till half past two.

Of course she could have—should have—gone downstairs to complain. Sure. Just as she could have complained the last time Jennifer tested the upper limits of her amp, or all the times before that. But she never had.

Wendy sighed. She had to face it. She just wasn't cut out for confrontations.

The sigh stretched into a yawn. Warm waves of sleep rippled over her, a lulling glissando felt rather than heard. Her eyelids slid shut. The room was spinning, spinning . . .

Don't do it, she warned herself. *Come on now. Wake up.*

Reluctantly she opened her eyes, rolled onto her side, kicked off the covers. With groaning effort she hauled herself out of bed and shuffled down the hall to the bathroom, where she splashed handfuls of cold water in her face to scare sleep away. That done, she tugged off her pajamas and ran the shower till it was hot, then stepped under the spray and shocked her body alert.

Toweling off, she studied her reflection. Caught in the steam-frosted mirror was a small woman; "petite" was the word her mother always used, a word Wendy hated but had never dared to challenge. She stood a fraction of an inch over five feet tall, weighed a hundred and two pounds. Throughout her childhood and adolescence, her diminutive size had led her to be mistaken for a younger girl. Now, at twenty-nine, she could have passed for a woman in her late teens.

The face that returned her critical stare was that of a child, or a child's doll. Wide china blue eyes, pert mouth, button nose. She'd been told she was appealingly cute and innocent, but she didn't believe it; her impression was that she looked half-formed, like a featherless chick, all raw skin and vulnerability.

Turning away from the mirror, she set to work drying her ash-blonde hair with vigorous strokes of the towel, like a carwash attendant buffing chrome. Then briskly she brushed it, combed it, coiled it in a bun at the nape of her neck, and clipped it in place. She always wore her hair that way. Jeffrey had suggested that she let it fall loose over her shoulders, but she was afraid to try. Loose hair could behave in unpredictable ways; it might blow in the breeze or swing in front of her face. A chignon, tightly knotted and clipped, allowed no such wild, dangerous license.

After spraying herself liberally with antiperspirant, she returned to her bedroom and picked out a two-piece tan suit from her closet. She rarely wore bright colors, even on sunny days like this one. There was something assertive, vaguely frightening, about the hot pinks, burnt oranges, jades, and citrons favored by the other women at the office.

Low-heeled sensible shoes and a well-worn purse completed her ensemble. She put on lipstick; then, concerned that she'd applied too much, she patted her mouth with a tissue, removing most of the color. She wore no other makeup.

Once dressed, she went into the living room, an icy cave of white pile carpet and bare white walls. There were no paintings or posters, no hanging rugs, no shelves cluttered with knick-knacks, nothing to suggest the imprint of a distinctive personality on the room.

In her narrow kitchenette, under the steely

glare of a fluorescent lighting panel, she nuked breakfast. As she unwrapped the sausage-and-egg sandwich and put it on a tray, she worried briefly about cholesterol.

She carried the tray into the dining area and set it down on the drop-leaf table. With the leaves up, the woodgrained Formica tabletop would expand from four feet to six. Wendy had never put the leaves up. That was the kind of thing you did when you were having company over for dinner, wasn't it?

She sat with her back to the living room, in her favorite chair. Her apartment was an end unit, and from this vantage point she faced two corner windows framing the branches of a fig tree. As she ate, she watched the dark green leaves rub against the windowpanes softly, sensuously, like cats against legs.

After breakfast she returned to the bathroom and brushed her teeth, digging the toothbrush bristles into her gumline to root out plaque, then gargled Listerine, wincing at the raw acid burn. Mouthwash was awful stuff, but not as awful as the thought of walking around with bad breath; she was certain everyone would notice.

Before leaving the bathroom, she took a final glance in the mirror. The woman she saw shocked her just for a moment. Dressed, groomed, and wide-awake, she looked attractive and intelligent, clear-skinned and clear-eyed; when she smiled in surprised pleasure, her cheeks dimpled sweetly.

That's me, Wendy thought as she experienced a flash of positive self-appraisal so rare as to feel almost hallucinatory. *I can be pretty, see?*

Then she shook her head, dispelling the thought and the mirage in the mirror.

From the hall closet she grabbed her coat; from the refrigerator she plucked a brown-bag lunch, her first name neatly printed on it in Magic Marker. She left her apartment at eight-thirty-five, taking care to shut the door firmly and secure the dead bolt.

She hurried along the outdoor gallery, then down the stairs. As she reached ground level, the door to the apartment directly beneath hers swung open, and Jennifer Kutzlow, patron saint of the hearing-impaired, emerged.

"Hey, Wen!" Jennifer flashed a Pepsodent smile. "How's it going?"

"Hi, Jenny." Wendy's voice lilted up, making the words a question. *Why the hell did you play your stereo so loud last night?* she wanted to say, but didn't.

She glanced at the suitcase swinging loosely in Jennifer's hand—an overnight bag, it looked like. Under her light spring coat, her blue stewardess's outfit was visible, glamorous as a comic-strip crime-fighter's costume half-concealed beneath street clothes. Wendy envied the lifestyle implied by that uniform, the casual trips to distant places, the casual affairs in hotel rooms with men who smelled of Brut or Lectric Shave.

"Off to Seattle today," Jennifer said, as if reading Wendy's thoughts and confirming them. "Probably be raining up there."

"Probably."

"They get lots of rain. I knew this guy once, he was from Seattle, and he told me—"

A Mazda hummed up to the curb, and a horn blatted.

"Oh, hey, there's my ride." Jennifer ran for the car, her strawberry-blond hair raveling behind her in slow motion, a TV-commercial cliché. "See you!"

Her free hand flapped a wave. She hopped into the passenger seat, and the Mazda sped off.

Wendy stared after it. Her mouth, she noticed, was still smiling. Very weak-willed, that mouth. It had this pitiful, childish need to be liked. She was very annoyed with her mouth right now.

At the side of the building, she found her blue Honda Civic sedan parked in its assigned space. She climbed behind the wheel, snugged her seat-belt firmly in place, and backed carefully into the street, checking both the rearview and sideview mirrors.

She drove west on Palm Vista Avenue, past rows of apartment buildings. The radio was on, turned to KFWB, the all-news station. The newscaster informed her that the recent spell of warm weather, unseasonable for mid-March, would continue through the end of the week; a Santa Ana condition was predicted for later this afternoon. Wendy frowned. She hated the Santa Anas, those dust-dry devil winds that blew in from the desert, whistling through the canyons like banshees to suck the moisture from the air and leave eyes red and skin parched.

At Beverwil Drive she turned north, easing into a sluggish stream of traffic. The newscast reported a shooting at an automatic teller machine. A customer making a withdrawal after dark had been ambushed; apparently he'd offered resistance. Now he was in critical condition at Cedars-Sinai.

Not me, Wendy thought reflexively; she always had the same reaction to stories like that. *I wouldn't put up a fight. If they want my money, they can have it.*

Of course, she reminded herself, *I wouldn't have visited an automatic teller machine after dark in the first place.*

She hooked left onto Olympic Boulevard. Before her, the twin Century Plaza Towers leaped up, crowding out the sky. They were three-sided modernistic high rises, the sharp edges of their roofs cutting the morning mist like scalpel blades, forming a starkly modern backdrop to the rows of townhouses and shops lining the street—older, homier buildings, almost Victorian in appearance, that reminded Wendy for some reason of false fronts on a Hollywood studio lot.

After an irritating commercial in which the toll-free 800 number was repeated at least ten times, the newscaster updated the story that had dominated local news for weeks. The serial killer known as the Gryphon remained at large; no apparent progress had been made in the case since the discovery of his third victim, Elizabeth Osborn, thirteen days ago.

Wendy clicked off the radio. She wished she hadn't heard that report. She should never listen to the news. The things that went on today were too awful. It was better not to know.

Still, she couldn't help thinking about that killer. His three victims had all been women in their twenties or thirties, and they had all lived on the Westside—her part of town. Unconsciously her hand strayed to her neck, as if feeling her head to confirm that it was still attached.

She reminded herself to double-check the locks on her front door and windows before she went to bed tonight. Of course, she always double-checked them anyway.

A sign marking the Avenue of the Stars glided

into view. Flashing her directional signal, she turned right. She checked the dashboard clock. Eight-forty-seven. She would make it easily. Not that it would be any big deal if she were a few minutes late. Except she hated being late, because she always made such profuse apologies for it. She couldn't seem to help herself.

"God, what a wimp," she said aloud, sighing.

She wished she weren't so . . . so damn timid. She wanted to be strong and confident and free, yet it seemed she felt safe only when alone in her apartment with the door locked, huddled in her hidey-hole like a rabbit in its den. The city scared her; it was so big, so loud, so full of senseless violence—like that serial killer with his hacksaw and his heads. But she couldn't fool herself, couldn't place all the blame on L.A. and its craziness. She'd grown up in the suburbs of Cincinnati, and she had been afraid there, too.

A headache was coming on. Suddenly the car was stuffy and too warm. She thumbed a button on the dash, and fresh air jetted through the vents, cooling her face. She felt a little better. But the bad thoughts, the unwanted, unkind, unsparing thoughts, still pressed in on her.

She was afraid of life. It was that simple. Her fear had stunted her, crippled her, cut her off at the knees and left her half a person, an invalid wary of human contact, shunning closeness and intimacy, avoiding love or simple friendship. So she'd learned to live through books and videocassette movies and crappy TV shows, which offered an escape of sorts—but she knew they were an escape to nowhere, a dead end.

For the most part she could brush aside that knowledge and go on sleepwalking through her days; but sometimes, late at night, when darkness had fallen like a hush over the earth and she lay awake, unable to sleep, in an apartment that had become a cage of shadows, her mind turned restlessly to the life she wasn't living, the chances left untaken and the things left undone, the years of her youth passing by, never to be hers again. She would press her face to the pillow and listen to the slow rhythms of jazz playing low on her bedside radio, a lonely saxophone crying for her in its mournful voice, as she thought of the city beyond her four walls, the great sprawling expanse of lighted streets and glass towers, of nightclubs where couples danced till the sky ran red with dawn, of neon signs aglow with promise, beckoning her—all the mysteries and wonders of this city she hadn't dared to know. She felt old on those nights; she knew the hollowness of a life lived only in dreams.

Those bad nights would pass, as would the nagging sense that she was living her life with blinders on, imposing a kind of tunnel vision on herself, moving through the blur of her days without risking a glance at anything she hadn't seen before. But the fear, the constant tension twisting her gut, would remain.

How long could she continue this way? How many more years would she waste, hiding from the world, eating dinner alone and talking to herself and watching too much TV? Would she still live as she did now when she was forty? When she was sixty? Was this the shape the rest of her life would take?

"No," Wendy whispered, chilled by the thought. "No, I won't let it be like that."

She sat up straight at the wheel. A wild notion

seized her. She would not go to work today. She would stop at a pay phone, call in sick, then drive up the coast to Santa Barbara—she'd always meant to go there, and it was only two hours away—and spend the day wandering the city, exploring out-of-the-way shops, buying presents for herself. Perfume, maybe. Or a necklace. A beautiful gold necklace. She'd wanted one for so long, and Jeffrey never gave her jewelry. He never gave her anything at all.

Well, she'd find a necklace she liked and buy it for herself. Perhaps she would even stay overnight in a hotel, make it a real adventure. And she'd never tell anyone, not Jeffrey, not her friends at work, not her parents. Nobody would ever know. It would be her secret. Her special day.

She would do it. She was entitled to go a little crazy once in a while, wasn't she? Sure, she was.

Wendy smiled, pleased with the idea. She kept thinking about it, adding detail and nuance, imagining every shop she would visit in Santa Barbara and all the charming knickknacks she would buy. She was still mulling it over and smiling when she pulled into the parking garage of the Century City office building where she worked, took a ticket, found a space, and parked.

On her way to the elevator, she checked her watch.

Eight-fifty-five.

She was on time. Of course.

3

The morning had not gone well.

Delgado should have known he was in for a bad day when at six A.M. he was awakened from a troubled sleep on his office cot by shouts and running footsteps in the hall. It seemed that a juvenile offender on his way to the holding cells at the rear of the station had somehow appropriated a can of tear gas from the arresting officer's utility belt. A dozen cops had the kid surrounded, but he kept yelling that if they tried to take him down, he'd Mace them.

Delgado decided to put some of his conflict-resolution training to work. He ordered the other officers to back off, then approached the kid and began speaking softly, reasonably, in the calming voice of gentle authority. He tried not to think about the Beretta 9mm service pistol snugged in the pancake holster under his jacket. There was a chance that the kid could blind him with a shot of Mace, then grab the gun away from him while he was incapacitated.

Their conversation lasted seven minutes, a span of time that, to Delgado, seemed much longer. Finally the kid handed over the tear-gas canister, and the uniforms converged on him in an angry rush. Delgado waited till the kid had been locked up, then returned the Mace to the officer who'd lost it. "Try keeping an eye on this," he told the man dryly.

Not long afterward, a disappointing piece of news reached him. Albert Garrett was not the Gryphon. Of course Delgado had known that Garrett was a long shot. Even if a man was charged with beating his wife into unconsciousness, and even if that same man happened to work in an art store, where he'd displayed a knack for modeling clay curios, he was not necessarily the city's most notorious serial killer. But when a blood test identified Garrett as AB positive, a match with the Gryphon, Delgado had permitted himself cautious optimism.

A seven A.M. telephone call had extinguished his hopes. Garrett had been positively alibied for the night of the Osborn murder; moreover, it appeared that his whereabouts on the day of Julia Stern's murder had also been accounted for.

The rest of the morning had been taken up with phone calls and hurried conferences that wasted a great deal of time and seemed to accomplish nothing. Delgado wondered why so much of policework was like that. Bureaucracy was part of the reason. Cops were only bureaucrats with guns anyway. A depressing thought; but then, it had been a depressing day.

He sat at his desk, a pile of notes spread on his stained and dog-eared blotter, steam rising from a Styrofoam coffee cup. Behind him was a laminated noteboard that had become an abstract artwork of half-erased flow charts and scribbled phone numbers. Outside the closed door of his office, the station echoed with the clamor of ringing telephones, bursts of static from police radios, and boisterous voices, mostly male and often profane.

He glanced at his watch, confirming that the time was eleven A.M., then swiveled slowly in his chair to survey the seven men and one woman assembled before him. A few were seated in metal chairs they'd brought in from the squad room; most stood leaning against file cabinets or walls. None looked happy.

He was seeing the key members of the special task force hunting the Gryphon. All of them were veteran Homicide detectives. Individually or in pairs they supervised teams of less-experienced detectives and uniformed cops.

There was one man in the room who was not part of the task force. The division commander, Captain Bill Paulson, sat in a corner sipping herbal tea from a seemingly bottomless mug.

"All right, everybody." Delgado's calm, authoritative voice instantly silenced the low babble of conversation. "Let's go over what we have."

He summarized the situation they were faced with. Nearly two weeks had passed since Elizabeth Osborn's murder, and with the elimination of Albert Garrett as a suspect, the task force appeared to be no closer to finding the killer.

The only recent development, one that was not unexpected, had been the delivery on Friday of the third tape. Over the weekend Delgado had listened to it many times; he now had a new voice to haunt his sleep.

Frustration was building. Delgado did his best to boost morale. "The case could break wide open at any time," he reminded them. "So let's hear what you have. Eddie?"

Eddie Torres frowned. "The spotters at the fu-

neral saw a few unfamiliar faces, but we've
checked out those guys, and they're clean. The
photos SID snapped of the gawkers at the Osborn
crime scene haven't yielded diddly. We've com-
pared them to the crowd shots from the first two
murders, and we can't make any matches. Two
black-and-whites are running regular patrols of
Osborn's neighborhood, and they've caught a
few thrill seekers nosing around, but nobody
interesting."

"And the hardware stores?"

"No luck on the hacksaw or blades." Torres
sighed. "Basically, Seb, we're batting zero."

"Maybe not for long," Delgado said, trying to
sound reassuring. "Donna, Harry, how about
you?"

"Still at it, Seb," Donna Wildman answered.
"Going through Osborn's Rolodex. She had a lot
of friends and even more business associates."

"We've finished interviewing her neighbors,"
Harry Jacobs added. "They barely knew her, as
usual in the big city. And we've found her datebook, so we're calling up her old boyfriends and,
I think, scaring the shit out of them."

"That can't be helped."

"As for linking her with the other victims—so
far, nothing."

"Her ex-husband?"

"Alibied," Wildman said. "Yeah, that occurred
to us too. Guy cools the first two just to make the
third one look random. But it turns out that only
happens on TV."

"What else are you pursuing?"

Wildman shrugged. "What *aren't* we? Her medical records, family history, recent vacations. The
works."

"Okay. Tommy?"

Tom Gardner, the task force's liaison with Forensics, looked up from the Bic pen he was rolling restlessly between his palms.

"We've printed all of Osborn's friends and neighbors," he said, "anyone who might have been in that house. There was a lot of glass, and SID found plenty of latents. We're working on eliminating prints now. Donna and Harry got me a list of the people in the Rolodex and the datebook, and we're printing them too. It's a hell of a job, and the evidence techs say this bastard wears gloves anyway."

Delgado ignored his last comment. It was true that smooth glove prints had been found at the crime scenes, but there was always a chance that the killer had removed his gloves before or after one of the murders and left traceable latents. Gardner knew this, of course; he was just blowing off steam.

"I'm looking for more than that from you," Delgado told him. "I need an analysis of the crime scene—any changes in the pattern, evidence of progression or deviation, anything at all that might spark a better understanding of how this man's mind works and what he might do next."

"I hear you," Gardner said.

"Rob?"

Rob Tallyman shifted his weight, and his chair creaked. "The cranks are really crawling out from under their rocks on this one. Ten seconds after KFWB broke the Osborn story, the hotline phones were ringing off the hook, and they haven't stopped since. Needless to say, the confessions are all bullshit, and so far none of the leads has panned out."

"Have you got enough uniforms to fill in the tip sheets?"

"I could use another couple jakes."

"I'll see what I can do. Ted, Lionel, you're still working the art angle?"

"Working it to death, Seb," Ted Blaise said sourly. "We've been in so many art galleries and boutiques the last couple months, people are starting to think we're a little swishy."

Robertson straightened his huge shoulders in mock annoyance. "Speak for yourself, sucker."

Mild laughter greeted that remark.

"Me, I like this detail," Robertson added. "Paintings and statues are a lot prettier to look at than your typical homeboy."

"They're the only thing about this case that looks good," Delgado said grimly.

At noon the meeting adjourned. Delgado talked briefly with a couple of the detectives as the others filed out. Then they too departed, and only Bill Paulson remained, still sipping his tea.

Delgado sat on the corner of his desk and waited, watching the captain. Paulson was a big, thick-necked, large-mustached man, gray and paunchy, but still formidable, like an aged but untamed grizzly. Delgado knew he would speak when he was ready and not before. Deliberation was his style in speech, in movement, in planning an arrest or composing a memo. Everything about him was slow except his mind.

"So let's hear it, Seb," Paulson said finally. "How's it really coming? No pep talks, please."

"We're following up every possible lead," Delgado replied. "My people are running themselves ragged. But a case like this . . ." He spread his hands. "It's not normal policework. You know that, Captain."

Paulson nodded. Normal policework was ninety percent snitches and squeals. Or it involved solving a crime with an obvious motive or a clearcut personal connection. The Gryphon killed randomly. No apparent motive, no personal acquaintance with his victim, no likelihood of being involved in a criminal network.

"We have minimal physical evidence," Delgado said, "which we're exploiting for all it's worth. We have the BSU profile, the charts and extrapolative materials they sent us, which make interesting reading but have been of limited practical use. We have no eyewitnesses, no IdentiKit sketch, no vehicle description or license number. We're doing what we can."

He heard defensiveness in his voice and regretted it. Six weeks of uninterrupted work on the case had worn him down.

"Okay," the captain said. He walked slowly toward the desk, his footsteps heavy, loose change jingling in his pockets. "I'll be straight with you, Seb. Our friends at Parker Center are under a lot of pressure. You know the score. Angry letters from concerned citizens. Nasty editorials in some of the smaller papers—not the *Times* yet, but the *Outlook*, the *Daily News*, and that Spanish rag, *La Opinion*. And the TV creeps are putting a little more bite in their stories. I was hoping this man Garrett might be our guy. Apparently he isn't. Which means we're still no closer to catching the bastard—and we're running out of time."

He met Delgado's eyes. "What it comes down to is this. The big boys are looking for a scapegoat. You're it. They want you eighty-sixed. Want me to put another man in charge."

Paulson's words hung in the room, gathering weight. Delgado knew he hadn't spoken lightly. If he said it was time for a new man to take over the task force, he meant it.

Still, there might be a way to change the captain's mind. Delgado had to try. Losing the command would be a heavy blow to his career, the career that had cost him his relationship with Karen and, along with it, any hope of a life outside his job. But even that was not his main concern now. His main concern was the work of the task force itself. If someone else were brought in for political reasons, time would be lost, work needlessly duplicated, exhausted avenues of investigation reopened for no good reason. And while that happened, the Gryphon would go on killing, the intervals between murders frighteningly short.

Slowly he stood up, facing Paulson from a yard away. He spoke quietly, choosing each word with care.

"You're telling me what *they* want. The brass and the politicians. But how about you, Bill?" It was a risk, using Paulson's first name, but Delgado felt the need for informality between them. "This is your precinct. All three murders have been committed in your territory. You're the one in charge. What do *you* want?"

Paulson grunted. "I want you to catch the son of a shit."

"So do I."

"I know you do. But so far you've gotten nowhere. Maybe another man could come up with a new approach, an angle you haven't thought of."

"Maybe. Or maybe by the time he's brought up to speed, the body count will stand at four. Or five. Or higher."

"It won't take that long to get caught up."

"It won't take that long to get more bodies either."

Paulson returned his stare steadily, then sighed, conceding the point. "No, I guess it won't. How long till the next one turns up?"

"You're asking me to guess?"

"Yes."

"It could happen anytime. But I think it will be soon. Perhaps even within twenty-four hours."

"Shit."

"He's riding high. He thinks he can't be stopped."

"So tell me, Seb: Is he wrong? Can you stop him?"

"Yes."

"What makes you so sure?"

"I know him."

Delgado waited. There was nothing more he could say.

After a long moment, Paulson nodded. "All right. I'll hold them off a little longer." He frowned. "But not forever. You'll have to show some progress soon. Understood?"

It was a reprieve. Not much of one, but a stay of execution nonetheless. Delgado kept his face expressionless. He could not show how much this meant to him.

"Understood," he answered evenly.

"Okay, then." Paulson was all business now. "You're holding a news conference at two o'clock.

That's early enough to make the afternoon news shows."

Delgado had no doubt that the news conference originally had been scheduled for the purpose of announcing his replacement.

"You don't need to take any questions," Paulson was saying. "Just make a statement. Keep it vague: The investigation is ongoing and the task force is currently exploring several promising leads, no further details to be released at this time for fear of jeopardizing the case, et cetera."

Delgado nodded. "Anything else, Captain?"

Paulson paused in the doorway.

"Just catch him, for Christ's sake," he said coldly. "I want that feathered motherfucker grounded—permanently."

A moment later the door banged shut, and Delgado was left alone in the room.

He returned to his desk and sighed. A little longer, the captain had said. What span of time was implied by those words? Another couple of weeks? Perhaps not even that much, if the Gryphon kept busy. Could he solve the case, make an arrest, in a matter of days? Not unless one of the leads unexpectedly panned out, or the killer started making mistakes, big ones. Well, he could only proceed with the various strategies he'd been following, and hope.

He leaned back in his desk chair and looked around slowly at the narrow windowless room, a room daylight could never reach. One of the overhead fluorescent panels had gone out; the other hummed and buzzed, singing insect songs. In the dreary half-light, the metal file cabinets and institutional-green walls seemed more depressing than usual.

His gaze, tracking restlessly, settled on the nodule of agate he kept on his desk. The egg-shaped stone had been split neatly in half by some accident of nature to expose a mirror-smooth oval of cryptocrystalline quartz banded in concentric circles of green, gold, and neon blue.

Delgado had found the stone in the Mexican desert when he was eight years old, and had invested many hours in its sanding and polishing. He'd been fascinated by the colors, the patterns, and the mystery of the forces that had formed them. If such beauty could be hidden inside a dusty chunk of rock, he'd sometimes asked himself as he stared into the agate's depths, then what other, greater wonders might the world conceal?

He smiled. Picking up the nodule, he ran his thumb and forefinger lazily, sensuously, over the flat, glassy surface. Handling the stone relaxed him, helped him to think. He kept on rubbing slowly as he reviewed the facts known about the Gryphon.

There was no point in going over it all again, no reason to expect a sudden brainstorm, the mental click of a new understanding or a new approach. But he would do it anyway.

All right. Start at the beginning.

Saturday, December 1. Shortly after nine A.M., Robert Stern drove to a municipal golf course to play eighteen holes with some friends, leaving his wife alone in their apartment. Julia Stern, twenty-four years old and seven months pregnant, took a shower at nine-thirty, according to a neighbor who heard the whistling of water through the pipes. At the same time, the Gryphon easily defeated the simple latch bolt on the apartment's front door. When Julia, wrapped in a towel, emerged from the bathroom, the killer was waiting. In midafternoon Robert Stern returned to find the front door ajar, the lights on. His wife's decapitated body lay on the carpet near the bathroom doorway, a clay gryphon in her hand.

Delgado winced, recalling his own first look at the corpse. The hump of the belly. The ragged trunk of the neck.

At the time, no one could have been certain that the killer would strike again. Even after the tape arrived in the mail and Delgado heard the Gryphon's mocking challenge, he'd found it possible to believe that the murder had been an isolated occurrence. As days passed, then weeks, some of the psychological consultants on the case began to speculate that the Gryphon had committed suicide and rid the city of his presence.

But that was before Friday, February 8. At six-fifteen that evening Rebecca Morris, thirty-one, arrived home from work while her roommate was fixing dinner. Rebecca was in a hurry. Less than a month earlier, she had been promoted to vice president of a computer software firm; that night she was scheduled to attend a reception thrown by the firm's biggest client. Quickly she changed into a formal ice-blue gown that stressed her statuesque figure and set off her fiery hair and emerald eyes. Her roommate later reported that Rebecca had never looked so enthused, so healthy, so alive. At six-forty-five Rebecca, running late, rushed to the one-car garage stall at the side of the building where her Mazda RX-7 was parked; she lifted the garage door by hand and entered. Apparently she was unlocking the car when the Gryphon slipped into the garage

through the open doorway and attacked from behind. At seven-thirty Rebecca's boss called the
apartment to ask where the hell she was. Her
roommate, concerned, went down to the garage
to see if the Mazda was gone. She discovered a
woman's naked, headless corpse stretched across
the two front seats, one hand clutching a clay
gryphon. At the morgue she could make a positive I.D. only from the ring on Rebecca's finger,
a ring Rebecca had bought for herself in celebra-
tion of her promotion and her exciting new life.

After the second murder, there could be no
doubt that the Gryphon meant to go on killing till
he was stopped. The task force had been formed,
with Delgado in charge; the miscellany of unre-
lated cases he'd been investigating had been
handed over to other detectives, most of whom
groused about the additional caseload for days.
The second tape had arrived within a week, the
FBI had been contacted, and Delgado had begun
working twenty-hour days and sleeping on the
cot in the corner.

And then the week before last, on Wednesday,
March 6, Elizabeth Osborn had lost her life.

Delgado shook his head slowly.

If the women had died in street muggings or
bungled burglaries, their deaths might not have
seemed so difficult to accept. There was a kind of
logic to events like that, a motive and purpose
that could be, if not defended, at least divined.
Here there was no logic, no motive, no purpose.
There was only the terrifying randomness of a
restless evil that claimed lives as arbitrarily as an
airborne virus or a cloud of poison gas.

All three victims had been young middle-class
women; but other than that, no common denomi-

nator appeared to link them—not occupation, not background, not religious affiliation, not business associates or friends or doctors. Although all three had been attractive, their physical features had varied as well: Julia Stern, dark-haired and pale-skinned; Rebecca Morris, redheaded and freckle-faced; Elizabeth Osborn, blond and salon-tanned.

As far as Delgado could tell, the three women had had nothing in common except the fact that they were young and vital and alive. Presumably that had been enough.

He turned to a map of the city tacked to the far wall. Three red push pins marked the locations of the murders and suggested the parameters of the Gryphon's field of operation. It was an area of roughly six square miles, extending west to Bundy Avenue, where Julia Stern had lived; east to Rebecca Morris's apartment on Beverly Glen Boulevard; south to Elizabeth Osborn's neighborhood near National Boulevard. Everyone on the task force assumed that the killer lived somewhere on the Westside and was operating reasonably close to home. He was not a drifter; he was settled, using a house or apartment as his base of operations. And he was mobile; he must own or have access to a vehicle.

The three victims had been Caucasian, a fact that virtually guaranteed that the Gryphon was white also; serial killers only rarely crossed racial lines. Julia Stern's murder had taken place on a Saturday morning; Rebecca Morris had been killed at about six-forty-five in the evening; Elizabeth Osborn had died in the middle of the night. Those time periods suggested the possibility that the Gryphon held down a daily nine-to-five job, which would restrict his activities to nights and weekends.

It seemed clear that the Gryphon watched each house or apartment building for at least a short while before acting. He must have seen Robert Stern depart with his golf clubs, just as he'd seen Rebecca Morris open the garage door and hurry inside. Presumably he'd observed Elizabeth Osborn's house as well, lingering nearby until the lights were out and she was asleep. Only once he had determined that his victim was alone and vulnerable would he strike.

By all odds, somebody in one of the neighborhoods should have noticed a strange man, an unfamiliar vehicle—something, anything, out of the ordinary—during the period when the killer watched and waited. But the Gryphon's luck had been excellent—the luck of the devil, Delgado thought. Nobody had seen a thing.

The murder weapon remained unknown. The victims' heads were severed at the base of the neck, so if a knife or razor had been used to slash their throats, as Delgado suspected, there was no way to confirm it now.

The tool used to decapitate the bodies was a hacksaw. Thanks to the lab, Delgado even knew the specific brand. Microscopic analysis of the torn flesh had revealed minute particles of tungsten carbide, which had been matched to those found in a commercially available hacksaw blade. The blade, twelve inches long, was made of high-carbon steel to which tungsten carbide was metallurgically bonded to form a highly effective cutting edge. It could cut easily through cast iron, hardened steel, reinforced cement, and, of course, bone.

Delgado had ordered Eddie Torres and the officers working under him to trace every purchase of that hacksaw and its replacement blades that had been made in the Westside during the past six months. The number of customers was large, the records poor, the job nearly impossible.

At each of the crime scenes, evidence technicians had picked up short-nap rayon carpet fibers, industrial gray; the cheap material, ubiquitous in low-rent offices and homes, was impossible to trace. The Gryphon had left no fingerprints, but the techs had found a few dark brown head hairs. And they had found semen in the dead women's vaginal vaults as well as, in one instance, the anus. Postmortem examinations indicated that penetration and ejaculation had occurred after the victims were dead. Like eighty percent of the male population, the Gryphon was a secretor, meaning that analysis of an antigen secreted with his bodily fluids could determine his blood type. His blood was AB positive.

Then, of course, there were the clay statues. Delgado had given Blaise and Robertson the assignment of making inquiries at art galleries and gift shops, looking for any local artist who could conceivably fit the Gryphon's profile. They were still on the detail; so far no useful leads had developed.

Delgado had given himself a crash course in mythology to better understand the symbolism of the gryphon. The peculiar hybrid of eagle and lion, he had learned, had haunted the minds of human beings for four thousand years. Its point of origin was the Levant; from there it had been conveyed to Asia and eventually to Greece. The Athenian playwright Aeschylus had his Prometheus warn of the hounds of Zeus, the sharp-beaked gryphons; the animal, thought to be the guardian of treasure hoards, was ever-vigilant, cruelly predatory, capable of a swift, deadly attack in which its ruthless talons would slash its victim to bits.

It was a symbol of blood and death, of patient observation and sudden violence, of the lion's cunning and the eagle's swiftness. Regal and vicious, mythic and monstrous, a creature to be both feared and revered.

Now the city of Los Angeles was experiencing the same primitive terror Aeschylus's audience had known: terror of the sharp-beaked, bloody-clawed Gryphon, the beast that struck without warning and killed without remorse.

Delgado shook his head. Having learned all that, perhaps he understood the killer's psychology slightly better, but he was no closer to catching the man.

The other major phase of the investigation focused on earlier unsolved homicides that might roughly fit the Gryphon's pattern. In a city as large and as violent as L.A., there was no shortage of brutal attacks on women; but two cases struck Delgado as particularly intriguing. Last June a Culver City woman had disappeared while on a shopping errand, then had turned up dead in a trash dumpster several days later, her neck deeply gashed and nearly severed by what might have been a hacksaw. Six months earlier, in December, a teenage Santa Monica girl was found dead in an alley behind the video rental store where she'd worked; her right hand had been lopped off and stuffed in her mouth. In each case the victim had been sexually abused after death, and the killer's blood type had been established as AB positive.

The task force was also looking into out-of-state crimes that might be connected with the Gryphon's activities. So far a murder in Idaho two years ago seemed the likeliest connection. The body of a female hitchhiker had been discarded in a roadside ditch; the girl's tongue had been cut out, her fingers methodically removed. Again, the body had been used as a sexual object by a man typed as AB positive. The Idaho authorities had formed a small task force of their own and were digging through their files to find similar crimes. A number of possibilities had cropped up—a call girl, Lynn Peters, raped and strangled in Nampa three years ago; a high-school teacher, Georgia Grant, stabbed to death on a hiking trail in the Sawtooth National Recreation Area in the summer of 1987; a Twin Falls waitress, Kathy Lutton, bludgeoned to death in a parking lot at Christmastime in 1986—but none could be definitely linked to the current investigation.

Well, that was hardly surprising. Nothing definite had developed anywhere. And while Delgado's task force pored over arrest records and filled in tip sheets and canvassed neighborhoods and made inquiries at art galleries and gift shops, that man was out there, the brown-haired man who eluded them, mocked them. Even now he might be at work. At any moment the phone might bring word of another corpse.

Slowly Delgado replaced the chunk of agate. His gaze traveled to the tape recorder on his desk. He looked at it for a long moment.

Then, while he watched as if from a distance, his hand opened the top drawer of his desk. Inside lay a pair of foam-cushioned miniature head-phones and three audiocassettes. The cassettes were copies; the originals were locked in storage, as evidence.

The tapes had come by first-class mail, ad-dressed to Detective Sebastián Delgado, care of this precinct house; the words had been printed in large block letters with a felt-tip pen. There had been no return address, of course, and the two postmarks had been different. The existence of the tapes had never been made public, and so far the Gryphon had chosen not to contact any of the local news services. Only one fact pertaining to the tapes had leaked out, and that was the name selected by the killer to identify himself.

Delgado stared at the tapes. He didn't want to hear them. He'd played them many times, too many, and it was pointless, an exercise in self-torture, to play them again.

But he would anyway.

His hands shook only a little as he removed the headphones from the drawer and slipped them on.

4

From nine to twelve Wendy worked steadily, rarely looking up from her word processor. She typed briskly and accurately, using two fingers; in time with the tapping of the keys, columns of radium-green characters marched across the display screen, forming sentences, paragraphs, chapters. But not the great American novel or anything—just another booklet for Iver & Barnes Consultants, Inc.

Iver & Barnes was an actuarial firm specializing in pension plans for medium-size corporate clients. The people in the communications department, Wendy among them, had the task of explaining the complex plans to the clients' employees. The most common approach was a pamphlet ten or twelve pages long, written in simple declarative sentences and illustrated with goofy little cartoons. Once you got the hang of it, the actual writing was ridiculously easy, almost mindless; long ago Wendy had learned that each new job involved merely rearranging the same basic phrases in slightly different patterns.

The department functioned as a halfway house for aspiring writers. They arrived fresh out of college, worked for a year or two, and moved on. All of the people who'd been there when Wendy arrived five years ago were long gone. Many had gone into publishing; a few of the braver ones had saved up money, then embarked on a free-lance writing career.

But she remained, grinding out paragraphs and pages, going nowhere.

At noon she broke for lunch. She pushed the keyboard away from her and rose from her chair, yawning hugely, then damned Jennifer and her stereo system for the hundredth time. God, was she ever tired. Maybe food would revive her.

She walked the length of the department, passing rows of particleboard cubicles identical to her own. Her lunch was stashed in the compact refrigerator under the water cooler. Kneeling, she opened the fridge and found the brown bag marked with her name.

She was turning to go when she saw two of the newer writers, Kirsten Vaccaro and Monica Logan, approaching. They were deep in whispered conversation. As they came closer, Wendy caught a reference to the Gryphon.

Oh, no. She didn't want to hear this. But before she could walk away, Monica spotted her.

"Hey, Wendy, you live on the Westside, right?"

Glumly she nodded. "Half a mile from here."

"So are you scared out of your wits or what?"

"I . . . I guess so."

"Sure glad I'm out in the Valley. You know, I'll bet when they get this guy, he turns out to be one of those released mental patients."

Kirsten frowned. "What makes you say that?"

"Because he's obviously crazy. I mean, totally insane."

Kirsten was thoughtful. "I don't know. He's got

to be at least somewhat rational to avoid getting caught."

"Rational? Him? No way. He's foaming at the mouth."

Having lingered long enough, Wendy felt she could permit herself to leave. She had taken her first tentative step away from the water cooler, the paper bag clutched in her fist, when Kirsten turned to her.

"What do you think, Wendy?"

She froze.

"Me?" she asked stupidly.

"Yeah. Is the Gryphon a certified psycho or not?"

She faced the two women, who were watching her expectantly. Hot panic swelled inside her. Nobody ever asked for her opinion. She had no idea what to say. Her mind had gone blank.

"Well, I . . ." She groped desperately for words. "I think . . . I think he probably can't help doing what he does. Because none of us can really help it, right? Whatever we do. It all goes back to our childhood."

Monica pursed her lips. "You're saying the Gryphon is a victim of his childhood?"

Was she saying that? She supposed she was. It sounded kind of ridiculous, didn't it? Or maybe not. She wasn't sure. Monica and Kirsten were still looking at her, still waiting.

"He might be," Wendy said cautiously, searching for a way to squirm free of the snare of words. "I mean, you could look at it like that. But it's just an idea, that's all. I guess I'm not really sure one way or the other. . . ."

Her voice trailed off into embarrassed silence.

"Well," Kirsten said dryly, "I don't feel sorry

for him, no matter how lousy his childhood might have been." She turned back to Monica. "And I don't think he's crazy either. I think he's just bad news, and when they catch the guy, they ought to string him up by his balls."

"Ouch," Monica said. "Nasty."

"That's me. The Torquemada of the typewriter."

The two women laughed. Discussion continued. Wendy slipped away unnoticed. She was trembling.

She returned to her cubicle and sank into her swivel chair. She stared at the computer screen. A paragraph of text stared back at her, the cursor winking maliciously like an evil eye.

Slowly she opened the brown bag and removed a chicken-salad sandwich sealed in Saran Wrap, a can of Diet Sprite, two paper napkins, and a banana. While she ate, she scrolled through the work she'd done this morning, not seeing it, not seeing anything except her own humiliation.

She asked herself why she'd always been so deathly afraid of taking a stand, any kind of stand. Why she froze up like a deer in a splash of headlights the minute anybody asked her anything more controversial than the time of day.

She sighed. The answer, she supposed, was obvious enough; it was contained, in fact, in what she'd said at the water cooler, even though her presentation had been so inept that the logic of the idea had been impossible to follow.

Childhood was the key, the key to everything. The origins of any adult's secret terrors and painful inadequacies could be traced back to those few precious years when a young life was molded and shaped like clay on a potter's wheel.

That serial killer must have had a horrible childhood; people like him always did.

But not just people like him.

Wendy could point to no physical mistreatment that had scarred her as a child. No whippings, no molestations, no incarcerations in locked closets. But there were other forms of abuse.

For her entire adult life, she'd found it painfully difficult to think about her childhood or even to remember it. Those years were masked by a fog of amnesia. She hated that fog. Pieces of herself lay concealed behind it, hidden from her—stolen from her—erased from memory as if they'd never existed. But when she tried to poke holes in the fog bank, when she tried to see the truths veiled by smoke and darkness, her mind usually would make a sharp detour, and all of a sudden she would find herself thinking about what to make for dinner or what to wear at work. Oh, the mind was a wonderful thing, all right, and what it was most wonderful at was protecting itself. It put up walls and smokescreens and No Trespassing signs to keep you away from dangerous, forbidden, hurtful memories.

But sometimes she forced her mind to stay on track, to bring up the past and relive it, no matter how frantically some small scared part of herself tugged like a dog on a leash, fighting to pull free of such thoughts. Then, for a little while, she became a girl again, the timid, frightened girl who'd grown into the woman she was.

That girl's father, Stanley Marshall Alden, had been the products inventory supervisor for the Cincinnati office of a nationwide manufacturer of metal containers. Wendy had never quite known what a products inventory supervisor was; she'd been afraid to ask. Stan Alden did not take kindly to any question that could be taken as a derogation of his responsibilities, his attainments, his earning power, or his manhood; all these concepts, she'd understood in the wordless way of a child, were intimately bound together in his mind.

Her mother, Audrey, had been a housewife and a Red Cross volunteer. Her duties at the Red Cross, which were never clearly specified, conveniently required her to be out of the house during most evenings and many weekends. Wendy was ten years old before she realized that Audrey Alden used her charity work as an excuse to avoid contact with her husband. She was fifteen before she permitted herself to know that her parents hated each other.

Why they'd stayed married, Wendy had no idea. That was another of those things she'd never dared to ask. She knew they were unhappy, though they tried desperately not to show it. She remembered her mother's smile, a smile made of gritted teeth, and her father's medicine cabinet, the shelves lined with antacids and headache pills. The internal pressure of all that unvoiced, unadmitted anger must have been considerable. To survive, her parents had needed a safety valve. They found one; it was named Wendy.

Their common misery, the one thing they shared and nurtured together, had been taken out on their only child. Her parents had been her constant critics, their appraising eyes and chilly voices the ceaseless barometers of her own worthlessness.

Whatever she did was wrong. If she got good grades she was called a perfectionist, a know-it-all, a smarty-pants; if she let her schoolwork slide, she was accused of being lazy, stupid, undisciplined. When she was quiet, she was told to stop acting so damn sullen; but if she forced a smile and fumbled her way through a joke, she was ordered to pipe down. She tried to please her parents by anticipating their criticism and using it on herself, remarking humbly on her clumsiness and obstinacy. "Show some self-confidence, for God's sake," her father would growl. Desperately she complied, fixing her hair and wearing her best dress, then announcing how pretty she looked. "Bragging doesn't become you, young lady," her mother would say in a flat scolding tone.

She couldn't win. There was no way to satisfy them. If she changed her behavior, they changed their standards.

At times her parents, perhaps skewered by guilt, actually found something positive to say about her. The rare, unexpected praise only made things worse. She could have learned to accept any amount of criticism, as long as it was consistent; at least then her world would have been predictable. But switching signals were impossible to live with. She felt like a laboratory rat tortured by electrical stimuli that changed without warning from pleasure to pain. She could never adjust to a universe as plastic and shape-shifting as a nightmare.

And so, gradually, she retreated inside herself, hiding from life. As she grew older, she rarely went out, lost the few friends she'd made, began living vicariously through TV shows and books. She became afraid of people, not just her parents but people in general, all people. They were unpredictable and dangerous. She feared their watchful eyes, their closed faces, their secret judgments.

Yet at rare moments, impelled by some unstated need, she still had dared to reach out for life, to take risks. Small risks, to be sure, like a toddler's mincing hesitant steps, but risks nonetheless.

Moving to Los Angeles had been the biggest chance she'd taken. After four friendless years at a local college, she kissed her folks goodbye, boarded a DC-10, and watched the Ohio River shrink into the haze of spangles frosting the airplane window. She'd never been sure, then or later, quite why she'd chosen L.A. as a place to relocate. Perhaps because it was a place where people went to start over, a big anonymous place without history or tradition, a place where the past didn't count. Or perhaps merely because L.A. was about as far from Cincinnati as it was possible to get.

Whatever the reason, she'd chosen to make some kind of stand in this city, to become a new and better person, to leave childhood behind. But making a fresh start was harder than she'd expected; changing her life turned out to be more difficult than changing her address. And childhood, she learned, could not be left behind. Not ever.

The sudden shrilling of the phone on her desk startled her. She blinked, coming out of her reverie, and picked up the handset.

"Communications Department," she said.

"Communicate with me," a male voice purred.

"Hello, Jeffrey," she said, automatically lowering her voice, even though there was no company rule against taking personal calls.

"Hello, dollface."

Nervously she swiveled around in her chair, away from the doorway of her cubicle. "Don't . . . don't call me that."

"You like it."

She didn't, actually, and she'd told him so, but Jeffrey never listened.

"You doing anything tonight?" he asked.

Silly question. Of course she wasn't doing anything.

"No," she answered.

"How about dinner, then? Six o'clock at the Mandarin House?"

"Okay."

"Remember where it is?"

"I think so. The dragon place, right?"

"Yeah."

"I remember."

The dragon in question was a large papier-mâché model that hovered over the central part of the restaurant, suspended from the ceiling by what looked like monofilament fishing line. She and Jeffrey had agreed it was the tackiest *objet d'art* they'd ever seen.

"Look, I've got to go," Jeffrey said suddenly. "I think the key spot is melting the wax fruit. See you."

He hung up before Wendy could reply.

As she cradled the phone, she found that she was smiling. She was glad Jeffrey had called. Even if he never gave her jewelry or . . . or much of anything.

With a shake of her head, she brushed that thought aside, then tossed the remnants of her lunch in the wastebasket, shrugged on her coat, and left for her walk. She took a walk every day on her lunch hour; and she always walked alone.

Quickly she made her way through the suite of offices to the reception area, then out into the long gray corridor. The elevator dropped her eight stories to the lobby, a mausoleum in brick and marble, enlivened by a few trees in large planters. She passed by the security guard at the front desk, pulled open the glass door, and stepped outside, blinking at the brightness of the day.

Within a short walk of the high rise was the Century City Shopping Center, an outdoor mall crowded with art galleries, clothing stores, a multiplex movie theater, and three department stores, Bullock's, Crane's, and the Broadway. She entered the mall and strolled down the main concourse, passing carts stocked with popcorn, hot pretzels, and cappuccino. A man selling flowers was serenading potential customers with a rendition of "On the Street Where You Live" in a loud, pleasant voice. Pausing to listen to the song, Wendy considered buying herself a flower; she decided against it. Too expensive.

As she reached the section of the mall devoted to restaurants, she encountered crowds of office workers from the nearby high rises. She disliked crowds. On impulse she entered Crane's, hoping the store would be emptier.

It was. She wandered among the racks of women's fashions, picking idly at dresses she knew she would never wear. Nearby was a glass display case crowded with wristwatches, cufflinks, rings, bracelets, and necklaces. Necklaces . . .

She stopped, staring at a necklace of gold squares strung together on invisible thread. It was exactly the sort of thing she'd been wanting for so long. The sort of thing she would have bought for herself in Santa Barbara, if she'd had the courage to go there.

"Oh, God, it's gorgeous," she whispered to herself, then glanced anxiously over her shoulder, afraid someone might have heard.

She took a step toward the display case, imagining how it would feel to have that necklace—so beautiful, so luxurious—touching the bare skin of her neck. Her hand rose, trembling, to her throat.

A thought ran through her mind, a crazy thought: *How much does it cost?*

She shook her head. It didn't matter. Whatever the price, it was more than she could afford, even if she did pull down thirty grand a year and even if she did have a great deal of it squirreled away in a savings account—such a nice, safe, federally insured place to put your money, a place with no risks, no challenges, no excitement . . . like the lifestyle of a certain someone she could name.

I'll think about it, she told herself.

She almost walked out of the store, then stopped, knowing that if she left, she would never come back.

Her gaze returned to the necklace. She touched her purse, silently reminding herself that inside it she would find a Crane's charge card.

"No," she whispered. This time she did not look around to see if anyone could hear. "You can't. It's crazy. It's too . . . too impulsive."

But that was the whole problem with her life, wasn't it? She was never impulsive. Here at last was a chance to go a little wild, to buy a costly present for herself on the spur of the moment, for the sheer hell of it—a chance to blow a small chunk of her savings on something utterly impractical, something she didn't really need, something she just wanted, yes, *wanted*, in the simple, uncomplicated way an animal or an infant wants food.

She had to have that necklace, dammit, simply had to. She ached to clasp it on her neck and feel its sinful weight against her breastbone.

"No," she said again, but she barely heard herself; she was already walking up to the counter near the display case, where the male sales clerk was installing new batteries in an elderly man's wristwatch.

She waited restlessly till the watch was ticking and the customer was satisfied. Then the clerk turned inquiringly to her. She asked in a voice that trembled only slightly, "How much is that necklace?"

He smiled. "Two hundred forty-nine dollars. It's on sale."

Oh, that was far too much. She couldn't possibly. Just couldn't. There was no way.

"I'll take it," she said.

The clerk raised an eyebrow. "Would you like to try it on first?"

"No. It's fine. I'm sure it's fine."

He shrugged. "Okay." He reached inside the display case and removed the necklace. It glittered magically. "Will that be cash, check, or charge?"

"Charge."

The card was already in her hand. She gave it to the clerk, who ran a scanner over the bar code. Information on her charge account came up on the display screen of his computer terminal. The amber light glinted on his glasses as he briefly checked the file to see if her account was in good

standing. It was, of course. She always paid on
time.

The clerk smiled, apparently arriving at the
same conclusion. "Here you are, Miss Alden," he
said, handing the card back.

A moment later the necklace was in a box, and
the box was in a shopping bag, and the bag was
in her hand.

"Thank you for shopping at Crane's," the clerk
said as she walked away.

She nodded in reply, afraid to say anything,
afraid to slow down, afraid she might change her
mind, ask for her money back, do some crazy
thing. And then she was out the door, free of the
department store, having made her purchase, and
she felt fine.

I did it, she thought proudly. *I didn't chicken out
this time. I really for-God's-sake did it.*

When she went back to work, the words came
easily. She tapped her foot as she wrote, keeping
time to some melody playing in her head, a high,
sweet, wonderfully secret melody only she could
hear.

5

After a moment's hesitation, Delgado selected the copy of the first audiocassette he'd received. He loaded it in the tape recorder. His finger pressed the button marked Play. Tape hiss rose in his ears like the phantom ocean caught in a conch shell. An anonymous official identified the tape as a duplicate before reciting the case number and other details.

Then a louder hiss sizzled through the headphones, signaling the start of the dubbed portion of the tape.

Julia Stern's voice faded in. She'd stepped out of the bathroom, fresh from her morning shower, and the killer had grabbed her from behind. He must have told her not to scream for help, that the first sound she made above a whisper would mean death. Delgado could picture the young pregnant woman standing just outside the bathroom doorway in her blue terry-cloth towel, drawing shallow scared breaths as the Gryphon hissed in her ear and held the knife—if it was a knife—close to her throat.

Perhaps Julia had tried to reason with him, tried to find out what he wanted. The killer had told her. He wanted her to beg. To plead for her life.

Delgado doubted that the Gryphon had mentioned the tape recorder. But he'd been carrying one, all right—probably a small portable unit, either tucked in his coat pocket or snugged to his belt. It was unlikely that he'd used a handheld microphone; he would have needed one hand to grab Julia and the other hand for his weapon. But a built-in omnidirectional mike, standard in portables, would have worked just fine.

For about five minutes, the killer had recorded Julia's voice as she asked him to please let her go. Five minutes was not a long time, but it must have stretched to hours for Julia Stern and her pounding heart.

Excerpts from that recording now crackled and hissed in Delgado's ears.

". . . didn't see your face. So I can't identify you. We've got a lot of nice things here. You can have any of it. There's silverware in the kitchen. A color TV, a stereo. In the closet I've got some birthday presents for my husband: a camera, a watch, a new coat. Oh, God . . . Please, take anything you want and just go"—her voice cracked on that word—"and you'll never get caught. I swear. I won't even tell the police. I won't tell anybody. Only, don't hurt me . . . and my baby. . . ."

Slowly Delgado fisted his hand, then raised his fist to his mouth. He chewed on his knuckles and finger joints. He wanted to turn off the tape, turn it off and throw the goddamned obscene thing in the garbage can and set fire to it, but he couldn't. He listened. He had to hear it.

The killer's words had been excised from the tape. The cuts and transitions were neatly done, indicating the use of a mixing board. There were

too many audiophiles in L.A. to make it possible
to track down the equipment.

Julia was begging now. There was a theatrical
quality to her voice, even though her fear was
unquestionably genuine. It was obvious that the
Gryphon had explained the exact words he wanted
Julia to say, words she'd haltingly recited.

"Please don't kill me," Julia Stern was saying.
"I don't . . . want to die. I'll do whatever you
say. I know you're much more powerful than . . .
than I am. You're so strong. You frighten me.
You're the strongest and most terrifying person
I've ever . . . encountered in my life."

A momentary drop-off in volume indicated another edit. In the excised segment, the killer must
have delivered new instructions. Based on what
followed, Delgado assumed Julia had been told to
say something personal about herself, her aspirations, her reasons to go on living. That was a
particularly cruel aspect of the psychological torture the Gryphon inflicted. He let his victim remember and express, clearly and in detail, all the
values life had to offer; then he ended that life.

"I'm only twenty-four," Julia whispered. "I've
got a husband, and we love each other; we really
do. We got married two years ago this April, and
we promised it would be forever, and it will be.
And . . . and I've got a baby coming. A boy.
We're going to name him Robert. That's my husband's name . . . If you don't care about me, at
least think about my baby. You wouldn't hurt a
baby, would you? Would you?"

Desperation spiked her voice. Tears were audible, thickening the words to paste. Her breathing
was faster, huskier. Perhaps the knife had been
pressed closer, the blade drawing blood.

Another edit in the source material. Next came the bad part, the unbearable part. The killer must have let Julia in on his little secret, must have informed her that, despite her compliance with his demands, she was going to die. When she spoke again, Delgado heard her hopeless, helpless terror.

"No . . ." Less a word than a moan. "It's not fair. I did what you wanted. I said all those things. You promised . . ." A sobbing little-girl voice. A whimper. The beginning of a scream: "Please—"

The scream tightened into a gargle. Wet. Rasping. Then faded out. Gone.

In the silence, a new voice, a man's voice. The voice of the Gryphon.

He had not recorded his commentary at the crime scene. Analysis of the tape had shown a measurable difference in room tone as the recording segued from Julia's murder to the Gryphon's remarks.

The killer spoke in a whisper, his mouth apparently pressed close to the microphone, and nothing about his normal speaking voice could be determined except that he had no obvious accent or speech impairment. Occasionally the breathless words were interrupted by sloppy smacking sounds as the Gryphon licked his lips.

"I hope you enjoyed that performance, Detective Delgado. I found it exquisite. Mrs. Julia Stern conveyed real emotion, don't you think?

"Oh, but forgive me; how terribly inconsiderate. I haven't introduced myself. Call me the Gryphon. I suppose the *objet d'art* I left with Mrs. Stern is sufficient to make the reference clear.

"You may wonder what I'm up to. Well, I'll tell

you. I'm playing a game. A wonderful game I invented. The object of the game is to take living women and turn them into dead ones.

"Have you ever killed anybody, Detective? In the line of duty, I mean. If so, you may understand what I've learned from the game I play, the transcendent truth I've discovered.

"Other men, lesser men, measure power in terms of money or political influence or sexual conquests. But I have seen what true power is, and it is not found in checkbooks, voting booths, or bedrooms. No, true power is the power of life and death. Now, consider Mrs. Julia Stern. She wasn't important, merely one anonymous soul among millions, never to be missed. But when I ended her life, I ended a universe. Yes, a whole universe. The private cosmos that had been Mrs. Stern's world. The earth, sun, and stars, human history, culture, and art . . . all of it had existed, for her, only in her own mind. Now Mrs. Stern is dead, and, for her, those things exist no more.

"That is the secret I have learned. To wield power, ultimate power—the power to erase existence, void reality, blot out stars and galaxies with one stroke—it is not necessary to bring on Armageddon. It is necessary only to take a life.

"The God of the Old Testament is said to have created the world in six days. But I can wipe out a world in less than a minute, and I can do it whenever I please. Who, then, is the more powerful? Who is the greater god? The creator of one world—or the destroyer of many?

"Well, enough of this philosophizing. We're practical men, Detective; you have your work to do, and I have mine. Let's both get on with it. I know I will. You'll be seeing more art objects, many more. I hope you'll take the time to admire their beauty. Art adds so much to our enjoyment of life, doesn't it? Art and myth and ritual—see how neatly I've blended all three. Or perhaps you don't share my taste in aesthetic matters? Then try to stop me. Do your best.

"Catch me before I kill again."

The tape faded out.

Delgado switched off the tape recorder, then tugged off the headphones, grateful to escape them. Quickly he returned the cassette and the headphones to the drawer, slamming it shut.

He'd learned nothing new. But he hadn't expected to. He already knew what little the tapes could tell him.

After the second murder, Delgado had asked the FBI's Behavioral Science Unit in Quantico, Virginia, to prepare a psychological profile of the man who called himself the Gryphon. As part of its Violent Criminal Apprehension Program, or VI-CAP, the BSU had amassed files on every modern serial killer, and its experts used the known tendencies of those who had been caught to extrapolate the probable behavior and personal characteristics of the ones still at large.

The BSU analyst, a glib, chatty man named Landers who gave the impression that he enjoyed his work too much, had called Delgado to go over the profile with him. The evidence was necessarily sketchy, the results largely guesswork. Still, it was better than nothing.

"Most serial killers," Landers told Delgado breezily over the buzz of the long-distance connection, "are adult males in their twenties, thirties, or forties. Typically the younger ones strike quickly, while the older ones draw out the murder, often making their victims beg. On this basis I'm tentatively placing the Gryphon in the upper age bracket. Thirty to forty is my working hypothesis."

Delgado listened, taking notes, saying nothing.

"The tape indicates that he's intelligent, fairly well educated. Good verbal skills. Pronounces difficult words without strain—even *objet d'art*, for Christ's sake. The name he's picked for himself suggests a knowledge of mythology, the classics, maybe ancient or medieval history. Let's see, what else? It's hard to say for sure, but I think I noted signs of effeminacy in his choice of words. Also a strange sense of humor—well, I guess you'd expect it to be strange, wouldn't you? Puckish. That's the word I'm looking for. You know what I mean, Detective?"

"Yes."

"Now, this is a guy who broke into Julia Stern's apartment during the day, when he knew she was home. You have to ask why he would do that. Why not ring the doorbell, pretend to be a salesman or a new neighbor? Two possibilities occur to me. One is that he lacks even elementary social skills; he's withdrawn, a loner—what we call a 'disorganized asocial' personality type. For a man like that, breaking in might seem easier than talking his way inside. The other possibility is that he's actually deformed, disfigured in some way. It's a long shot, but it could explain the decapitation of the victims. Maybe he projects his self-loathing onto these women and takes their heads as a punishment of himself.

"Of course, there are other possible reasons why he decapitates the bodies. He may use the heads as totems, as sexual objects, or as objects of further violence. There was one guy who hacked off his mother's head and used it as a dartboard. Or—I hope you've got a strong stomach, Detective—he may consume the heads, or parts of them, in order to gain his victims' life force; conceivably he eats their brains to gain knowledge or their eyes to gain vision."

"Or perhaps," Delgado said slowly, "there is a simpler explanation."

"Such as?"

"I was ten years old, Mr. Landers, when my family moved to the United States from Mexico. That was in 1965. On our way north we stopped to visit Disneyland. I kept the ticket stub for years afterward. I probably still have it somewhere. Every time I looked at it, I remembered the excitement of that day, the escape I'd found from everyday life. For the Gryphon, his victims' heads may serve the same purpose."

Landers chuckled. "You ought to be in my line. You can think like them. That's the whole secret, right there."

It was a secret Delgado had never wanted to learn.

"Is there anything else you can tell me?" he asked heavily.

"Only the classification," Landers said. "We classify lust murderers—our term for serial killers—according to their presumed motives. There are four categories we recognize. The first is the so-called visionary killer, the guy who hears voices or sees visions that compel him to kill. Personally I'm skeptical about this category; most of the visionaries turn out to be faking it. But it's irrelevant anyway, because your man doesn't mention any voices in his head.

"Then there's the mission-oriented killer. He feels it's his sacred calling to eradicate a specific group of people. You get a nurse who pulls the plug on terminal patients, or a Jack-the-Ripper type who kills prostitutes. Well, the Gryphon doesn't say there was anything about these women that caused him to single them out, so we can ignore this category too, at least for now.

"Third, the hedonistic killer. He murders for sexual gratification and usually performs sex acts with the victim or the victim's body. Obviously, the Gryphon fits this profile—up to a point. But he doesn't mutilate the women's genitals, buttocks, or breasts, as we would expect a classic hedonistic type to do.

"Finally, the power-oriented killer. This is the guy who kills because he likes control, likes to dominate his victims. I think it goes without saying that your man, the Gryphon, is definitely into power and control in a major way. He says he's greater than God, after all, and he makes his victims pay homage to him before he kills them.

"So my tentative conclusion is that he's a mixture of the last two categories. A sexually twisted sociopathic personality working out his frustrations by means of a violent power trip."

"All right, Mr. Landers. Thank you. I take it you've covered everything I need to know about serial killers."

"Except for one last point."

"Which is?"

"They're damn hard to catch."

In the final analysis, however, Delgado based his understanding of the killer not on the BSU's psychological profile, but on a fragment of ancient history that he remembered from one of his college classes—a small, bloody episode that merited barely a footnote in most texts, but which had been printed indelibly on his mind.

In A.D. 408 the grand minister Olympius had ruled the western half of the Roman Empire through the intermediary of the retarded and ineffectual emperor, Honorius. A lifetime of manipulation, scheming, and murderous betrayal had lifted Olympius to a position of nearly absolute power. Only one significant threat still faced him, the threat posed by the militant Goths, who wanted to claim the Empire for themselves. The Gothic armies had the manpower and the martial skills to defeat any forces loyal to the emperor. But they were held in check by the knowledge that their wives and families, sixty thousand women and children who had settled in Italian towns, were at the Romans' mercy.

Olympius had everything he wanted. He controlled the Empire. He ruled the world or what was then known of it. As long as those sixty thousand hostages were his, the Goths could do nothing.

Olympius ordered the hostages killed.

There was no logic to what he did. In murdering those sixty thousand, he ensured his own downfall. He freed the Goths to move against him and avenge their loved ones. He must have known the consequences of the orders he gave; yet he gave them anyway.

Delgado's teacher, perhaps embellishing the story, had reported that as the slaughter was carried out, the bodies heaped high, and the mass graves filled, Olympius capered in his palace, exulting with frenzied glee: "This is greater than the Empire!"

Delgado believed the Gryphon was a man like that.

People assumed that anyone capable of senseless murder must be deranged. The popular stereotype, endorsed to a large extent by psychologists and sociologists and bright young experts like Landers of the BSU, was that of a man driven by irresistible impulses, unable to control his wild urges.

Delgado disagreed. Whatever his inner compulsions, the Gryphon was in final control of his actions. He knew what he was doing, just as he knew how to reach the police if he wanted to confess, or a psychiatrist if he wanted to get help. He planned his crimes with care, taking elaborate pains to avoid leaving evidence that might lead to his arrest. Afterward he showed no sign of remorse or even regret for what he'd done. Quite the contrary. Like Olympius, or like Hitler, Stalin, Mao, and Pol Pot, he reveled in death, intoxicated by the bloody elixir of the suffering he caused.

There was a word for such a man, a word so simple it had been all but forgotten in this complex modern age. A word Delgado's grandmother in Guadalajara had known.

Evil.

Delgado nodded. Oh, yes. There was good and evil in the world. Underlying each of these three murders was the will of the man responsible, his private volition, his conscious choice to do violence to the innocent. He had felt the need to kill, and rather than resist that urge, he had given in to it, had acted on it three times and laughed about it later. His compulsions did not drive him; he allowed himself to be driven by them. And for what? An illusory sense of power, a sexual thrill, a few hours of fun. He was a man who took pleasure not in living, but in denying life to others.

Delgado stared moodily at the map on his wall, at the three red dots scattered across L.A.'s Westside. Somewhere in that sweep of lookalike houses and anonymous apartments and gas stations and stores, there was a killer who struck with the brutal impersonality of accident, an Olympius for a meaner and sorrier age. He fashioned his clay sculptures and then he played his game, choosing victims by some means Delgado could not guess, stalking them, killing them, and taking his hideous souvenirs.

Delgado knew everything about that man, except his name.

6

Franklin Rood stepped dripping out of the shower.

He took a shower every afternoon at four-thirty, immediately after getting home from work. He had a strong belief in the importance of personal hygiene. Many of the world's problems, he felt, could be solved or at least significantly ameliorated if the common herd of people simply learned the value of cleanliness. Instead, just look at them, greasy and unwashed, sweat-stained and foul-smelling, the filth and dreck of the human cesspool. Disgusting.

Briskly he dried himself with a clean white towel, a towel as fresh and new as any that might be found in a hotel bathroom; Rood had no tolerance of dirty laundry, of anything dirty. He was, he supposed, a rather fastidious man. That was a nice word, wasn't it? Fastidious. He said it out loud, enunciating each syllable clearly, then grinned at the mirror. What a fine smile he had. He looked lovingly at himself, freshly washed, his brown hair tousled and ropy, the skin of his shoulders flushed with the heat of the shower spray.

In the bedroom he put on his glasses, snugging the stems behind his ears, then dressed briskly in blue denim jeans, a plaid shirt with the sleeves rolled up to expose his muscled forearms, and white Reebok running shoes. The Reeboks were excellent for his purposes, permitting rapid movement while ensuring relative silence, and he'd sprayed them liberally with a silicon formula to keep off the worst of the stains.

On his way out of the bedroom, he paused to execute half a dozen pull-ups on the bar screwed into the doorframe. He did them easily, feeling no strain. Every morning and evening he performed a minimum of twenty chins and twenty squats to keep his arms and legs in condition.

He walked through the living room into the kitchen, and stopped before the refrigerator. Arctic air gusted against his face as he opened the door to the freezer compartment and peered inside. The freezer was crowded with unidentifiable leftovers in aluminum-foil wrapping. At first he couldn't find the Swanson Hungry Man chicken pot pie he wanted. He rummaged in the freezer, looking past plastic trays of ice cubes and cans of orange juice. Then, with a delighted smile, he saw the corner of the box sticking out from behind the frozen blue mass of Miss Elizabeth Osborn's head.

Rood slid the chicken pot pie out of the package, punched a few holes in the pie crust with a fork, and placed his dinner in the oven.

Checking his wristwatch, he saw that the time was now one minute to five. There were local newscasts at five. Couldn't miss them. He hurried back to the living room, turned on the TV, loaded a blank videotape into the VCR, and settled into his armchair with the wireless remote in his hand. He pressed the button marked Record. The VCR started with a whir just as "Eyewitness News" began.

The female news anchor was afraid of him. Rood could see the fear furrowing her forehead, tugging at the corners of her mouth, moistening her lips. Every woman in the city was afraid. Well, they ought to be.

The top story was a fire in Topanga Canyon, fanned by the dry desert winds. Rood was disappointed. Fires were common. Fires had no business taking priority over the Gryphon.

He waited impatiently for the real news, the only news that counted. Finally it came on—the daily update on the city's waking nightmare.

He quickly gathered that there were no new developments in the case. Ignoring the reporter's meaningless commentary, he focused on the snippets of file footage, mostly pertaining to Miss Osborn's murder.

Her bungalow, looking seedier in daylight than it had at night. The crowd of spectators, like vultures, disgusting. The camera peering past the yellow crime-scene ribbon, panting for a voyeuristic glimpse through the doorway. A metal gurney, and on it a black plastic body bag. The doors of a coroner's wagon slamming shut.

Then an unexpected treat: Detective Sebastián Delgado standing outside the police station, delivering a statement to the press.

Rood leaned forward, studying the man's face, a face he'd seen in other newscasts and in newspaper photos, but one he found endlessly fascinating. The black hair swept back from the high forehead. The sharp nose, hawklike. The angry mouth bracketed by chiseled grooves.

"Catch me, Detective," Rood whispered. "Catch me before I kill again."

The newscast continued, but it was not about the Gryphon anymore. Rood flipped through the other channels and caught a few seconds of other, similar reports. Then there was nothing. Ah, well. He could get more air time whenever he liked.

There would be newspaper stories too, of course. He'd brought home today's edition of the L.A. *Times*, the *Evening Outlook*, the *Daily News* and, although he could not read Spanish, *La Opinion*. More clippings for his scrapbook.

He rewound the tape and played the "Eyewitness News" story again. As he watched, he leaned back in the chair, lacing his fingers behind his head, smiling. The game was such fun.

For most of his thirty-two years Rood had found little that brought him pleasure or pain. His life had been a blank, his days drudgery, his nights dreamless. He had been a zombie shuffling through the motions of living, dead inside.

His first kill, five years ago, had changed all that. Freed from the strait jacket of normal existence, hunting his prey, Rood felt alive—wonderfully, intoxicatingly, dizzyingly alive—more alive than any other man had ever been. He was a god, vertiginously elevated above ordinary humanity, towering over the teeming mob as an average man would tower over a nest of squirming maggots. He was in total control of every aspect of reality, free to do as he pleased, utterly unconstrained. Nothing could compare to the exhilaration of taking a woman's life, then using her body while the flesh was still warm, the blood still wet. It was a thrill as dark and heady as black wine.

A knock on the door interrupted his thoughts.

He froze. Suddenly he was afraid. Nobody ever visited him. In his two years in L.A., he'd never once had company. The very idea seemed unreal. In a distant, rather abstract way he was aware that people did such things; they learned one another's addresses and dropped in now and then to say hello. But the ritual was as alien to him as the social habits of bees in a hive.

He had no idea what to do. Perhaps if he made no sound, whoever was out there would go away.

There was another knock, then a faint, muffled voice. A woman's voice.

"Franklin? It's me. Melanie. From next door."

Rood swallowed. Oh, God. What was *she* doing here?

He'd exchanged pleasantries with Miss Melanie Goshen on a few occasions while entering or leaving his apartment. She was a tall, pale blonde who spoke quietly, rarely meeting his eyes. Very shy and innocent. Or so she seemed. But Rood knew that her innocence was an act. On more than one night, she'd had a man over at her place. Rood had heard the noises of their love-making through his bedroom wall.

"Franklin?"

He didn't want to answer, didn't want to talk with her at all, but he felt he had to. Vaguely he thought it might seem suspicious if he didn't. Lately he'd grown extremely conscious of avoiding any activity that might raise suspicions of any kind.

He tried to imagine what a person would say when company called. After a moment's thought, the correct response came to him.

"I'm coming," he said loudly, his voice pitched

an octave higher than normal, his vocal cords stretched taut by nervous tension.

He rose from his chair and switched off the TV, then hurried to the door and opened it. Miss Goshen was standing on his front steps, lit by the porch light, the empty courtyard behind her. Her sleeveless blouse was much too tight. Indecently tight.

Fear squirmed in his gut. He felt droplets of sweat squeezing out all over his body.

"Hello," he said, straining for calm.

"Hi." She smiled, and her cheeks dimpled sweetly. "Sorry to bother you, but I'm making dinner, and the recipe calls for olive oil. Which I thought I had, but it turned out that all I've got is peanut oil. Which won't do at all."

"You . . . want to borrow some?"

"That's what I'm trying to say. Yes. If you've got any, that is."

"I'm . . . I'm sure I do." Don't look at her breasts. Don't think about the noises from her bedroom, the groans of pleasure, the creaking mattress springs. "Just a moment."

He meant to have her wait in the doorway, but as he headed for the kitchen, he realized she was following him.

"Thanks so much," she said. "I appreciate this."

"Don't mention it."

The oils were kept in a cabinet over the sink. He saw the jar of extra-virgin olive oil immediately. He reached for it, fighting the panic that sent ripples of light-headedness radiating through him.

"You've got something in the oven." Her voice startled him, and he nearly dropped the jar.

"Uh-huh." Speech was difficult. He cleared his throat. "Chicken pot pie."

He could feel his body shaking, knees liquefying, fingertips tingling. It was intolerable to have her in here with him. The kitchen was too small, and she was too close. The nearness of her body, a woman's body, not safely dead but warm and living—he couldn't stand it. He wanted to run. To run and hide in the bedroom with the door closed until she went away.

"It figures," she was saying. "Bachelors always go for those pot pies. Hungry Man, right?"

"Right." The word was a dry cough.

"Bet you've got a big appetite, a big guy like you."

His fear receded before a flare-up of anger. What did she mean by that? She'd insulted him just then, hadn't she? Hadn't she, the little bitch?

Big, she'd called him. But he wasn't big. Five-ten wasn't big at all. So what had she really meant? That he was fat? He wasn't. A hundred eighty pounds was not excessive for his height. And a good deal of it was muscle. His upper body, particularly. Strong arms. Powerful hands. Hands that could snap this cunt's neck with one twist of the wrists. One twist—

Suddenly he wasn't afraid anymore. He had never been afraid. She couldn't frighten him. No woman could. He was Franklin Rood. He was the Gryphon.

He smiled and handed her the jar of olive oil. "Here you go."

"Thanks so much."

"Is there anything else you need?"

"No, this'll do it."

"I've got some fine things in my freezer."

"Yeah, you single guys always go for frozen food."

"Want to take a look?"

"Uh, no. Not really."

"Why not?" He put a hand on the freezer door. "Lots of nice things."

She was looking at him strangely now. She was afraid of him now. And she ought to be. They all ought to be.

"No," she said, as she took a sliding step toward the doorway to the living room, "seriously, the olive oil is all I need. Hey, look, I'd better get going. I've got stuff on the stove."

He almost did it. Almost grabbed her by the hair and jerked open the freezer door and made her look. Then he would throw her to the floor and beat her to death, the same way he'd beaten the whore-bitch waitress who'd been his first kill.

But he couldn't.

Her disappearance would raise questions. The police would be sure to interview the next-door neighbor. And they would know.

With effort he damped down the fires inside him. He followed her to the front door.

"Hope your recipe turns out okay," he said.

"Oh, I'm sure it will." She flashed a nervous smile, keeping her distance. "Thanks a lot. I'll return this to you . . . uh . . . tomorrow."

"The jar's nearly empty. You might as well keep it."

"You sure?"

He nodded.

That frightened smile flickered again. "Okay. 'Bye."

Then she was gone. Rood shut the door and released a long shuddering breath.

He tried to relax, couldn't. He paced the living room, breathing hard, perspiring freely. Once or twice his glasses threatened to ski off his nose; each time, with a swipe of his hand, he knocked them back into place.

The feelings were strong in him, too strong to be denied. He needed to release them—now, immediately—and there was only one way to do it. Only one.

He could not kill his next-door neighbor without risking capture. But he could kill another woman instead. He even knew who it would be.

Flipping open his wallet, he removed the scrap of paper marked with the name and address of the next contestant in the game. He stood staring at it for a long moment.

Previously he had waited longer between kills. He didn't care for the idea of hurrying the process. That was the way to get sloppy, to make mistakes. He really should wait another week or two.

Yes. Should. But wouldn't. Couldn't.

Eyes shut, he watched Miss Melanie Goshen's lips split as his fists hammered her face. Slowly his fingers moved, squeezing air, as in his mind he fondled the soft mounds of her buttocks. His tongue clucked at his lips as he imagined himself licking her wet secret parts.

He had to play again. And he had to do it tonight.

"And so," Franklin Rood breathed while a grin like a grimace warped his face, "let the game begin."

From a cabinet under the kitchen sink he removed a package of modeling clay. He set the bag down on the counter, then put on a pair of thin rubber gloves. It would hardly be a good idea to chance leaving impressions of his fingerprints in the material as he worked it.

He opened the bag and tore a hunk of soft brown clay off the large mass, then modeled it quickly, expertly, with his nimble hands. First the general shape of the beast—four limbs, two wings, beaked head. Then the subtleties of musculature and texture. With a pencil point he etched ruffles of fur into the creature's hindquarters and suggestions of feathers into the wings. Last he pushed the pencil gently into the head on each side, creating two small black holes that passed for eyes.

Normally he would have let the sculpture dry overnight, but this time he could not wait that long. Heat would harden the model faster than air alone.

Rood placed the clay gryphon on a baking sheet and slid it into the oven. While he waited for it to bake, he consumed the chicken pot pie, barely noticing the taste.

Finally he tested the model with a spoon and judged it done. The clay was no longer soft and yielding, but rock-hard. With oven mitts he removed the baking sheet. He let the figure cool for half an hour.

Then he picked it up and studied it in the light of the overhead fluorescents. He admired the stylized simplicity of the artwork. A lovely thing. His best work so far. Any woman would be proud to have it. But it was not meant for just any woman.

"For you, Miss Wendy Alden," Rood whispered. "Only for you."

7

At five o'clock the communications department began to empty out. Most of the writers headed off to the Avenue Saloon across the street, where they often went after work. Nobody asked Wendy to join the group, not because she wasn't liked, but because she'd turned down such offers so many times in the past. She always said she just didn't care for bars—the noise, the swirl of smoke and people, the harsh, raucous atmosphere—and all of that was true enough; but the deeper truth was that she was afraid to go along, afraid to be part of a crowd, afraid the others would gang up on her, taunt and jeer, make her feel ridiculous. The fear was irrational—of course it was—but she felt it anyway.

Well, none of that mattered tonight. Tonight she had something better to do. She was going to see Jeffrey . . . and when she did, she would be wearing her new gold necklace.

She lingered in the office till five-thirty, fiddling with a paragraph that didn't need fixing, then left the office clutching the shopping bag with the necklace inside. The elevator carried her to Level A of the underground parking garage, where she fetched her Honda.

She drove west on Santa Monica Boulevard,

turned south at Beverly Glen, and hooked west
again on Pico, heading into the glare of the setting
sun. The predicted Santa Ana condition had developed on schedule; moisture had vanished from
the air, and the breeze through her open window
had the rough sandpapery feel of a desert wind.
The night wouldn't be hot, but it would be dry;
before bedtime she would have to apply Vaseline
to her lips and splash cold water on her face to
relieve her burning eyes.

Just past the intersection of Pico and Overland,
she eased the Honda into a curbside parking
space. She switched off the engine, then sat behind the wheel, summoning her courage.

Slowly she opened the shopping bag, removed
the small cardboard box inside, and took out the
necklace. It gleamed, catching the last light of
day. With trembling hands she hooked it around
her neck. She felt its weight on her breastbone,
the coolness of the metal against the bare skin of
her throat.

Her heart was beating fast—fluttering, almost.
Her mouth was dry. She was a little dizzy.

Tilting down the rear-view mirror, she studied
her reflection, the band of glittering gold plates
ringing her throat. So glamorous. So daring.

And it's mine, she told herself proudly. *I saw it,
I wanted it, I bought it. Just like that. Totally on impulse. Didn't even stop to think. Not much, anyway.*

She hoped Jeffrey liked it. She hoped he said
all the right things—how lovely the necklace
looked on her, how well it set off her hair and
eyes, how bold she'd been to have made such a
costly purchase. She hoped . . .

A hand shot through the open window and
closed over her arm.

Wendy whipped sideways in her seat and came face to face with the man leaning in through the window. It was only Jeffrey.

"Oh, Jesus," she hissed. She let her head fall back on the headrest while she fought to catch her breath.

"What's the matter?" Jeffrey Pellman asked innocently. "Did I scare you?"

"Only enough to put me in cardiac arrest."

"Sorry." The grin on his face said he wasn't. "I saw you sitting there in a daze, and I figured you could use something to wake you up."

"Oh, thanks. Thanks a bunch."

His grin faded. "You really *are* mad, huh?"

"Oh, I . . . I guess not."

She was, though. Scaring her that way had been such a stupid, thoughtless, childish thing to do. And it wasn't the first time either. Jeffrey was always tricking her, springing practical jokes, messing with her head. Playing games. God, did she ever hate that. But she'd never told him off, just as she could never bring herself to ask Jennifer to turn down the volume on her stereo.

"Am I forgiven?" Jeffrey asked in a tone of voice a shade too sincere to be believed.

No, she wanted to say, but didn't. Instead she merely smiled—a wan, forced smile, the smile a survivor of a plane crash might summon for the TV cameras—and said, "Forgiven."

She cranked up the window and got out of the car. Jeffrey was already feeding change into her parking meter. Which, she supposed, was considerate of him.

A moment later he turned, looked her over, and smiled.

"You look nice tonight."

It was the same thing he told her every time they went out together. The same exact words.

He hadn't noticed the necklace. Hadn't even seen it.

"Oh," Wendy said. "Thanks. So do you."

She told herself she ought to feel disappointed. She didn't. She felt nothing. Nothing at all.

Hooking his arm in hers, Jeffrey led her down the street toward a display of cursive letters in red and green neon that formed the words "Mandarin House," "Chinese Cuisine," and "Open." He held the door for her, as he always did.

The Mandarin House was not particularly crowded tonight. A young couple sat at one table, speaking quietly, lost in each other. At the far end of the restaurant, two tables had been butted together to facilitate a gathering of several generations, all talking loudly and more or less simultaneously in fluent Chinese.

Jeffrey selected a table by the front window, with a view of the traffic streaming past the garish neon facade of the Westside Pavilion across the street. He held Wendy's chair for her, another of his small courtesies, then seated himself. The waiter, smiling nervously and shifting his weight as if in need of a trip to the rest room, took their order for drinks. Wendy asked for an iced tea, and Jeffrey decided on a beer, specifying Heineken to show that he was too sophisticated to drink an American brand.

Once the waiter had hurried off, Wendy settled back in her chair, glancing around at the restaurant, adjusting to the place by slow degrees. A bas-relief of a pagoda hung on the far wall. In a corner a brass Buddha prayed for enlightenment under the spreading leaves of a potted fern. Chinese music tinkled like raindrops, rising over the hiss of steam from the kitchen.

"You know," Jeffrey said suddenly, "I just noticed something."

Her heart kicked. The necklace. He'd seen it. He'd finally seen it.

"Oh?" she said as casually as possible. "What's that?"

He cocked his thumb at the ceiling. "The dragon. It's turned into a fire-breather. I don't remember that from last time."

A small, private death took place inside her. Indifferently she lifted her head to the beam ceiling. Yes, Jeffrey was right. The large papier-mâché Chinese dragon, suspended over the center of the room by strands of fishing line, was now exhaling a tissue-paper plume of orange flame.

"A new touch," she said softly. "Nice."

All of a sudden her lower lip was trembling. She couldn't let him see that. She opened her menu and held it in front of her face, feeling like a fool. There was no reason to be so upset. It was only a necklace, for God's sake. It wasn't important. Besides, she must have been crazy to think he'd notice. Nobody ever paid any attention to her. If she hadn't raised her hopes unrealistically high, none of this would have happened. The whole thing was all her fault for being so . . . so immature.

"Made up your mind?" Jeffrey inquired after a few moments.

"Almond chicken for me," she answered, and was relieved to hear that her voice was steady, safely devoid of emotion.

"I think I'll have the shrimp with lobster sauce."

Putting the menu aside, she smiled, a calm, easy smile which, she was sure, betrayed no hint of pain. "Whenever we go to a Chinese restaurant, you always order the shrimp with lobster sauce."

"I'm reliable. Sue me." He shrugged. "Anyway, I'm too tired to be experimental. This shoot today was murder. Took me six hours, and I still don't think I got what I wanted. The thing is, I decided to go for a soft-focus look, but I didn't want to lose too much detail, so . . ."

Jeffrey went on telling her about his current assignment, invariably the principal topic of conversation when they were together. He was a freelance photographer who did magazine spreads for a living and more consciously artistic work on the side, some of which had been exhibited at the smaller local galleries. The galleries provided little income, but the magazines, glossy large-circulation publications with exorbitant advertising rates, paid well—well enough to cover the rental of a two-bedroom house in the Hollywood Hills north of the Sunset Strip, a good neighborhood. The house served as both residence and studio; Jeffrey had converted one bathroom into a darkroom, and used the garage for many of his photo sessions.

On assignment he would shoot anything in any style or format desired, but when he worked for himself he limited his medium to high-grain black and white and confined his subjects to the buildings and monuments of the city; "urbanscapes," he called the results. To get such shots, he often worked in the early morning, when the streets

were empty; no human beings could be permitted
to clutter up his vision of the city. Jeffrey positively hated photographing people, because with
people, he felt, a photographer could not be in
complete control. And as Wendy knew only too
well, Jeffrey Pellman was a man who needed to
be in control.

Maybe, she'd often reflected, it was his passion
for control that made him play tricks on her, in
order to keep her off balance, dependent on his
whim. Maybe—she didn't care for this thought,
but it sometimes came unbidden, especially late
at night when she was alone—maybe that was
the only reason he'd ever gone out with her.
Maybe he liked the way he could dominate her,
control the course of any conversation, hold court
with no fear of being challenged by a stronger
personality with an opinion of its own. Yes. Just
maybe.

Their drinks arrived. Jeffrey made an elaborate
show of testing the beer with a connoisseur's
wariness, then pronounced it acceptable. The
waiter took their order. Wendy asked for an egg
roll as an appetizer, followed by won ton soup
and almond chicken. Jeffrey chose pan-fried
dumplings, hot and sour soup, and of course,
shrimp with lobster sauce.

The waiter returned to the kitchen, vanishing
through a swinging door into a haze of steam and
a clatter of pans. Jeffrey resumed his monologue
as if there had been no interruption, describing
in considerable detail the specific lenses and filters he'd used, even though he must have
known that the technical jargon meant nothing
to her. Wendy found herself tuning him out.
She didn't think she was being rude; as far as

he knew, she was still listening in rapt attention. Anyway, he mainly wanted to hear himself talk. She was merely the wall off which his voice was bounced.

Still pretending to listen, occasionally prompting him with a word or two—"Yes." "Uh-huh." "Really?" "Did you?"—she let her thoughts drift back to the gourmet cooking class where she and Jeffrey had met three months ago. Even signing up for the class had been a major accomplishment. She remembered how she'd procrastinated about sending in her check, desperate to escape the prison of her loneliness even if only for one night a week, yet afraid to commit herself to the unknown. Finally she'd gone through with it. She'd been proud of herself, although as things turned out she was too much of a klutz in the kitchen to learn much of value.

Jeffrey, on the other hand, mastered each new recipe with ease. He began showing her how it was done; looking back, she supposed he must have enjoyed playing the part of teacher, master, guru, with Wendy herself safely relegated to the supporting role of the humble apprentice at his side.

At the time, she'd been both astonished and flattered by his attention, while the other single women in the class were clearly envious. Jeffrey was trim, tall, certainly good-looking enough. His eyes, half-concealed behind wire-frame glasses, were a pleasing shade of blue-gray. He wore his sandy blond hair in deliberate disarray, as if stressing his indifference to the superficialities of grooming. His wardrobe consisted mainly of dusty jeans and white shirts, often with a sport jacket tossed on, seemingly at the last minute, to suggest the hurried, harried elegance of a successful man on the move.

And beyond all that, he was a gentleman. He opened doors for her, he always picked up the tab, and he had never gotten fresh, had never pressured her to go further than the brief parting kiss they shared at the end of most of their dates. Perhaps he sensed that if he tried coming on to her, if he even suggested the possibility of greater closeness between them, she would be frightened away like a bird launched into flight by a clap of hands.

And it was true. She would fly from him. She might not want to, but she would. Intimacy scared her, any sort of intimacy, and physical intimacy most of all.

Jeffrey was still detailing the difficulties posed by the photo session when the waiter delivered the appetizers and soup. Cutting into her egg roll, Wendy squinted at the jet of escaping steam. She blew on forkfuls of food to cool them, wary of burning her tongue.

She told herself she ought to quit grousing about Jeffrey's inattentiveness, ought to be happy he'd taken an interest in her. Certainly it was an interest no one else had ever shown. In high school, in college, in L.A., she'd had no boyfriends, no dates. She'd never imagined that anyone of the opposite sex could be attracted to her—and certainly not a successful photographer, handsome, confident, worldly. When Jeffrey had asked her out for the first time, she had been stunned, simply amazed, then so excited she'd kept fearing she would throw up, literally throw up, during their evening together. But gradually her excitement had turned to disappointment as she realized that Jeffrey was not aware of her as a person, that he never saw or heard her, that he merely wanted a silent respectful audience, a role she played so well.

After disappointment came self-reproach. She asked herself how she ever could have thought Jeffrey would be interested in her anyway. Was she good at conversation? Was she worth listening to at all? Did she have anything worthwhile to say, to give, to share? The silent questions, asked and answered on many sleepless nights, were like hammers, padded in soft velvet, striking again and again at her face, leaving no visible scars, but numbing her; in that numbness she found an odd sense of relief.

A few minutes before seven o'clock the main course was served. Wendy spooned steaming white rice onto her plate, then piled on a hot mixture of skinless chicken chunks and chopped almonds, water chestnuts and sliced carrots, celery and onion, in a mildly spicy sauce. She ate slowly, appreciating the taste and texture of the food, the pleasing contrast of the stir-fried chicken and the crunchy nuts and vegetables.

"How's yours?" Jeffrey asked.

"Really good."

"Mine too. I'm glad I found this place." Jeffrey always treated the Mandarin House as his personal discovery, even though he'd once let it slip that he learned of the restaurant's existence through a favorable review in the L.A. *Times*. "I like it, tacky dragon and all."

"Hey"—she attempted a joke—"the tacky dragon is what makes it work."

The line fell flat as predictably as any of her

occasional stabs at humor. She wished she'd kept quiet. It was always safer to—

"You know," Jeffrey said suddenly through a mouthful of shrimp, "that necklace is really something."

Her heart was ice, her breath frozen. She stared at him.

"You . . . you noticed?"

"Sure." He smiled. It was the same smile she'd seen through the car window. "I could hardly miss it, could I? You've been fiddling with the darn thing all night."

"I have?" She hadn't realized she'd been doing that.

"Uh-huh. Anyway, I saw it right off. As soon as you got out of the car. Must be brand new."

"Yes. It is. I bought it today. I went shopping. Well, not really shopping. I was just out for a walk. At lunchtime. I went into the department store, and there it was. It wasn't cheap. But I figured, you know, you've got to splurge once in a while. . . ."

The words came in fits and starts, barely coherent, while a confusion of feelings whirled inside her. Of course she was glad Jeffrey had noticed the necklace, glad he'd asked her about it and given her tacit permission to talk about the one big event of her day. Yes, thrilled about all that. Except . . . except . . .

I saw it right off, he'd told her. As soon as you got out of the car.

So why hadn't he said anything then? Why had he strung her along for more than half an hour, chatting about his f-stops and exposure times, while she waited in an agony of suspense for some word of acknowledgment?

She thought she knew the answer. It was simply one more tactic he employed to maintain control. He'd known what she wanted him to say, and he'd found pleasure in withholding that small gift as long as possible, like a sadist who dangles a morsel of food near his starving victim, just out of reach.

In that moment Wendy hated the man across the table from her. Yet in a strange way she loved him too. Because at least he *had* noticed, and now he was letting her talk, and—oh, God—did she ever need to talk. She needed it badly enough even to put up with his manipulations and smiling lies.

She went on talking and talking and talking, telling him every detail of her purchase. Probably she was boring him or making a complete fool of herself or doing something else that was utterly wrong; but for once, she didn't care.

8

At six o'clock, having finished his dinner, Rood set about making his preparations for the night's work.

From his bookshelf he pulled out a copy of the 1990 Thomas Guide for Los Angeles County, a spiral-bound map-book with an alphabetized directory covering every street in the county. He pinpointed Miss Wendy Alden's address—9741 Palm Vista Avenue—and marked it in red ink.

Then he peered into the large canvas drawstring bag he used for carrying his tools and trophies, taking inventory of its contents.

The hacksaw, fitted with a fresh tungsten-carbide blade. Two spare blades, in case the first one broke; bone was tough. The clay gryphon, carefully wrapped in plastic. His Toshiba tape recorder with a built-in omnidirectional microphone, loaded with a blank thirty-minute cassette; he would clip the tape recorder to his belt before the kill. A jumbo two-gallon Baggie, in which Miss Alden's head would be sealed. A wire twist tie for the Baggie. Saran Wrap for the hacksaw, which would be bloody, dripping; no use getting the bag soiled. A metal loid and wire tool for opening locked doors. A roll of electrician's tape and a hammer, useful for breaking windows with a minimum of noise; he'd tried that technique for the first time at Miss Osborn's place, and it had worked wonderfully well. A Tekna Micro-Lite miniature flashlight, four inches long. A pair of night-vision binoculars for scoping his victim from the street.

His weapon and his leather gloves were tucked in the side pockets of his black winter coat, which he now shrugged on.

Yes, he decided as he reviewed a mental checklist. He had everything.

He left his apartment, shut and locked the front door, and let the screen door bang shut. In the newly fallen darkness he crossed the courtyard, a patchwork of cracked concrete and rectangular grass strips. From the apartment across the way came the steady barking of Mrs. Weiman's German shepherd, Sherlock. The dog was often allowed to wander the courtyard, and Rood invariably stopped to scratch him behind the ears. He loved animals. In truth, he vastly preferred them to human beings. He had never been what one might call a "people" person.

His car was parked on the street. It was a 1963 Ford Falcon, the Futura Sports Coupe model, a white two-door hardtop with a tan interior. When viewed from the front, the Falcon looked squarish, almost boxy, but in profile its lines were as sleek and streamlined as a Fifties rocketship, the kind that was always setting down on a planet of nubile young women and enlarged iguanas, amid the alien vegetation of Griffith Park.

The word FORD was emblazoned in silver capitals across the hood, above the chrome grillwork and the huge round glassy headlights. Under the hood, a V-8 engine lay concealed, quiet now, like a somnolent animal, but poised to awaken with a growl at the turning of a key. More bold silver spelled out FALCON across the rear end of the trunk lid; below it gleamed the taillights, each one a red circle of molded plastic with a plastic knob embedded in its center, looking uncannily like a nipple. Arrowlike strips of chrome had once graced the sides of the car, but these had fallen off, leaving empty grooves in the metal.

Rood had bought the Falcon in Idaho a month before his move to L.A. two years ago. He was not a connoisseur of classic cars, but he appreciated old-fashioned workmanship, the solidity of a thing made to last. At the time of his purchase, the Falcon's odometer had registered eighty-six thousand miles; he'd realized, of course, that the car must have clocked far more mileage than that, with the odometer resetting to zero every hundred thousand miles. Yet even after the decades of hard service the car had delivered, it remained dependable; never once had it broken down.

What had drawn him to the car most of all, however, had been neither its design nor its durability, but that name: Falcon. The bird of prey, riding the high thermals, quartering the land below, then swooping out of the sun, its shadow the black shape of death, claws extended to snatch up the squeaking innocent, and rising, wings spread, talons streaked with blood. Falcon. Yes. Rood liked the sound of that.

Unlocking the door, Rood placed his canvas bag carefully on the floor of the backseat, then slid into the driver's seat and started the engine. When he closed his fists over the simulated wood-grain steering wheel, he smiled, pleased with the hard smoothness of it.

He turned the key in the ignition, switched on the headlights to cut the night, and motored south for a few blocks, hooking east on Olympic Boulevard. As he drove, he tuned the radio to a pop-music station. Rood liked songs, nice songs, not this modern rap garbage or this heavy-metal ugliness.

"Desperado" came on, sung by Linda Ronstadt. The song was one of his favorites. He admired the romanticized portrait of the outlaw, the loner, the man who refused to play by the rules. Of course the message of the song was that the loner was wrong, that he should give up his life and settle down, become ordinary. But Rood was sure that the message had been inserted only to appeal to the gutter filth who bought popular records; their mean prejudices and narrow outlook must be appeased.

The same cowardly appeasement could be seen in Hollywood movies. At the end of nearly every one, the villain got killed in some messy and horrible way, and the audience clapped their hooves and baaed and bleated in satisfaction. But, in truth, the villains were the real heroes, because they stepped outside society's boundaries, they dared for greatness, they endured the loneliness of the outcast, just as the musical desperado did; and though their lives ended in blood and fury, they died as martyrs to a great cause, the cause of superiority to the mundane.

Better to reign in hell than serve in heav'n, Rood thought, quoting Mr. John Milton, who in turn had been quoting Lucifer.

He turned south on Beverly Glen Boulevard, passing the apartment building where Miss Rebecca Morris had lived. The sight evoked pleasant memories; he smiled in warm nostalgia. Miss Morris had made a fine kill, but there were far finer ones to come. What he had done in the past few years was only the beginning. Dimly he'd glimpsed his future, and it was magnificent. Songs and poems would commemorate him. Some unborn Homer would pen his odyssey. Statues would be raised in his image, and monuments in his name.

It had been a long road he'd traveled to reach the threshold of such greatness. As a child he could never have predicted his awesome destiny. He had been weak then. Yes, weak from the beginning.

His mother had often told him the story of his difficult birth, three weeks ahead of schedule, and how the small, wet, shriveled, wailing thing in her arms had not been expected to survive for more than a few days. An inauspicious arrival for one who would someday become the destroyer of worlds.

He had survived, of course, and grown; but he had not grown well. His weakness as an infant hung on like a stubborn illness. He developed into a skinny, nearsighted child blinking at life through thick lenses in owlish frames. He couldn't run more than a few yards without tiring, couldn't bat a ball or throw one, couldn't chin himself even once. He had no skill at sports, no confidence in any aspect of life pertaining to physical activity. His body was an alien vessel in which his mind was trapped.

The only escape for him lay in imagination. Fantasies became his life. In daydreams he was strong, strong enough to take revenge on those who wronged him daily. He could shape his private inner world to whatever specifications he desired, edit and alter it at will, control the outcome of any situation. He could be a god.

Reality was less malleable, and for that reason, it was terrifying. He remembered the day in gym class when the teacher had ordered the kids to climb a rope. The others had done it with varying degrees of ease, most of them nimble as monkeys, a few grunting and straining but getting the job done. Then it was his turn. He stared up at the knotted line that extended to the ceiling a million miles high. He knew he couldn't do it; and what was worse, he knew that the others knew it also. He felt the pressure of their eyes on him, the tension of their suppressed laughter straining for release.

"Hurry up, Frankie." It was the gym teacher's voice, empty of compassion. "Get going. Quit fooling around."

He managed to climb five feet before his meager strength gave out. Then he just hung there, unable to go higher and afraid to slide down. Around him rose the sound he feared more than anything, the sound of children's laughter, the ugly, hooting, chattering laughter heard only in treetops and playgrounds.

Afterward, in the locker room, the others ganged up on him. Holding him by his arms and legs, they slammed his head into the steel door of a locker again and again while his small fists flailed uselessly.

Weakling, they called him. Baby girl. Faggot.

Finally they shut him in the locker and left him there. For two hours he was trapped in that lightless coffinlike place, breathing through the

vents and whimpering softly. Eventually the jani-
tor heard him weeping and let him out.

Rood winced at the memory and tightened his
grip on the steering wheel.

There had been many such incidents. Children
were evil creatures; they sensed weakness and
preyed on it. In any group of youngsters, there
was one who would be cast as the outsider, the
loser, the perpetual victim. In the small town
where he'd grown up, in the school that had been
his prison, he had been assigned that role, and
there was no escaping from it.

He was twelve years old when he developed
an interest in the opposite sex, an interest confined to sexual fantasies; he was sure he had no
chance with any of the girls in town. They knew
too much about him. They knew he was a sissy
because he was the one picked on by the other
boys. They knew he was weird because he kept
to himself and rarely spoke above a mumble.
They knew he was a fairy because he wore glasses
and was no good at sports. Oh, yes, they knew
everything.

He did his best to satisfy his urges in secret.
His collection helped, at least for a time. He spent
many hours pressing his lips to the satin smoothness of stolen panties and running his tongue
over the cups of bras. But articles of clothing, no
matter how seductively feminine, were not enough.
He needed a woman, a woman who would love
him and whisper tender words to him and stroke
him in the dark. He needed love.

Only three times in his life had Rood tried to
establish any form of intimacy with a woman. He
made his first attempt while in the tenth grade.
After helping a girl with her homework on several

occasions, he summoned all his courage and asked her to a school dance. The look on her face when she turned him down—that mixture of discomfort and shock and imperfectly concealed amusement—was a splash of acid burned into his memory.

His second attempt came four years later, on the night of his twenty-first birthday, when he visited a whorehouse. He still wanted a woman, wanted one desperately, but he was terrified of facing rejection again.

The whore did not reject him. His wallet was full; that was all she cared about. But when she took him to bed with her, a terrible thing happened, a thing that shamed him worse than any humiliation of his childhood. He was impotent with her. His manhood, which had never failed him when he huddled alone in the bathroom, was limp and unresponsive. The whore told him that it was all right, that it happened all the time; but he heard the contempt in her voice, the words she had not spoken, the words she must have been thinking.

Sissy. Weakling. Faggot.

His third and final attempt took place on a winter afternoon six years ago, the day when he dared to ask Miss Kathy Lutton to a movie. At the time he hadn't known her last name; he learned it a year later from news reports of her murder in the parking lot outside the restaurant. A murder that had never been solved.

Miss Lutton had rejected him, but he had not taken rejection and humiliation passively that time. At last he'd found a way to exercise power over women. The ultimate power, the power of life and death, the power of a god.

Even as a child, Rood had known of the power that was his when he did things to animals. He'd thrilled at their helplessness, their frantic squirming and final convulsions. He'd known other varieties of power as well—the power that came from shoplifting, from breaking into homes, from setting fires and watching the flames leap up.

But none of that had been enough to make him truly strong. Murder was different. Murder was the medicine that cured him at last of the disease of weakness.

Now he was more powerful than any of the bullies who'd beaten him, more powerful than any of the frigid, sexless, man-hating bitches who'd done their best to emasculate him. He'd strengthened his body with a rigorous exercise regime, and he'd strengthened his character with ever greater tests of his courage and cunning. Over the past five years he'd taken many lives, each time refining his technique and polishing his skills.

There had been Miss Georgia Grant, whom he'd encountered on a hiking trail in 1987. After that, the teenage girl he'd kidnapped outside of Boise; he'd seen to it that her body would never be found. Then, in 1989, two kills: Miss Lynn Peters, the escort-service whore in Nampa, and Miss Stacy Brannon, the hitchhiker on Route 15.

Shortly afterward, he'd moved to L.A., where he'd found new opportunities. A nameless female transient he'd buried in Griffith Park. A few months later, Miss Erin Thompson, the UCLA student whose body must still be moldering in a cave near Paradise Cove. Then Miss Kelly Widmark, who'd worked at a video store in Santa Monica, and who'd died in the alley behind the store. Her murder, unlike most of the others, had been impulsive and unplanned; the sight of her as she stood at the checkout counter, so young and virginal and yet so very ripe, had jolted him with desire, and he'd simply left the store without renting a tape, then waited in the alley, hoping she would leave via the rear door. She had. And more recently, less than a year ago, in fact, there had been Mrs. Carla Aguilar, the housewife from Culver City. He'd seen her on the street and followed her for hours before ambushing her in the parking garage of a shopping mall.

His first kill in Twin Falls had been rushed and rather sloppy. Only gradually had he learned to draw out each murder by means of physical or psychological torture, to enjoy the corpse afterward, and to take parts of it with him for purposes of preservation; he'd always taken pleasure in keeping the animals' remains. At first fingers and tongues had seemed particularly appealing; the possibility of taking the head had not occurred to him until lately. He'd tried it first on Mrs. Aguilar, but the hacksaw blade had snapped in half, defeated by the unyielding vertebrae of the neck. Only once he'd bought a tungsten-carbide blade had he been sure of taking the trophy he most wanted.

Now the Gryphon would strike again. And the city would tremble before him. And he, Franklin Rood, would laugh.

Power, yes. He had power. Unlimited power.

He was the most powerful man in the world.

As he headed east on Pico Boulevard, approaching Miss Alden's neighborhood, he found himself humming along with the new song on the radio, which was "Sweet Dreams."

9

After dinner Wendy and Jeffrey crossed Pico Boulevard, jaywalking at his insistence, and entered the Westside Pavilion, a cavernous postmodern shopping mall echoing with footsteps and the blare of Muzak from trendy little stores. They rode the escalators from floor to floor, people-watching and window-shopping, stopping once to purchase two strawberry frozen-yogurt cones. They ended up at the multiplex theater facility on the top floor, where they debated seeing a movie—or, rather, Jeffrey knocked around the pros and cons of the idea while Wendy listened impassively. There was no shortage of first-run films to choose from, but none of them really appealed to Jeffrey, so he concluded that they didn't want to go to a movie after all. Wendy agreed.

"Well," Jeffrey said, which was what he always said when they reached the terminal point in one of their dates.

"Well," she echoed foolishly.

"You've got yogurt on your nose," he informed her.

She wiped it off. "Thanks."

"So I guess we've had our fun for tonight, huh?"

"I guess so."

He walked her back to her Honda. They stood on the curb watching random cars whiz past, headlights tracing white comet tails in the darkness. The dry wind was stronger than before; trees rustled ominously, and scraps of newspaper cartwheeled like tumbleweeds down the street.

"There's still some yogurt on you," Jeffrey said.

"Where?"

He kissed her mouth gently. "There."

"Gone now?"

"Not quite."

He kissed her again. His lips lingered. Her sudden awareness of his body, so close to her own, was frightening. Nervously she pulled away; then, to compensate for breaking contact so abruptly, she smiled.

"Thanks for dinner."

He nodded, showing nothing in his face. "I'll call you."

Quickly she got into her car, turned the key in the ignition, switched on the headlights. She pulled away from the curb and left Jeffrey standing there, alone on the sidewalk, his hand lifted in a wave.

She'd been planning to drive straight home, but on impulse she took a detour into Westwood Village, where the sidewalks were always crowded, even on a Tuesday night. She cruised past movie theaters dressed in neon radiance, bars and restaurants throbbing with the electronic pulse of amplified music, storefront windows framing pyramids of record albums and platoons of T-shirts gliding on automated racks. A sudden inexplicable urge seized her, the urge to get out of her car, join the crowds, become part of that cheerful chaos just beyond her windshield, just out of reach.

The feeling passed. After she'd circled the Village a few times, crawling at five miles an hour in the sluggish traffic, she had no urge to do anything except go home and climb into bed.

She took Wilshire Boulevard east to Beverly Glen, cut south to Pico, and pulled into her parking space at nine-thirty. She got out of the car, carrying the shopping bag from the jewelry store, which now contained only an empty box; she stuffed the bag in the trash dumpster at the side of the building.

As she passed Jennifer Kutzlow's apartment on the ground floor, she noted with relief that the lights were out, the place silent. Then she remembered having seen Jennifer leave this morning. Off to Seattle, she'd said, swinging her overnight bag. Well, there would be no rock and roll tonight, thank God.

Wendy checked her mail and found nothing but the usual assortment of bills and advertising circulars. She climbed the outside staircase, walked along the second-floor gallery, and unlocked her door. Stepping inside, she flipped up the wall switch; light flooded the living room. Automatically she glanced around to see if the place had been burglarized; it hadn't.

She hung up her coat in the hall closet, then went into the bathroom to pour a glass of water. Her reflection in the mirror over the sink caught her eye. She stared at herself. The necklace sparkled like spilled wine. It really was beautiful. Beautiful—but wasted. Wasted on her. Because nobody would ever look twice at her, necklace or not.

"It was better off in the display case," she whispered. Quick tears stung her eyes. "Shouldn't have bought the thing." Her fingers fumbled at the clasp. "Waste of money, is what it is. Goddamn waste."

She yanked off the necklace and flung it to the floor. Then she sat on the closed lid of the toilet, shoulders slumping, and lowered her head, not quite crying but wishing she could.

After a few minutes she collected herself, then knelt and picked up the necklace. As far as she could tell, it was undamaged. She stroked it gently, almost tenderly, as if seeking to apologize for having been so rough with it.

In her bedroom, she opened the jewelry box in the top drawer of her mahogany dresser and laid the necklace inside. She pulled off her tan suit, then changed into white satin pajamas and a blue terry-cloth robe. Groping on the floor of her closet, she found a pair of cushioned Deerfoams and slipped them on her feet. She unclipped her hair and let it fall loosely around her shoulders.

Then she left the bedroom to fix herself a snack. She wasn't particularly hungry, but an apple might be nice. In the kitchen, in the shadowless light of the overhead fluorescents, she cored and sliced a red Delicious. She switched on the portable TV for the company of a human voice. The ten o'clock news was already under way.

". . . search continues for the Gryphon. Thirteen days have passed since the body of Elizabeth Osborn was found . . ."

Wendy snapped off the TV, letting silence settle over the apartment once more.

She put the apple on a plate, poured a glass of skim milk, and sat at the dining table in her usual chair, facing the two corner windows. Chewing slowly, not noticing the taste, she stared out at the leafy branches of the fig tree swaying and creaking in the wind.

She thought about Jeffrey and the games he played with her, the mind games, the power games. He was wrong to act like that, but she was equally wrong to let him get away with it. Why hadn't she simply asked him straight out, "How do you like my new necklace?" Why had she been afraid to solicit a compliment from him? But she supposed she knew the answer. She remembered how, as a little girl, she'd dressed up for her parents, hoping to hear words of approval, only to be criticized for being a show-off.

A sigh escaped her lips like a hiss of air from a punctured tire, the weary sound of something shrinking, flattening, losing shape and firmness, a sound that matched the way she felt inside. No longer hungry, but determined to finish her snack, she picked up the second-to-last wedge of the apple and raised it to her mouth, and then from somewhere in the room at her back, she heard a noise.

The noise was faint, so faint as to be nearly inaudible, yet she had no difficulty identifying it in an automatic, almost instinctual way. It was the sound a joint makes when cartilage snap-crackle-pops. The crick of a spine, perhaps, or . . . or the creak of a knee.

A *human* sound.

Somebody is in here, she thought in slow, creeping horror. *Somebody is . . . in the apartment . . . with me.*

But that was crazy. Insane. There was no way anyone could have gotten in. The door had been locked. There'd been no sign of forced entry. She had to get hold of herself.

Her hand closed over the cold glass of milk. She took a sip, tried to swallow, couldn't.

Because she was thinking that, yes, the door had been locked when she'd left and locked when she returned—but locks could be picked, couldn't they? A man could get in and shut the door behind him, and she would never know. Not until she heard the crackle of bones in the stillness of her living room.

Holding the glass in one hand, she sat motionless in her chair, listening. She heard no further sound. Which, of course, proved nothing. Nothing at all.

Suppose, she thought, *now just suppose for the sake of argument that somebody really is in the apartment with me. Hiding. Crouching down, say, his knees getting stiff. Where would he be? In the hall closet? No. Closer than that. Somewhere in this room.*

She tried to visualize the layout of the room at her back, but it was difficult; her mind seemed to have gone blank. She'd moved into this apartment five years ago, bought every stick of furniture in the place, spent nearly all of her free time here—yet at this moment she had no idea what the room looked like.

Of course she could see for herself, simply by turning in her chair. But she didn't want to do that. Because all of a sudden she had the feeling that as long as she didn't see whatever was there, it couldn't hurt her. She was a child again, pulling the covers over her head so the monsters wouldn't be real.

All right, Wendy, she ordered herself. *Get it together*.

She shut her eyes. She forced herself to construct a mental picture of her apartment.

She started with the front door. To the left of the door there was the doorway to the hall that led to the bathroom and bedroom. To the right, there was the kitchen, divided from the living room by a chest-high counter. Near the entrance to the kitchen was the table where she was now seated. Directly behind her, perhaps five yards from where she sat, was the sofa she'd gotten at Sears. It was flush with the wall; no way for anyone to hide behind it. In front of the sofa was a glass coffee table; it, too, was useless as a hiding place. And at the far end of the sofa, near the doorway to the hall, was her little reading nook: a floor lamp, the fake schefflera tree, and that big old armchair and ottoman she'd picked up at a garage sale and reupholstered. . . .

She drew a sharp breath.

Those two things—the potted plant and the chair—formed a kind of bracket, didn't they? A man could conceal himself there, screened from view by the bulk of the chair and by the schefflera's polyester leaves. Couldn't he? *Couldn't he?*

Wendy shivered.

No, the hard, stolid voice of reason insisted. *It's absurd. And you're going to prove to yourself just how nonsensical it is. Right now.*

She put down the glass of milk with a loud, oddly reassuring clunk. Slowly, deliberately, she turned in her chair and stared at the other end of the room.

Nothing stirred. No one was there. No one she could see anyway.

She considered getting up and looking behind the easy chair, then dismissed the idea. If somebody were there, why would he still be hiding? He would come out and get her, wouldn't he? The whole thing made no sense. She was just overtired. She hadn't gotten enough sleep last night.

Calm once more, mildly amused at herself, she ate the last of her apple, then washed it down with the milk. She was still thinking about how silly she'd been to overreact that way when she heard the noise again.

Crick.

Her lower lip began to tremble. She bit down on it, hard.

Old wood, she told herself. *Old wood settling in for the night. That's all it is. That's all. Please. Let that be all it is.*

As casually as possible, Wendy shifted her position in her chair, turning her head just enough to catch a glimpse of the other side of the room.

Her heart froze.

Because for a split second she'd *seen* something behind the armchair—a wisp of curly brown hair—the top of somebody's head ducking quickly out of sight.

Oh, my God.

She turned back to the windows, trembling.

He is there, she told herself as panic rippled over her. *He must have been there the whole time, ever since I got home. He's been watching me, watching from behind the chair. For Jesus Christ's sake, there's a strange man in my living room and he's hiding behind the fucking chair!*

Okay, girl. Don't lose it now. Don't lose it.

With effort she stayed in control. Just barely.

She tried to determine her options. She could attempt to get into her bedroom and lock the door, then call the police. But suppose he heard her making the call and came after her. The bedroom door was only cheap plywood; anyone could break it down. Response time in this neighborhood was eight or nine minutes at least. Too long.

All right, then. She would make a run for it. Yes, even though she was wearing only pajamas and a robe. She would get out the front door and run, run like hell.

But she had to be smart about it. Had to act natural, con him into thinking she suspected nothing. In order to reach the front door she'd have to cross the living room, which meant she would pass right by the chair; if she betrayed any hint of what she knew, the man would pounce on her and bring her down, and then God only knew what he would do.

But if she could make it past the chair, then the front door would be less than five feet away. That would be the time to break into a run. All she'd have to do was get to the door, down the stairs, into the street. And scream. Scream for help. Yes. That was all.

But it sure was enough.

She took a breath. With studied nonchalance, she picked up her plate and her glass, carried them into the kitchen, and put them in the sink. To her astonishment she realized she was humming a melody—that old song, "Full Moon and Empty Arms," which had been taken from the theme of Rachmaninoff's Second Piano Concerto, hadn't it? Now why would a tune like that have chosen this particular moment to pop into her head? The human mind sure was an amazing thing, yes, indeedy. Simply remarkable, what the old cerebral cortex could come up with to amuse itself in moments of extreme stress.

Nausea burned in her stomach. The back of her neck was icy; her forehead, feverish. She had the absurd impression that her heart had leaped out of her chest into her skull and was beating there; she could feel its hard steady rhythm against her temples, her jaw, the crown of her head, each beat a separate knock, shaking her body.

Still humming softly, she ran cold tapwater in the sink, banged her breakfast dishes around in a noisy pretense of washing and drying them, and shoved them into the kitchen cabinets. Then, prompted by a sudden thought, she picked up the knife she'd used to core and slice the apple, and hid it in the pocket of her robe.

Now for the hard part.

She tried to estimate how far it was to the front door. A good fifteen paces, she figured. All she had to do was cover that much distance, and she would be home free.

Heart pounding, she left the kitchen, keeping her face averted from the armchair and potted plant up ahead on her left. She could feel his eyes on her. Could sense his closeness, the closeness of a camouflaged jungle animal poised to spring for the kill.

She padded through the living room, still humming the tune, which in her ears had segued from a cheerful melody into a series of stifled screams. She was aware with preternatural alertness of every object she passed. The coffee table, its glass surface scattered with copies of *Elle* magazine. The sofa, still bearing the plastic slipcovers that had come with it. The end tables where ceramic lamps glowed, casting cones of yellow light over the bare white wall.

She wished she were not wearing her pajamas and robe. The bedtime clothes made her feel even more vulnerable, almost naked. Naked before him, exposed to his staring eyes.

The door was only six feet away. But closer still, there loomed the armchair. She wanted to veer around it, but if she did, *he* would know something was up. She forced herself to walk right by the chair, passing so close that the hem of her robe brushed its legs. Abruptly something cold and smooth touched the bare skin of her neck, and she was sure it was his hand reaching out for her—but no; it was only one of the schefflera's plastic leaves. She hummed louder. The noise was maddening in her ears; it throbbed in time with the pulse of roaring blood.

Then—hallelujah—she'd gotten past the chair. The hallway was coming up on her left. He would expect her to turn down that hall. When she didn't, he would know she was on to him, and he would strike.

She took a step toward the hall, and then with a burst of speed she raced for the front door.

Behind her she caught a flash of motion, and without even looking back she knew he'd sprung to his feet, bobbing up from behind the chair like a malignant jack-in-the-box. She reached the door. Her hand fisted over the knob. She jerked it savagely. The door didn't open. The dead bolt—oh, God—she must have thrown the dead bolt.

Behind her, footsteps. Closing in. Fast.

She drew the bolt and tried the knob again.

This time the door opened. She was going to make it. Going to make it—

At the edge of her vision, a blurred white shape. A sneaker lashing out in a kick. Thump of impact, rubber on wood. The door slammed shut.

Wendy grabbed the knob again, trying to turn it, to pull open the door and escape into the night just beyond her reach, and then suddenly two gloved hands flew past the sides of her face like brown bats, leather-winged and blood-spotted, and something threadlike and viciously sharp was looped around her neck, cutting into the tender skin, drawing blood.

"Let go of the door, Miss Wendy Alden," a male voice whispered in her left ear, "and don't make a sound."

My name, she thought in cold shock. *How does he know my name?*

Slowly she released her grip on the doorknob. She let both hands fall to her sides, fingers splayed. She was unnaturally aware of the position of her body, her slippered feet planted wide apart on the floor, her back arched, her head leaning back under the pull of the sharp slender cord—a loop of wire, she realized—lashed around her throat.

The man was directly behind her. She could smell the stale greasy odor of his sweat, could feel his breath hot on her cheek. But she couldn't see him. Couldn't see anything except the black specks pinwheeling crazily before her eyes.

"If you cry for help," he said softly, his voice so low she could barely hear it over the staccato beating of her heart, "if you try anything foolish, I'll kill you."

His last words echoed in her mind: I'll kill you,

kill you, kill you. No, he couldn't have said that. But he had. She'd heard him. She was sure of it. He'd said he would kill her. But that was crazy. She couldn't . . . die. Could she?

"Your lovely neck," he went on quietly, "is now encircled by a foot and a half of stainless-steel wire. A garrote, you see."

Garrote. Like in *The Godfather*.

"Homemade," the stranger whispered, "but most effective nonetheless. The wire is threaded through two wooden dowels, which serve as handles. Simply by twisting those handles, I can exert pressure"—the wire tautened slightly for emphasis—"as much pressure as I like. Steel wire is wickedly sharp; it can slice flesh like wax. Do you understand what I'm telling you? Say yes."

"Yes." The word a croak. It startled her. Someone else's voice.

"Good. Very good. Are you afraid of me, Miss Wendy Alden?"

A choked sound was all she could utter.

"Are you?" he inquired more sharply, as once again the garrote tightened almost imperceptibly, but just enough.

"Yes. Oh, yes."

"Of course you are. Do you know who I am?"

"No."

"I am called the Gryphon."

Dizzying fear. Waves of it. Her knees weakening. Feverish heat in her forehead. Vision doubling. Heart pounding. She fought to keep from passing out.

This wasn't happening. Not to her. It couldn't be. The Gryphon—why, that was something she heard about on the news, something that involved other people, something remote and distant, a headline or a few seconds of tape shot by a wobbly camera, scary but not immediate, not a threat, not part of her world.

"Oh. Oh. Oh." Who was saying that? She was. Funny. Why was she repeating that one word, that empty sound, over and over? She wanted to stop, couldn't. "Oh. Oh. Oh." The sounds coming faster now, uncontrollable, like hiccups.

"Shut up." His voice like a slap.

She shut up. She waited for him to kill her. He would, of course. He always killed his victims. Killed them and . . . and cut off their heads.

"Now listen to me, Miss Alden. You've seen the stories in the news. You know what happened to the other women I've encountered. But for you I may make an exception. I may let you live . . . if you'll do what I say. Will you?"

An exception. Then there was a chance. A hope. If she would do what he said. Well, of course she would. She would do whatever he wanted. Even let him molest her, rape her. It didn't matter. Nothing mattered except staying alive.

Everything was clear, vivid. Terror had sharpened her senses, heightened her awareness, slowed time to a spider crawl. The smallest details around her stood out sharply like photographic close-ups. She saw the light glinting on the brass doorknob a foot away, saw the blurred, contorted, upside-down images of herself and the man behind her cupped in the knob, two indistinct shadowy shapes backlit by the lamps on her end tables. She saw the white pile carpet, and the seam where the carpet met the molding of the wall, and the brownish dust that had collected there, where her vacuum cleaner hadn't reached; she would have to use the Dustbuster on that mess, uh-huh. She heard the hum of the refrigerator and the buzz of the fluorescent lighting panel in the kitchen. Outside a car rattled past, engine noise fading with distance, leaving an impression of motion and freedom, cruelly tantalizing.

"Will you?" the Gryphon asked again.

She realized she hadn't answered. Her voice was stuck in her throat. Her tongue was paste. She forced out sound.

"Yes."

"You're most cooperative, Miss Alden. I like that. Your chances of surviving this rendezvous are improving all the time." His lips drifted closer to her ear. She felt the heat of his breath on her earlobe. "Of course, if you saw my face, then I would have no choice but to kill you. You didn't see my face, did you?"

"I didn't. I swear." Oh, God, it was no use, he'd never believe her, even though it was true. "You've been behind me the whole time," she said desperately, pleadingly, "and there was no way I could see you, really, I don't have any idea—"

"Fine. I only wanted to be sure."

Did he believe her? Did he really? There was no way she could know. She had to hope, that was all, just hope.

"Now," he said softly, "here's what I'd like you to do."

She waited, praying it wouldn't be too bad, whatever it was he wanted. Distantly she was aware of the searing pain in her throat where the wire had dug into her skin, and the warm trickle leaking from the wound. She could feel the strength of his arms in the pressure of the garrote around her neck. The garrote that, at any moment, could cinch tight, tear open her throat like a paper bag, slice arteries, stop breath.

"I want you to say some words for me," he told her. "Some very special words. Words that please me and leave me satisfied. I'll say them first, and you'll repeat them for me. Do that, and I'll release you unharmed. Fair enough?"

Fair enough? she thought. *Oh, God, yes, more than fair enough. Just saying some words, why, that's easy, that's nothing.*

"Yes," she said. "It's fair. Very fair. Thank you." She felt ridiculously grateful to this faceless stranger who was giving her a chance, who wanted nothing more from her than a few words. "Thank you very much."

"Why, you're most welcome, my dear. And most charmingly polite. All right, repeat after me: Please don't kill me."

"Please . . ." She stumbled. This was harder than she'd thought. Those words were difficult to say. They named her emotions too exactly. They made the danger facing her fully real. "Please don't kill me," she said with effort.

"I don't want to die," he said.

Suddenly her eyes were burning. Tears threatened. "I . . . I don't want to die."

"I'll do whatever you wish. Anything at all."

"I'll do anything . . ." No, that was wrong. *Dammit, Wendy, get the words right.* "I'll do whatever you want. Wish. Whatever you wish. Anything at all."

She was messing up. She couldn't concentrate. The wire testing her throat, it was tight, too tight. Hard to breathe.

"You are far greater and more powerful than I."

He spoke in a slow, measured, ritualistic cadence. "You frighten me. I've never been so terribly afraid. You're the strongest, the most awe-inspiring being I've ever conceived of." His voice was growing sluggish, torpid, the voice of a leech battening itself on blood. "I'm blinded by your radiance, prostrate before you. Overwhelmed, chastened, humbled. Say it."

It was too much to absorb; she couldn't retain it all. Her head was spinning.

"You . . . you're much greater than I am, much more, uh, powerful. You scare me. I've never felt so afraid. You're the . . . the strongest and most . . . most . . ."

"Awe-inspiring," he prompted.

"Most awe-inspiring being I've ever imagined. I'm blinded by your . . ." What was the word? "Radiance. Blinded by your radiance. Blinded and humbled . . ." No, there was something before that, something about kneeling, but not kneeling, some other word, what was it? She didn't know, couldn't think, she'd blown it, oh, God, what a jerk she was. "I'm sorry," she said helplessly, "I'm all mixed up. Could you repeat the last part? Please?"

"Never mind." An edge in his voice. A growl. Anger.

He would kill her now. She knew he would. She had to make him give her another chance.

"Oh, come on, tell me again," she pleaded, hating the tremulous eagerness in her voice. "I'll say it right this time, I'll say all of it, I just couldn't remember . . ."

He made no reply. She waited for the sudden agonizing bite of the wire.

"Please," she said again, hoping for some answer, any answer. "Oh, please, I promise I won't disappoint you. Uh, let's see. I'm blinded by your radiance, I'm, uh, overwhelmed and humbled . . ."

"There, there, my dear," the voice behind her said with surprising kindliness. "It's all right. No need to go on with this part of the program. You've recited enough borrowed words."

She understood that he was not angry with her after all, that he was not going to tighten the garrote, not yet anyway. Relief weakened her.

"Now," he said, "I wish to try something a little different. More creative. I want you to tell me exactly why you ought to live. Why your life matters. Why it's important. I'm not talking about your value to society or to mankind; this isn't the Miss America pageant we're running here, in case you hadn't noticed. Tell me why your life is important to *you*. What do you love? What are your aspirations? Your dreams? Your prayers? Tell me."

Dreams? Prayers? She didn't know. She hadn't dared to dream in so long. Her mind was blank.

"I . . . oh, Jeez, I . . . I'm not sure what to say. . . ."

"Well, you'd better think of something, Miss Wendy Alden." The garrote tightened again, the razor-keen steel burning. "And you'd better make it good."

Even though she couldn't see him, she knew he was smiling; she could *feel* the slow upward curve of his lips, the feral flash of teeth. She had no choice but to give him what he wanted, if she could find the words. And she had to find them. Just had to.

"Okay," she said. "I'll tell you. I . . . I want to

live, because . . . because . . ." No words would come. "Because . . ."

Nothing. Nothing at all. *Did* she want to live? Did it matter? Did anything matter?

"I'm waiting, Miss Alden."

Talk, she ordered herself. *Say any goddamn thing, will you? Come on, dammit. Come on.*

"Santa Barbara," she said, then rushed on, afraid to stop. "I want to go there. Want to see Santa Barbara. Oh, God, that sounds stupid, doesn't it? I mean, it's not that far away, and why didn't I ever go when I had the chance? But I didn't. Because I was afraid. Afraid to live. I haven't lived yet, not really, not ever. Haven't done anything. And now I'm sorry, so sorry, for all the things I've missed."

"What else?" the voice breathed.

"I want to do something with my life. Get a better job, challenge myself, I don't know. I'm afraid to die not knowing what I could have done, what I could have been. And I . . . I want to fall in love. I've never been in love, never even known what love is. This probably isn't good enough, is it? What I'm saying, I mean. I know it's not. I should have some big exciting plans, when all I've got are these stupid little things that don't mean anything, except they're what seem to matter most, the things I've never done. . . ."

She was crying. Crying for the first time in years, the first time since childhood, and perhaps for the last time ever. She was still afraid, yes, but underlying her fear was sadness, a profound and all-consuming sense of loss. She mourned for herself and for her life. She was an unborn child; she had never really lived; and now she never would. Her brief flame, never bright, would be snuffed out, leaving behind no memory of its burning. She'd spent twenty-nine years on earth, twenty-nine years of days and nights, but out of all those days, how many had she known when she truly felt alive? How many hours? Not enough, not nearly enough. Oh, but if he only would let her go, she would cherish every day, hour, minute, second, every breath of life; never again would she let time go by unappreciated and unused. And she would have time, so much time—years, decades—who ever said life was short?

Please, God, please make him let me go. . . .

"I want to live," she said, her voice thick. "I do. Really. So much. I never knew before—how much. And if you . . . kill me, I won't get the chance to live, to change. If I can change. I don't know if I can. Maybe I can't. Maybe nobody can. Maybe we're all victims, me and you, everyone. Maybe it's too late . . . for all of us. But I'm not sure. I have to find out. Please let me find out. I'm not making sense, am I? I know I'm not. I wish, I wish, I *wish* I knew what to say. . . ."

"Hush now. You've done fine, Miss Alden. The Gryphon is well-pleased."

She hitched in a breath. What did he mean by that? Would he let her go? He'd promised he would, if she satisfied him. She waited, tears standing in her eyes, feeling a desperate hope.

"You're very innocent," he breathed in a voice soft as velvet, "aren't you, my dear? I like that. You're not at all like the others in this polluted city. You're so wonderfully untouched, uncorrupted. Your purity makes me ashamed of having lied to you."

Her heart twisted. "Lied?"

"I do apologize."

"What . . . did you . . . lie about?" But she knew. She knew already.

"Letting you go. Sparing your life. There never was any chance I would do that."

Her last hope crumbled, crushed under heavy despair. She moaned. Her mind was a bruise slowly turning black-and-blue.

"You're far too fine a specimen," he whispered. "You'll be such a wonderful addition to my collection."

Specimen? she thought numbly. *Collection?*

Then she understood. Her head. That was what he meant. He collected heads. The heads he took from his victims. And now he would take hers.

She tried to speak, couldn't. Her mouth worked, but no sound came. She closed her eyes, trying to shut out the world and flee this nightmare, then opened them immediately, afraid of the dark that had fallen behind her eyelids, the dark that was so much like death.

The steel wire was tightening slowly, slowly. She was going to die here, in this room, tonight—die before she'd lived—and there was nothing she could do.

"You're mine now, Miss Wendy Alden," the Gryphon breathed, his voice like dust, like death. "Mine forever."

10

The Detective Unit office was a large windowless room partitioned into smaller sections by rows of shoulder-high filing cabinets, many of them topped with bound volumes of the Municipal Code and potted plants that did not require sunlight. Metal desks butted up against one another, sharing their clutter; swivel chairs that rolled on steel casters were scattered here and there like driftwood.

Delgado sat in one chair, turning slowly in his seat, back and forth, back and forth, while two of the task-force detectives, Donna Wildman and Tom Gardner, tossed ideas at him. It was a brainstorming session, the kind of thing cops did when they had run out of strategies. Phones rang in other parts of the room, and people hurried in and out of doors, trailing plumes of cigarette smoke and the odor of sweat.

"So how about working the statues harder?" Wildman said. She was eating a granola bar, and she spoke through a mouthful of molasses and nuts.

"Harder, how?" Delgado countered. "Torres and Blaise have visited every gallery and art school on the Westside."

"But only looking for somebody who's a sculptor. What about approaching it from another

153

angle? Wait a minute. The lab report is here someplace." She dug through a mound of papers on her desk, found a manila folder, scanned its contents. "It says the statues were made of a specific brand of modeling clay. Why don't we go to art-supplies stores and track down everybody who bought a box of that stuff?"

"I was told it's a common brand, sold everywhere."

"If he used a particular kind of sculpting tool to put in the details, we could look for purchases of that."

"The experts say it was probably a pencil."

"Maybe we should run in everyone who's bought a pencil," Tom Gardner cracked.

Wildman glared at him.

"Okay," he added, "we'll limit it to number-two pencils only."

"Come on, you two," Delgado said. "Give me some better ideas. Amaze me."

"I say we post unmarked cars at all crime scenes, twenty-four hours a day," Gardner said. "Just watching. He may show up again."

"Why would he?" Wildman asked, sounding irritated at Gardner because he'd shot down her idea.

"These guys do that. Like Ted Bundy. He would go over to a crime scene and fantasize about the murder, relive it, get off on it." He fingered the tape dispenser on his desk, removing bits of tape and sticking them on his blotter. "I think he brought little souvenirs with him, like the victim's ballpoint pen, say, or a grocery list— something he'd taken that was never missed. He'd sit there in his car and fondle this thing and think about how good it had felt to kill that girl."

"We've already got beat cars cruising past those buildings every fifteen minutes," Delgado said.

"Suppose he's there for only five minutes, and they miss him."

"What are we going to do?" Wildman asked. "Arrest everybody who parks on the street?"

"Only the ones who look suspicious."

"Whatever that means."

Delgado cut off Gardner's reply. "I don't think we can spare the manpower right now. But I'll keep it in mind."

"I say we push the limits of the physical evidence," Wildman said. "Physical evidence is what always trips up these guys. For instance, those carpet fibers. I think we were too quick to brush them off."

"The fibers will convict him," Gardner said, "not catch him."

"Maybe they'll do both. I say we start checking likely places where this guy works. Operate on the assumption that he's an art aficionado. Look at the galleries, art stores, and other operations like that, and see what kind of carpeting they've got. If we find a fiber match, we start checking out the employees—" Her desk phone rang; she grabbed it. "Wildman."

Delgado was watching her, and he saw her face change as she slowly put down the uneaten portion of her granola bar. She looked at him.

"Another one, Seb."

He drew a sharp breath. "Damn. God *damn*."

"Female Caucasian, decapitated, in a one-bedroom apartment at nine-seven-four-one Palm Vista Avenue. That's a couple of blocks south of Pico, near Beverly Boulevard."

"Farther east than the others," Gardner said.

"I'll go on ahead," Delgado told them. He was already rising from his chair, shrugging on his coat. "You two call the rest of the task force, get them out of bed or wherever the hell they are, then hustle everybody over there as fast as possible."

He did not wait to hear their replies.

The address was twenty minutes from the West L.A. station. As he drove, Delgado felt anger rising in him, the cold familiar anger at the taking of an innocent life. He knew he shouldn't let himself feel that way; he should remain calm and professionally detached. But he couldn't help it. He had always become personally involved in the cases he worked. His need to see justice served was a whip cracking over his head, lashing his back, driving him to put in fourteen-hour days and seven-day weeks, never to rest, never to be satisfied.

Yet objectively he knew that there was more to his motivation than moral passion alone. There was his stubborn, angry need to prove himself, to solve every case, to be the best.

He remembered how close Paulson had come to removing him from the investigation this afternoon. At the time Delgado had been sure that his insistence on retaining command of the task force was based purely on a professional commitment to getting the job done. Now he wondered. To what extent had he been moved by motives less noble—pride, grandiosity, an unwarranted self-confidence, and, underlying it, the secret terror of failure and public humiliation?

Stupid greaser couldn't cut it after all, said an ugly voice in his mind. *Always said he was a loser, the spic bastard.*

He knew that voice. He had heard it many times—in high school, in college, at the police academy in Elysian Park, in the station-house locker room. It was the voice of unthinking, irrational hostility, focused on him for no reason other than his dark complexion and sharp accent, markers of his place of origin that had made him an outcast in a country not his own.

In Mexico things had been different. There he had been popular, at least as popular as a boy given to remoteness and intellectual abstraction could be. Even so, he had not been happy growing up in Guadalajara. He remembered being bored most of the time, bored with his elders and his peers, impatient to discover a more interesting part of the world. Mexico had been long behind him when he learned to his surprise that Americans found Guadalajara exotic and fascinating, "the Pearl of the West."

There was little romance in the slum neighborhood where he was raised. There were vendors selling *pulque* on hot summer afternoons, children playing the hopscotch game *bebeleche*, flyblown dogs napping in swatches of shadow. Parchment-creased grandmothers sat on stone steps telling stories of Pedro de Ordinales, the wily shepherd who could outwit God and Satan, and La Llorona, the Wailing Woman, who would come in the night to steal away any child who misbehaved. The streets were narrow, the buildings dark, and so were the minds of the people who lived in that part of town, acting out roles scripted by traditions they neither understood nor challenged.

Young Sebastián had been told he should be proud of those traditions and of his heritage. He was a *mito mita*, half-and-half, his mother descended from the Yaqui Indians, his father from the Conquistadors. A locked box in the parlor was purported to contain a sheaf of yellowed papers that recorded his father's genealogy, tracing his ancestry to a Spanish captain named Delaguerre who had explored the coast of Mexico in the sixteenth century. But the box had never been opened in Sebastián's presence, and even as a boy he had doubted there was anything inside. From the beginning, skepticism was natural to him; perhaps he was fated to become a cop.

He was ten years old when his parents took him to live in the United States, aided by an uncle who had become a naturalized citizen, and a prosperous one. In Tucson or Houston or any of a dozen other places, Sebastián might have lived among Mexican immigrants like himself, blending with them; but his uncle's home was in Indiana, where a boy with a funny way of talking and a strange cast to his skin could not help drawing furtive, suspicious looks.

Grade school was hard; high school was harder. Sebastián became good at fighting; and not just with his fists. The real fight was the fight for respect; and he was smart enough to know that he would win it only if he honed his mind. He studied hungrily, earned top grades, and delivered the valedictory address at his high-school graduation. Two of his classmates, denied a diploma and sentenced to summer school, tried to beat him up after the graduation ceremony. Delgado broke both their noses.

His academic achievement opened the doors of every college in the country to him. He chose UCLA, because Los Angeles was warm and the Indiana winters had been too cold. Even in L.A., three hours from the Mexican border in a city named by Spanish settlers, he discovered prejudice. But it was manageable. Everything was manageable as long as he worked harder than anyone around him.

He was finishing college, uncertain of his future, when the LAPD recruited him. The department needed more minority cops to patrol the *barrios*, where WASP rookies automatically became targets.

Again racism plagued him. He heard a lot of wetback jokes in his days as a uniformed cop, jokes that bit like small dogs and left scars. But he knew the solution. To fight back with hard work, as he had done in school. To outperform those who looked down on him. To log more hours, take more Academy classes, spend more time on the shooting range or in the gym, read more books and write more reports. To work nights and weekends, sacrifice his social life, forgo any existence at all outside his work. That was the way to win.

His ambitiousness had served his career well. He'd risen swiftly, making detective at twenty-six, then spending two years in Narcotics and four years in Robbery before his transfer to Homicide. At thirty-four he'd earned the rank of Detective 2; if he solved this case he might well become a D3, one of the youngest ever made in the LAPD.

But the price he'd paid had been high, too high, and the worst of it had been losing Karen. She had offered her love to him, and what had he done with that precious gift? Wadded it up and tossed it away—because he could not escape his work.

Now he had been handed the most important assignment of his career, the toughest challenge, the case that would make him or break him—and he was failing. Failing.

And another woman was dead.

Delgado guided the Caprice up to the crime-scene ribbon, then switched off his engine. He sat unmoving in the car for a long moment, looking at the apartment building before him. Squad cars and uniformed cops were everywhere; police-band crosstalk crackled and sputtered nervously from car radios and portable handsets. The media had yet to arrive, but a restless, murmuring crowd of onlookers loitered at a barely respectable distance, held back by patrolmen with unfriendly stares. Some fool with a flash camera was clicking off snapshots, perhaps in the hope of selling them to the *Times* for a small payment of blood money, or perhaps as personal mementos, to be preserved under acetate in his photo album between last year's trip to Yosemite and next year's vacation at Walt Disney World.

Suppressing his disgust, Delgado left the car and crossed the yellow ribbon. He flashed his badge at every uniform he passed, not stopping for conversation with any of them. He was in no mood for talk.

The apartment wasn't hard to find. The door was ajar, the lights on. Half a dozen cops milled around outside; their muttered conversation died away as they saw Delgado approach. Wordlessly they parted to let him through. He reached the doorway and looked in.

Just inside the door, a young woman's naked, decapitated body, limbs in disarray, lay sprawled on a white pile carpet soaked with glistening blood.

There was no clay statuette in her hand.

Delgado blinked. No, that couldn't be. The Gryphon never failed to leave his calling card.

A chill shivered through him as he considered the possibility that this killing had been the work of a copycat, some maniac inspired by the news coverage to imitate the Gryphon, but failing to get one key detail right.

He didn't want to believe it. One maniac was enough to deal with.

With a sigh, he banished that line of speculation. For the moment he would proceed on the assumption that the Gryphon was responsible for this latest crime. Most likely, the killer had simply altered his usual pattern for some reason known only to him.

Carefully, Delgado stepped through the doorway into the apartment and looked around. It was a modest mid-rent place, neatly kept and unimaginatively furnished. His circling gaze took in a sofa, a coffee table, a potted plant. Corner windows framed a leafy fig tree. A chest-high counter divided the living room from the kitchenette, brightly lit by overhead fluorescents.

In a corner lay a heap of torn, bloody rags. The victim's clothes, obviously, which the Gryphon had ripped off her body and cast aside. Delgado couldn't tell what kind of outfit it had been without handling the clothes, and he wouldn't do that, of course. There was always a chance the Gryphon had neglected his gloves this time and left a nice bloody fingerprint for Frommer and his SID team.

He knelt by the body. The woman was a young

Caucasian, probably in her twenties, perhaps five feet tall. She was slender, as all the Gryphon's victims had been, with shapely legs and small pert breasts. No doubt she had been attractive. They always were.

Delgado wondered what her name was, what her life had been like, what dreams she'd nurtured. He would learn the answer to such questions soon enough, he supposed. Her name would be determined at the morgue; her lifestyle would be reported by friends, neighbors, and relatives; and as for her dreams . . . A tape would come in the mail, a recording of her last words, and when he listened to her whispery plaintive voice, Delgado would know what she'd wanted out of life, and what she would never get.

How many more voices would he have to hear?

He got up slowly, feeling tired, very tired. He backed away from the corpse, careful to disturb nothing around it, and returned to the doorway, where the uniformed cops were watching him intently, as if trying to read his thoughts in his eyes.

"Who were the first officers to arrive at the scene?" Delgado asked, fatigue thickening his voice.

Two men stepped forward. "We were, Detective," one of them said.

Delgado recognized the pair. The cop who'd spoken was named Branden. He wore wire-rim glasses and longish hair that tested the limits of departmental regulations, giving him the appearance of a disaffected intellectual of the existentialist stripe, the sort who could go on at tedious length about Plato's cave or Dostoevski's underground man. There were a lot of them in L.A., and a few had even found their way onto the police force, for motives impossible to guess.

Branden's partner, Van Ness, was a farmboy, or should have been; he had the kind of build the word "strapping" had been coined to describe: thick neck, broad shoulders, huge meaty fists like hams. Excitement shone in his eyes. Clearly he was getting a kick out of being involved in a case with this much heat on it.

Flipping open his memo pad, Delgado fixed his gaze on Branden, whom he judged the more intelligent of the two. "Let me have your report."

"We were cruising this neighborhood," Branden said, "when a call came over the radio. Some civilian nine-elevened a report about the Gryphon. Apparently he was seen at this address—"

"Seen?" Delgado interrupted, his heartbeat speeding up. Nobody had ever seen the Gryphon before. A description would be invaluable. If an artist could work up an IdentiKit sketch . . .

Branden shrugged. "That was how I understood it, sir. But the details were fuzzy as hell. Frankly, we didn't think there was anything to it anyway; people have been calling in false alarms for weeks."

"The whole Westside is scared shitless," Van Ness added. "Jumping at shadows. We figured somebody saw a drunk taking a leak in the bushes, and got spooked."

"All right." Delgado tried to hold impatience and frustration at bay. He would find out about the alleged sighting later, from somebody better informed than either of these two. For the moment he would dig out whatever information they had. "You arrived at the scene at what time?"

"Ten-thirty-four," Branden answered.

"Go on."

"We checked out the grounds of the building first, then the apartments. That was when we saw the stiff. Couldn't miss her. The door was wide open, and the lights were on."

"He always leaves the place lit up like that," Van Ness said. "Like a frigging laundry-mat." That was how he put it: laundry-mat.

Delgado ignored him. "You found the body. What then?"

"Van Ness called in the homicide. In about two minutes, we had more backup than I've ever seen in my life."

"Everybody wants to be in on this one," Van Ness said, smiling.

"Everybody except the victims," Delgado replied coolly. He returned his attention to Branden. That 911 report still teased his curiosity. "Do you have any idea who tipped us off? Could it have been somebody in the building?"

Branden shook his head. "We asked all the neighbors. Nobody here saw anything."

"Did they tell you who rents this apartment?"

"Yes, sir. It's a woman, and the description they gave us matches the deceased. I mean, as far as you can tell."

"Did she live alone?"

"According to them, yes. And there's only one name on the mailbox."

"Which is?"

"Kutzlow, sir. Jennifer Kutzlow."

"They say she was a stewardess," Van Ness added.

11

This was bad. Very bad.

Franklin Rood sat in his car, breathing hard, fighting pain and weakness. His shirt was untucked, his belly exposed to the pale yellow glow of a streetlight. Blood oozed from a jagged vertical gash in his side. Not a great deal of blood, but enough to have trickled down his pants and pooled on the driver's seat, soiling the tan upholstery. He hoped he could remove the stain.

He'd driven at least a mile from the apartment building on Palm Vista Avenue before parking on a quiet side street to inspect the wound. He couldn't tell how serious it was, though it sure hurt like the dickens.

He sighed, a low wheezing sound that startled him, the kind of sound an invalid would make. He had to admit that the last round of the game had not gone exactly as planned.

Shortly past eight o'clock Rood had arrived in Miss Wendy Alden's neighborhood and parked in a curbside space. Before leaving the car, he clipped the cassette recorder to his belt. He played the blank tape for a few seconds to get past the leader, then pulled on his gloves and checked the pocket of his coat to confirm that the garrote was inside.

He smiled. Ready to go.

Holding the bag by its strap, he got out of the car and walked toward the apartment building where Miss Alden lived. It was a simple two-story frame structure, put up back in the late fifties or early sixties, in those simpler times when nobody felt the need for a security gate or an intercom system or any protection at all. The doors opened directly onto the street—or, in the case of the apartments on the second floor, onto a gallery that could be reached easily enough via the outside staircase.

How wonderfully convenient.

As the building drew near, Rood became aware of raucous rock music blaring from a ground-floor window. He wondered if Miss Alden were throwing a party. He hoped not. If she were, he'd have to wait for her guests to leave.

A few yards from the building Rood stopped, removed the night-vision binoculars from his bag, and squinted through the eyepieces. The world was suffused in a green fog; the brass numbers affixed to the apartment doors shone brightly in the enhanced luminescence of the streetlights. He rotated the focusing knob, bringing the numbers into crisp resolution, then located the door marked 204. Miss Alden's apartment.

She lived in an upstairs corner unit directly above the noisy apartment. The curtains in the side window were drawn, the place dark and silent. She must be out.

Rood replaced the binoculars in his bag and considered his options. He could wait in his car till he saw the lights go on in the apartment. Eventually the window would darken again when she retired for the night. An hour or so after that, he could silently break in and surprise her in bed. She would awaken from a dream into a nightmare.

Yes, he could do it that way. But there was another, more interesting, slightly riskier possibility. He could pick the lock on her door, conceal himself in the apartment, and wait for her to come home. There was danger in an ambush; suppose she returned with her boyfriend or with a group of friends. But then again, suppose she didn't. He could watch her from his hiding place, then pounce for the kill. What fun.

He decided to chance it.

Briskly he walked up to the staircase. He'd just put his foot on the lowest step when the door to the ground-floor apartment swung open in a blast of frenzied guitar chords and a young woman emerged with a bulging sack of garbage in her arms. She stopped short, her eyes fixed on Rood from a yard away.

"Oh," she said very simply, as her eyes tracked from his face to his gloved hands, mottled in dried blood.

"Hello," Rood said pleasantly. "What's your name?"

The bag slipped from her fingers and hit the ground with a moist plop. She whirled. She was almost inside the doorway of her apartment when Rood caught her from behind. He pushed her forward into that cave of crashing stereophonic sound. She fell sprawling on hands and knees. He kicked the door shut, tossed his bag on the floor, advanced on her. She tried to crawl away. He grabbed her by the hair and yanked her head back. She screamed. It was a healthy scream, the shriek of a vital young animal, a high, ululant

wail that ordinarily would have alerted the neighbors, who might have summoned the police. But
the stereo was awfully loud; Rood was certain nobody outside these four walls had heard a thing.

Still clutching a fistful of reddish-blond hair, he
pulled the woman to her feet. She screamed
again, a lovely trilling sound registering pain and
terror, infinitely sweeter than that raucous noise
she seemed to regard as music. He spun her to
face him and clapped a hand on her mouth, then
swept his gaze over the living room, a place of
white pile carpet and teakwood occasional tables,
lit by ceramic lamps and the fluorescent panel in
the adjacent kitchenette. A hallway led to what
must be a bedroom and bath. Corner windows
looked out on the lower branches of a fig tree.

The apartment appeared empty. He saw no
sign of company. Well, she had company now.

Gripping her thin shoulders, Rood pulled the
woman close.

"Tell me your name," he ordered.

She swallowed. A tremor ran over her face, like
a current of wind rippling through a field of tall
grasses.

"Jennifer."'

"Your *full* name."

"Jennifer Kutzlow," she said hastily, then
caught herself and corrected, "Jennifer Ellen
Kutzlow."

Rood nodded. Still holding her by the shoulders to prevent any attempt at escape, he examined Miss Jennifer Ellen Kutzlow. He estimated
her age at twenty-five and her height at five-two,
a head shorter than Rood himself. Her feet were
bare, the toenails painted pink, a detail he found
oddly alluring. White beltless shorts showed off

her lithe, shapely legs. A low-cut blue T-shirt was pasted to her breasts, the thin cotton pinched by the hard knobs of her nipples. Small brown freckles stood out prettily on her cleavage, her pert nose, her flawless cheeks. Her green eyes made a pleasing contrast with the strawberry blond of her hair, long silken hair so marvelously luxuriant it seemed to beg you to put your hands in it and feel its gossamer softness, its spun-gold delicacy.

"Lovely," Rood said softly.

Miss Jennifer Kutzlow shuddered. Her lower lip went spastic, squirming and writhing, a worm on a hook. Rood felt the trembling of her shoulders in his fingertips.

"No," she whispered. "Please, no."

She thought he was going to rape her, Rood realized. But he wouldn't. He wasn't even going to make her beg or recite the words he liked to hear. That ritual was reserved for those whom he chose as contestants in the game; Miss Kutzlow was merely an innocent bystander. Besides, the noise of the stereo would make a decent recording impossible. No, it would be a swift, clean kill this time.

"Don't worry, my dear." He smiled kindly. "I won't try anything. I just happened to notice how attractive you are, that's all."

His words did nothing to reassure her. She trembled violently in his hands. Her body shook as if with palsy.

"And I wanted to know," Rood went on smoothly, "if you don't mind my asking, why such a charming young lady as yourself would be home all alone, taking out the garbage, when she ought to be on the arm of some dashing young gentleman, enjoying life."

"I . . . I was supposed to be out of town tonight."

"Where?"

"Seattle. I'm a flight attendant, see? But my flight was canceled. Mechanical problems . . ."

"That's too bad."

"Yes." She giggled. "It is, isn't it? I . . . I really wish I'd gone to Seattle."

"I'll bet it's nice up there," Rood said. "Beautiful." His smile widened. "Like you."

Miss Kutzlow swallowed. "Look. Don't hurt me, okay?" She spoke so softly that her words were covered by the thunder of the stereo, and Rood had to read her lips to make out what she was saying. "You can take all my stuff, take everything, but please don't hurt me."

He didn't answer her directly. Instead he asked, "Who's that you're listening to?"

She blinked, surprised by the question. "Guns N' Roses."

Rood rather liked the way those words went together. Guns, roses. Guns meant death, and roses meant love. Death and love—he could hardly imagine one without the other.

"I'm afraid I'm not familiar with them," he said mildly.

"They're pretty famous. They've got a real unique sound, you know? They . . ."

Her words trailed off as she appeared to grasp the absurdity of discussing the merits of Guns N' Roses with a man whose leather-gloved hands were clamped on her shoulders like an animal's claws.

"They *are* good," Rood agreed, although in truth he found such ugly, discordant noise intolerable. "But that music is awfully loud. I'm afraid it's giving me a headache. Would you do me a favor and turn it down?''

"Turn it down?'' Miss Kutzlow echoed as if she were unfamiliar with the concept, which, all things considered, might very well be the case. Then she smiled and nodded with desperate affability. "Oh, sure. No problem.''

Rood released her shoulders. She turned toward the stereo, and in one practiced motion he plucked the garrote from his pocket, grasped the wooden handles firmly in both hands, and tossed the noose over her head. She staggered backward, her hands flailing wildly, fingers scrabbling at the garrote in a desperate, doomed effort to pry it free. Rood twisted the handles clockwise, and the wire bit deep, severing the carotid arteries. She whipped her head crazily from side to side, gargling bloody froth, while her reddish-blonde hair was stained a purer shade of red.

Blindly she thrust her hands backward, seeking to claw Rood's face. Laughing, he dodged her stabbing fingernails. She balanced on one leg and kicked backward with the other, striking again and again with the ferocious determination of the dying. The heel of her bare foot bruised Rood's ankles and shins, but he barely felt the blows; the momentary twinges of pain were lost in the buzzing, humming cicada song of euphoria rising in his brain.

Rood tugged harder at the garrote, choking off the last of Miss Jennifer Kutzlow's blood and breath and life. He felt the burning strain in his forearms and biceps and shoulders, felt the muscles of his neck standing out in sharp relief, felt the pressure of his gloved fingers on the garrote's wooden handles. Looking down through a mist of sweat, past the bloody mop of the woman's hair, he saw the tanned and freckled cleavage exposed in the vee of her T-shirt, her small firm breasts jogging frenetically while her body spasmed and sunfished and jackknifed. Whose hands, he wondered, had fondled those lovely breasts? Whose lips had kissed them? What secret pleasures had she known in lovers' beds? She would not know pleasure again, any kind of pleasure, ever.

She was still struggling, but more weakly now, her energy ebbing, life and strength spiraling away, her arms and legs moving sluggishly, with the slow-motion languor of an underwater dancer. Finally her knees buckled, her legs folding under her like broken flower stems. Her body sagged. For a last moment her lithe arms beat listlessly at air, and then her head lolled back on her shoulders, her hair matted and sticky with blood, her eyes open, her green gaze lifted to Rood as if in supplication. He stared down at her, studying those round hopeless eyes brimming with tears, the tongue protruding from her mouth as if in a last futile gesture of defiance, the freckles on her nose and cheeks standing out against the blood-less paleness of her skin. Her death rattle was swallowed by the stereo.

Rood lifted the garrote from around her neck, peeling the blood-slick wire free of the deep wound it had gouged.

"You're mine now, Miss Jennifer Kutzlow," he whispered, his voice suddenly husky and so low that the pounding music rendered it inaudible even to his own ears. "All mine."

Tenderly he kissed her forehead. Then slowly his mouth traveled down her cheek to her lips, then farther down, to her neck, her cleavage, the round hill of a breast. He licked her skin, tasting the salty sweat glistening there. He pressed his lips to the T-shirt, his tongue probing her nipple through the thin fabric. She was beautiful. So beautiful.

A sudden frenzied need possessed him, the same need he'd felt after every previous kill. With frantic haste he tore at the T-shirt, stripping it from her body, then ripped off her shorts and pawed at her panties till they shredded in his hands. He tossed the bloody rags of her clothes in a corner. Gulping air, heart pounding, he lowered her body to the carpet and kissed her naked breasts, her smooth belly, her tanned legs. His gloved hands fumbled with the zipper of his fly. He mounted her and thrust himself inside, grinding his hips and gasping. An instant later it was over; he was empty and flaccid and satisfied.

Exhausted, he lay atop her, breathing hard, planting more wet kisses on her face. After what seemed like a long time, he got to his feet and zipped his pants again.

"Thank you, my dear," Rood breathed, smiling down at the corpse. "I hope it was good for you too."

He'd shared something with Miss Kutzlow tonight, something so special it must be honored. Although she was not on his list, he wished he could leave a statuette with her; she deserved that tribute. But he had only one clay figure, and that one was for Miss Alden upstairs. Well, he could take her head, at least.

Rood shut off the stereo, grateful to hear the throbbing din finally subside, then reached into his bag and removed the hacksaw. He set to work, guiding the tungsten-carbide blade back and forth in swift, regular strokes. When the head was finally detached, he dropped it in the jumbo Baggie he'd brought with him, then tied the plastic bag shut with a wire tab.

He looked down fondly at Miss Kutzlow's remains, lying in a tangle of limbs on the white carpet that was now a lake of blood. When he checked his watch, he saw that the time was nearly nine o'clock. He'd spent more than half an hour with Miss Kutzlow. At any moment Miss Alden might return home, if she hadn't already, and the opportunity for the ambush would be lost.

Quickly he went around the living room, switching off all the lights. Normally, when leaving the scene of a kill, he left the lights on and the door open, proudly displaying his work to the timid, craven world of sheep and ants. But for the moment he wanted the apartment dark and uninviting, to discourage visitors. It would hardly do to have someone find Miss Kutzlow's remains before Rood had taken care of her upstairs neighbor.

In darkness he returned to the front door, stepping carefully over the body in his path. He found the canvas bag and hefted it. The bag was heavy, bulging with the trophy he'd won.

Opening the door a crack, he peered out. He saw no one. He stepped outside and shut the door behind him, careful to leave it unlocked so he could return later to switch on the lights before he left.

The sack of garbage lay on the ground where Miss Kutzlow had dropped it. Afraid the sack might attract attention and curiosity, Rood picked it up, carried it around to the side of the building,

and deposited it in a trash dumpster. Then swiftly
he mounted the outside staircase and hurried to
Miss Alden's apartment. The side window was
still dark; no sound was audible from within. As
best Rood could tell, she wasn't home yet. To
make certain, he knocked loudly, rapping his
gloved knuckles on the door. No answer.

Her door was protected by a common mortise
lock with a spring-latch bolt and a dead bolt, both
of the pin-tumbler type. Defeating the dead bolt
would require a delicate touch. Rood took off his
gloves and flexed his fingers rhythmically, then
rummaged in his bag until he found a tension
wrench and a homemade wire tool. The tool was
a six-inch length of medium-gauge wire that he'd
bent with pliers into a hooked shape. The design
wasn't original; he'd followed a diagram in a book
on locksmithing he'd found in the public library,
a book that had told him everything he needed
to know about picking locks.

Carefully he inserted the tension wrench in the
keyway of the dead bolt, applying gentle pressure
with his index finger in the direction of the lock's
rotation. With his other hand he slid the wire tool
into the keyway, then drew it back and forth in
a rapid sawing motion.

In theory, what he was doing was quite simple.
Inside the lock there was a row of pins set in tiny
pin wells, holding the lock cylinder and the central plug together. The right key would nudge
those pins up into the pin wells, liberating the
plug from the cylinder and allowing it to turn in-
dependently, thus retracting the dead bolt. Rood,
of course, had no key. But if his wire tool could
bump the pins into the desired alignment just for

an instant, the pressure of the tension wrench should be enough to turn the plug.

Yes, easy in theory. But although he'd practiced the technique on the locks in his own apartment for many hours, this was the first time he'd tried it in the field. Mrs. Julia Stern had not engaged the dead bolt before taking her shower. Miss Rebecca Morris had obligingly opened the garage door for him. And most recently he'd chosen to break Miss Elizabeth Osborn's window rather than struggle to defeat the intimidating locks on her front door.

Rood was sweating now. His glasses slid down his nose. He jiggled the wire hook desperately. Nothing happened.

Suppose he couldn't open the door. The only way he could then get inside would be to break the window, and that was no good; when his quarry saw the damage, she would never fall for his trap. No, he had to defeat the lock, simply *had* to.

With a click of tumblers, the plug rotated ninety degrees, and the dead bolt was released.

Rood smiled, expelling a shaky breath. He'd done it.

Now only the latch bolt remained.

From his bag he removed a small sheet-metal loid, which he slipped between the door and the strike plate. He pushed, exerting pressure on the bevel edge of the latch. The latch depressed, the doorknob turned, the door swung open.

He was in.

Before entering, he pulled on his gloves once more, then wiped off the doorknob and the locks, in case he'd inadvertently left prints. Then he crept into the darkness, closing the door behind him. The spring latch snicked into place automatically. Because he wanted to leave no sign that the locks had been tampered with, he turned the knob that slid the dead bolt back into its socket.

He didn't dare turn on a lamp. If Miss Alden saw a light in her window, she would know someone was inside. Instead he removed the Micro-Lite miniature flash from his bag and switched it on, cupping the beam with his hand to narrow its focus.

He directed the flashlight at different parts of the living room. As best he could tell, the apartment's layout was identical to that of the unit below. The same kitchenette, the same corner windows, the same hallway leading, presumably, to a bedroom and bath. He swept the faint funnel of light over a sofa, a coffee table, an armchair positoned beside a potted plant nearly as tall as he was. A man could easily hide behind that chair, concealed by its bulk and by the plant's leaves. Perfect.

With nothing else to do while he waited, Rood prowled the apartment, examining the contents of closets and drawers, trying to get a sense of Miss Alden's personal life. He noted few dates marked on the calendar in her bedroom, few scribbles on the notepad by her phone. Apparently she was not a very social person.

Returning to the living room, he observed a telephone answering machine on an end table by the sofa. The red LED was not blinking; no messages had been recorded since the machine had last been used. Still, there might be old messages on the tape, messages that had never been erased.

Curious, Rood pressed the button marked Playback. A man's voice crackled over the speaker.

"Wendy, this is Jeffrey. Calling to see if you wanted to catch a movie tonight. There's a Kurosawa film playing at the Nuart. I'll be home all afternoon." He gave his number, then hung up. The tape beeped. A prior message, partly recorded over, came on in midsentence. The same man's voice. ". . . thinking of checking out this Ethiopian place on Melrose." As before, Jeffrey left his home number. Another beep, then the tail end of a still earlier message. ". . . not usually real big on these equity-waiver shows, but I've heard this one's not bad." Once more, his number, the click of a cradled handset, a beep.

Silence.

Rood wondered if it was only coincidence that all three messages had been left by this Jeffrey person. Didn't Miss Alden have any other friends, any family?

He shook his head sadly. He had a feeling that the woman led a lonely life. Well, she would not be living it much longer.

The rumble of a car engine cut into his thoughts.

He padded across the living room to the corner windows. Pressing his face to the glass, he peered out. Through the scrim of the fig tree's branches, he saw a blue Honda Civic park in a reserved space at the side of the building.

A moment later Miss Alden emerged from the car.

"You're mine," Rood told the distant figure. "All mine."

Hastily he concealed himself behind the chair, shoving the potted plant out of the way to get into position, then pulling it back into place. With a stab of disgust he realized that the plant was fake, a plastic replica, a lifeless thing. Such artful

imitations repelled him. He would no more have
a phony plant in his home than take a manne-
quin's head as his prize.

Crouching low on his haunches, hugging the
drawstring bag close to him, running his hands
over the lumpy shape inside, Rood waited.

Footsteps pattered up the stairs, then drummed
on the gallery. A key rattled first in one keyhole,
then the other, drawing back both bolts. The door
opened. The lights came on.

From behind a mesh of leaves, Rood stared at
Miss Wendy Alden. She paused in the doorway,
glancing nervously around the living room in a
way that reminded Rood of a startled doe scenting
the woods for danger. For a second he was sure
she sensed his presence; then he realized she
must always enter a room this way, alert to any
possible threat.

A moment later she relaxed visibly, and Rood
knew she had no inkling anything was wrong.

She entered the apartment, shut and locked the
door behind her, and vanished down the hallway
immediately to his left. Rood remained hidden,
even though he knew it would be easy enough
to kill her now. He wanted to watch her a little
longer.

As he awaited her return, his right hand crept
into the pocket of his coat and closed over the
garrote, gripping it tight.

A considerable length of time passed before
Miss Alden emerged from the hall. When she did,
she was wearing white satin pajamas, a blue
terry-cloth robe, and slippers, an outfit that made
her look girlish and vulnerable and appealing.
Her hair had been unclipped to fall loosely over
her shoulders. Idly Rood reflected that she ought

to wear it that way all the time. The advice would do her no good now, of course. But he would keep it in mind when he prepared her head for display.

She crossed the living room, taking dainty steps, soundless as a shadow. Entering the kitchenette, she turned on the overhead light, then fixed herself something to eat. Rood peered out from behind the chair, observing her over the chest-high counter that divided the kitchen from the living room. The portable TV on the counter came on, and a newscaster's voice said something about the Gryphon; with surprising abruptness Miss Alden snapped the TV off. Rood frowned, disappointed; he would have liked to hear that report.

He watched as she put a sliced apple on a plate, poured a glass of milk, and carried her snack to a table in the far corner of the room. She sat with her back to him, eating and looking out the windows at the leaves of the windblown fig tree scraping the glass. He wondered what she was thinking.

After a while he became aware of a certain stiffness in his legs, bent in a half-crouch. Slowly he bobbed up and down, trying to exercise his muscles and loosen his joints. His right knee creaked loudly in protest.

Miss Alden stiffened in her chair.

She heard that, Rood thought, dismayed. *She must have*.

He sank down, well out of sight, and remained there for a silent count of fifty. His heart was beating fast, his body charged with tension. He was ready to leap into action if she showed the slightest hint of alarm.

But when he looked out from behind the chair, he found she'd gone back to her snack.

He breathed easy once more.

A few moments passed, during which time Rood promised himself he wouldn't shift his position again no matter what, for fear of making another telltale sound and bringing this most pleasurable round of the game to a premature conclusion. But he couldn't help it. He could think of nothing but the numbness in his ankles where blood was pooling, the tingly pins-and-needles sensation stitching pain up his calves. His legs seemed to be going to sleep below the knees, and he knew he couldn't allow that; it was imperative he have the mobility to strike at will.

As quietly as possible he flexed his knees to restore his circulation. But his caution was wasted. His right knee creaked as it had before.

Damn.

He decided to risk a peek in her direction to see if she'd heard. As bad luck would have it, he peered over the top of the chair in the exact moment when she was turning in her seat. He ducked. He didn't know if she'd seen him or not. She might have.

There was nothing he could do but wait. If she showed any sign of alarm, he would have to finish the job right now.

But she did nothing suspicious. She merely sat there for a few minutes, then carried her plate and her glass into the kitchen. Rood heard running water and the low clatter of dishes. She was humming softly, some tune he didn't recognize, a pleasant, soothing melody, perhaps a love song or a lullaby. Whatever it was, he much preferred it to Miss Kutzlow's high-volume noise.

Still humming to herself, she left the kitchen and recrossed the living room. Rood huddled behind the chair, feeling the floorboards vibrate gently under the soft tread of her slippered feet.

Then suddenly, shockingly, she broke into a run, racing for the front door.

She's onto me, Rood's mind screamed.

And she was quick, yes—but not quick enough. Rood leaped to his feet, covered the distance between them in two strides, and kicked the door shut as it was opening under her hand. Then the garrote was around her neck, and everything was fine, just fine.

He had great fun making her say the words he liked to hear; her stammering terror, her confusion, her inability to remember the lines he fed her, all served only to increase his enjoyment of the ritual. And her pathetic little monologue listing all the trivial, inane reasons that justified her continued existence—that was deliciously amusing as well. Rood was almost sorry to end their encounter. But he was tired; though tonight's game had gone wonderfully well, it had taken a lot out of him. He was ready to go home and put the two new heads in the freezer next to Miss Osborn's, then relax in bed with his memories and smile himself to sleep.

Rood slowly pulled the garrote tight, taking care not to gouge deeply enough to open her arteries, not yet; first he wanted to hear her choked, gargling protests, wanted to get them on tape. He was still reveling in the effortless pleasure of the kill when silver flashed in Miss Alden's right hand. Her fist arrowed backward. Pain hit him. A shaft of hard, steely pain in his side, like a hot wire plunged into his flesh. He looked down in

numb bewilderment and saw a knife jutting out
of his body at a crazy angle.

A *knife*.

She'd stabbed him—drawn blood—the bitch.
The evil, butchering little *bitch*.

The jolt of mingled shock and agony loosened
his grip on the garrote. The handles slipped from
his fingers. Miss Alden pulled free of him, leaving
the knife embedded in his side, and lunged for
the door. Rood watched as if in a trance. He knew
she was getting away, knew he ought to stop her,
but he seemed unable to react; he stood staring
as if from some great distance as she yanked the
door open and ran outside onto the gallery. Her
footsteps beat a ragged tattoo on the stairs, then
faded with distance, diminishing to silence. She
was gone.

Gone.

Blinking, Rood snapped alert.

Slowly he closed his fist over the handle of the
knife and pulled the blade free. Blood leaked from
the wound. His own blood. The sight sickened
him. He coughed, doubled over, as black spots
flickered before his eyes. He was going to pass
out. But he couldn't. If he did, they would find
him here. They. The police. They would find him,
arrest him, throw him in a cell. And when he
regained consciousness, he would find Detective
Sebastián Delgado staring down at him, smiling
in triumph.

No. No. *No*.

Steadying himself, Rood forced down the waves
of faintness that threatened to wash him away.
After a few moments he was certain he was all
right. He felt a trifle light-headed, and there was

a liquid looseness in his knees he didn't like, but he was still strong, still in control.

He had no idea how long it would take Miss Alden to summon help, but he surely wasn't going to hang around and find out. He retrieved the garrote from the floor and slipped it in his pocket, then dropped the bloody knife in his canvas bag. Carrying the bag, he lurched out the door and down the staircase.

He reached Miss Kutzlow's apartment, pushed open the unlocked door, then quickly circled the living room and the kitchen, switching on all the lights. Part of him knew it was absurd to waste precious seconds on this ritual, so meaningless now, when the police might be racing to the scene. But he didn't care. He would not run like a rabbit before the hounds. He would depart with dignity—at least, as much dignity as possible under these trying circumstances. He would show them that despite his regrettable failure in the apartment upstairs, he was still a man to be feared; he was still the Gryphon.

He left Miss Kutzlow's door wide open, the light spilling out onto the walkway, inviting any passerby to look inside and get a glimpse of hell. Then he staggered down the street to his Falcon, climbed behind the wheel, and sped off.

For twenty minutes he drove aimlessly, putting distance between himself and the crime scene, before finally parking on a quiet street to examine the wound. It was not bleeding too badly. He had been lucky, he saw; the blade had missed his abdomen and merely passed through the small fold of fat at his waist—what some people would call a love handle. The injury was painful, but not serious; no arteries or internal organs had been damaged.

Of course he ought to go to the hospital anyway, but he didn't dare. The police would alert the staffs at all the local emergency rooms to be on the lookout for any man with a stab wound. No, he would have to deal with this little problem on his own. Like the physician of the proverb, he was obliged to heal himself.

He removed the knife from the drawstring bag and held it up to the glow of a streetlight, studying it. A common kitchen knife. Kitchen. So that was where she got it. When she was in the kitchen, humming to herself and pretending to do the dishes. She must have hidden the knife in her robe. Then, when he ambushed her, she in turn had ambushed him. And had beaten him, quite literally, at his own game.

But how could she have been capable of a deception like that? He'd seen no evidence of icy coolness or low cunning or even simple courage in her. Quite the contrary. She'd been so witlessly flustered and starkly terrified she couldn't even get her lines straight. Unless her fear had been only an act. Yes. That must be it. She'd never been afraid at all. She'd been toying with him, feigning innocence and helplessness, while poised to strike and kill. Kill . . .

For the first time, Rood realized how close he'd come to dying tonight. If she'd stabbed him in the stomach . . . or the heart . . .

Suddenly his hands were shaking. For a moment, just one moment, he considered forgetting all about Miss Wendy Alden. He could count Miss Kutzlow as his victim and call tonight's contest a success.

Then he shook his head, angry at himself. The rules of the game were clear. Miss Alden, not Miss Kutzlow, was the player he'd selected. Now he must play out the game to its conclusion.

Besides, he wanted revenge. He hated that bitch.

She'd tried to *kill* him, for God's sake.

But she'd failed. And that was her mistake. A fatal mistake. He would not rest until he had her in his hands again. And when he did, he would take her life slowly, not with the garrote, but with the knife she'd used on him. He would cut her to pieces while she grunted and groaned, unable to scream; it was hard to scream without a tongue.

"You'll be sorry, Miss Wendy lying-slut Alden," Rood said aloud, his voice hollow in the confines of the car. "Oh, yes, I swear, you'll be oh-so-very sorry you fucked with me."

12

The police station on Butler Avenue was a bedlam of ringing telephones, clacking typewriters, and screams. The screams were in Spanish, and they came from a man in handcuffs as he was led away toward a lockup area. His head whipsawed crazily; streamers of spit sprayed from his mouth. Wendy stared at him in paralyzed fascination.

Patrol Officer Sanchez touched her arm. She jumped.

"This way, Miss Alden."

She followed obediently. Sanchez showed her into a small, windowless office smelling of stale coffee. One of the two fluorescent panels was out, leaving the room half in shadow.

"Would you like something to drink?" Sanchez asked, then smiled. "I mean coffee, tea, juice. I can't offer you the hard stuff."

"Just water would be fine."

He returned with a glass of water and handed it to her.

"Thanks," she said, sipping it gratefully.

"The detective will be with you in just a minute." Sanchez left, shutting the door.

Wendy sat in a straightback chair. She shivered, feeling wet and cold. Her pajamas and robe, tacky with sweat, clung to her skin in damp patches.

Her bare toes poked through a hole in the one slipper she was still wearing. She wrapped herself more tightly in the blanket she'd been given, then sneezed.

Wendy, she told herself, *are you ever a mess*.

But at least she wasn't dead.

The garrote had been tightening around her neck when she remembered the knife. The knife she'd used to carve and core the apple. The knife she'd stowed in a pocket of her robe before leaving the kitchen. In her panic she'd forgotten it. Forgotten the only weapon she had.

Her right hand dived into her pocket and closed over the handle. With all her strength she thrust her arm backward and drove the blade into the killer's body.

He made a sound that was more than a croak, not quite a shout. The garrote fell from his hands. She flung open the door and fled.

The gallery streaked under her feet like a sheet of ice. She bounded down the staircase, taking the steps two at a time, an act of sheer recklessness she'd never attempted before in her life, not even as a child. When she reached ground level she shot a terrified glance over her shoulder, certain the Gryphon would be following her, wielding the bloody knife in one fist and the garrote in the other. No one was there.

Maybe she'd killed him. Maybe he was lying dead on the floor. Oh, God, she hoped so.

But she knew he wasn't dead. Just knew it. A man like that wouldn't die so easily. If he could die at all.

She looked around frantically, trying to decide what to do, where to go. Her car. She had to get in her car and speed to the nearest police station, wherever that was. No, wait. She didn't have her car keys, did she? They were in her purse, and her purse was in her apartment, where *he* was.

All right then. Run. Go on, Wendy, run!

She stumbled blindly along Palm Vista Avenue, not looking back, then reached Beverly Boulevard and headed north, sprinting uphill, gasping. Apartment buildings blurred past, buildings crowded with people she didn't know. She could pound on some stranger's door and yell for help. But she was afraid to stop. Afraid the Gryphon might be right behind her, gaining on her, ready to bring her down. She was sure she could hear his racing footsteps, his panting breath.

She ran faster. Somewhere along the way she lost one of her slippers, like Cinderella after the ball. She didn't notice.

At the corner of Beverly and Pico she found a Mobil station, an oasis of light amid the shadowed streets. The smell of auto exhaust and gasoline bit her nostrils as she staggered across the floodlit asphalt, past the two service islands, into the snack shop. She caromed off a wire carousel, spilling candy bars on the tile floor. The clerk looked up from the magazine he was reading and started to say something, and then Wendy was screaming, screaming in terror and release, screaming about the Gryphon. She was still screaming when the clerk dialed 911.

Several endless minutes passed before a police car arrived, domelights flashing. By that time Wendy was calm, yes, remarkably calm, except for the sudden unpredictable tremors that racked her body and set her teeth chattering for no reason at all.

Somehow she mustered the clarity of mind to

condense what had happened into a few simple declarative sentences, not unlike the ones she was always writing in those stupid little booklets of hers. The two patrolmen, plainly skeptical, radioed a report of a possible sighting of the Gryphon at 9741 Palm Vista. Another squad car, en route to the scene, volunteered to take a look.

"Tell them to be careful," Wendy said. "Very, very careful."

"They will be, ma'am," one of the cops said in a soothing voice, the voice of a man doing his best to comfort a small trembling animal.

His partner was studying Wendy's neck. "Guess you'll need to see a doctor about that, huh?"

About what? she wondered blankly.

Raising a hand to her throat, she felt warm liquid. For the first time she realized she was bleeding. The garrote had gouged a hairline wound in her neck. She swayed, light-headed, overcome by the sudden visceral awareness of how near death had been, how narrowly she'd escaped.

The two cops steadied her. Kindly they gave her a blanket from the trunk of the patrol car. She draped herself in it and rubbed her legs together to keep warm as she rode in the backseat on the way to the hospital.

The car had just pulled into the parking garage at Cedars-Sinai Medical Center when the radio crackled with a Code 187. The unit at 9741 Palm Vista was calling in a homicide that matched the M.O. of the Gryphon.

Homicide, Wendy thought blankly. *But he was after me. And I got away. So . . . who?*

From the report, she gathered that the Gryphon himself had fled the scene. She hadn't expected to hear otherwise. It would take more than the thrust of a knife to stop that man.

Between bursts of radio crosstalk, the two cops turned in their seats to introduce themselves; their names, they said eagerly, were Sanchez and Porter. Condescension had vanished from their voices, replaced by admiration, even awe. Clearly they now realized Wendy was not the nutcase they'd made her out to be. She was someone who'd taken on the city's most notorious killer and survived.

They asked how she'd gotten away. She told them about the knife. "I stabbed him. Somewhere around the waist, I think."

Porter got on the radio to relay the information. "Every hospital in town will be looking for him now," he said briskly. "If the asshole tries to get medical attention, he's screwed, blued, and tattooed. Uh, sorry, ma'am. Pardon my French."

Wendy sat with Sanchez in the crowded waiting room while Porter phoned the station house for further instructions. She was still shivering, not with cold.

"You know, Miss Alden," Sanchez said quietly, "I've had some bad experiences in this job. You want to know how I handle them? I close my eyes, and I imagine I'm in my favorite place in the world. It has to be a peaceful place. A place where nothing bad ever happens. You have a place like that?"

"I . . . I think so." She was thinking of a park in Beverly Hills where she liked to spend her summer afternoons, a green place of trees and laughing children.

"Can you go there now? In your mind, I mean?"

She smiled. "I can try."

Eyes shut, she visualized the park. She felt the velvet grass and smelled the flower-scented air.

"You there?" Sanchez asked.

"I guess I am."

"Feeling a little better?"

"A little." She studied herself and found that the shivering had stopped. "Yes, definitely. You ought to be a shrink."

"The pay's not good enough. Police work is where the real money is."

She grinned at that, and then she just sat there, in the park. Not long afterward a nurse summoned her.

"Porter and I will still be here when they get done looking you over," Sanchez assured her. "We wouldn't leave without you, Miss Alden. Believe me."

She doubted that the average crime victim received such personalized service from the LAPD. It was funny, wasn't it? The Gryphon had attained a twisted kind of celebrity status in this city; as his intended victim, Wendy had become a celebrity of sorts as well. She wondered if her picture would be in the papers, if she would be interviewed on the news. Maybe there would be a TV movie about her. Who would be cast in the lead? Somebody blonde and much better looking than she was. Meg Ryan, maybe.

The nurse led her into a ward lined with examination tables separated by pleated privacy curtains. Wendy reclined on a table, resting her head on a pillow, and asked for a mirror.

"This isn't a beauty parlor," the nurse said testily. "You don't have to fix your hair for the doctor."

Wendy fingered her throat. "I just want to see what . . . what he did to me."

The nurse softened. "Of course you do. It's not too bad, honey. Believe me, I'd trade my looks for yours any day."

She hurried off and returned with a hand mirror. Nervously Wendy raised it to her face. The eyes that gazed back at her were not the eyes she'd seen in her bathroom mirror this morning, the eyes of a woman who'd always looked younger than her years. The fragile innocence they'd always reflected was still there, but overlying it she saw anger and determination and something more—a hard, glassy quality midway between ice and steel.

She tilted the mirror to examine her throat, neatly bisected by a thin red line still oozing droplets of blood. For some reason she was reminded of Elsa Lanchester in *The Bride of Frankenstein*, her head sewn onto her body, the stitches plainly visible. The comparison disturbed her. Wendy Alden, the living dead.

Her hands were shaking as she put the mirror aside.

A doctor looked her over, pronounced the wound superficial, and treated it with antiseptic before applying medicated adhesive strips. "No need to worry," he said briskly. "It won't leave much of a scar."

Wendy knew better. There would be a scar. A bad one. A scar, not on her body, but on her soul.

When she returned to the waiting room, Sanchez and Porter revealed that they had orders to deliver her to the West L.A. station, where she would meet with a Detective Delgado. The name seemed vaguely familiar. She couldn't quite place it. She was too tired to try.

As the squad car cruised west on Santa Monica Boulevard, Wendy sat with her head thrown back against the seat, listening to the beat of her heart in her ears. It was a sound she hadn't expected to hear ever again.

"Aw, shit," Porter said as the car turned south onto Butler Avenue.

She blinked alert. Looking past the two cops, she saw a row of TV news vans and a milling crowd of reporters.

"Knew our luck couldn't hold out forever," Sanchez said. "We got a break just getting out of Cedars without those pricks hassling us."

"But"—Wendy swallowed—"how could they have heard about me so soon?"

"They monitor the radio chatter," Porter replied. "Of course, they probably don't know your name or any of the details. That's why I used the landline—the telephone, I mean—at Cedars. A little more privacy that way."

She looked down despondently at her robe and pajamas. "Am I going to have to be on TV like this?"

Sanchez shook his head. "Uh-uh. Don't you worry, ma'am. Situation's under control."

Halfway down the block, he spun the wheel, guiding the cruiser into the station-house parking lot. Slant-parked patrol cars and unmarked sedans glided past, leeched of color by the glareless sodium-vapor lights.

"Cop cars are pulling in and out of this place all night long," Porter said. "One more won't make any difference. Anyway, those camera jockeys can't come in here. Restricted area."

At the rear of the windowless two-story building, safely out of sight of the street, Sanchez parked. He and Porter escorted Wendy inside via a back door.

Now here she was, in the detective's office. She looked around slowly, trying to make the room real. A noteboard littered with incomprehensible diagrams was mounted behind a neat, uncluttered desk. A pair of battered file cabinets stood near an unmade cot in a corner; apparently Delgado slept here sometimes. On one wall hung a map of Los Angeles, studded with three red pins in the West L.A. area. With a small shock Wendy realized that each pin must mark the location of one of the murders.

There could have been a pin for me, she thought numbly. *A marker for my life. What else would have marked it? Anything? Anything at all?*

The door creaked open. Into the office stepped a tall, whipcord-thin man in a brown suit. He nodded at her, bowing slightly, a gesture suggesting an air of formality alien to L.A.

"Miss Alden, my name is Delgado. Detective Sebastián Delgado."

"Pleased to meet you," she answered automatically.

"Not half as pleased as I am to meet you."

She studied him as he shrugged off his coat and tossed it on a coat rack in the corner. He was in his mid-thirties, she guessed, though at first glance his face made him look older—a long, narrow, angular face, vaguely patrician, lined with worry and saddened by heavy-lidded gray eyes under finely traced brows. His skin was dark; his hair, swept back from his forehead, was a deep lustrous black.

She'd seen that face before. Suddenly she knew why his name had been familiar.

"You've been on TV," she said, then instantly regretted it. What a stupid thing to say.

But Delgado didn't seem to think so. Turning to face her, he smiled, a surprisingly warm smile made of small white teeth. Quite an attractive smile, really.

"I'm afraid I'll never have my own series, though," he answered. The trace of a Spanish accent tinged his words; she liked it.

He kept looking at her, and she realized he was studying her, sizing her up. His eyes were alert, perceptive, intelligent. They were his best feature, she decided. Well, that and his smile.

She shifted nervously in her chair.

"I've never met a detective before," she told him, for no particular reason except that she felt the need to say something, anything, right now.

"Well, I've never met anyone who survived an encounter with the Gryphon."

"I came pretty close to not surviving."

"Close doesn't count. You made it. You're alive."

"I guess I am. It seems hard to believe. In fact, I'm not sure I do believe it yet. Any of it. It's like . . . like a dream."

He grunted. "I wish it were. For your sake and mine and . . . everybody's. How's your throat?"

She touched the bandage self-consciously. "It hurts a little. But it's not serious. The garrote"— she drew a quick breath—"didn't cut very deep."

"Garrote?" He sat on the edge of his desk, leaning forward, and flipped open a memo pad. "Is that the weapon he used?"

"Uh-huh. Why? Does he usually do it some other way?"

"We've never known what the weapon was. I'd assumed it was a knife for, uh, for various reasons. But there was no way to tell."

"Oh. Of course." No heads, she remembered. Her stomach rolled.

"Can you tell me anything more about the garrote?" Delgado asked.

"I didn't really get a look at it, but . . . but he described it to me. See, the garrote was around my neck, and he was standing behind me and whispering in my ear. He said it was a foot and a half of steel wire." A shiver radiated through her as she remembered his low voice, his hot breath, the garrote's chilling touch. "And he said—let's see—he said it was homemade, and it had wooden dowels at both ends, for handles, and he could tighten the wire by twisting the handles."

Delgado nodded slowly, scribbling in his notepad. "Homemade. That makes our job more difficult. If he'd bought it on the street, we might be able to . . . well, never mind."

Wendy sighed. "I take it you don't have any idea who this man is. No clues, no leads . . . ?"

"Clues and leads, yes, a few. But if you're asking me if we have a specific individual in mind, or even a list of individuals, the answer is no."

"Must be tough to track down a killer with no motive."

"Tough?" Delgado chuckled without humor. "Yes, you could say that. But perhaps you can make it a little easier. Did your assailant give any indication of why he'd chosen you?"

"No."

"Did he suggest in any way that you might have met him previously?"

"You mean at a party or something?"

"Perhaps. Or in some business connection."

"No. No, he didn't say anything like that." She closed her eyes briefly. "I'm sure I've never met him. I couldn't have."

"You didn't recognize his voice?"

"No."

"Don't answer too quickly. Think for a moment. Are you sure his voice didn't remind you, even slightly, of someone with whom you might have come in contact, either in person or over the telephone? Perhaps an anonymous phone caller . . . or the mailman . . . or a neighbor you barely know."

She shook her head. "It didn't remind me of anyone. But he was whispering. I guess everybody's voice sounds pretty much the same in a whisper."

"Did any of his statements reveal personal knowledge of you?"

"Well, he knew my name."

"How did he refer to you?"

"Miss Wendy Alden. Or just Miss Alden. He always said it that way, very polite." She clucked her tongue against her teeth. "Doesn't that sound crazy, calling him polite? But you know what I mean."

"Yes." His gaze was suddenly faraway. "Yes, I know exactly what you mean."

Delgado stared into space a moment longer; she wondered what he was thinking of. Then with sudden energy he stood up.

"All right," he said briskly. "What I'd like to do is go over this from the beginning. I want to know everything in detail, as much detail as you can remember, starting with . . ."

"Wait." She swallowed. "There's something I have to know first." She took a breath, then asked the question that haunted her. "Who was killed in my apartment building tonight?"

Delgado looked down at his desk, his lips pursed, and made no reply.

"I know somebody was," she went on urgently. Despite the water Sanchez had brought, her mouth was suddenly dry. "I heard about it in the police car, on the radio. Homicide, they said. A homicide at my address."

"Miss Alden," Delgado said slowly, "you've already been through a lot tonight. Wouldn't it be better if . . . ?"

"No, it wouldn't be better. I need to know." She would not be put off. Yesterday she would have meekly dropped the subject, but not now. She had faced the Gryphon. She could face this. "Who got killed instead of me? Tell me. Please."

Delgado met her gaze. "As best we can determine, her name was Jennifer Kutzlow."

Wendy stared at him, trying to take in what he'd said. A rush of blood thrummed in her ears with a conch-shell roar.

Jennifer.

Jennifer, who was always playing her record albums at a million decibels. Jennifer, who'd smiled at her just this morning, making small talk about the weather, before hurrying off to the airport. But Jennifer couldn't be dead in her apartment; she was in Seattle, wasn't she? *Wasn't she?* She couldn't have gotten back this soon. And, anyway, if she'd been home tonight, she would have been making a racket, like always.

Unless she was dead already . . . Unless he'd killed her first . . .

Did he kill Jennifer because he thought she was me? Wendy thought in trembling horror. *Is that it? Did he think she was me?*

"Miss Alden?" The voice was Delgado's, and it came from some great distance. "Are you all right?" She couldn't answer. "Miss Alden?"

"Don't call me that," she heard herself say. "That's what he called me. Just say Wendy. That's my name. Wendy."

A hand was touching her arm. "Are you all right, Wendy?"

She looked at the hand. His hand. She realized he was leaning over her. Concern showed in his gray eyes.

"Yes," she whispered. "I . . . I'm fine."

"I'm very sorry," he said gently. "Was she a friend of yours?"

"No. Not really. Not at all, in fact. To tell you the truth, I thought she was kind of a bitch. . . ." She hitched in a breath. "Oh, God, I don't even know what I'm saying."

"You're doing just fine."

She lowered her head. Her eyes were burning. "I hate this. I hate this so much."

"I know it's hard," Delgado said softly. "But at least you got away. You made it. You've got to hold on to that. You're alive."

She looked at him. A new thought entered her mind.

"For how long?" she asked quietly.

"What do you mean?"

"He's still out there. He wants to kill me. He'll try again."

"Not necessarily. You gave him a lot more trouble than he bargained for. After tonight he may not want to tangle with you a second time."

"Or he may want to get me back. Even the score."

Delgado nodded, not with his head but with his eyes, dropping the heavy lids in a way that signaled assent. "I won't argue the point. Anything is possible. We won't know for certain what he's thinking till we find him."

"How will you do that? You don't know who he is. You don't know anything about him."

"Sooner or later he'll make a mistake."

"And in the meantime?"

"I'll assign uniformed officers to watch you around the clock on triple shifts. You'll be constantly protected. You won't have to face this thing alone."

She didn't answer. Couldn't. But she knew Delgado was wrong.

Of course she would face it alone.

She was always alone.

13

Rood arrived home at eleven-twenty. He parked the Falcon at the curb, then staggered across the courtyard of his apartment complex, lugging the heavy canvas bag.

Once safely inside his apartment, he went immediately into the bathroom. He placed the bag on the counter by the sink, took out the bloody knife, and held it up to the ceiling light. He smiled as he read the words STAINLESS STEEL printed on its handle. Already he was much relieved. Stainless steel didn't rust, thus reducing the danger of tetanus.

He stripped off his clothes. Naked, he examined himself. The wound was still bleeding slightly. In his medicine cabinet he found a package of sterile cotton balls. He used them to sop up the blood, tossing each one in the toilet as soon as it was soaked through.

When the wound had been thoroughly cleaned, he stepped under the shower, parted the skin flaps of the bloody cavity, and let icy water stream inside. He stood there, gritting his teeth against the pain, thinking of nothing, while blood and water streamed down his bare legs.

After a full five minutes, he turned off the

shower and toweled himself dry. He was not bleeding anymore.

He rummaged in the medicine cabinet till he found a tube of bacitracin ointment, then spread the antiseptic around the edges of the gash, though not in the cavity itself.

Those precautions ought to minimize whatever risk of infection he faced. Now to dress and bind the wound.

He got out more of the cotton balls, placed them directly on the cut, and glued them down with Band-Aids. Next, he found an old bed sheet in his hall closet, tore it into strips, and wrapped the strips tightly around his waist, a makeshift bandage.

That ought to do it for now, although he might need to repeat the whole procedure two or three times until the wound healed. His side still ached; it would probably hurt for days. He swallowed two aspirin tablets, then tried to put the pain out of his mind.

His clothes were blood-spotted and useless. He tossed them in the garbage and selected a new outfit, retaining only his white Reeboks and his coat.

Once dressed, he carried the drawstring bag into the kitchen, removed Miss Kutzlow's head from the jumbo Baggie in which it was sealed, and placed the head carefully in his freezer. He looked slowly from Miss Kutzlow to Miss Osborn. They made a pretty pair.

Then he considered his options.

He was reasonably certain Miss Alden was at the police station on Butler Avenue right now. Detective Delgado, after all, would be anxious to speak with her. Rood doubted she could identify him; he didn't think she'd ever gotten a look at his face, and he'd kept his voice in a whisper the whole time.

Sooner or later she would leave the station. Perhaps, Rood thought hopefully, he could ambush her then. But no, that wouldn't work. The detective was sure to arrange a police escort. Besides, with the news media watching for any sign of her departure, the cops would have to spirit her away unobserved. Rood could neither attack her nor follow her under such circumstances.

Well, where would she go? Back home? Impossible. For one thing, detectives and forensic technicians would be combing her apartment for the rest of the night in search of clues. For another, still more members of the news media would congregate outside her apartment building in an all-night vigil. And because the police would expect him to return to the apartment and strike again, no doubt Miss Alden would be told to avoid going home not only for tonight but for several days.

She would need a place to stay. A motel, perhaps. Or a friend's home. A friend . . .

Three messages had been left unerased on the reel of tape in Miss Alden's telephone answering machine. Three messages from the same man. A man named Jeffrey.

She might very well stay with him. And even if she didn't, she would certainly contact him soon enough to let him know where she was. Once this man Jeffrey knew her whereabouts, Rood would find it simple enough to extract the information from him by whatever means necessary.

That left only one small problem. Rood had no

idea who Jeffrey was or where he lived. He didn't even know the man's last name.

But he did have one piece of information. Jeffrey's home telephone number. The man had recited it with every message he left. Rood had an excellent memory for numbers.

He dialed the seven digits. A sleepy voice answered.

"Hello?"

"Jeffrey?"

"Yes? Who is this?"

"Sorry to call you so late. I wanted to apologize for not making it to the party last weekend."

"Party? What party? Who's calling, please?"

"Isn't this Jeffrey Booker?"

"My name is Pellman. Jeffrey Pellman."

"Oh, I'm *so* sorry. I must have dialed the wrong number. I hope I didn't wake you."

Rood cradled the phone.

Mr. Jeffrey Pellman.

Rood flipped through the residential listings in his telephone directory, hoping Mr. Pellman would not be one of those uncooperative souls with an unlisted address. He wasn't.

According to the listing, he lived in the 2100 block of Nichols Canyon Road. Rood knew that street. It wound through the hills above Hollywood Boulevard. Not terribly far away.

He could get there in no time.

14

"Did you hear me, Wendy?" Delgado asked softly. "I said you won't have to face it alone."

He gazed down at her, curled up in the chair, huddled in her robe and the borrowed blanket. The news about the Kutzlow woman had hit her hard, triggering a sudden desperate fear for her own safety. That fear was far from irrational. Although Delgado had done his best to persuade Wendy that the Gryphon wasn't likely to come after her again, he knew he hadn't been entirely convincing—perhaps because he was by no means convinced, himself.

The Gryphon was a man who craved power. Such a man, Delgado believed, was driven by a terror of his own fundamental weakness and by the need to avoid confronting that weakness at any cost. He had to see himself as a master of reality in some cosmic sense in order to compensate for a basic, unconfessed inability to deal with reality on the mundane, everyday level. He had to be a god because he could not live as a man. Failure, any failure, was a threat to the extravagantly grandiose identity he'd crafted, his precariously artificial sense of self; and as a threat, it would be met with anger, with blind, furious rage, rage projected outward at the most obvious target.

For the Gryphon, that target would be the small, frail, trembling young woman who sat before Delgado now.

"I heard you," Wendy whispered. She brushed a loose strand of hair from her face. "But I'm still afraid. He can find me again if he wants to. He knows where I live. . . ."

"Well, that's something I wanted to discuss with you." Delgado picked his words with care. "It would be best if you could make arrangements to stay somewhere else for a while."

"Somewhere else?" She blinked. "Oh. Of course. You're right. I can't go back there. And even if I could, I wouldn't want to. Not so soon. I don't know what I was thinking of."

"Maybe you had a few other things on your mind."

"If I can use your phone, I'll call a . . . a friend of mine right now and see if I can sleep over."

"Be my guest."

He handed her the desk phone. She balanced it on her lap and punched in a number. He could hear the faint ringing of the phone at the other end of the line, then the flylike buzz of a voice.

"Jeffrey?" Wendy said. "It's me."

Abruptly Delgado turned away. He realized he'd been hoping the friend she called would be a woman. He didn't want her to have a boyfriend.

Now why would he care, one way or the other?

Out of the corner of his eye he studied Wendy Alden. Her face was pale, her eyes huge and frightened. A scared little girl. Yet the impression of helplessness was at least partly an illusion. She'd fought off a killer—stabbed him with a kitchen knife, according to what she'd told Sanchez and Porter.

So what is it, Seb? he asked himself. *Do you admire her because she beat the Gryphon? Or do you feel sorry for her after what she's been through?*

Both, he decided. Her open vulnerability made him want to protect her; her inner strength challenged him to pursue her. The combination, rare and paradoxical and intriguing, was one he'd never encountered before.

Delgado believed he had a pretty fair idea of who Wendy was and what kind of life she'd made for herself. She lived alone. That much he knew from having explored her apartment after Porter's phone call from Cedars-Sinai had cleared up the confusion at the crime scene. He'd learned other things while in the apartment. She did not drink; no alcoholic beverages were stored in the refrigerator or pantry. No sign of drugs either; having put in two years in Narcotics, Delgado knew where to look. She read a great deal; paperbacks were lined two deep on the shelves of the bookcase in her bedroom. Self-help books predominated; she had personal problems she needed to solve, and she felt she must solve them alone. She was neat; she liked order—everything in its place.

Frowning, Delgado turned his attention to setting up the tape recorder on his desk. There was no point in thinking about her. His three years with Karen had left him painfully aware that he was unfit for a serious relationship.

Many times in the sixteen months since he'd last seen Karen, Delgado had tried to imagine the pain he had unthinkingly put her through. Her love for him must have been like the unrequited love one feels for the dead. That was what he'd been to her—a dead man, a ghost who materialized occasionally in the bedroom of their apartment, tired and preoccupied, a ghost who left her questions hanging unanswered in the darkness, who rarely responded even to her touch.

Hostility became her only means of contact with this man who was not there. She got angry at him with increasing frequency. Sometimes her sarcasm cut too deep, and then he would snap at her, and she would retreat into another room, a slammed door between them.

Still he paid her no attention. He was busy getting ahead, proving himself, being the best.

And so he lost her. Literally lost her—she was something he'd misplaced in the clutter of his life, like a file folder buried under a stack of more urgent priorities, and by the time he thought to look for her, she was gone, leaving no note and no address where she could be reached.

But he had learned a truth about himself, at least. His obsession with his work had left him no room in his life for anything else. Not even for the beautiful young lady in his office now.

Anyway, he reminded himself, *she has a boyfriend*.

"I'm at the police station," Wendy was saying. "Yes, the police." A pause. "No, Jeffrey, I wasn't arrested."

Delgado smiled.

"Something bad happened to me," she went on, "but I wasn't hurt. Well, not much. Look, I'll explain later. The thing is, I need to stay with you tonight. I mean, I can't stay at my apartment, and I don't know where else to go. That's all."

Delgado noted the care she took to spell out exactly what she meant by staying the night. Her caution suggested that she and this man Jeffrey were not lovers. Perhaps Jeffrey wasn't even her boyfriend, just somebody she worked with or knew socially. He felt a brief, furtive stab of hope.

"Uh, let's see," Wendy said. "It's on Butler Avenue, just south of—"

"Wait a moment," Delgado interrupted. "He doesn't have to pick you up."

Wendy put her hand over the mouthpiece. "I think he wants to."

"No, that will only make things more complicated. Tell him to stay where he is. The officers who brought you here will escort you to Jeffrey's place. And they'll stay there, parked outside, till another unit relieves them. Somebody will be on duty all night. Just in case."

"I'm feeling better already." She spoke into the phone again. "Jeffrey, the police are going to take me there. . . . No, it's okay; it'll be easier to do it their way. Anyway, I don't know how long I'll have to be here. I've got to make a statement. You know."

She was quiet for a moment, listening to the voice in her ear. Delgado saw her swallow.

"Me too," she said quietly. "I . . . I'll see you."

She hung up.

What had Jeffrey said to her at the end? "I love you," perhaps. Probably. Then again, it might have been something as innocuous as "I'm glad you're all right."

Cut it out, Seb, he ordered.

Delgado took back the phone and sat behind his desk. Briskly he flipped open his spiral notebook and uncapped his pen.

"Even though I'm taking notes, I'd like to record our conversation, if you don't mind."

"Sure, that's fine."

He switched on the tape recorder, took down Wendy's date of birth and other particulars, and led her slowly through the events of her day.

She told him she'd gotten up at the usual time and left for work without incident. "I ran into Jennifer as I was leaving. I wanted to yell at her for playing her stereo too loud the night before. Now I'm so glad I didn't."

At the office she'd talked with two of her co-workers about the Gryphon, eaten lunch at her desk, and made a date with Jeffrey. That was what she called it: a date. He must be her boyfriend, then.

"After lunch I went for a walk in the shopping center next door to the office building. I bought a necklace at Crane's." She fingered her neck self-consciously, touching the bandages there. "Funny—I thought that was the most exciting thing that would happen to me today."

She'd worked till half past five, then gone to dinner with Jeffrey at a Chinese restaurant, and returned home at nine-thirty.

"Were the lights in Jennifer's apartment on when you got back?" Delgado asked.

"No. I noticed that her place was dark. And I remembered she said she was going to Seattle."

"We checked with her airline. The flight was canceled."

"Canceled?"

"Mechanical problems."

"You mean, if not for that, she would . . . ?"

"Go on, please," Delgado prompted gently.

At home she'd changed into pajamas and robe, then fixed a snack. She was in the living room when she heard the creak of a knee.

As she continued the story, her words came more fitfully. Her hands, knotted in her lap, twisted and writhed.

Delgado was impressed with her presence of mind under stress. She hadn't panicked, hadn't bolted for the door. Instead she'd pretended everything was normal. She'd even gone through the motions of washing the dishes—a nice touch. In the kitchen she'd stashed the carving knife in the pocket of her robe, an action that had saved her life.

Listening to her describe the ritual the Gryphon had performed, the lines she'd repeated and the secrets she'd confessed, Delgado tried not to think of how near he'd come to hearing her voice speak those words on a cassette tape mailed to his office.

". . . and so I told him all the reasons why I wanted to live," she whispered. "He told me he was satisfied—'well-pleased' is how he put it. Then he said he was sorry he'd lied." She ran a shaky hand through her hair. "He wasn't going to let me go. And he said . . . he said . . ."

"What, Wendy? What did he say?"

"He said I was too good a specimen. He wanted me for his . . . his collection."

Delgado winced.

Wendy stared at him with brimming eyes. "His collection of heads. That's what he meant, isn't it?"

Delgado's own voice was hoarse when he answered, "I believe so."

She nodded weakly. "That's what I thought. Oh, well, I guess that part doesn't matter. I mean, who cares what happens once you're dead? Who cares what he does with you then? Except . . . I can't help but think about it. About him having part of me like that. And about . . . the body. I mean, what do they do at your funeral? Do they just bury you without . . . ?''

Delgado did not reply.

"Anyway, that was when he started tightening the garrote. I could feel it digging in deeper and deeper. I'd forgotten all about the knife in my pocket. I'd forgotten everything. All I knew was that I was going to die. And . . . and I was so afraid. . . .''

Something broke inside her. She slumped forward in her chair and cupped her face in her hands, weeping, her voice ragged with the catch-and-gasp sobs of a child. Delgado rose from his chair and reached out to her. She took his hand. He said nothing. There was nothing to say.

During his fourteen years on the force, Delgado had endured many discussions with psychologists and psychiatrists, sociologists and criminologists, all the vaunted experts smelling of books and grants who maintained with erudite complacency that criminals of every variety were sick, diseased, dysfunctional, that they were the products of cruel childhoods or damaged brains or an unfeeling society, that they merited pity, not contempt, and treatment, not punishment. Men who robbed and raped and killed for kicks were not autonomous agents but helpless victims, he'd been told, victims crying out for understanding, begging for release from the prison of their psyches, a prison they'd played no role in creating. And if he didn't see it that way, if he insisted on judging and condemning, then he was intolerant, close-minded, arrogant, cruel; he was a man devoid of compassion, a man with a heart of ice.

But where were those experts now? Why weren't they here, in this room, holding Wendy Alden's hand? Why did their compassion, which they prized so highly, extend only to the perpetrators of evil, and not to the innocent ones whose lives evil ensnared? When the Gryphon was caught, those anxious humanitarians would gladly devote hundreds of unpaid hours to the job of treating him, reclaiming and redeeming a man who murdered for pleasure; when he was put on trial, they would eagerly testify for the defense, peering into the Gryphon's past or into his skull to find extenuating circumstances that would relieve him of all responsibility, legal and moral. Not one of them would speak on Wendy's behalf. Not one.

In the Mexico of Delgado's boyhood, the parish priest had delivered many long, stammering sermons with the same message: that the man of God must love the sinful, and the greater the sin, the greater the love that was called for. And Sebastián Delgado, nine years old, had listened, frowning. He felt no love for evil, nor for those who willfully committed evil acts; and if God commanded him to feel such love or fake it, then God must be the devil in disguise. A blasphemous thought, yes, but one he would not disown.

Compassion? he asked himself now. Yes, there must be compassion. Compassion for the innocent. For the victims. But not for those who'd made them victims. Not for the killers, the torturers, the predators. Not for the Gryphon. No compassion for him. To treat him as a social product, as no more than a victim himself, was to give him the psychological excuse and the moral justification he needed. To feel love for him, or pity, or sympathetic concern, was to aid and abet him in his monstrous crimes, and in so doing, to become a kind of monster as well.

He waited for Wendy to regain some measure of composure, then said quietly, "I think we've covered enough for tonight."

"Yes." She coughed and rubbed her red eyes. "I . . . I'm a little tired."

"You have every right to be. Look, tomorrow, when you're rested, we'll go over it all again and see if there's anything you missed. For now, I think you'd better try to get some sleep."

"I don't even want to think about the nightmares I'll have."

"Maybe there won't be any. Maybe you won't dream at all."

"I hope not."

He took down Jeffrey Pellman's address and phone number, then told Wendy to sit tight a moment longer. Leaving his office, he talked briefly with Lieutenant Grasser, the night-watch commander, then found Sanchez and Porter waiting near the water cooler.

"Time to roll, Detective?" Sanchez asked.

"Soon. First there are a few things we need to get clear. Number one, you leave the same way you came in, via the rear door. I want the cruiser pulled up nice and close, so Miss Alden doesn't have to walk more than two steps. Two quick steps. Got it?"

"Sure." Porter was plainly puzzled. "You afraid some creep with a telephoto lens might be trying to snap her picture over the wall?"

"Something like that. Once Miss Alden is in the car, she lies prone on the backseat. Before moving out, get on the radio—on the simplex setting— and show Code Twenty twice. On that signal, three other cars will leave from different exits and split up, heading in various directions. I've already worked it out with Lieutenant Grasser."

Sanchez smiled. "Decoys. You don't want any of those TV creeps to put a tail on us, right?"

"That's part of it." Delgado hesitated, then decided to be straight with the two men. "Part, but not all. The Gryphon knows I work out of this station. He's got to figure Miss Alden was taken here. He may be watching."

"Shit." Porter's dark face had lost some of its color. "It's not a telephoto lens you're worried about. It's a goddamn rifle scope."

Delgado ignored the comment. "Once you're certain there's no pursuit, radio a Code Four. But even if you get away clean, I don't want you to let down your guard. You're going to stay alert every minute till your relief shows up. Every damn minute. You hear me?"

"Yes, sir," Sanchez said.

"As you may have guessed by now, this detail you've pulled isn't a PR job. The Gryphon wants Miss Alden very badly. I don't believe there's any way he can predict where you're taking her, but I could be wrong. Perhaps he's way ahead of us."

"How could he know?" Porter asked.

"ESP. Lucky guess. Divine inspiration. This son of a bitch is capable of anything. Oh, one more thing. I don't want Miss Alden to know we're even thinking about a possible threat. As far as she knows, you're only there to make her feel better. That's the way I want you to play it when she's with you."

"After all this shit," Porter said, "that'll take some acting job."

"Well, you're in the movie capital of the world. Acting should be no problem. Right?"

"Right, sir," Sanchez said crisply. "No problem at all."

Delgado led the two men into his office.

"Wendy," he said pleasantly, "I think you know these gentlemen."

She stood up, smiling. Her tears, Delgado noted, were almost dry. "Yes, I do. You just can't get rid of me, can you?"

"We don't want to," Porter said with an answering smile of his own. "You're a lot better looking than the usual suspects we get paid to round up."

He was playing the part fine, just fine.

"Ready to go?" Delgado asked her.

"I think so. Not that I don't like it here or anything."

"What's not to like?" Sanchez cracked.

Delgado took Wendy's arm and guided her out of the office. Walking with her down the hall, he became aware, for the first time, of how small she was. The top of her head barely reached his shoulder. Her hair looked very soft.

At the rear door he waited with her while Sanchez pulled the squad car close.

"We think the TV people may have set up cameras to take some footage when you leave," Delgado lied smoothly. "For that reason it would be a good idea if you could get into the car as quickly as possible, then lie down till you're well away from the station house."

"Yeah, I definitely don't look my best for a TV debut."

"It's not just that. If these reporters know which car you're in, they may follow you to Jeffrey's. Then, if they give away the address, you'll have to go somewhere else."

"Would they do that? Report the address?"

"They might. Their sense of civic responsibility can, at times, leave something to be desired. That's why it's important for you to keep your head down till the two officers tell you to look up."

"Okay. I will." She shifted her weight nervously.

Delgado tried to lighten the mood. "Look, don't worry about it. Everything will go fine. Tomorrow morning I'll call you at Jeffrey's. In the meantime, do your best to put this whole miserable experience out of your mind."

"I'll try." She pulled her features into the pale imitation of a smile. "But I'm making no promises."

Delgado watched tensely as Sanchez and Porter led Wendy to the squad car. Within two seconds she slid into the backseat. She ducked her head immediately and stayed down. So far, so good.

The patrol car pulled away with Sanchez at the wheel. Porter's voice crackled over Delgado's radio handset: "Eight X-ray Forty-four. Code Twenty, Code Twenty."

An endless minute passed while Delgado waited for the all-clear signal.

"Eight X-ray Forty-four. Code Four. Repeat: Code Four."

Delgado expelled a shaky breath. Done.

He returned to his office, shut the door, and sank wearily into his desk chair. Rubbing his forehead, his eyes, his neck, he tried to think.

He now knew why no clay statue had been left in Jennifer Kutzlow's hand. Wendy, not Jennifer, had been the Gryphon's target from the start.

That much was clear from the fact that the Gryphon had known Wendy's name and from the details of the ritual she'd described. Poor Jennifer had merely gotten in the way somehow. The Gryphon had killed her and turned the lights off in her apartment—Wendy had said the place was dark when she arrived home—then turned them on again before fleeing the scene.

Delgado made an effort to review his notes and put together the rest of what he'd learned in the interview. But he couldn't concentrate. He could think only about Wendy. From her date of birth he knew she was twenty-nine; she seemed younger. Young and shy, yet tough too, tougher than she herself might have realized, tough enough to punch a bloody hole in the Gryphon, depriving him for the first time of the prize he sought. How the discovery of her secret strength would affect her, Delgado couldn't say; but he suspected she wouldn't be reading as many self-help books in the future. She would be less shy, less timid, not so easily cowed by the world. Having faced death, she would learn to live.

Then he thought of the Gryphon, still running loose, still holding on to the clay statuette he'd made for Miss Wendy Alden. And he was afraid. His fear was groundless; of course it was. Every reasonable precaution had been taken. There was no possible danger to Wendy tonight. He knew that.

He was afraid anyway.

15

Rood crouched low in a thicket of wild buck-brush, watching Mr. Jeffrey Pellman's house from across the street.

The lights in the house were on, and Rood could see the silhouette of a moving figure projected on the yellow window shades behind iron security bars, passing first in one direction, then the other, over and over again. Pacing.

He had little doubt the figure in question was Mr. Pellman, awake and restless. But why? Perhaps after having been awakened by Rood's phone call, the poor man had found himself unable to get back to sleep. Possible. But Rood thought it far more likely that Mr. Pellman had heard from Miss Alden and was worried about her.

Still, if he'd heard the news, why hadn't he rushed to the police station to be at his sweetheart's side? Why had he remained in the house, walking the floor? Rood didn't know.

His knees stiffened up as he crouched, as they had in Miss Alden's apartment. Out here, at least, he could flex his joints without fear of being overheard. There was nobody around. There was nothing for a quarter mile in any direction save

220

Mr. Pellman's house and stands of weed and the parched Santa Ana wind.

Nichols Canyon Road was one of several winding two-lane strips of macadam that traversed the Santa Monica Mountains, the modest range dividing L.A.'s Westside on the south from the San Fernando Valley on the north. Unlike Coldwater Canyon Avenue and Laurel Canyon Boulevard, Nichols Canyon Road was not yet crowded with houses along every inch of its switchback trail. The lower stretches, just north of Hollywood Boulevard, were densely built up, the stucco bungalows sardined together, guarding their fragile privacy with high walls and lush gardens. But as the road rose higher into the hills, the homes thinned out, giving way to sections that were entirely undeveloped, merely chaparral-choked chasms on one side and sheer cliff faces on the other.

Mr. Pellman's house stood alone in one of these forgotten areas. It was an old, sad, one-story frame building with an attached one-car garage. A white Camaro was parked in the driveway. Mr. Pellman's car, Rood assumed.

Rood had encountered no difficulty in finding the house. After crawling past it at a mile an hour to confirm the address, he'd driven on up the road till he found a narrow, lightless side street, where he'd parked the Falcon. He'd removed his canvas bag from the backseat, then retraced the route to the house on foot, ducking into the roadside chaparral whenever car headlights swept by.

Directly across from Mr. Pellman's house there was a dusty turnout sprouting gray stalks of deerweed, buckbrush, and chia. At the rear of the turnout stood a wall of rock, colorless in the wan starlight, tufted with rare clinging shrubs like flecks of mold on a hunk of stale bread.

Rood retreated to the rock wall and hunkered down in the brush. Invisible from the road, he enjoyed a clear view of the house. If Miss Alden showed up, he would see her easily.

So far, however, he'd seen nothing but Mr. Jeffrey Pellman's shadow sweeping like a pendulum across the window shades.

While he waited, Rood considered his next move. If Miss Alden did arrive, then he would simply watch till the lights went out and the two were in bed, either asleep or satisfying their coarser needs like rutting animals. At that point it would be a simple matter to silently break in and kill them both—the boyfriend quickly, Miss Alden with the exquisite slowness she deserved. Then his hacksaw would claim its prize, and the clay gryphon, still wrapped in plastic in his drawstring bag, would find its proper home in her hand.

But if Miss Alden failed to make an appearance, the situation would become considerably more complicated. Rood could practice the art of ungentle persuasion on Mr. Pellman to extract his whore's whereabouts. But the man might not know where she was, and then Rood would have gained nothing. He had no interest in killing Mr. Pellman just for the fun of it; a man's head held no mystique for him. The specimens he collected were objects of art, each capturing the delicate beauty that only an attractive young woman's features, twisted by the final extremity of terror and pain, could convey.

There were other possibilities. He could follow

Mr. Pellman the next time he left home. The man might lead him to Miss Alden's safehouse. Or . . .

Tires hissed on the macadam. A northbound car pulled slowly around a curve in the road, then cut its speed and turned into the driveway, parking behind the Camaro with a yelp of brakes.

A police car.

Rood retreated still farther into the brush, dragging his bag with him, and lay on his belly peering out from between two clumps of bedstraw. He fumbled the night-vision binoculars out of his bag and raised them to his face.

The car doors opened. Two uniformed policemen got out warily, their bodies stiff with tension.

From the backseat Miss Wendy Alden emerged, looking tired and bedraggled, a blanket wrapped incongruously over her night things. A bandage on her throat marked the garrote's work. Rood hoped the wound hurt.

"Hello, my dear," he whispered. "So nice to see you again."

The front door of the house banged open. A man hurried down the steps into the twin funnels of the patrol car's headlights. He was tall, about thirty, with wire-frame glasses and sandy hair standing up in dry patches that spoke of interrupted sleep.

"And hello, Mr. Pellman," Rood said.

Mr. Pellman embraced Miss Alden briefly, perhaps a shade self-consciously in the presence of the two cops.

"What happened to you?" the boyfriend asked as they parted. His voice carried clearly in the night stillness.

She shook her head. "Later." She turned to the policemen and handed them the blanket. Now she was clad only in the robe and pajamas Rood remembered. "Thank you, Officer Sanchez. Officer Porter. Thanks for everything."

"Our pleasure," replied the one she'd called Officer Sanchez.

Mr. Pellman took Miss Alden's hand and led her inside, shutting the door with a solid thump that reminded Rood, most appropriately, of the closing of a casket lid.

The two cops lingered in the driveway, beaming flashlights first at the bushes in the front yard, then at the encircling eucalyptus trees. Each man kept a hand on his hip, where a gun was holstered. Rood was suddenly glad he hadn't chosen to conceal himself close to the house.

Finally Officers Sanchez and Porter seemed satisfied. Switching off their flashlights, they climbed inside the squad car, which backed out into the street.

"Good night, officers," Rood breathed. "And thank you very much for a job well done."

Naturally he expected the car to execute a U-turn and drive off, down the mountain, back to the station or to wherever cops went when they were through delivering delightful young ladies to their death. And that was why he was so badly disappointed when, instead, the patrol car swung into the turnout, tires crunching on dirt like hungry mouths, and parked ten yards from Rood's hiding place. The engine was silenced, the headlights darkened. He heard a low creak as the windows were cranked down, then the quiet conversation of the two men inside.

They weren't leaving. They were going to stay all night. Stay and watch the house.

Rood pursed his lips, fighting an absurd and

quite undignified urge to cry. It wasn't fair. Miss Alden was so close—he could see her silhouette dancing on the window shade along with Mr. Pellman's now—so tantalizingly close, yet still out of reach.

Then he steadied himself. He was Franklin Rood. He was a man superior to all others. His temporary failure with Miss Alden had shaken his confidence, true, but that was all the more reason to persevere and redeem himself.

He must not be denied. He must have his revenge. And he must have it tonight.

There had to be a way.

Calm once more, relaxed and in control, he contemplated his next move. It occurred to him that he had one advantage over Officers Sanchez and Porter. He knew exactly where they were and what they were doing, while they had no idea that he was even in the area, let alone that he was positioned thirty feet from their car. Nor were they likely to discover him, even if he crept closer. Their attention would be focused on the house and the road, not on the dry brush rustling at their backs.

A plan of action was already forming in his mind.

Rood replaced the binoculars, then rummaged in the bag till he found Miss Alden's kitchen knife. A good weapon, as he ought to know. More efficient than the garrote. Perfect for a swift, silent kill.

He shoved the bag behind a patch of weeds, out of sight. Later he would come back for it; now he needed to be unencumbered as he wriggled on his stomach through the dirt, snaking toward the car and the two men inside it, who were still speaking softly, trading jokes and sharing laughter and watching the empty road.

16

Wendy didn't feel really safe until she was inside
Jeffrey's house with the door shut and locked to
keep out the darkness.

Aimlessly she circled the living room, grateful
for the table lamps blazing everywhere. Like the
rest of the rented house, the room was small and
musty and cluttered. The white walls were covered with photographs, some framed, most simply tacked up with pushpins, all of them Jeffrey's
own work and all of them in black and white, a
medium he preferred for complex, idiosyncratic
reasons he'd once explained to her at tedious
length. A few sticks of worn, mismatched furniture were scattered across a lusterless hardwood
floor patterned with an intaglio of decades-old
scratches. The floorboards creaked under her restless motion.

"All right," Jeffrey said briskly, clapping his
hands once. "The first thing to do is get you into
something dry to wear. Sound okay?"

"I think I'd like to freshen up a little. Wash my
face. I want to . . . feel clean."

He looked at her, his face an unasked question.

"No," she said quietly. "I wasn't raped, if that's
what you're thinking."

"I'm not sure what to think."

"I just feel dirty. Like I've been touched by"—death—"something bad."

"You can take a shower."

"Uh-uh." She touched her neck. "The doctor said I can't get the bandages wet for twenty-four hours. Just a washcloth and a sink full of water will be fine."

"Well, I believe I can arrange that. Follow me."

"Oh, wait a second. I want to check on something."

She peeled back a corner of the window shade and peered out through the security bars. She saw Sanchez and Porter slamming the doors of the squad car. As she watched, the car reversed out of the driveway, then parked in a weedy lot across the road.

"What is it?" Jeffrey was right behind her.

"Those policemen who brought me here—they're going to watch the house."

"Watch it?"

"Uh-huh."

"What for?"

"It's just a precaution."

She expected him to press her for details, as anybody would; but strangely he didn't. When she turned away from the window at last, she read distance in his eyes, distance and what might have been pain.

He seemed to realize she was staring at him. His expression cleared.

"Ready to get cleaned up now?" Jeffrey asked, his voice normal, too normal.

"You bet."

He led her down the hall. More photographs glided by, interrupted by the doorway to the half-bath Jeffrey had converted into a darkroom, then the closed door of the guest bedroom, which, Wendy knew, contained no furniture, only cartons of junk he'd never bothered to unpack. In the one-car garage he used as his studio, still more boxes were piled high against the walls. He'd once told her, while working on his third bottle of beer, that he saved all his notes and conceptual sketches because he believed his photographs would make him famous someday, and then his papers would be of historical value.

At the end of the hall Jeffrey opened the door to the master bedroom and showed her inside. The bed was scattered with tangled sheets and blankets hastily thrown aside.

"Sorry I had to call so late," Wendy said pointlessly. "You must have been sound asleep."

"Actually, no. I got a wrong number just about five minutes before you called me. That's what woke me up."

Adjacent to the bedroom was the master bath. Jeffrey opened the bathroom door and switched on the overhead light. The ceiling fan came on simultaneously with a rattle and whir.

"Your wash basin, madam. As for a change of clothes, I'm afraid the selection of outfits available at Chez Pellman is limited, basically, to blue jeans or pajamas."

"Pajamas, I guess. I'm not sure I can sleep, but I'd better try."

"One pair of clean, dry, much-too-large men's pajamas coming up." He removed a folded pair from a dresser drawer and handed them to her with ceremony. "Followed by one slightly ratty bathrobe." He plucked a robe, not ratty at all, from a hanger in the closet. "And slippers. No, that won't work. They'll be way too big for you. How about thick wool socks?"

"Perfect."

He found a pair. "Anything else?"

"I think you've got me covered. So to speak. I'll be right out."

"Take your time. And, Wendy . . . like I said on the phone, I really am glad you're okay."

"Me too," she answered, using the same words she'd spoken earlier.

He hesitated, as if feeling the need to say something more, then apparently decided against it. He shut the door behind him. Wendy heard his footsteps recede down the hall.

She kicked off her one slipper and stripped out of her robe and pajamas, then hung them from the shower head. Turning to the bathroom mirror, she studied her face. The new hard glint in her eyes, which she'd first detected at the hospital, was still there.

She filled the sink, then methodically ran a damp washcloth over her legs, arms, breasts, face. The cool water felt like a process of healing. She dried herself, enjoying the towel's rough texture. Finally she wetted, dried, and combed her hair. Jeffrey had always said she ought to let it fall around her shoulders. She wondered how he liked it this way.

Returning to the bedroom, she unfolded Jeffrey's pajamas, a pair of blue cotton trousers and a matching long-sleeved shirt. With difficulty she pulled them. He was right: they were much too large. They hung on her like a clown's baggy suit. She rolled up the pantlegs and sleeves till she felt marginally less ridiculous, then donned the robe and belted it tight. The socks came last; they warmed her feet instantly.

"Want something to drink?" Jeffrey asked when she returned to the living room.

"No, thanks. I've had enough stimulation for one night."

"It doesn't have to be a *drink*-drink. I've got fruit juice, coffee, probably some hot chocolate somewhere, mineral water, the works."

"I'm okay. Really."

"All right." He sat on the edge of a battered armchair, under a grainy close-up of a half-crushed beer can. "So."

"So."

"I guess it's time we talked."

"I guess." She thought about taking a seat, didn't. She stood before him, putting her hands in the pockets of the robe and taking them out, shifting her weight restlessly. "Look, Jeffrey, I know this is going to sound hard to believe. . . ."

"It was the Gryphon, wasn't it?"

She felt her jaw drop, actually drop. "How did you know?"

"Oh, Jesus, Wendy. Oh, Jesus."

"Come on, tell me. How did you know?"

His glasses were in his hand. He rubbed his eyes, wincing, shaking his head.

"Jeffrey. How?"

With effort he answered her. "After you called, I had nothing to do except wait. So I turned on the radio. The news came on. They were reporting that the Gryphon went after two women in the same apartment building tonight. He killed one; the other one got away. They didn't give the address, but the neighborhood sounded like yours. Of course I wasn't sure. When you told me those cops would be watching the house, I thought . . . But I couldn't really believe . . . I mean, it sounds so insane. . . ."

"It *is* insane. All of it. So insane I still can't believe it myself."

Jeffrey sat looking down at his glasses, the wire frames glinting in the lamplight. Then he tossed the glasses aside and rose to his feet in one crisp motion. He must have crossed the room to her, but Wendy didn't see him do that; she knew only that one moment he was standing by the sofa and the next moment he was holding her in his arms, rocking her back and forth, kissing her forehead, her cheek, her mouth.

"Wendy. Wendy. Wendy . . ."

She swayed with him, hugging him tight, then buried her face in his chest, needing the warmth she found there, needing to be close to his heart. Distantly, past the buzzing haze filling her brain, she heard a quiet, emotionless voice—her own— telling her she'd been wrong about Jeffrey, terribly wrong. He might not have shown it, but he did care for her, cared a great deal, far more than she'd known, perhaps more than she'd wanted to know.

"Wendy," he said again, the word whispered like a prayer.

After a long time they parted. She looked at him through a prism of tears. When he spoke, he made an effort to sound casual, almost business-like, as if nothing had happened between them; but his voice was hoarse and cracked, giving the show away.

"Look, you don't have to tell me the details tonight. Unless you want to talk about it."

She'd thought she did, but in that moment she

knew she'd been wrong. She couldn't go over it again, couldn't relive the experience as she'd relived it in Delgado's office. She felt worn through, like old cloth.

"No," she answered. "I don't want to talk about it. Not right now. In the morning, maybe. It'll be easier for me—everything will—in the morning."

"Would you like to get some rest or stay up for a while?"

"Rest, I think."

"You take the bed. I'll sleep on the sofa."

"I'm sorry to put you out like this."

He laughed. Low helpless laughter that had no hilarity in it. After a startled moment she joined him.

They were still giggling softly as Jeffrey accompanied her down the hall to the bedroom. His arm was around her waist, and her head was resting on his shoulder. For the length of the walk, Wendy hoped the hallway would be endless, the bedroom forever receding, this moment stretching like elastic and never breaking.

At the doorway they stopped. She lifted her head from his shoulder, and felt his hand glide free of her body. The last of their laughter dribbled out and was gone. Then they were just two people standing there.

"If you need anything during the night, holler," Jeffrey said.

She smiled up at him. "I will. Good night."

He kissed her again, then hesitated, his hand brushing her hair. She wondered if he would try anything.

I won't mind if he does, she thought. *I won't try to stop him.*

Now that was a new attitude, wasn't it? Not in keeping with the old Wendy at all. But the old Wendy, the one who was always a victim, was not the Wendy she'd seen in the hand mirror at the hospital or in the bathroom mirror just minutes ago. She was not the Wendy birthed in bloody trauma tonight.

His fingers lingered in her hair for another moment, then vanished, leaving only the memory of their touch. He took a step back. She knew he would not try anything, would not take advantage of her when she was tired and confused and perhaps willing to do something she might later regret. As always, he was a gentleman.

"Good night," he echoed softly, then turned with involuntary abruptness and walked too quickly toward the living room, where the sofa was.

Wendy's heart was beating fast, and her face felt flushed. She stepped into the bedroom, shut the door, and leaned against it, drawing rapid, shallow breaths. Though Jeffrey was gone, she could still see him behind her closed eyelids, gazing down at her with sympathetic concern. "Are you all right, Wendy?" she heard him ask, his calm baritone edged with a hint of an accent. . . .

She blinked. It was not Jeffrey she was imagining. It was Delgado.

Why would she be thinking of him now?

A tremor danced lightly over her shoulders like a shrug. She dismissed the question.

Carefully she draped the robe over a chair, then climbed into bed. Lying on her back, her hands folded on her belly, she stared up at the ceiling with its cobwebbed corners. One of those gray fuzzy things that floated perpetually before everybody's eyes drifted across the white blankness of the ceiling like a cell on a microscope slide.

After a while she heard the creaking of the sofa and realized Jeffrey had settled down for the night. She wondered if he'd turned off the lights in the living room. Of course he had.

Oh, God, he shouldn't have. She ought to tell him—

Then she remembered Sanchez and Porter, her guardians. She felt better. Nobody would get inside the house or anywhere near it as long as they were posted across the street.

To prove she was no longer afraid, she switched off the bedside lamp. Darkness pressed down on her. She listened to the faint, regular sound of her own breathing. Images flashed in her mind like heat lightning, silent, vivid, fragmentary. A wisp of curly brown hair behind the armchair. Gloved hands flying past her face as the garrote was tossed over her neck. The crimson thread ringing her neck where the wire had bitten and fed.

She shivered and rolled onto her side, crushing the pillow to her face.

Forget about it, she ordered herself. *Sleep.*

But I'll have nightmares, another part of her mind protested in a child's frightened voice.

No, you won't, she answered soothingly. *You already had a nightmare, Wendy. A bad one. The worst you'll ever have.*

And it's over now.

17

"Still can't figure how she did it. Just an itty-bitty little thing."

"Must be a scrapper, though."

"Damn straight. She stabbed him, she said. Little street fighter. Amazing."

"Hope she got him good."

"Hell, maybe he's dead right now. Maybe he only lived long enough to get out of the building, into some alley, and he croaked there like a damn stray dog."

"You better believe Delgado checked all the alleys."

"Yeah. Well, maybe he's dead anyway. Dead in his goddamn house. Maybe he offed his pretty self."

"Hey, man, we can dream."

Rood smiled. Yes, they could dream. Soon they would dream forevermore.

Officers Sanchez and Porter were so pathetically impressed with Miss Wendy Alden's survival skills. Mr. Porter, especially. "An itty-bitty little thing," he'd just called her, and earlier he'd remarked admiringly on her "Kewpie-doll face and bad-ass attitude," while insisting in a humorous way that "she's got to have some Zulu blood in her, man, plain *got* to." He and his partner had spoken of little else during the past hour, while Rood lay on his belly at the rear of the squad car.

He'd crawled there unobserved, the knife clamped in his teeth, his eyes fixed on his prey, a guerrilla warrior weaving through jungle brush. His progress had been slow, every inch a trembling effort to maintain absolute silence; his enemies had been the rustling of his coat, the brittle weeds that crackled under him like twigs, and the gusts of wind that threatened to carry such telltale sounds to the open windows of the patrol car. Although the night was cool and dry, not much time had passed before jewels of sweat were tracking down Rood's temples, his cheeks, his neck. Periodically he'd paused to snug the black stems of his glasses behind his ears.

Finally he'd reached the rear bumper, where he could lie unseen, eavesdropping on the two cops' witless conversation and awaiting his opportunity to strike. As he waited, he removed his blood-spotted leather gloves from the pockets of his coat and slipped them on.

From his hiding place he could still see Mr. Pellman's house across the street. Shortly before two A.M. the lights in the front windows snapped off. The two lovers had gone to bed, it appeared. Rood could picture them locked in grunting passion, their bodies striped with sweat.

He wondered how it felt to make love with a living woman. A woman who would whisper his name as tenderly as he whispered hers. A woman who would say she loved him, gazing on him with adoring eyes. The eyes of the dead held no adoration. They were glass marbles, nothing more.

For the first time in many years he remembered how much he'd wanted Miss Kathy Lutton, the waitress in Twin Falls. Wanted her not as a victim but as a lover. How good that would have been. Not as great, as noble, as the work he was doing now, of course. But even so . . . how nice to have someone he could love. Just once.

"Hold the fort, will you?" Officer Porter said suddenly. "I've got to make some rain in this desert."

Rood tensed, pushing away those unfamiliar thoughts. The passenger-side door swung open. The car rocked lightly on its springs as Officer Porter got out. He took a few steps into the brush. Rood heard him unzip his fly.

Raising himself to a half-crouch, Rood peered cautiously inside the car through the rear window. Officer Sanchez was looking away from his partner, toward the dark, silent house. Rood swiveled his head to study Officer Porter. The man's broad back was turned, his hands planted on his hips; falling water sizzled on the dry brush.

Vulnerable. Both of them. As vulnerable as they would ever be.

Still, two armed men . . . two men trained in self-defense . . .

Rood had never killed a man before. Many women, but never a man, any man, let alone a cop.

For a moment he nearly lost his nerve. He told himself he could sink back into the brush unnoticed and try to come up with another, better plan. Or he could forget Miss Alden entirely. Or . . .

He gritted his teeth. Fear was unworthy of him. An ordinary man would feel fear. Not Franklin Rood. Franklin Rood would do what had to be done.

So do it, he ordered himself. *First one, then the other. Both kills quick and silent. Now.*

Doubled over, staying low, Rood covered the two yards that separated him from Officer Porter. The cop was fumbling with his zipper, his head down, when Rood rose up behind him. Rood was close, inches away; even in the chancy starlight he could see individual kinks of hair curling over the nape of the man's thick muscular neck.

His right hand tightened its grip on the knife. The stainless-steel handle was stiff and hard like an erection. Rood felt good. There was no more fear. There had never been fear. Voltage crackled behind his eardrums. Invisible power lines hummed and sparked. Electric currents passed over him and through him. He was pure energy. He could not be defeated, could never be denied.

Rood seized Officer Porter from behind, cupping his mouth with one hand, while with the other he jammed the knife blade into the cop's neck and yanked it sideways, ripping open his throat in a spurt of blood.

Easy. So easy.

Officer Porter, who had such high praise for Miss Wendy Alden and who hoped the Gryphon lay dead in an alley like a mongrel dog, spasmed and twitched and danced. No doubt he was trying to scream, but with his throat cut no sound came except a series of low choking gasps muffled by Rood's hand. Blood spattered on the ground, sounding very much like the sprinkle of urine a moment ago.

Another universe, erased. Another private cosmos, canceled. Another taste of omnipotence.

The carcass in his arms stopped writhing within seconds, its feeble energies exhausted. Rood lowered the body gently to the ground, then moved immediately toward the open door of the squad car.

He slid into the passenger seat. Officer Sanchez sat at the wheel, still looking at the house.

"Guess when you've got to go," the cop said without turning, "you've got to go. Right?"

"Right," Rood answered.

Officer Sanchez heard the unfamiliar voice and swung around in his seat, his hand scrabbling at his holster.

"And you," Rood said, "have got to go."

He thrust the knife into the cop's left eye. There was a small pop as the eyeball burst. Rood leaned on the knife, driving the blade in deep. He felt a momentary obstruction, then a sudden release as the stainless-steel tip punched through the thin shell of bone at the back of the eye socket, into the brain.

Officer Sanchez surrendered his grip on the butt of his gun. He stared at Rood with his one remaining eye, his face a silent shock mask. He was still staring when Rood withdrew the knife by slow degrees, twisting the handle to wrench it free. He was staring even when he slumped in his seat, listing forward in comical slow motion till his forehead banged the dashboard with a hollow thump.

Rood held up the knife. The serrated blade was smeared with blood and pus. He licked it clean, then let his head fall back against the headrest as he expelled a shaky breath. He was trembling.

After a few minutes he was calm again. Calm and vastly pleased with himself. He'd carried out his mission with remarkable expertise. There were not ten men in the world who could have accom-

plished what he'd done. When his story was told
by future generations, as it would be, the execution of Officers Porter and Sanchez would occupy
a prominent place in the myth. And the two cops
themselves would achieve a kind of immortality,
a place in history they had not earned, but which
Rood, in his magnanimity, would not begrudge
them.

With effort he roused himself. He could hardly
afford to slow down now.

He left the car and retrieved the drawstring
bag. He needed the bag, which contained his
tools for entering the house, as well as the hacksaw with which he would take his grandest
trophy.

Crossing the street, he approached the house
and circled it. Although he would have liked to
break in through a window, as he'd done at Miss
Osborn's place, he found he couldn't; all the windows on the ground floor were protected by the
iron security bars he'd noticed earlier. Well, the
locks on a house so old and poorly maintained
should give him no trouble.

They didn't. Within two minutes he'd defeated
the rusty latch bolt and dead bolt on the front
door. Cautiously he entered the dark living room,
then stopped, his attention caught by the low
burr of a snore. The noise came from the sofa,
where Mr. Jeffrey Pellman lay fast asleep. Alone.

So Miss Alden wasn't sleeping with him, after
all. For some reason Rood was relieved. He
wasn't sure why. He supposed he wanted the
woman all for himself. Yes. That must be it.

Well, he would have her soon enough.

18

Wendy couldn't sleep. Her body hummed with adrenaline. Though she'd lain in bed for over an hour, pressing her face to the pillow, she'd been unable to nod off. She felt the need to talk, not about what had happened tonight, but about other things. That park she liked so much, the one Sanchez had reminded her of—she wanted to talk about the summer afternoons she'd spent there, and about how much she loved summer, June especially, when the daylight lasted so long that anything seemed possible. She wanted to say things she'd never dared to say, reveal secrets long hidden even from herself. Then cry a little— she was getting good at that—and let herself be held.

But she didn't feel right about waking Jeffrey, even though she was sure he wouldn't mind. She hated to interfere in his life any more than she already had. Or maybe she hated to admit that she needed him, needed anyone.

Anyway, morning would come soon. It always did.

She smiled at the thought, appreciating the optimism contained in it, the optimism always so foreign to her in the past.

At the other end of the house, in the living room, a floorboard creaked.

She rolled over on her side and listened. She heard another creak, then another.

Footsteps.

Jeffrey was awake. Apparently he couldn't sleep either.

Slowly she raised herself to a sitting position. Since he was up anyway, she decided there was no reason not to seek his company. Maybe he would fix her a cup of that hot chocolate he'd offered earlier. She could picture the two of them seated at his kitchen table, earthenware mugs steaming in their hands, talking in hushed voices till the sky was glassy with dawn. The scene was vivid in her mind, like a clip from a movie.

Smiling, pleased with the prospect, Wendy rose from bed and crept across the bedroom in her socks, holding up her loose pajama pants with one hand. Jeffrey's robe felt warm and comfortingly heavy as she shrugged it on.

She stepped out of the bedroom and looked down the hall. At the far end, in the doorway of the living room, stood an indistinct figure in a field of grainy darkness. Ambient starlight glinted on his glasses. His breathing was low, almost husky.

"Jeffrey?" she called softly. "Have you got insomnia too?"

"Uh-huh," came the whispered reply.

"Guess I can't blame either one of us."

She walked swiftly toward him. The photographs on the walls glided past her, glossy squares, faintly luminous, like pieces of dreams.

"Hey, you think maybe I could have some of that hot chocolate now?"

"Okay." The word a breath.

As she got closer, she noticed that he was wearing a robe, bulky and shapeless, which made his shoulders look broader. She thought it was funny the way he was standing there, unmoving, his hands at his sides. His gloved hands.

Halfway down the hall she froze.

Not Jeffrey.

Him. *Him*.

"Hello, Miss Alden," the Gryphon whispered.

She couldn't breathe. Tightness in her chest. Squeezing pain.

"I'm afraid," he said quietly, "the hot chocolate will have to wait."

A scream struggled to take shape at the back of her throat. She heard it rising and falling like a siren, but only in her own mind.

He'd found her, tracked her down, even though there was no way he could have known where she was. He'd broken into the house, past Sanchez and Porter, stationed outside. That wasn't possible either. None of it was possible. None of it was real. Of course not. She was asleep in Jeffrey's bed, asleep and dreaming.

The Gryphon was coming toward her now. Floorboards squeaked like mice. The folds of his robe—no, not a robe, a coat, a bulky winter coat—rustled around him. Silver glinted in his right hand. A knife.

She stared at him as he approached. She knew she ought to run, but she couldn't. Her knees were locked, her muscles rigid. Anyway, there was no point in running. He would always catch up with her. She could never escape him. Never. She could board a plane bound for the other side of the world, and when she disembarked in Australia or Singapore or Taiwan, she would find him waiting at the airport, holding up a sign with her name on it, a name written in blood.

The knife swam out of the darkness, cutting a silent wake like a shark fin. Her knife—she recognized it as it loomed closer—the knife from her kitchen drawer, the one she'd used against him. He would cut her with it. Cut her to pieces. Then take her head and leave a clay gargoyle in her hand.

No. *No.*

Her paralysis broke. She turned. Ran. Nearly tripped over her baggy pajama pants. Fast footsteps behind her. The bedroom was too far. She'd never make it. Ahead, a doorway. She ducked inside, slammed the door, locked it. Her hand swatted the wall switch. An amber safelight snapped on. Seven and a half watts. The darkroom. That was where she was. The door thumped. A fist or a shoe. Again. Louder. He was going to break it down.

She ran for the window, covered in black paper to make the room light-tight. Her fingernails peeled the paper away in curling strips of confetti. The window looked just large enough for her to climb through. If she could get it open. The door thumped again. She unlocked the window and tugged at it. Stuck. She was making noises like sobs, though her eyes were dry. She tugged harder. The door shuddered under another blow, but held, and in the same moment the window popped free and slid up. She grabbed the sill, hoisted herself off the floor, and came up short against the iron security bars. Her hands fumbled at the bars, groping for a latch, some way to open them from the inside. There had to be a way—

fire hazard if there wasn't—but this was an old house, pre-code; fire hazards all over. There was no latch. None she could find, anyway. She was caged like an animal.

She thrust her face at the bars and hammered them with her fists and screamed.

"Help! Police! Help me! He's in the house, oh, Christ, get in here, hurry, *he's in the house!*"

They had to hear that. Even from across the road they had to hear it on a still night.

The door boomed, and she heard the pop of a hinge, and she knew the two cops wouldn't, couldn't, reach her soon enough. Unless she could buy herself some time. But how?

Maybe she could hide from him. She scanned the converted bathroom in the amber glow of the low-wattage bulb. Toilet, sink, counter. No place offered concealment.

All right. Then she would fight. What she needed was a weapon.

Her gaze flicked over the scattered objects in the room. A paper cutter; could she use the blade? Something that looked like a microscope mounted on an easel—an enlarger, she realized; it might serve as a blunt instrument. Three plastic trays on the counter, worthless. A pair of tongs, some empty bottles, a row of jars. Jars. Chemicals.

She squinted at the labels in the weak light.

Dektol. Chromium Intensifier. Hypo Test Kit. Ektaflo Fixer. Glacial Acetic Acid.

Acid.

Below the bold print, a stylized skull and cross-bones. Words in italics: *Causes Severe Burns*.

The acid was stored in a sixteen-ounce glass jar with a metal twist-off cap. The jar was half-full.

She could splash him with it. Burn the skin

right off his face. Get him in the eyes and blind him. Blind the motherfucker.

Her heart was banging in her head like a migraine. She unscrewed the cap and held the bottle in both hands, hands that were almost steady. She positioned herself near the door, then flipped down the wall switch. The safelight winked out. Darkness gave her an advantage. She would know he was in the doorway, but he wouldn't be able to see her for a split second, at least. She would have that long to act.

Distantly she was aware that she wasn't doing this. She couldn't be. Less than twenty-four hours ago she'd been afraid even to express an opinion about the Gryphon.

The door exploded open. He came in fast, the knife leading him.

His eyes. Get his eyes.

Wendy pistoned out both arms and released a looping tongue of acid from the jar. The Gryphon grunted in surprise and spun sideways, shielding his face with his forearm. Acid hissed on his sleeve. Only his sleeve.

She'd missed. Missed his face completely. Done no damage at all.

You fuck-up, Wendy, she thought in miserable terror. *You blew it, blew it, blew it.*

She shook the bottle. Nothing left but drops. She threw it at him, a pointless gesture. He knocked it aside with a swing of his arm and lurched forward, the knife shining like teeth.

"Bitch," he gasped.

He advanced on her. She backed up as he closed in. The hard lip of the Formica countertop banged into her spine. She reached behind her, searching the counter for a weapon, the paper cutter maybe, or—

The enlarger.

She closed both hands over the central steel column, eighteen inches long, and swung the instrument like a club. The laminated baseboard slammed into the Gryphon's forehead and broke off with a rifle crack. Waves of vibrations radiated through her wrists, echoes of his pain.

The knife leaped at her. She batted it down, then whipped steel across his face. His head snapped sideways. He stumbled backward. The knife dropped from his splayed fingers. She lashed out again. This time he blocked the blow and grabbed the enlarger. She let go of it and ran, brushing past him toward the open door. With a snarl he lunged for her. He seized the belt of her robe, but the loose knot instantly came undone and the belt snaked through the loops like kite string through a child's fingers, gone.

Then she was out of the darkroom, running down the hall. Stumbling, tugging at her loose pants like a movie clown. Caroming from wall to wall. Breath coming in torn gasps. She looked back, but he was not in pursuit, not yet. Maybe he was groping for the knife on the floor, or maybe he was hurt too badly to follow at once.

She'd held him off, all right. Long enough for Sanchez and Porter to get here. So where the hell were they? They had to have heard her screams. Had to.

Unless they were dead. Oh, Jesus, they must be dead.

She was on her own, then. No cavalry on the horizon.

What could she do now? Get outside and run.

But where? No other homes nearby. If she fled into the canyon behind the house, the Gryphon would hear her thrashing in the chaparral and hunt her down. Okay, then take a car. Jeffrey's car. Parked in the driveway because the garage was his studio. Yes, that would work, had to work. She was thinking very fast, everything clear. She didn't want to die.

She stumbled into the dark living room. Jeffrey lay on the sofa, fully dressed save for his shoes, his head resting limply on a pillow. For a split second Wendy had the impression he was asleep, and a hot needle of anger stabbed her: How could he sleep through all this? Then she realized that of course he couldn't, nobody could, and as she lurched closer she saw the wetness smearing his neck, the parted skin flaps, the chocolate puddle on the floor.

She had no energy left for grief or horror or even shock. She took in what she saw and registered it—*yes, he's dead, Jeffrey's dead, what did you expect?*—and she knew she would have to feel something about it later, but not now, because now there were footsteps in the hall.

She needed his keys. His car keys. She leaned over him and thrust her hands into his pants pockets. The smell of his blood was strong in her nostrils.

I'm sorry, Jeffrey, so sorry I got you involved.

Her questing fingers fished out a key chain. She sprinted for the front door. For the first time she noticed that it was open. The Gryphon had picked the lock and walked right in. Those were the footsteps she'd heard. While she'd been rising from bed and pulling on her borrowed robe, while she'd been imagining hot chocolate and quiet conversation at the kitchen table, Jeffrey had been shocked out of sleep by a knife thrust that left him strangling on his own blood.

Don't think about it. Don't.

As she ran down the porch steps, she heard the Gryphon pound into the living room. It wouldn't take him long to guess where she'd gone.

The rough gravel of the driveway bit the pads of her feet through Jeffrey's wool socks. She tugged at the driver's-side door of the Camaro, praying it was unlocked—but no, Jeffrey had locked it; of course he had; nobody left a car parked anywhere in L.A. without locking it. She fumbled with the keys on the chain, feeling their shapes.

"Come on," she whispered. "Come on, dammit."

She selected what felt like a car key and tried to use it, but in the darkness and in her mounting panic she couldn't find the keyhole.

Heavy footsteps drummed on the porch. He was coming.

Finally the key slid into the slot. She turned it and heard the click of the door lock's release. She groped for the handle. Where was it? Where the hell was it?

Ragged breathing chugged down the driveway. She looked back and saw the Gryphon loping toward her. A canvas bag swung by its strap from one fist; he was rummaging in the bag as he ran.

She found the handle at last. The car door swung open. She threw herself behind the wheel and slammed the door and locked it. The ignition key was the next one on the chain. She inserted it on the first try and jerked it savagely. The engine coughed and sputtered but wouldn't turn over.

"Jesus. Oh, Jesus."

The driver's-side window shattered into a spiderweb of cracks. Her head jerked up, and she saw the Gryphon standing beside the car, the hammer in his hand raised for a second strike.

Hammer? Where had he gotten that? From the bag, of course, the bag.

The hammer swung down. The steel knob punched a hole in the window, smashing glass like ice. Frantically Wendy jiggled the ignition key. This time, thank God, the engine caught. The hammer burst through the broken window into the car, the steel claw pecking at her like an angry bird. She screamed and shifted into reverse and hit the gas. The Camaro skidded backward, tearing the hammer out of the Gryphon's grasp. Wendy spun the steering wheel. The Camaro fishtailed off the driveway onto the lawn, bounced over the curb, and rocked on its shocks in the middle of the street. She slammed the gearshift into drive and shot forward, speeding north, higher into the hills.

Relief surged over her in a cresting wave.

"I made it," she said aloud, the words tentative and tremulous, like a child's prayer. "Oh, God, I made it, I really did, I got away."

She was rounding the nearest curve when headlights flared in her rear-view mirror. Domelights twinkled. A siren rose in a ululant wail.

The police car. But Sanchez and Porter were dead. Weren't they?

Then she understood.

The Gryphon had taken the car. He was still after her. He refused to give up.

Wendy laid her foot on the gas, demanding speed, while behind her the blue and red beacons spun closer, gaining ground.

The road coiled into a series of tight turns. She shifted into low gear for better traction and climbed higher. She knew she'd made a mistake in heading north. Should have gone south into the city. Nothing she could do about it now. She would have to get over the mountain and find help in the San Fernando Valley on the other side.

The Camaro shuddered with a sudden impact from behind. Wendy looked in the rear-view mirror. Saw the patrol car accelerate to ram her again. A sharper blow this time. The steering wheel jerked free of her hands. The road skewed sideways. The Camaro skidded into the shoulder, tires kicking up sand and gravel. A telephone pole expanded in the funnels of her headlights. Wendy swerved left. The pole brushed past, shearing off the Camaro's side-view mirror on the passenger side.

Close one, she thought shakily.

The sour taste of vomit rose in her throat. Her stomach bubbled.

She crested the mountain and was swept onto Mulholland Drive, the winding ribbon of road that ran along the spine of the Hollywood Hills. The dark, hunched shapes of houses whipped past, first on one side, then on the other. In those houses were people who had no part in any of this. The thought seemed unreal.

The patrol car, domelights blazing, siren caterwauling, rear-ended her again. Wendy was flung forward in her seat, the Camaro wobbling drunkenly toward the white guardrail. Beyond the rail, nothing but black space and a sheer drop. The

Camaro thudded into the rail and skidded along it with a screech of tortured metal, shooting up white pinwheels of sparks. She spun the wheel hard to the left and swung back onto the road.

The siren was abruptly cut off. "Got you now, you bitch!" boomed a thunderous male voice, God's voice, loud in the sudden stillness. "Got you now!"

Jesus, what the hell . . . ?

The loudspeaker. In the squad car. Not God. Just him. Just the Gryphon.

"Got you!" he roared again. The squad car accelerated as the siren screamed to life once more.

"No, you don't," Wendy breathed. "You motherfucking bastard, you don't."

She veered into the other lane, then hit the brakes. The patrol car rocketed past her, taillights streaking like a time exposure, siren lowering its pitch.

Wendy was behind him now. She could execute a U-turn, try to get away. The most logical thing to do. Of course it was.

She arrowed the Camaro at the squad car. Shot forward. Punched a dent in its rear bumper.

"How do you like that, you asshole?" she yelled, her voice high and thin and ragged, keening like the rush of air through the shattered window. "How the hell do you like *that*?"

She rammed him again, again, again. She thrilled with the impact of steel on steel, enjoying the hard shock of contact. She was fighting back, going on the offensive, not running anymore. She'd run for too long, too many years, her whole life. The world had abused her, and she'd responded by hiding her pain, curling up inside herself, learning fear and smallness. Now at last she was taking action, lashing out, and it felt good, so good.

"Fuck you!" she shouted as she hit him once more, crunching one of his taillights like a sea shell. "Fuck you!" Another impact; his left rear tire blew and shredded. "Fuck you!" His trunk lid sprung a latch and popped up, flapping fitfully.

She no longer knew if she was screaming or laughing or both, and she didn't give a damn. She was free. Free.

Over the siren's wail, a sound like an engine backfiring. A gunshot.

A hand hung out of the squad car's window on the driver's side, a gloved hand with a pistol in it. The gun kicked again. The Camaro's windshield exploded. Wendy threw a hand over her face. Glass shards bit her palm.

"Fuck you," she said again. She would not be intimidated. Would not back off.

She put on a burst of speed and plowed into the black-and-white, delivering a blow hard enough to crack both cars' axles. The gun retreated as the Gryphon tried to steady the cruiser, now weaving wildly, the shredded tire smoking, the one taillight tracing red curlicues like the burning end of a cigarette in a restless hand.

Wendy careened into the patrol car again, her fender a shark's mouth chewing metal, and then, because she knew it was the last thing her adversary expected, she dropped back, giving him room to maneuver. He straightened out the car and cut his speed, falling back to pull alongside her on her right, no doubt intending to squeeze off another shot from closer range, but before he had the chance, she angled the nose of the Camero at the squad car's door and lunged forward, crushing the door like a tin can and shoving the cruiser off the road into the shoulder, where it ought to have smacked into the guardrail, except there was no guardrail this time; there was only dry brush edging the void of a bottomless descent as deep and dark as the black well of death.

The two cars barreled off the shoulder onto a thin strip of dirt scruffy with weeds. The abyss loomed. Wendy wrenched the steering wheel sharply to the left. For a bad moment she thought her bumper had locked with the twisted metal of the black-and-white's door. Then with a grinding roar it tore loose, and she was skidding back onto the road while the police car, propelled by momentum, kept going, racing toward oblivion, one brake light glowing uselessly, siren whooping in terror.

The cruiser dipped abruptly. The single taillight shot high into the air like a red signal flare as the car's front end lurched down. An instant later the car was gone.

Wendy stood on the brake pedal with both feet. The Camaro spun completely around and came to a dead stop straddling the double yellow line. Then she was running in her wool socks across the road. At the edge of the cliff she looked down and saw it, the crackling glow on the mountainside two hundred feet below, where the twisted remains of the police car had impacted. A rumble, a shock wave, and the ground shivered as fire bloomed in a blue-red cloud like the domelights' last furious display. The gas tank had ruptured, caught, blown, and now the car was a fireball, blossoming red, reminding her of a flower with petals unfolding, a red hothouse flower that, like a carnivorous jungle plant, was consuming the car and its contents, consuming the man who'd killed Jennifer and Jeffrey and Sanchez and Porter and who'd tried to kill her, tried and tried again, but had failed each time, and who'd finally paid with his life.

"Fuck you," Wendy said one last time, her voice groggy and slow.

She staggered back to the Camaro and sank into the driver's seat, thinking vaguely that she had to go somewhere, call someone, do something. But she couldn't concentrate; her mind had gone blurry; weakness was spreading through her like the sudden onset of flu. She let her head fall back on the headrest. Her eyelids fluttered weakly, then shut, and a buzzing roar closed over her, all but drowning out the siren rising in the near distance.

Siren.

She jerked half-awake with a last jolt of adrenaline and terror.

The police car hadn't crashed. The Gryphon was still after her, still chasing her with his siren shrieking, the gun hot in his hand. . . .

No. This was a new siren. An ambulance, probably, or a fire engine. Someone coming to help her, not to slash and kill. Of course. Of course.

Calmness returned, and with it a drowsiness she could no longer resist. She felt no fear, none at all.

Her last thought before losing consciousness was that she would never be afraid again.

19

Drifting. She was drifting. Weightless, bodiless, free. No pain, no fear. Around her, blackness and shades of gray. From somewhere, from everywhere, a rushing-air sound, a conch-shell hiss, monotonous and soothing.

The hum reminded her of the ocean. Slow rolling waves. Sheets of bubbly foam tickling a white shore. Sea birds like chips of broken glass, pieces of the sky. Far down the beach, laughing people. She watched them, saddened by their distance, wishing she could join the crowd. She didn't dare. She was safer alone. Always alone. Alone and afraid.

No, wait. That was wrong. That was the old Wendy. Something had changed her, shocked her out of hiding, made her come alive. The Gryphon. Yes. Fear was behind her, and all because of the Gryphon.

Her eyes fluttered open. The ocean and the people were gone. She lay in an unfamiliar bed, her left cheek resting on a starched pillowcase.

Without lifting her head, she took in her surroundings. Beige carpet, yellow walls. In a two-dollar frame, a painting of a farmhouse with a red barn. A long wooden bureau. A doorway to what must be the bathroom, and, near it, a closed door.

Behind the door, the squeak of rubber-soled shoes on tile. A hallway. A nurse walking past. A hospital. She was in a hospital room. Of course she was. She knew it even before she rolled her head languidly to the right and saw the bed beside her, unoccupied, its white privacy curtain hanging open.

On the other side of the empty bed, there was a window. Although the shade was drawn, enough pale pinkish daylight filtered through to wash the room clean of darkness. The light was the color of dawn, of promise. Was it springtime yet? No, still March. Spring would come soon, though. Wendy smiled.

For what seemed like a long time she lay motionless, staring at the corkboard ceiling panels. There had to be a call buzzer within reach; she could summon a nurse if she liked. She chose not to. She wanted to think. Wanted to reconstruct what had happened to her and figure out how she'd wound up here.

She remembered watching the police car explode on the mountainside. Then she'd stumbled back to the Camaro and collapsed into the driver's seat, feeling suddenly weak. After that, a stretch of darkness. Her next memory was of lying with eyes closed in the back of a moving vehicle, her body draped in the soft heaviness of a blanket. The blanket was good because she was terribly cold, shivering. Her skin felt damp, clammy, almost slimy. Like sushi. She wondered if only a Californian would think of that.

Sounds of activity swirled around her as she was wheeled on a gurney into a room smelling of disinfectant and ringing with voices. The voices seemed gratingly loud. She wanted to open her eyes, but found she couldn't.

Snatches of hurried conversation faded in and out like a weak radio signal.

"Respiration twenty-two."

"Pulse eighty. Strong and regular."

Static thrummed in her ears. She went away somewhere. When she came back, hands were crawling like spiders over her fingertips, her lips.

"No cyanosis."

Pressure on her wrist.

"Distended veins prominent."

A python squeeze on her left arm.

"Blood pressure one-twenty over sixty."

"It was one-fourteen over forty-eight in the wagon . . ."

The static rose to a roar, drowning out the voices, then receded.

"Vasoconstrictor indicated?"

"No, she should be all right, now that she's supine. Give me another BP reading."

The rubber python coiled around her arm again. "One twenty-two over sixty-four."

"Better all the time. You're going to make it, honey."

Of course I'll make it, Wendy answered voicelessly. *I knew that. I can't die now. Not after what I've been through. It wouldn't be fair.*

The voices went on, but the static was rising once more, the signal dissolving in the ether. She thought of Pioneer, of Voyager, those robot spacecraft sent out to explore the solar system, and how they'd glided ever farther from the sun, finally losing radio contact with Earth's voice and spinning on into the void among the stars, that great and silent darkness. She slept.

And awoke in this bed, in this room, in the first light of day.

Well, she thought with a smile, *the doctor was right, and so was I. I made it. I survived. Everything is going to be fine now. Everything.*

Except . . .

She went cold.

"Jeffrey," she whispered.

She'd forgotten about him. No, not forgotten. She'd pushed the memory out of her mind, not wanting to face it, not wanting to feel the pain.

She asked herself if she'd been in love with Jeffrey. She wanted to answer yes, but she knew the truth. He'd been someone to go to dinner with, someone who broke up the lonely routine of her days, someone who liked to talk and who'd found a lady willing to listen. That was all.

Then she remembered the concern he'd shown for her last night. The way he'd hugged her when she cried . . .

He might have loved me, she thought. *He really might have.*

And I got him killed.

She flinched from the thought. It wasn't right to hold herself responsible. After all, she'd nearly died too.

But suppose she hadn't telephoned Jeffrey from the police station last night. Suppose she'd decided to stay in a motel. Perhaps the Gryphon wouldn't have been able to track her down at all. And even if the Gryphon had found her, even if he'd killed her, Jeffrey would still be alive.

His death was her fault. Indirectly and unintentionally, yes, sure, of course; but her fault nonetheless.

Her fault . . . and her guilt.

The dawn light flaring around the edges of the window shade didn't look quite so bright anymore. And springtime no longer seemed so close.

A creak of hinges drew her attention to the door. A nurse was looking in.

"You're awake," the nurse said with a pleasant smile. "How are you feeling?"

"Tired. But okay." She was surprised at the hoarse rasp of her own voice, the dryness of her mouth.

"Well, you've been through a lot. Everyone on the staff is talking about you. You're a regular celebrity." The nurse stepped lightly to the bed and attached a blood-pressure cuff to Wendy's arm, then pumped it up and took a reading. "Looking good."

"What happened to me exactly?"

"You went into shock." She consulted the clipboard in her hand. "Says here, neurogenic shock brought on by a syncopal episode. In English, a syncopal episode is a fainting spell. Normally if you were to faint, you'd fall over. But you were sitting in a car, so you stayed upright. That caused the blood to pool in your legs, and not enough was getting back to your heart."

"Sounds dangerous."

"Can be. But fortunately the paramedics got there fast." The nurse listened to Wendy's heart with a stethoscope, then nodded as if pleased. "They pulled you out of the car and put you on a stretcher. Once you were laid flat, normal venous flow was reestablished. In other words, you got better."

"Why did I sleep so long?"

The nurse briefly checked the beds of Wendy's fingernails and the veins of her wrists. "Well, I'd say you were flat-out exhausted, for one thing. But you didn't sleep straight through. You had a bad dream, and it woke you up."

"I did?"

"You've forgotten that, huh? Well, there's only so much a person can take. Must have been a doozy of a dream, the way you were yelling."

"Screaming, you mean? I was screaming?"

"Were you ever." The nurse crossed to the window and raised the shade, inviting in the slanting sun rays, the fragile salmon light. "Anyway, we gave you a shot of Valium, and you slept just fine after that."

Wendy blinked. The entire incident—the nightmare and the fit of hysteria that followed—had been erased from her memory. She supposed it was just as well. She had enough nightmares stored in her gray cells as it was.

"Is there anything you need?" the nurse asked.

"I'd like to get out of bed, use the bathroom."

"Okay, hold on. You're going for a ride."

The nurse cranked up the bed till Wendy was in a sitting position, then lowered one of the side rails. She took Wendy's hand and helped her get up. For the first time Wendy noticed that her palms were bandaged. She remembered shielding her face from flying glass when the windshield blew apart.

The semiprivate room had its own half-bath. Wendy found the nurse waiting for her when she emerged.

"I'm wide awake now," she said. "I don't need to go back to bed." But as she took a step forward, she tottered with a wave of vertigo.

The nurse steadied her. "Looks like you do. The tranquilizer hasn't worn off completely."

Wendy allowed herself to be eased back under the sheets. She sat upright, a pillow at her back, fighting spirals of dizziness.

"Which hospital am I at, by the way?"

"Cedars-Sinai."

"My home away from home."

"Well, you can go back to your real home soon enough. I'm sure you'll be discharged as soon as the Valium is out of your system . . . and as soon as the doctor has had a chance to look you over, of course. In the meantime relax and take it easy."

"Not much else I can do."

"If you get bored, call your friends." The nurse nodded to the telephone on the nightstand. "I'll bet a lot of people will be anxious to hear from you."

She shut the door on her way out.

Wendy sighed. She wished the nurse had been right. But with Jeffrey dead, how many people did she have in her life who cared about her? Was there anyone? Anyone at all?

My parents, she thought with a chill of concern. *If they've heard the news* . . .

And they probably had heard by now. The Gryphon had been a national story; what happened to her must have been on all the morning shows back East.

She picked up the handset, dialed an outside line, and punched in a long-distance number with a 513 area code, charging the call to her phone-company credit card. The phone at the other end of the line rang three times before her mother's voice answered. "Hello?"

"Mom? It's Wendy."

"You're calling awfully early in the A.M.," Audrey Alden said in a dry, needling tone. "Must be six o'clock out there."

"Yes. I . . . I just got up."

"Something the matter?"

They knew nothing, obviously. That was good. Better to learn about it over the phone than from a TV newscaster.

"Yes," Wendy said carefully, "you could say so. I mean, there was something the matter, but it's all right now."

"Speak English, will you? What did we send you to that college for, if you can't make yourself clear about the simplest things?"

"I'm sorry." What was she apologizing for? "A lot has happened, and I guess I'm confused—"

"Boyfriend trouble, I'll bet. That Jamie's no good for you."

"His name is Jeffrey, and you've never even met him, and—" And he's dead, she wanted to add, but she couldn't force the words out.

"Those photography people are all, you know, peculiar," her mother went on, unhearing. "Of course I suppose beggars can't be choosers."

"What . . . what's that supposed to mean?"

"It means you're not getting any younger, and with all the trashy sweet things out there in Hollywood sashaying around on Sunset Boulevard, you've got to settle for what you can get."

Wendy shut her eyes, swallowed her anger. "I only called because I have something important to tell you. Last night—"

"It's Wendy," Mrs. Alden said suddenly, her voice muffled. "Yes, calling this early. Sounds half asleep, but then she always does. Pick it up on the extension, why don't you?"

A moment later her father's voice came on the

line. "I'm on my way to work," he said without greetings or preamble, "so I haven't got much time. What's the matter, darling? Short of cash?"

"No, I—"

He chuckled. "Figured you might be, what with that job of yours. How much are they paying you there? Twenty-five, is that it? Nobody can get by on twenty-five a year, not these days, not in the big city. There are jobs that pay a whole lot better, but a person's got to have gumption to get ahead in this world, is what I say."

"I make thirty grand a year," Wendy said coldly. "Not twenty-five. And I'm not calling about money anyway. For Christ's sake, don't you people own a television set? Don't you—"

"How dare you address your father in that tone of voice," Mrs. Alden interrupted. "Taking the Lord's name in vain—where did you learn manners like that?"

"Not from us, that's for certain," Stan Alden put in.

"From that Jamie, I'll bet."

"Shut *up!*" Wendy hissed. "Can't you just *listen* to me for once? I'm trying to tell you—"

"Keep this up and you won't be getting any money from us, daughter of mine," Mr. Alden said darkly. "Not one red cent."

"I don't *want* any money. Why do you keep talking about money?"

"Ease off, Stan," his wife told him. "The girl is upset. She's got boy trouble."

"No, I do *not* have boy trouble! That has *nothing* to do with . . . with anything."

Wendy was losing her composure. Suddenly she was a small child again, helpless, intimidated, being told what she thought and what she wanted and what was wrong with her, and being given no choice in any of it.

But I'm not a child, she reminded herself as she tightened her grip on the hard plastic shell of the telephone handset. *Not anymore.*

"Look." She kept her voice low and even. "I got into some trouble last night, and I wanted you to know—"

"Trouble?" her mother interrupted, a strange note of eagerness in her voice. "What sort of trouble?"

"Whatever kind of jam you're in," her father said sternly, "it's up to you to get yourself out of it. I'll do what I can, but I can't bail you out every time. I'm not made of money, you know."

"Are you pregnant?" Audrey Alden asked. "Or is it AIDS? That's it, isn't it? AIDS? That Jamie—I knew he was one of *those* types. The artistic ones always are."

"If you'd learn to keep your head on straight and not act like such a damn fool," Mr. Alden said, "you might be able to take care of yourself for a change."

"I warned you about Jamie, but did you listen?"

"All it takes is the sense God gave a goat, but sometimes I think that's more sense than you've got."

Wendy took the phone away from her ear, looked at it for a long moment, then raised the mouthpiece to her lips.

"Mom," she said quietly. "Dad."

There was something in her voice, some quality of steely hardness, that silenced them.

"For twenty-nine years"—she listened to herself from some great distance, wondering what she was about to say—"you've been taking out your problems on me. Giving me grief because it's all you've got to give. Making me crazy."

"We never—" her mother protested, but Wendy cut her off.

"I don't want to hear it. Any of it. I'm not putting up with your bullshit anymore. You hear me? I'm through being treated like a nobody. Because I'm not a nobody. And if you can't understand that, then it's your problem, not mine."

The line was quiet save for the buzz of the long-distance connection.

"Is that what you called to tell us?" her mother asked finally in a small, oddly subdued voice.

"Yes," Wendy said after a moment's thought. "As a matter of fact, it was."

"Then what was all this guff about the trouble you're in?" Her father sounded as if he didn't know whether to be hurt or angry.

"You can read about it in the paper," she said coldly. "On the front page."

She hung up before they could say anything more.

Then she threw her head back on the pillow and marveled at what she'd done.

I told them off, she thought, astonished. *I let them know exactly what I think, how I feel. I got them off my back. At last.*

The accomplishment seemed as significant as surviving the Gryphon's attacks last night.

She shut her eyes, her lips parted in a tremulous smile. She felt light and free.

"Good morning, Wendy."

Her eyes flashed open. Sebastián Delgado stood in the doorway, watching her.

"Oh. Good morning, Detective."

He stepped into the room, closing the door. She

noticed he was wearing the same brown suit she'd seen last night. Dark crescents bruised his eyes. She remembered the cot in his office and doubted he'd had the chance to use it.

"The nurse down the hall told me you were awake," Delgado said. He pulled up a chair and sat at her bedside. "Are you feeling all right?"

"Not bad. A little woozy from the Valium they gave me."

"Nothing more serious than that?"

"Uh-uh. Apparently the paramedics did their job."

He nodded. "They reached you almost immediately. There's a firehouse only half a mile from the scene of the . . . the accident."

"Believe me, Detective, it was no accident."

Delgado smiled. "I didn't think it was. You ran him off the road, didn't you?"

"Yes." She remembered herself screaming obscenities as she slammed the Camaro into the squad car again and again.

"He stole the patrol car and pursued you after you escaped from the house?"

"That's right."

"Did you get a look at him?"

She thought about it. "No," she said finally, "I never did. In the house it was dark, and when he was chasing me, there was too much going on."

"I can imagine."

She took a breath. The next question had to be asked, even though she knew the answer. "Jeffrey is dead. Isn't he?"

"Yes, Wendy." He spread his hands and let them drop in his lap. "I'm sorry."

She nodded.

"I should have protected you better," he said softly. "I should have posted more than two men outside the house. But I didn't think the Gryphon could find you there. And I assumed that, if he did, two men would be enough to stop him. I was wrong on both counts."

"I'm not blaming you, Detective. Nobody is."

He made a noncommittal sound. It was clear he was blaming himself.

"What about Porter?" she asked. "And Sanchez?"

"Porter's body was found in the brush across from the house, where the car was parked. He got out of the car for some reason, and the Gryphon ambushed him. We haven't found Sanchez yet, but we don't hold out any hope for him either. His body is probably in the wreckage of the car."

"Probably? You mean you haven't looked?"

"We've been unable to get near the car. When the fuel tank exploded, it ignited a brushfire. The winds spread the flames pretty fast; in a Santa Ana condition, that dry chaparral is like tinder. The whole mountainside was set ablaze. The fire department is still damping down the last of the hot spots."

"Was anyone hurt in the fire?"

"No. It was contained before it could threaten any homes."

"But if you can't get to the car, you don't know for sure that he died in the crash." She heard the mounting panic in her voice but couldn't quell it. "What if he got away somehow? What if he's still out there?"

Delgado leaned forward and took her hand. "Believe me," he said quietly, his voice as gentle as his touch, "there is no way anyone could have survived that explosion."

The red flower of flame bloomed again in her mind. "I guess you're right."

"Of course I am. I'm a cop. I'm always right." The words were spoken lightly, but she could see the sudden bitter self-reproach in his eyes, the brief, ugly twist of his mouth, and she knew he would not forgive himself for the mistakes he felt he'd made.

Wishing to reach out to him as he'd done for her, she raised her free hand and ran her fingers over his knuckles. "It was sweet of you to come see me."

He shrugged, a shade too casually. "I was in the area, so I thought I'd drop by the hospital and check on your condition." He glanced in the direction of the bureau. "When you're ready to go home, look in the top drawer. You'll find a set of clean clothes from your closet. I had one of my officers—a female officer—pick out some items for you." He smiled. "I thought you might be tired of wearing pajamas."

She returned the smile. "Are you always so solicitous toward the civilians you deal with?"

His eyes met hers. "Not always."

She felt the shiver of a spark between them. They both broke eye contact at once.

"Look, I'd better get going," Delgado said briskly. "The mop-up operation on the mountain must be nearly done by now." He released her hand and rose from his chair. "Later I'll take your statement about what happened last night. The ladies and gentlemen of the press are rather eager to know the details as well. For the moment we're keeping them at bay; nobody except staff members is being admitted to this wing of the hospital. But I'm afraid I can't hold them off forever. Before long you'll have to face the media."

"After last night, I can face anything."

He nodded, unsmiling now. "I know you can."

20

Delgado drove east on Hollywood Boulevard, then turned north onto Nichols Canyon Road, returning to Jeffrey Pellman's house.

As he drove, he replayed the conversation with Wendy in his mind. He'd lied to her about one thing. He hadn't stopped off at Cedars-Sinai because he was in the neighborhood. He'd gone out of his way to see her. He suspected she knew it too.

Ran him off the road, Delgado thought with a slow shake of his head.

Of course he'd already assumed that she'd gone on the attack in the car chase. Having spent the past few hours reconstructing the events of the previous night, he believed he knew what had transpired at nearly every turn.

Ralston, the coroner's assistant, had been preparing to perform an autopsy on Jennifer Kutzlow, and Delgado and Tom Gardner had been waiting restlessly in the chilly, echoing morgue, when the phone rang. Lieutenant Grasser, the West L.A. night-watch commander, was on the line with news that Jeffrey Pellman's nearest neighbor had reported hearing a woman's cries for help.

Delgado left Gardner to oversee the autopsy

and preserve the chain of evidence that would be necessary for the eventual prosecution of the case. By the time he jumped behind the wheel of his Caprice, the radio was crackling with word of a car crash on Mulholland Drive, the details still unclear.

He drove directly to the scene of the accident, bypassing Pellman's house, and arrived there only minutes after Wendy had been taken away in an ambulance. He had no idea of her condition. The Camaro she'd been driving—Jeffrey's car, according to the documents in the glove compartment—was in bad shape. What kind of shape was Wendy in? Was she bleeding, hemorrhaging, going into cardiac arrest, entering a coma? Was she dying even as he stood there in the windy darkness above the blazing brushfire? Perhaps she was dead already, pronounced DOA in the emergency room.

He was scared. Distantly he was astonished at how very damn scared he was.

With trembling effort he pushed fear out of his mind and focused on the job at hand. As he took notes on the scene of the accident, four engine companies from Hollywood and other nearby communities roared in, responding to the alarm. Pumping engines, Range Rovers, brush breakers, pump water tenders, and the big fire trucks known as quads and quints lined the road; lines of lightweight flexible hose, two and a half inches thick, were quickly stretched across the macadam.

The fiery mountainside was bracketed by Mulholland Drive to the south and, to the north, a smaller road of lower elevation called Thornwood Place. Between the two roads was a steep slope choked with chaparral. In the dry weather the chaparral, with its high oil content, had caught easily.

The engine crews' strategy quickly became clear. Using Mulholland and Thornwood as firebreaks, they first targeted the leeward fringes of the fire, spraying streams of water at the upslope flames and driving them back. Helicopters racketed out of the night, dumping thousands of gallons of di-ammonium phosphate to knock down the worst of the hot spots. Brush strike forces were formed, teams of smokechasers masked in bandannas and wearing yellow Nomex fireshirts; working with grub hoes, hatchets, shovels, and McLeod fire rakes, they cleared the brush in advance of the fire, digging firelines eight feet wide, then set backfires to consume excess fuel. From time to time Delgado saw the smokechasers staggering out of the chaparral, sweat-soaked and gasping, the fire having consumed much of the oxygen in the air. After sucking on air packs and guzzling bottled water, they would tramp back into the hell of whirling embers and superheated air to con-tinue raking and shoveling. Delgado was glad he would not be joining them.

Having completed his examination of the scene on Mulholland, he left the fire crews to their hot and hazardous work, and drove to Jeffrey Pell-man's house. He found it swarming with uni-forms. The first TV vans and print reporters were already there, as were the key members of the task force, disheveled and jittery, running on adrenaline and black coffee. Tom Gardner was among them, having just arrived after witnessing the autopsy.

"Give me the details," Delgado said tersely.

"Porter is dead," Donna Wildman answered as

she led him inside the house. "Throat slashed. Sanchez is missing. We're assuming his body was in the patrol car when it crashed. And here's another one."

She gestured toward the living-room couch, draped with a white sheet.

"Jeffrey Pellman?" Delgado asked.

"Yes. The neighbor who called in the report has already been over to I.D. him."

"Same wound as Porter's?"

Wildman nodded. "Cut throat. Nasty."

As Delgado moved through the house, reconstructing the events that had taken place there, he became aware of an ugly tension around him, the tension that always developed in any crowd of police officers when one of their own had been killed. Or in this case, two of their own; nobody had any serious expectation of finding Sanchez alive.

The Gryphon had added a pair of cops to his roster of corpses; and the men and women who had worked alongside Sanchez and Porter, who had sat beside them at the night-watch roll call and swapped stories with them in the locker room, were upset and angry and seething to obtain the rough justice of vengeance. Delgado caught whispered remarks concerning what would happen to the Gryphon when he was eventually caught.

Of course, Delgado had known the two officers as well. Other than Wendy and her boyfriend, he must have been the last person to speak with them. In a sense he had sent them to their deaths. The thought cut him like glass. Despite himself, he felt stirrings of the same wild anger that simmered around him, the animalistic fury that, unchecked, would drive a lynch mob. With effort he suppressed those feelings, slamming the lid on any thoughts of the two patrolmen. He had to stay in focus. There was a job to do.

"Something happened in the darkroom," Eddie Torres was saying. "We think she locked herself in, and he broke down the door."

Delgado peered into the half-bath, past the door leaning on shattered hinges, and saw that the black paper sealing the window had been stripped off, the window raised.

"She tried to escape, but the security bars stopped her," he said.

"Goddamn firetrap," Ted Blaise muttered.

"There's a latch," Harry Jacobs said, "but she must have been too panicky to find it."

Wildman grunted. "Can't say I blame her. Suspect was chasing me down an alley once, and I could barely remember how to pop the strap on my holster."

"I'll bet you did remember, though," Torres said.

"Yeah, and shot the bastard in the knee. He'll never play soccer again."

"What's that on the floor?" Delgado asked.

Rob Tallyman followed his gaze. "Frommer says it's acid."

"She tried to splash him, turn him into the Phantom of the Opera, I guess," Jacobs said.

Blaise frowned. "He wouldn't have been any scarier that way than he was already."

"You can see somebody took a swipe at somebody else with that photographic enlarger." Wildman was pointing at a dented chunk of metal on the floor. "My guess is she brained him with it."

Delgado got down on hands and knees. He

peered under the sink, then pulled on a glove and carefully retrieved a knife. "Take a look at this."

"Kitchen knife, it looks like," Tallyman said.

Delgado studied the serrated blade. "This could be what he used to kill Porter and Pellman, and quite possibly Sanchez as well. It may even be the same knife Wendy wounded him with, the one from her kitchen drawer." He bagged and labeled it.

Spots of blood mottled the floor of the hallway. "The lab's doing tests on them right now," Lionel Robertson said. "Ten-to-one odds they match the Gryphon's blood type."

"Or Wendy's," Delgado said quietly.

The blood trail, cordoned off by evidence tape, led them back into the living room and out the front door. In the driveway, the beam of Tallyman's flashlight picked out a pile of shattered safety glass.

"The Camaro had a broken window on the driver's side," Delgado said.

"Then it all fits together." Wildman sounded pleased. "She ran for the car and got in. He caught up with her and broke the window, but she got away."

"Pulled out fast, bounced over the curb," Gardner said. "See the tread marks in the lawn?"

"After that, the Gryphon ran across the road to the black-and-white," Delgado said. "He had already taken care of Sanchez and Porter before entering the house. He jumped behind the wheel, pushing Sanchez's body into the passenger seat if necessary, and took off in pursuit."

"Most of the locals heard the car chase," Tallyman said. "High-speed pursuit. The Gryphon was using the siren and maybe even the loud-speaker; somebody heard what sounded like an amplified voice."

"And gunshots," Blaise put in. "He was firing at her."

"Probably using Sanchez's gun," Delgado said. "The Camaro's windshield was blown out, and a nine-millimeter Parabellum round was embedded in the headrest of the passenger seat."

Gardner rubbed his chin. "If the bullet entered through the windshield, he must have been in front of her. That doesn't make sense."

"Maybe they were careening back and forth, jockeying for position." Wildman shrugged. "Who knows?"

Delgado had another idea. He thought Wendy had deliberately maneuvered behind the Gryphon and rammed him, forcing him off the road. But he kept that opinion to himself.

"Then the guy loses control of his car," Robertson was saying, "and takes the big plunge. Ka-bam! The car goes up like a drum of gasoline and rockets him straight to hell."

"Think that's it, Seb?" Wildman asked.

"Yes," Delgado answered slowly. "That, or something very much like it."

"Guess what, folks?" Eddie Torres wore a huge grin. "I think gryphons just became extinct."

"I've got just one question," Tallyman said. "Why did he take the patrol car, and not his own?"

"Because obviously his car was parked some-where else," Gardner replied. "On a side street, I'd guess."

"If so, then it will still be there," Delgado said.

"And that means you talented people are going to find it."

Wildman groaned. "We'll have to check out all the cars parked on the street within a two-mile radius. Wake up everybody in the neighborhood to determine the ownership of every vehicle in sight."

"I'm afraid so."

"A lot of people who managed to sleep through the rest of the excitement are going to be awfully upset at being dragged out of bed," Torres said.

Delgado smiled faintly. "Well, isn't that just too damn bad?"

Shortly before dawn, Delgado finally received word of Wendy's condition. He was told she'd suffered a mild case of shock but had come out of it unharmed. She had no broken bones, no internal bleeding, no serious cuts or contusions. All she needed was rest. He experienced a wave of relief so intense it was physically draining.

He arranged for a female beat cop to deliver a set of Wendy's clothes to her hospital room, then ordered the staff at Cedars-Sinai to restrict access to that wing of the medical center. He was no longer concerned about the Gryphon, but he wanted no one from the media sneaking into Wendy's room to wangle a secret interview or snap a photo of her in bed.

At daybreak the blaze on the mountain was declared to be "confined and controlled," though not yet extinguished. The task force would not be permitted to examine the wreckage for at least another hour. Delgado took the opportunity to drive to Cedars-Sinai and look in on Wendy. She was pale and thin, her hands bandaged, her eyes too large for her face. He thought she was lovely.

He wanted to hold her in his arms, but he contented himself with merely taking her hand lightly in his. For now, that was enough. For now.

Smiling slightly, pleased to find himself in a world where the Gryphon was dead and Wendy Alden was alive, Delgado arrived at the 2100 block of Nichols Canyon Road. He threaded his Caprice through a corridor of parallel-parked TV vans and came to a stop at the cordon sealing off Jeffrey Pellman's house.

Inside, he found Frommer and the SID team still methodically bagging and tagging. Frommer seemed more irritated than usual, perhaps because he'd worked three crime scenes in the last twenty-four hours, but more likely because none of the physical evidence he'd collected had played the slightest role in the Gryphon's demise.

From the kitchen Delgado heard the familiar voices of the task-force detectives. If they were back, then they must have completed their rounds, which meant they had located the car. From the license number, the Gryphon's identity could easily be traced. At his home, the heads of his victims would be found. The last pieces of the puzzle would snap into place.

Delgado entered the kitchen and saw the eleven investigators scattered around the large sunlit room. He sensed their moody restlessness at once, even before Donna Wildman spoke.

"Bad news, Seb."

His gut tightened.

"What is it?" he asked, already knowing the answer.

"We checked out every car, truck, van, motor scooter, and tricycle within two miles of this location, and all the owners are accounted for."

"Every vehicle." Ted Blaise sighed. "Every god-damn one."

"No," Tallyman said. "There was one I didn't check." They all looked at him, and he smiled. "Cop humor."

"Hilarious." Wildman was not amused.

Neither was Delgado. He leaned against the refrigerator and rubbed his forehead. He was tired suddenly, more tired than he'd ever been.

"It doesn't make sense," he muttered. "The Gryphon must have had transportation to get here."

"We were talking about that," Jacobs said. "We came up with a few ideas."

"Such as?"

"He might have lived in the area," Robertson said. "Within walking distance. Then he wouldn't have needed the car."

Delgado grunted. "Pretty tall coincidence, don't you think? He just happens to live a few blocks from the home of Miss Alden's boyfriend?"

"Not necessarily," Robertson persisted. "Maybe she used to come up here a lot, to be with this Pellman guy. If the Gryphon lived nearby, he would have seen her hanging around. That could be why he chose to go after her in the first place. And it would explain how he knew he'd find her here."

"There's no reason to think any of the other women ever came to this neighborhood."

"This could be a special case."

"It's possible," Delgado conceded. "But I still think it's farfetched."

"How about this?" Blaise offered. "Suppose he parked on a side street, and while he was otherwise occupied, the car got lifted."

Delgado smiled without humor. "Now *there's* a coincidence."

"I admit that. But L.A.'s the car-theft capital of the world. And there are a lot of nice wheels garaged in these hills. You never know."

"I'll file that one under Improbable. Any other suggestions?"

"An accomplice," Gardner said. "Let's say the Gryphon worked with a friend. He parks, leaves the friend in the car, and when the friend hears sirens, he gets nervous and takes off."

"Nearly all serial killers work alone," Delgado said slowly. "And we have no indication of any teamwork in these killings."

"Can't rule it out, though. Remember Bianchi and Buono."

"I acknowledge the possibility, Tommy. But I'm still not convinced."

Gardner shrugged, not pressing the point. "So what do *you* think?"

"Perhaps . . ." Delgado hesitated, superstitiously reluctant to voice this thought and somehow make it real. "Perhaps the Gryphon took the car himself. Perhaps he didn't die in the crash after all."

"No way," Robertson objected. "The explosion—"

Delgado cut him off. "If the gas tank wasn't badly ruptured, he might have escaped from the car before it blew. In which case he's still out there, and . . ."

His words trailed away.

He was picturing Wendy in her bed, protected only by hospital security. Protected from the media, from tabloid journalists, nothing worse.

He reached for the wall-mounted kitchen phone. His radio handset would be more direct, but reporters would be monitoring the police bands, and he preferred to keep this communication confidential.

"What is it, Seb?" Wildman asked as Delgado punched in the number of the dispatch center in downtown L.A.

"I'm sending a uniform to pick up Miss Alden at the hospital right now, whether the doctors are through with her or not, and move her to the West L.A. station. I want a hundred cops around that woman—hell, a thousand of them—until we figure out what in God's name is going on."

21

Shortly after Delgado left, a doctor examined Wendy, looking her over like a mechanic inspecting a damaged but still functioning piece of machinery, and concluded she was well enough to go home. She was relieved to hear it. She'd always hated hospitals. No matter how much Lysol disinfected and deodorized the air, she was morbidly certain she could smell death in these places; and today of all days, she didn't like that smell.

Alone again in her room, she put on the clothes that had been left for her in the bureau. As she dressed, she found herself humming a melody, a strangely familiar one. Then she recognized it: "Full Moon and Empty Arms"—the same tune she'd hummed in the kitchen last night while she felt the pressure of a killer's gaze.

The police officer who'd delivered the clothes had selected an outfit typical of the old Wendy: white cotton blouse, gray pleated skirt, sensible low-heeled shoes. Wendy studied her reflection in the bathroom mirror with a muted sense of nostalgia. She felt as if she were looking at a photograph of herself from years ago, her college yearbook portrait, perhaps, or the faded photo on her driver's license. The drab uniform no longer suited her. From now on she would wear only bold colors and exotic styles. She wanted to stand out in a crowd, to be seen and admired. She wanted—

A knock on the door interrupted her thoughts.

"Come in," she said automatically, assuming her visitor was another nurse or orderly.

But when she stepped out of the bathroom, she saw a uniformed policeman standing at the threshold of her room.

" 'Morning, ma'am."

"Good morning," she answered uncertainly.

"Detective Delgado sent me to collect you."

"You mean, take me home?"

"Well, no, not exactly. He'd like to have you wait at the police station."

She blinked. "Wait there? Why?"

"Just a precaution."

"He didn't say anything about that to me when he was here."

"Well . . ."

Then she understood.

"Oh, Jesus," she whispered. Sudden fear jellied her knees. "He's still alive, isn't he?"

The cop moved his big shoulders. "That's the rumor. But don't tell the detective I said so, or I could be in some real hot water, if you catch my drift. . . ."

He went on speaking, but Wendy no longer heard him. His voice had receded, as had the walls of the room. The floor canted dangerously. Her head hummed.

"God. Oh, God." Was she saying that? "Oh, my God."

"Ma'am?" The cop took a step toward her. "You okay?"

That was a question. She had to answer it.

"Ma'am?"

"Yes." She drew a deep breath and let it out slowly. She regained some measure of control. "Yes, I'm fine."

"I shouldn't have shot my mouth off. Like I said, it's a rumor, that's all. I'm just a grunt; nobody tells me much."

"I understand."

"All I know for sure is that I've got to get you over to the station. And that it's for precautionary purposes only. Okay?"

"Okay."

"You got any stuff you want to take with you?"

"No. Nothing. Let's go."

As they walked down the hall, a new thought occurred to her.

"I'll have to arrange the payment of my bill before I leave."

"I'm afraid Detective Delgado's orders were to take you there straightaway. He was what you might call explicit on the subject."

"I can't just walk out without paying."

"As a matter of fact, you can." He tapped his shield. "Believe me, a badge can work wonders in a situation like this."

She didn't argue, because of course he was right.

They rode the elevator to the ground floor. At the front desk the cop talked briefly with the receptionist. Wendy signed a carbon-backed form she didn't bother to read, and then she was free to go.

The parking garage was directly adjacent to the lobby. The cop led her to a Dodge Aries coupe.

"The detective thought it would be a good idea

to use an unmarked car," he explained as he unlocked the driver's-side door. "There's a whole bunch of TV people out front, and if they laid eyes on a black-and-white, they'd be after it in a New York minute."

Wendy slid into the backseat. She watched the cop remove a tan coat from the passenger seat and shrug it on, concealing his uniform.

As he climbed behind the wheel, she leaned forward and said, "The TV people aren't the only reason for taking this car, are they?"

His face was all innocence as he turned to her. "Beg your pardon?"

"The real reason is that Detective Delgado is afraid the Gryphon will be waiting in the crowd outside. And if he is, then *he* might be the one to follow us. Or he might try something crazy, right on the spot."

The cop nodded sheepishly. "Guess there's no use trying to fool you, ma'am. And in case you're wondering, I'm wearing this beat-up old coat on account of the same considerations. I'm not supposed to look like a cop, see? And, uh, I'm not supposed to be seen with a passenger either."

She recalled the routine in the parking lot of the police station last night. "You want me to stay out of sight?"

"I'm afraid so."

With a sigh, she knelt on the floor and lowered her head. The narrow space between the front and rear seats was as claustrophobic as a coffin, the coffin that might yet be hers if the Gryphon learned her whereabouts again.

Suppose he *was* in the crowd outside, with the pistol he'd used during the car chase concealed under his jacket. Suppose, despite every safeguard, he somehow knew which car she was in. Suppose . . .

Don't think about it, she ordered.

Through the bandages on her palms she felt the four-cylinder engine shudder to life. The tires screeched as the Dodge reversed out of the parking space and pulled up to the gate. A moment later sunlight flooded the car's interior. Wendy waited tensely as sounds of traffic and rushing air flew past.

"Okay," the cop said after what seemed like several hours, "you can come up for air now."

Shaky with relief, she climbed back into her seat.

She looked out the window and saw that they were heading west on Santa Monica Boulevard. As she watched, the steel-and-glass towers of Century City glided into view on the left. She picked out the smaller office building where she worked. The sight of it reminded her to call the office and let everybody know she was all right.

"Nice part of town, isn't it?" the cop asked from the front seat. She noticed he was wearing sunglasses now, an unofficial part of the uniform of every L.A. patrolman. "Century City, I mean."

"I work there."

"Do you? What sort of job?"

"I write informational booklets for an actuarial firm, Iver and Barnes. It's pretty boring, actually. I've been doing it for five years, and I think pretty soon I'll be trying something new."

She realized what she'd just said. The words astonished her; and more astonishing still was the knowledge that they were true.

Rolling down the window, she gazed out at the morning. Last night's winds had died down, and a fresh breeze off the ocean had scrubbed the city clean, gifting L.A. with one of those rare perfect days unblemished by a brown haze of smog and unbleached by a white smear of sun. There was only a baby-blue sky streaked with herringbone filigrees of cloud.

She let her head drop back against the seat and surrendered herself to the crisp sunshine and the cool, healing air.

"Private joke, ma'am?"

At first she didn't understand. Then she realized she'd been smiling broadly; he must have seen her in the rearview mirror.

"No," she said. "Not a joke. I was just thinking that . . . well, that it's a good day to be alive."

"Every day is like that."

Yes, Wendy answered silently. *Every day from now on.*

22

Delgado was the first to reach the wreckage of the patrol car.

It lay on a broad shelf of granite a hundred feet above Thornwood Place, sprawled like a lazy cat, its chassis resting on the rock, its front end overhanging the lip of the outcrop. Fire had left the car a charred and smoking ruin. The domelights had melted; gooey tentacles of molten glass slimed over the roof. The tires were puddles of liquefied rubber. From inside the sedan came an acrid smell. Delgado wanted to believe it was the odor of burnt flesh, the Gryphon's flesh. He hoped the bastard had been roasted alive.

But he was no longer sure.

He and the members of his task force had been granted permission to hike up the mountain only fifteen minutes earlier. The twelve of them had made their way swiftly through the thinned and blackened brush, rarely speaking. The blistered landscape discouraged conversation. It was a study in charcoal, all stark tones and harsh contrasts, reminding Delgado of the engraved illustrations of Gustave Doré. And Doré, he thought grimly, had been particularly expert at depictions of hell.

In the pale morning light, the crust of fire retardant dumped by last night's helicopters looked pink and gelatinous, like the vast puckered surface of an amoeboid monster in a science-fiction movie. Wisps of smoke curled from rare places where spot fires still burned under the chemical coating. At various distances, fatigued fire crews could be seen tramping up and down the mountainside, dampening the last stubborn smokes with handheld soda-and-acid fire extinguishers.

As Delgado climbed higher, he observed that the grade of the mountain was not as steep as he'd first believed. What appeared from above to be a sheer drop was actually a gentler slope angled at about forty-five degrees. The patrol car would not have cartwheeled and somersaulted two hundred feet; instead it must have sledded down like a maniacal toboggan, chewing up clumps of blueblossom, greasewood, and Christmas-berry as it went. The tough, congested brush no doubt slowed its progress, preventing the buildup of lethal momentum. Only when the car struck the granite shelf had it received the powerful impact that had ruptured the gas tank. A fatal impact? Not necessarily. Delgado had seen cars folded into steel origami, from which the drivers had walked away with only minor scrapes and cuts.

Briefly he comforted himself with the thought that, even had the Gryphon escaped from the car before it exploded, he could not have outrun the brushfire that followed. But the wind had been gusting westward; if the Gryphon had headed east, away from the flames, he could very well have descended to Thornwood Place, then hurried through the network of intersecting streets till he hooked up with Nichols Canyon Road a

mile to the south. From there it would not have
been difficult for him to find his car, parked on
some dark side street, and drive off, unnoticed in
the confusion.

Yes, Delgado decided as he planted one shoe
on the spur of granite and stood looking at the
wreckage three yards away. The Gryphon could
indeed have done that. But had he?

There was one way to find out.

Slowly he approached the car. Without looking
back, he knew that the other detectives had
halted at the edge of the rock, watching him
tensely.

The car ticked and hissed and creaked, sounds
of the jungle or the swamp. Every window had
exploded in the intense heat, and the spray of
glass fragments littering the ground had melted,
fusing with the rock to form lumpy starbursts,
transparent as ice. Picking his way among the
slippery mounds, Delgado reached the driver's
side of the car, taking care not to touch the smol-
dering metal, and peered in through the twisted
window frames.

The front and back seats were craters of ash.
Plastic stalactites dripped from the dashboard.
Cinders drifted lazily in the air like dust motes.

There was nothing in the car. Nothing. No
human remains.

Delgado turned and shook his head once.
"Gone."

"The scumbag might be dead anyway," Tom
Gardner said with desperate optimism. "Even if
he jumped clear, he could have been torched. The
whole mountain went up like a bucket of super
premium."

Delgado shrugged. He wasn't hopeful. "Let's fan out and see."

They obeyed. Delgado remained at the car, circling it slowly, looking for clues he did not find. He wondered if this man could ever be killed.

"Seb!"

The cry was Donna Wildman's. She stood near the black remnant of a scrub oak thirty feet away, her outstretched arm arrowed at something in the brush.

Delgado clambered off the rock and ran to her. Looking down, he saw a body lying facedown on the ground, burned so badly that most of its skin had crisped like bacon and peeled off. The body was nude, the clothes apparently incinerated along with the flesh.

"Son of a bitch." That was Eddie Torres. Delgado glanced up and saw the other detectives ringing the scene. "We got Tweetie Bird, after all."

But Delgado didn't think so. An ugly suspicion was taking shape in his mind.

"Turn him over," he ordered, his voice ominously low.

Tallyman and Robertson donned plastic gloves and gently rolled the corpse onto its back. The front of the body was crusted with dark soil.

"Scrape him clean."

The two men wiped away the filth, exposing the corpse's face, preserved from the fire by the dirt. One sightless eye gazed up at them; the other was a bloody hole.

"Oh, Christ," Blaise whispered. "It's Sanchez."

Delgado nodded, unsurprised.

Harry Jacobs scratched his jaw. "Was he thrown here by the force of the blast, you think?"

"No." Delgado knelt by the body. "He was dragged."

With the flat of his hand, he wiped a long strip of grime from Sanchez's chest. The same dirt that had protected his face from incineration should have protected the front portions of his clothes, as well. But his uniform was gone. Only a soiled undershirt remained.

"Dragged . . . and stripped."

Then Delgado's radio was in his hand, his finger pressing the call button.

"Eight William Twenty. I need to have Eight Lincoln Ninety meet me on a Tac frequency."

He waited, heart pounding, while the female dispatcher selected an available frequency and contacted 8L90, the watch commander at the Butler Avenue station.

"Eight Lincoln Ninety"—the dispatcher's voice crackled over the handset's speaker—"meet Eight William Twenty on Tac six."

Delgado switched the handset to Tac 6 and keyed the mike. "Eight William Twenty to Eight L Ninety."

"Eight L Ninety, go," said the gravelly voice of Lieutenant Nat Kurtz.

"Nat?" Delgado fought to keep his own voice level. "I have some news here that won't wait."

"Hey, so do we, Seb. We've got what you might call a situation. The unit dispatched to Cedars just called in. The civilian they were sent to pick up is gone. Hospital staff reports she left with another officer less than five minutes ago. The guy was in uniform, but he's nobody we know. And here's the worst part. One of the security guards got a look at the mystery cop's nameplate."

Delgado closed his eyes. He barely heard the watch commander's next words. He didn't need to hear them.

"The name on the tag was Sanchez."

23

Wendy was gazing past the cop in the driver's seat, watching the modest high rises that lined Santa Monica Boulevard sweep by, when suddenly it came to her, wordless and unsettling—an eerie sense of déjà vu.

Blinking, she shifted her focus from the view framed in the windshield to the cop directly before her. She could see nothing of him but the top of his hatless head rising over the headrest. A few wisps of curly brown hair.

She stiffened.

The armchair in her living room. A glimpse of a stranger's head as he ducked down.

The same brown hair she saw now.

No. Crazy. Impossible.

She was turning paranoid, that was all. Probably half the male population in America had brown hair, for God's sake.

Calm down, Wendy. He's a police officer. He has to be.

But what if he weren't?

It occurred to her that a police car, even an unmarked car, ought to be equipped with a special radio, as well as a microphone clipped under the dash and other paraphernalia she remembered from Sanchez and Porter's cruiser last night. As surreptitiously as possible she peered between the two front seats. She saw no microphone, no squawkbox, only what looked like a perfectly ordinary AM/FM radio and . . . and a cassette player.

No police car would have a tape deck in it. She was certain of that. Almost certain. But suppose this car had been confiscated in a drug bust or something. Then it would have come with all sorts of options already installed. Okay, that made sense—maybe—but it still didn't explain the absence of a police radio. Unless the radios in unmarked cars were concealed in some way. That might be the answer.

But she wasn't convinced.

She glanced around at the interior of the car, looking for a way out. Just in case, she told herself, just in case.

There was no way out. She was trapped. Had the Dodge been a four-door model, she could have thrown open a rear door and jumped clear if necessary. But the car was a coupe, and from the backseat she couldn't reach the door handles.

She remembered lying on the floor and thinking of a coffin. Her coffin.

Oh, come on, she told herself shakily. *Take it easy, will you?*

But she couldn't take it easy. She kept staring at the brown curls above the headrest, while she thought of Officer Sanchez, whose body, according to Delgado, hadn't been found.

Had she checked the nameplate on this man's uniform? She knew she hadn't.

The car reached Sepulveda Boulevard. Abruptly the cop—if he was a cop—spun the steering wheel hard to the left, veering south.

But the police station wasn't south. It was west. Due west.

Wendy was trembling now. Trembling all over. She cleared her throat and tried to act casual and unconcerned. "Hey, aren't we, uh, heading the wrong way?"

"Well, yes, I guess you could say so," he answered laconically as auto-body shops and health spas ticked past. "Thing is, I believe we've got one of those TV news vans on our tail. So I'm taking a little detour to shake him loose."

Which made sense—sure, it did—except that when she glanced out the rear window, she saw no van. She saw only a wide, empty street.

Again the steering wheel blurred under his hands. The Dodge swung left onto Missouri Avenue, then immediately hooked right, nosing into an alley.

Wendy's heart was beating fast, very fast.

Gravel crackled under the tires. The alley was narrow, bracketed by fences and cement walls scarred with black spidery graffiti. Utility poles marched down its length, their power lines cutting the blue sky like cracks in a mirror.

Halfway down the alley, the Dodge eased to a stop behind a parked car. An ancient Ford, dressed in white paint and polished chrome.

Wendy swallowed. Pounding pressure filled her head. She wanted to ask him why he'd stopped, but her mouth was dry and she couldn't seem to form the words. Anyway, it didn't matter. She knew the answer already. She knew. She knew. She knew.

Slowly the man in the driver's seat turned to face her. In his right hand there was a gun, the blue-black Beretta 9mm from his holster. She heard a click as he thumbed down the hammer.

He smiled. His teeth shone white and looked cold, like chips of ice, below the black ovals of the sunglasses shielding his eyes.

"Hello, Wendy."

He whispered the words, and for the first time she recognized his voice.

She stared at the Gryphon, numbness spreading through her like an injection of painkiller.

"Now," he said softly, with the ominous politeness she remembered, "here's what we're going to do, you and I. First, we're getting out of this car. And you won't give me any trouble when we do that. Right?"

She didn't answer. Couldn't speak.

He nodded, apparently interpreting her silence as acquiescence. "Fine."

The door creaked open. He climbed out, then lowered the driver's seat so she could follow.

She hesitated, her mind racing as she considered what few options she might have. She could lunge forward, plant her fist on the horn, honk for help. No, hopeless; he would shoot her long before help came, if it ever did. All right, then. Grab the gun, wrestle it from his grasp. Dammit, that wouldn't work either; he was too strong for her.

"I'm waiting, my dear."

Nothing. There was nothing she could do.

She left her seat and stepped out of the car, looking around at the alley. On one side, a wire-mesh fence screened off an empty parking lot. On the other side rose a crumbling cement wall, and beyond it, a house with boarded-up windows.

The area was deserted. She could scream for

help, but her cry would echo down this stone corridor unheard.

The Gryphon jammed the gun in her side. "Now I'd like you to start walking. Please."

Her shoes crunched dead weeds and broken glass as he guided her to the passenger side of the Ford. The door was unlocked. He pulled it open.

"Inside."

If she got in the car, she was dead. He could drive her anywhere, kill her at his convenience. To live, to have any chance of survival, she had to do something, and she had to do it now.

She took a step toward the car, then spun sideways, away from the gun in her ribs, and pistoned out both arms, shoving the Gryphon off balance. He fell against the open door with a grunt of surprise. Then she was running down the alley toward the distant street, expecting at any second to feel a bullet in her back.

Behind her, the clatter of footsteps. Panting breath, hot and hoarse and close. Too close.

A hand closed over her arm and spun her around. She staggered, twirling in the killer's grasp like a drunken dancer. He jerked her toward him. Her face, twinned and miniaturized, stared back at her from the lenses of his sunglasses. She drove a knee into his gut. He released his grip, wheezing. She whirled. Started to run. He kicked her feet out from under her. The gravel-strewn pavement came up fast. Bright glassy pain burst in her hip as she hit the ground on her side.

She twisted around to a sitting position and looked up. A shadow slid over her. His looming figure eclipsed the sun. She heard his low breathing, like the grunting rasp of an animal. She breathed the sour stench of his sweat. Her stomach fluttered.

Reaching behind her, she groped in the trash lining the alley for something to fight him with. Her bandaged hands sifted through a scatter of broken glass, the shards too small to be of use as weapons. Near the glass lay a mound of rain-soaked newspapers. A record album broken in two pieces. A Styrofoam fast-food container. Somebody's shoe.

She picked up the shoe and pitched it at him, a final, desperate, meaningless gesture. He brushed it aside with a cough of laughter.

After that, she was finished; her pitiful last stand was over. She lowered her head and waited for him to do what he would. She hoped he would shoot her. A bullet would be quick.

Then softly he spoke to her, and strangely his voice was gentle, almost kind.

"Don't be afraid, Wendy. I'm not going to hurt you. Not this time."

Slowly she lifted her gaze and stared up at him through the webwork of hair plastered to her face.

"Oh, I admit I wanted to hurt you very badly last night. I wanted to do terrible things to you. But then I saw that I was wrong. That I'd missed the significance of what had gone on between us. That I'd failed to appreciate you properly. I saw that only a most exceptional woman could play the game so well."

"The . . ." Her voice cracked. "The game?"

"I saw," he went on, unhearing, the words dripping in a slow metronomic cadence, "that it could not have been an accident that I selected you. For out of all the lesser women I might have chosen, I had been led to the only one on earth who made a worthy adversary. Such things are never the product of chance. No, it was destiny that brought us together."

He chuckled, embarrassed by his own eloquence.

"That sounds so cornball, doesn't it? Like something in a Hallmark card. But I'm serious. I believe in destiny, in fate. I believe in a deeper meaning that transcends the ordinariness of life. And with that same faith, by the light of that same understanding, I believe we were meant for each other."

He gazed down at her fondly. He was smiling. A shy, almost boyish smile.

"What I'm trying to say is . . . I love you."

As Wendy watched, unable to move or speak or think, the Gryphon reached into the pocket of his coat and handed her a small clay statuette.

24

Wendy accepted the statue with numb fingers. She stared at it, turning it slowly in her hand.

"See the detail," the Gryphon breathed. "The delicacy of the carving."

"Very pretty," she said quietly.

"Like you."

She went on studying the figurine between her fingertips. Her body was a huddle of shock. Her mind was empty. She felt as if that hammer of his, the one he'd used to smash the car window last night, had slammed down on her brain and made it into mush.

"You . . . you said you love me," she whispered at last.

"Yes."

"But . . ." She almost choked on the words, on the idea of having this conversation with this man. "But that's impossible. That's . . ."

Crazy, she wanted to say, but didn't.

"Of course it's impossible, Wendy. Every great thing is impossible. That's precisely what makes it great. That's what greatness is: the act of overcoming. Overcoming the possible, the normal, the mundane."

She swallowed, barely hearing him, her mind

occupied with a new question. "Is this the statue you were going to give me last night?"

"Yes. But now it holds a very different significance."

"Does it?"

"Yes, it does. Then it was a marker of death. Now it is a token of my love to you. You must believe that, Wendy."

He kept saying her name, as if he took pleasure in pronouncing it. Her first name only; she wasn't Miss Alden to him anymore. The obscene familiarity implied in his choice of words revolted her.

She drew a sharp breath. "Look. If you're serious about . . . about what you said . . . then let me go. Let me just walk out of here."

"No."

"But if you"—say it, go on, say it—"if you love me . . ."

"I do love you. Honestly, I do. But I can't release you, because you don't understand what's happened between us. Not yet, anyway."

He knelt before her, tapping the pistol lightly against one knee. His sunglasses gazed blankly at her like insect eyes.

"I don't blame you. I don't question your lack of faith in me." He sighed heavily, a melodramatic, grandiloquent sigh. "This world is so choked with ugliness and pettiness and commonness. Sometimes it seems hard to believe that any genuine beauty or spirituality could exist here. But look, Wendy."

His hand closed lightly over her wrist, lifting the figurine closer to her face.

"If something as special as this can be shaped out of mud, out of dirt, then so can the love that is our destiny." He shrugged. "But until you see the truth in what I'm saying, until you're willing to accept it, I'm afraid I simply can't let you out of my sight."

His grip on her wrist tightened. He stood up and pulled her to her feet. Her legs felt weak and wobbly. There was a frightening tilt to the ground that hadn't been there before.

"Now, come along," he said as if to a hesitant child. He gave her arm a little tug. "Come on."

She let him lead her back to the white Ford, its door still hanging open. He released her hand, and she sagged against the car, her knees buckling. She had no idea what he would do next. She almost didn't care. Fear had drained out of her, leaving her hollow.

"Now, please . . . get in."

She obeyed. As she was settling into the passenger seat, he leaned in and tapped her arm. "Behind the wheel, if you don't mind."

She realized he wanted her to drive. He'd made her enter on the passenger side only to ensure that she would never be out of his reach.

With difficulty she climbed into the driver's seat. Sliding in beside her, he shut the door and handed her a set of keys. She stashed the clay statue in the pocket of her blouse, then turned the ignition key in the slot. The engine growled.

"Excellent," he said pleasantly. "I don't know about you, but I feel that this whole thing really is working out quite well."

His grating cheerfulness only made things worse. If things could be worse. If anything could be worse than this.

"Where are we going?" she asked flatly.

"I'll tell you in a second. But first, listen to me. Listen good."

She stared straight ahead, rigid in her seat.

"Look at me when I talk to you."

Reluctantly she turned toward him. For the first time she looked, really *looked*, at his face. She saw brown hair, curly and close-cropped. A high forehead. Thick brows. A fleshy nose, humorless mouth, square cleanshaven chin.

It was not the face of a monster, not a face that belonged in a lineup or a mug shot or a chamber of horrors. It was a face she could pass on any street, a face so ordinary it almost didn't exist.

Then, with a small, distant shock, Wendy realized she knew that face from somewhere. But she had no strength to think about it now.

"I know you still want to get away," the Gryphon was saying quietly. "And you'll think of all kinds of clever ways to do it. Send the car into a skid, drive off the road into a ditch—things like that. You're most resourceful, as I've already learned, much to my chagrin." His voice dropped lower, till it was nearly inaudible. "But there's one small detail you ought to be apprised of, Wendy dearest. Even though I've come to care for you very deeply, even though I cut you a good deal of slack just now, even with all that, my patience is not unlimited. To put it quite plainly, if you do attempt to pull off any of those clever schemes you're known for . . . I'll have no choice but to kill you."

The gun jerked forward, the muzzle biting the skin beneath her jaw like a hungry animal.

"I'll blow your fucking head off!" he snarled.

With his free hand, he whipped the sunglasses from his face, and suddenly she was staring into his eyes, gray eyes, small and flat and dull, like nailheads.

"Do you hear me, Wendy? Do you? *Do you*?"

She tried to nod, but the gun in the hollow of her jaw made it impossible. "I hear you."

"Good." He smiled, withdrawing the gun a few inches. His features smoothed out, and his voice was calm again, but hardly reassuring; she thought of the dangerous, unreal composure of an executioner. "I apologize for swearing. I wouldn't get so upset if I weren't genuinely concerned about your welfare. The thought of losing you after all I've gone through to make you mine . . . Well, it makes me a little crazy, I guess."

"I guess," Wendy echoed.

Her fear was back now. And with it came the knowledge that she still wanted to live. Despite everything that had happened or soon would, she wasn't ready to fold up and die. The thought astonished her and, in an odd way, made her proud.

"Now for those directions I promised," the Gryphon said matter-of-factly. "Go north on Sepulveda, over the hill, into the Valley. We could take the freeway, but I'd prefer not to travel that fast. Just in case I have to shoot you and seize control of the car. That could be dangerous at high speed."

"Yes," she agreed soberly, "it could."

"At the north end of the Valley, we'll hook up with San Fernando Road, which will take us to the Sierra Highway in the high desert. I've got a place out there, you see."

He chuckled. It was the sound of rattling bones.

"My special place."

She swallowed and put the Ford in reverse.

"Hey," he said sharply. "Wait a second."

She looked at him, wondering what he would want now.

"Buckle up," he said.

"Right." She fumbled with the strap.

"It's dangerous to drive without a seatbelt," he informed her with evident sincerity as he strapped himself in. "And besides, in California it's against the law."

Finally she got the buckle to snap. "Well," she whispered, her voice dark, "we wouldn't want to break the law, would we?"

She pulled out of the alley and turned onto Sepulveda, heading north. She tried not to think of anything at all.

The road was snaking into the mountains when the Gryphon turned on the radio. Music crackled through aged speakers. John Denver singing "Fly Away." The lyrics hurt, because they named her thoughts too clearly.

She wanted to fly away. Wanted it so badly.

"You like this song?" he asked.

"Yes."

"I like it too. You see, we have a lot in common."

Sepulveda carried them over the Santa Monica range. Wendy was careful to stay within the speed limit. She didn't want a motorcycle cop on their tail. She had a feeling the man beside her might react rather badly to that development.

"Pretty," he said suddenly.

She jumped a little, startled. "What?"

"The snow. See it?"

He pointed. She looked ahead and saw the distant cones of the San Gabriel Mountains, dusted white by winter storms.

"Yes," she said. "It is. Very pretty."

"But not as pretty as you."

She tightened her grip on the steering wheel.

"You know what they call snow when it's newly fallen?" he asked. "Virgin snow. Because it's still so pure. Not fouled and spotted with dirt. And its purity makes it beautiful and special." He looked at her. "I'm glad you made your boyfriend sleep on the couch last night. That was the right thing to do."

"Was it?"

"Uh-huh. Most women of your generation wouldn't display such a sense of decorum, of propriety. People nowadays, they're like . . . like animals. Like rutting goats. They disgust me."

"I didn't make him sleep on the couch," she whispered, not knowing quite what made her say it.

"Sure you did. He was there when I came in."

"But I didn't *make* him. It was his idea. He offered. He didn't want to take advantage of me. He was . . . a gentleman."

"Was he? Maybe. Or maybe he was just trying to con you. Gain your trust. Men do that, you know. They pretend to be your friend, when all they really want is . . . is . . ." He looked away, and Wendy realized with a stab of astonishment that he was embarrassed. "Well," he said vaguely, "you know."

"Yes. I know." Out of the corner of her eye she watched his face in profile against the blur of the roadside. "But you're different. Aren't you?"

"I am."

"So"—she spoke slowly, forcing out the words like paste through a tube—"what is it *you* want?"

He swiveled in his seat and looked right at her. "You, Wendy. I want you. But not in the way other men do. Lesser men. Men who could never appreciate you, could never hope to equal your strength of spirit. What you and I will have—oh, it will be something wonderful. A merging of minds, a commingling of souls. Nothing cheap or casual or meaningless. A partnership that will lift us both to new heights, heights neither one of us could have reached alone. That's what I want, Wendy. I won't take anything less. I want you. I want you. I want you."

Anger and terror and revulsion boiled inside her, reached a flashpoint and merged in a white heat of fury that made her reckless.

"But I don't want *you!*" she screamed, then stiffened, catching her breath, afraid of what she'd said and of what he would do.

But he merely smiled.

"You will," he said with finality. "Tonight."

She licked her lips. Her heart thumped in her ears. Sweat trickled down the insides of her arms, pasting the blouse to her skin. She hated to ask the next question, for fear of what the answer surely would be; but she had to ask it, because she had to know, just had to.

"What . . . what's going to happen tonight?"

He didn't answer. Instead he snapped his fingers with a sudden thought.

"Oh, gosh. I knew there was something I forgot to do. We're running low on gas, aren't we?"

Her gaze flicked to the fuel gauge, where the arrow was brushing the red zone.

"Almost empty," she reported.

"Darn. We'll have to fill up, then."

Fill up. At a gas station. With people around. Lots of people. He wouldn't shoot her there. Not in front of everybody. Would he? Maybe he would. But if she took him by surprise . . . if he didn't react quite fast enough . . .

All she had to do was throw open the car door and run, get inside the office or the service bay, and then—

"I know what you're thinking, Wendy."

A wave of light-headedness passed over her. She felt as if his fingers had been prying inside her brain. "I'm not thinking anything."

"Oh, yes, you are." He sounded amused. "It's written all over your face. Little Red Riding Hood thinks she's found the golden opportunity to get away from the Big Bad Wolf." The gun pressed deeper into her side. "But you're wrong, Wendy. Very wrong. Fatally wrong. I warned you about what would happen if you tried anything. I made myself explicitly clear. Didn't I? *Didn't I?*"

"Don't kill me," she breathed, the words coming out so spontaneously she was astonished to hear them.

"Don't make me," he answered coolly. "Lock your door."

She depressed the lock.

"Good. Now if you have any thoughts of making a break for it when we stop for gas, consider this. You're wearing a safety belt. Your door is locked. It'll take time to unbuckle that belt and unlock that door. A full second, at least. How long do you think it will take me to put a bullet in you?"

She didn't answer.

"How long?"

"Okay," she whispered. "I understand."

"You yell for help, you honk the horn, you do anything out of the ordinary—and you're dead."

"I understand," she said again, more sharply.

The Ford coasted down the mountain into Studio City. A few blocks ahead, the bright orange ball of a Union 76 sign hung against the sky like a setting sun.

"Pull in there," he ordered.

She guided the Ford onto the asphalt and pulled up alongside a full-service island, then shut off the motor, silencing Rosanne Cash, who was singing about a runaway train. Wendy knew about trains like that. She was on one right now.

"What now?" she breathed.

"When the attendant asks, you say you want a full tank." He was buttoning up his brown coat to conceal the policeman's uniform underneath. "And remember what I told you." The gun snaked behind her, the metal cylinder of the five-inch barrel hard against her lower back.

She cranked down the window, waited for an attendant to arrive, and asked him to fill the tank.

"Check the oil?" he asked briskly. "Tire pressure?"

A painfully false smile distorted her face. "No, thanks."

The attendant hooked up the gas-pump nozzle, then squeegeed the windshield with broad vigorous strokes. As he was scraping off the soapy water, Wendy turned toward the passenger seat.

"I don't have any money with me, you know," she whispered.

"That's all right."

"What are we going to do? Drive away without paying?"

"Wendy." He looked genuinely distressed. "That would be immoral. Of course we won't do anything like that." With one hand he fumbled in his coat pocket and gave her a well-worn wallet. "There ought to be enough in there to cover it."

The attendant rang up the total. Wendy handed him a couple of bills through the open window.

"Thanks," he said as he dug in his pocket for change. "Nice set of wheels."

He was looking right at her. She looked back. Their eyes met. In that instant she considered trying to signal him somehow, with a facial expression or a whispered word or . . . or something.

Courage failed her. She could imagine the shuddering blast of the gunshot as it tore through her spine.

"We like it," she said with another faltering smile.

"Yeah, they really built 'em back then. What is it, a sixty-two?"

"Sixty-three," the Gryphon said helpfully from the passenger seat.

The attendant nodded. "Nice condition."

"Well," the Gryphon said politely, "I've always believed that if you take care of your car, it'll take care of you."

"Hey, you know it." The attendant handed Wendy her change. "Have a nice one."

Wendy started the engine and steered the car out of the service station, rolling up the window. The deadly pressure on her back eased.

"Congratulations," the killer told her. "You're a very smart girl."

She took a breath. "You never answered my question," she said softly. "What's going to happen tonight?"

"Oh, nothing so awful." He was smiling again. "We're going to get to know each other a little better, that's all. We've been enemies, and now we're going to be friends. And something more than friends."

Her voice was a whisper. "Something more?"

"Lovers, Wendy," he breathed. "That's what we'll be. And I promise you, once you've known my passion and my power, then you will love me too."

25

Delgado was still at Cedars-Sinai when the Dodge Aries was found in the alley.

He'd arrived at the hospital at nine-fifteen, twenty minutes after Wendy's abduction, having left most of the task-force detectives at the scene of the wreckage with instructions to comb the area for clues. The chance of finding anything significant on the fire-ravaged mountainside was remote, but no possibility could be overlooked.

Plainclothes and patrol officers were crowding the lobby and parking garage of the medical center's North Tower when Delgado entered, accompanied by Tom Gardner and Rob Tallyman. Delgado hunted down the detectives in charge. They were Frank Nason and Chet Gray, who had taken him on a tour of Elizabeth Osborn's house two weeks ago.

"Fill us in on what happened," Delgado said brusquely.

"He came and took her," Nason answered, outrage in his voice. "The nerve of the bastard—he put on Sanchez's uniform and just waltzed right in here and signed her out."

"Fed the receptionist and the guards some cock-and-bull story about taking her to the station for safekeeping," Gray added. "Detective Delgado's orders, he claimed."

"The staff must have gotten a look at him," Delgado said.

Gray nodded. "Yeah, the IdentiKit artists are sharpening their pencils, but I don't think they're going to come up with much. The nurse on duty remembers he had brown hair and he was tall. The guards say the same thing."

"And the uniform," Nason said. "They remember that, for all the good it does us."

"Nothing else?" Tom Gardner broke in impatiently. "Nothing specific?"

Nason spread his hands. "You know how it is. One dude in uniform looks like any other."

"He would have been counting on that," Delgado said grimly.

"Yeah, he's smart, all right," Tallyman muttered. "And he loves taking chances, spinning that wheel."

"From what we can tell, even Miss Alden was fooled," Gray said. "No one observed any indication that she left under duress."

"How the hell did he even know where to find her?" Gardner asked.

"That one's easy." Nason shrugged. "Every TV and radio asshole in town has been broadcasting that information all morning. You should see these TV creeps doing their live stand-ups on the steps outside."

"Freedom of the press," Gardner hissed. "Fucking First Amendment gets on my fucking nerves."

"Funny how his cover story matched your orders," Tallyman told Delgado thoughtfully. "You think he was monitoring the police band and picked it up?"

Delgado shook his head. "I delivered those orders by landline. And the black-and-white was told to keep it quiet on the way over for exactly that reason. It's just a coincidence. Or perhaps he knows the way my mind works."

"Wish we could say the same about him," Gardner said.

In the parking garage, Delgado got a break. The attendant who manned the exit gate remembered one car in particular that had left within the appropriate time frame. It was a late-model blue Dodge Aries—he was pretty sure it was a coupe—and it had caught his attention because his girlfriend's mother drove one just like it. Yes, there had been a man at the wheel, but the attendant recalled nothing about his face. No, he hadn't been wearing a uniform; the attendant was certain he would have noticed that. And no, there had been no woman in the car—none who could be seen, anyway.

Delgado radioed Dispatch with orders to put every patrol car on the alert for a blue Aries coupe driven by a brown-haired man, possibly alone, possibly in the company of a blonde female.

He was interrogating the security guard who'd noticed Sanchez's nameplate, hoping to coax an additional detail from the man's memory, when Tallyman ran up to him, out of breath.

"News on the Dodge."

"They found it?" Delgado asked, forgetting the guard.

"No. But they know where it came from." Tallyman consulted a scrawled note on his steno pad. "Vehicle matching the Dodge's description was stolen at eight-fifteen, approximately one half hour before the kidnapping. Owner is a guy named Levy, Robert Levy. He parked outside a health spa on Sepulveda Boulevard—outdoor lot—and was struck from behind by a blunt instrument while locking the door. Regained consciousness roughly five minutes later; car was gone."

"Did he see the assailant?"

"No such luck."

"This man Levy should consider himself fortunate," Delgado said slowly. "The Gryphon doesn't normally leave his victims alive."

"Maybe he was in a hurry."

"Could be. All right, I want unmarked cars dispatched to cruise Sepulveda for at least five miles north and south of the spa. If the Gryphon was there once, he might have returned to lift a new car or ditch the stolen one. Tell them to look in the side streets, alleys, everyplace a car might be hidden, and take note of any suspicious vehicles, not just the Dodge."

"Right, Seb."

While he waited for word of the car, Delgado returned to Wendy's room. The empty bed pained him. He checked out the bathroom, opened the bureau drawers, and looked under the bed, being careful to touch as few things as possible; the room had not yet been dusted, and it was possible the Gryphon had left prints. He told himself that he was searching for some small item the Gryphon might have dropped, some clue that would magically reveal his identity, but he knew the truth. He simply wanted to be in a place Wendy had recently occupied, to feel some connection with her, however tenuous and unreal. He didn't want to feel he'd lost her forever.

In the middle of the room, between the two beds, he stopped, wondering for the first time if he had fallen in love with Wendy Alden.

No, he decided after a moment's reflection, he was not in love, not exactly. What he felt for her was the prelude to love, the wordless intuitive conviction that he could love her if given the chance.

It was a chance he might never have now.

There was a knock on the frame of the open door. He turned and saw Gardner standing there.

"Seb, they recovered the Dodge."

"Where?"

"About two blocks from where it was lifted. Parked in an alley just east of Sepulveda."

"And?"

"It's empty. Looks like it was abandoned there."

Delgado lowered his head. "Damn."

Obviously the Gryphon had anticipated the possibility that the car used in the abduction would be seen and remembered by someone. So he'd taken a sensible precaution. He'd stolen Levy's car, then switched to another vehicle—probably his own.

Delgado had no idea what kind of car or truck or van that might be. And he could not put out an APB on every brown-haired man in Los Angeles.

There was no way to track the Gryphon now. No way to guess where he might go. No way to find Wendy and save her.

No hope for her at all.

"Seb? Are you all right?"

Delgado didn't answer. Slowly he raised his

head and looked at the sun-streaked room around him, the room where he'd sat at Wendy's bedside only a few hours earlier, holding her lovely, delicate hand.

26

The time was exactly ten o'clock by Rood's wristwatch when Wendy guided the Ford Falcon onto San Fernando Road. His special place was less than fifteen minutes away.

The road swept into the lower fringes of the Mojave Desert, where windblasted rock formations jutted up at unnatural angles amid bleak stretches of pinkish alkaline sand. In the crisp, slanting sunshine the landscape was rendered forebodingly alien and slightly unreal, like a movie fantasist's vision of the surface of Mars.

Rood was fond of the desert. He liked its ugly desolation and arid inhospitality to man, the stony friendlessness of its monuments, the bite of the dusty air. But today he took little interest in the scenery around him. He had something far more interesting to occupy his attention.

Leaning back in his seat, he studied the young woman behind the steering wheel as she drove. He really did prefer her hair loose as it was now, not coiled in that dreadful chignon. He loved the innocence of her face, the smooth skin, the china-blue eyes. She was a porcelain doll. His doll. His to play with and fondle and hold. A life-size toy, all for him.

That was what love was. Wasn't it?

He was wonderfully happy. Everything had gone flawlessly so far. His good fortune seemed all the more amazing when he considered how close he'd come to the ultimate disaster last night. He'd very nearly lost the game for good. He could have been killed in the crash, yet incredibly he'd escaped without injury. He'd even shown the presence of mind to drag Officer Sanchez's body away from the car before the fuel tank blew. Then it had been a simple matter to remove the man's shirt, pants, shoes, and gun belt. Once back in his apartment, he'd scrubbed off the dirt and blood stains.

His initial plan was to impersonate a police officer in order to get into Miss Wendy Alden's room at Cedars-Sinai—where, according to the radio and TV reports, she was hospitalized in good condition—and kill her. But strangely he found he'd lost the desire to take her life. It seemed a shame to waste a player of such natural talent and unusual skill. No longer could he deny Miss Alden her due. She was unquestionably an extra-special opponent, a true challenge, almost his equal in certain respects. There were not many women who could have fought him off again and again. She might very well be the only one capable of such an achievement. In all the world, the only one . . .

Rood had shut his eyes in rapt contemplation of a sublime truth.

Out of all the hundreds, thousands, millions of women he might have come across, she had been the one he'd chosen. It could not have been coincidence.

She was meant for him. Not as a victim. As a lover. Of course.

"Wendy," he had said softly as he stood alone in his living room, his eyes still closed. "Wendy." Speaking of her that way, not as Miss Alden but simply as Wendy, had warmed him with a pleasant, almost intoxicating sense of intimacy. "Wendy. Wendy. Wendy."

Now she was his at last. He could hardly wait till he had her inside his special place, where they could begin to really get to know each other. He would keep her there indefinitely. During the day he would have to go to work, of course—he couldn't call in sick every morning, as he'd done today—but at night he could drop by and see her, and on every weekend too. He would feed her, comb and brush her hair, bring her gifts. She would hate him at first, but he would bring her around. Nothing was impossible. Not for him. Not for Franklin Rood.

Until she learned to love him, she would have to be kept under restraint whenever he was away. Well, that would be easy enough to arrange. In the beginning he would bind and gag her. Later he might invest in a cage. Yes, a good-size steel cage, the kind used for big dogs. The idea tickled him with dark pleasure. Before leaving for work, he would put her in the cage, like a doggie, *his* doggie, and wouldn't she be thrilled when her master came home in the evening and let her out to play? Unfortunately, while he was gone, she might scream for help. The easiest solution to that problem would be to cut out her tongue. So what if she couldn't talk? He would do the talking for both of them, and she would listen in humble silence. That was the way things ought to be.

Of course, Rood acknowledged realistically, even a love affair as exalted as theirs couldn't last forever. Sooner or later he would tire of Wendy's charms. When he did, he would have to get rid of her. But he preferred not to think about that just yet.

After all, he truly did love her, and the prospect of having to . . . well, it was depressing. Though he had to admit she would make a fine addition to his collection once the time came.

He was still contemplating the many bright facets of their future together when he realized that the junction with the Sierra Highway was coming up.

"Take the next right," he ordered.

Wordlessly Wendy obeyed. The car hummed across a bridge over an arroyo, white as bone, then rattled down the four-lane highway. Years ago, before the freeways were built, the Sierra Highway had been one of the main arteries serving the high Mojave. Now the cracked and rutted blacktop was all but empty of traffic.

"Turn right again. Here."

She hooked onto a narrow side road. An automobile graveyard passed by, rows of starred windshields and chrome grillwork glittering in the sun. An abandoned ranch appeared and vanished. Up ahead a windowless storage trailer, parked on the roadside on a parcel of dirt, slid into view.

"Pull over."

Wendy steered the Falcon off the road. She parked near the trailer. Clouds of pink dust boiled around the car.

"Shut off the engine. Give me the keys."

She did so. "Is this it?" she asked throatily, staring straight ahead.

"Uh-huh. When I moved to L.A., I purchased

this half-acre and this trailer. I wanted a hide-away, you see. A retreat. A place all for myself. You're the first guest I've ever invited." He opened his door. "Now we're both going to get out of the car. There's no use trying to run away this time. You've got nowhere to go. Okay?"

Without troubling to wait for her reply, Rood climbed out, then circled around the Ford to the driver's side, where Wendy stood waiting. The cool dry wind pasted her hair to her face in disorderly strands.

Tenderly he brushed the blond hairs from her forehead. He felt her shudder at his touch. Well, he would teach her not to shudder. He would teach her many things.

"Take a good look around, Wendy," he whispered. "Do you see any houses? Any shops? People? Anything at all?"

He watched her as she turned her head in a wide, slow arc. There was nothing to see in any direction. Nothing but the untraveled back road and the dirt and the distant shimmer of heat and sun.

"No," she said quietly in a voice like death. "I don't see anything."

"I just wanted you to be fully aware of how alone we are out here. It's just you and me now. So you'd better do what I say." He took her arm. "Come on."

He led her to the rear of the car and unlocked the trunk. Inside were the three items he'd brought with him when he left his apartment earlier this morning.

"Take out those bags." He pointed to them. "One in each hand. And don't drop them, or I'll be awfully upset."

She lifted the two plastic shopping bags. They sagged, heavy with secrets.

Holding the gun on her with one hand, Rood reached into the trunk and removed the third item, his drawstring bag. Awkwardly he shouldered the bag, then slammed the trunk lid. Then he stuck the gun in Wendy's back and marched her toward his special place.

The trailer was forty feet long and eight feet wide, supported by four tandem wheels and five pairs of metal support legs. Yellow and red reflectors studded walls of hot-dipped galvanized steel. A portable iron stairway—three rusty steps and a landing—was positioned at the rear, in front of the only door.

Rood guided Wendy up the steps, then fished the keys from his pocket. The door was secured by a pin-tumbler lock fitted with an antipick latch and a steel T-guard, backed up by a Segal vertical dead bolt. Together the locks would frustrate nearly any thief. The trailer was isolated and frequently unoccupied, and Rood didn't care to imagine what might happen if someone uninvited were to see what was inside.

He unlocked the door and pushed it open, exposing the cavelike darkness within.

"Well, this is it, Wendy. Your new home."

She hesitated on the threshold, her small body trembling.

"Go on, now," he whispered. "Go on."

Smiling, he gave her a gentle push into the dark.

27

When he was through at Cedars-Sinai, Delgado returned to the Butler Avenue station, having nowhere else to go. He shut the door of his office, sank into the chair behind his desk, and tried to think.

But the only thought that came to him was of Wendy, naked, headless, her hand clutching a clay figurine.

He turned to the map on the wall. His gaze flinched from the red pushpins marking the Gryphon's other victims. He glanced down at the papers on his desk and saw Ralston's preliminary report on the Kutzlow autopsy. He didn't want to look at that either. Averting his eyes, he noticed the tape recorder that had played the Gryphon's audiocassettes. When would the next tape arrive in the mail, the one mocking him with a new voice—Wendy's voice?

He had to stop this. Stop it right now. And think, dammit. Think.

But there was nothing to think about. He'd gone over the case a hundred times. A thousand times. He had no leads. No hope.

He called the Crime Lab, got Frommer on the line. "Anything?" he asked, his voice sharp.

"No." Frommer sounded weary. "At least,

nothing so far. The search of the mountainside has yielded no results. Well, we expected that. The fire would have erased any clues the Gryphon might have left."

"What about the Pellman house?"

"No significant physical evidence was obtained, except for blood spots on the floor—they're AB positive, the Gryphon's blood type—and the knife you found. It's Wendy Alden's. We matched it to a set of knives in her kitchen drawer. He was trying to kill her with it, apparently—poetic justice."

"Prints?"

"We dusted the knife with copper powder and got two partials on the handle, but they're so badly smeared as to be useless."

"How about the Dodge?"

"We dusted that too. The interior is littered with prints, but most of them presumably belong to the owner and his family. It'll take days, at least, to print everybody who might have been inside that car, and even then we may never get them all. A fingerprint can last for years, you know. There was a case where a woman's print on a glass remained intact for three decades—"

"Later." Delgado was in no mood for forensic folk tales at the moment. "So what you're telling me is there's no hope of a computer scan on any of those prints? A blind run, I mean, on all knowns in the database?"

"Impossible until we narrow it down, eliminate the prints we can identify. As I say, that'll take—"

"Days, at least. I heard you. All right, Eric. Keep at it."

He cradled the phone, then looked around him slowly. His hand closed over the nodule of agate on his desk. He picked it up and ran his fingers over the smooth core. There had been a time when the mysterious colors and eldritch patterns caught in that chunk of stone had seemed to hint at all the beautiful secrets guarded by the world. Now they signified nothing. The world held no secrets other than the ugly, evil kind he was paid to ferret out. And now even those secrets were eluding him.

He felt a surge of hatred for the agate, or for the innocent optimism it represented. With a quick reflexive motion of his arm, he hurled the stone across the room. It banged off a filing cabinet and skittered under a chair, the chair in which Wendy had sat last night—he could see her even now, wrapped in a blanket, curled up and watching him with her blue perceptive eyes.

Dead now. Or soon. Her blue gaze focused on nothing.

His eyes tracked to the tape recorder again.

He had to do something. No matter how pointless, how painful.

The desk drawer slid open under his hand. He put on the headphones. Loaded one of the Gryphon's cassettes into the machine. Then listened for the hundredth time to Julia Stern's pleading voice.

". . . can't identify you. We've got a lot of nice things here. You can have any of it. There's silverware in the kitchen. A color TV, a stereo. In the closet I've got some birthday presents for my husband: a camera, a watch, a new coat. Oh, God . . . Please, take anything you want and just go and you'll never get caught. I swear . . ."

No, he would never get caught. Julia had been right about that much, at least.

"Please don't kill me. I don't . . . want to die. I'll do whatever you say. I know you're much more powerful than . . . than I am. You're so strong. . . ."

Why are you doing this, Seb? he asked himself as the tape played on. *What purpose does it serve, other than self-torture?*

"I'm only twenty-four. I've got a husband, and we love each other; we really do. We got married two years ago this April, and we promised it would be forever, and it will be . . ."

No, it wouldn't, Julia. Nothing was forever. Nothing good. Only evil lasted. Only death was permanent.

". . . got a baby coming. A boy. We're going to name him Robert. That's my husband's name. . . ."

But there would be no baby. There would be no wedding anniversary to celebrate in April. There would be no birthday party for Julia's husband either, and the presents she'd bought for him would bring no joy, only a deeper grief.

Delgado blinked.

Birthday presents.

He rewound the tape.

". . . silverware in the kitchen. A color TV, a stereo. In the closet I've got some birthday presents for my husband: a camera, a watch, a new coat . . ."

He rewound it again.

". . . a camera, a watch, a new coat . . ."

Again.

". . . a watch . . ."

He shut off the tape.

A watch. She'd bought her husband a watch.

Why did that matter? Why was it teasing the nerve endings of whatever intuitive power he possessed? Why was it reminding him of Rebecca Morris?

Rebecca Morris, the second victim. Killed ten weeks later. Killed just as she was beginning to taste the success she wanted. She'd been promoted to vice president of her firm less than a month earlier.

Birthday. Promotion. Two events worth celebrating.

Julia Stern had bought a watch.

Rebecca Morris had bought . . . a ring.

The ring that was still on her finger when she lay on a slab in the morgue. The ring that had enabled her roommate to identify the headless body.

Delgado sat up slowly. For a moment no breath stirred in his body.

He was seeing Wendy in the chair again. Wendy, fingering the bandages on her neck as she told him she'd purchased a necklace on her lunch hour. At Crane's Department Store. The one in Century City.

Watch, ring, necklace.

Crane's.

He was getting ahead of himself. For all he knew, the other victims had never shopped at Crane's, had never bought anything there.

Then he remembered.

A smiling woman in a straw hat. The cheerful announcement: "Summer's On the Way!"

The cover of a catalog on the bureau in Elizabeth Osborn's bedroom. A catalog from Crane's Department Store.

His eyes were hot. The room blurred.

He knew.

There was no proof, not yet. But, dammit, he *knew*.

Crane's was the connection he'd been seeking.

He picked up the phone. Dialed 411. Obtained the number of Crane's Department Store in Century City. Got the manager, a Mr. Khouri, on the line. A computer search confirmed that, yes, all four women had charge accounts at Crane's. Delgado asked about Jennifer Kutzlow. No, she wasn't listed. That was all right. He'd always assumed Jennifer was a victim of circumstance. She hadn't fit the pattern. The Gryphon had left no statuette in her hand.

"I recognize the names of these women, Detective." The manager's voice was querulous and high-pitched. "They're all victims of that serial killer."

"You're most astute, Mr. Khouri. But I would appreciate it if you would avoid undue speculation."

"Yes, yes, of course."

"Would you kindly consult your records and tell me about any recent purchases these women might have made?"

"Certainly. One moment, please."

Delgado waited. He had no doubt that the store was the link. Still, knowing the common denominator of the crimes was not the same as finding the killer. It was possible the Gryphon simply liked to loiter at Crane's, probably near the jewelry counter, eyeing female customers till he spotted one he liked. Then he would follow her home to learn her address.

No, wait. That wasn't right. Because yesterday, after buying the necklace, Wendy had returned to her office, then had gone directly to her dinner date with Jeffrey. When she'd finally arrived home, the Gryphon had been there already, lying in wait.

He hadn't followed her. He must have learned her address by some other means. Probably through the purchase she'd made. If so, then he was almost certainly an employee.

But what kind of employee? Perhaps someone in the billing department, who would have access to all the customers' addresses. No, that seemed wrong also. All four women the Gryphon selected had been more than ordinarily attractive, a fact that suggested he picked them, at least in part, by their appearance. If so, he would have to be in a position to see the customers.

A sales clerk, then.

Khouri came back on the line. He sounded more frightened than before.

"Detective? All the accounts have been active within the past few months. Mrs. Stern purchased a wristwatch on November twenty-first. Ms. Morris charged a ring to her account on January twenty-third. Ms. Osborn made several purchases on different dates. On December eighteenth, some items from the lingerie department; on January tenth, a coffee maker; and on March third, a bracelet. And Ms. Alden purchased a necklace only yesterday."

"Are wristwatches sold in the jewelry department?"

"Yes."

"Then each woman bought something in that department: wristwatch, ring, bracelet, necklace."

"Yes, that's right."

"Would a clerk ringing up a sale have any means of knowing the customer's address?"

"In the case of a charge-account purchase, he would. There's a computer terminal at every counter. The salesperson uses a bar-code scanner to verify the charge card. When he does, information on the account appears on screen. The customer's home address is part of that information."

"How many clerks are assigned to the jewelry department?"

"We have two salespeople working two daily shifts, plus two more on the weekends, and on busy days—"

"Do you keep a record of which clerk handled any particular transaction?"

"Yes."

"Then tell me if the same clerk handled those four jewelry purchases."

"One moment, please."

Delgado waited.

Could it be this simple? This blessedly, damnably simple?

"Detective." Panic was jumping in Khouri's voice. "Yes. It was the same man each time."

"His name, please."

"Franklin Rood."

"Is he there today?"

"Why . . . no. He called in sick."

Bang.

"Did you speak with him when he called?"

"No. He telephoned my office before the start of business and left a message on my answering machine."

"What was his reason for missing work?"

"Illness. Nothing specific. I have no reason to mistrust him. He's one of our most reliable people." Khouri was babbling now. "He's been with us for over two years. I started him in Audiovisual"—Delgado thought of the cassette recorder and mixing board used to make the tapes—"and then one day we were short-handed in Jewelry, so I transferred him there, only temporarily, you understand." The mythical gryphon was a guardian of jewels; had Rood thought of that? "But he was so good with the wristwatches, and they make up half our receipts at that counter. You know how small the batteries are, how difficult to work with, yet he pops them in, just like that. He has such big hands, but a delicate touch." Delicate enough to pick locks. "So I left him there, even though it is perhaps unusual for a male salesperson to be stationed at that counter, but our female customers never minded, because, you see, Mr. Rood is unfailingly courteous, extremely polite. . . ."

Polite. The same word Wendy had used to describe the man who tossed a loop of steel wire around her neck. A man careful to address his victims as Miss or Mrs. while he tightened that wire to choke off their lives.

"Mr. Khouri," Delgado interrupted, "would you kindly give me Mr. Rood's home address?" Khouri did so. Delgado scribbled down a number and street in West L.A., near the intersection of Bundy Avenue and Santa Monica Boulevard. "Very good. Thank you for your help. I'll be in touch with you again shortly. In the meantime, please do not discuss this matter with anyone."

"You . . . you think he's the one, don't you?"

"I haven't said that."

"I can see how it must look to you. But let me assure you, Mr. Rood cannot possibly be responsible. He's not a killer, not the type at all. Quite the opposite, in fact. He's considerate of everyone.

Always punctual. Very neat. You should see him, every morning before the start of business, dusting the display case, whistling and . . . and . . ." Khouri gasped. "Oh, God in heaven. God in heaven."

"Mr. Khouri? Are you all right?"

"The display case, Detective." There was horror in his voice now. "The display case."

"What about it?"

"It's full of . . . of heads. Styrofoam heads with black velvet skin. They're all around him every day, and he dusts them off, dear God, and he whistles. Rows and rows of women's heads."

28

Wendy stepped into the trailer warily, the way she would have entered a house choked with gas fumes or a cellar smelling of rot. There were no windows, and the only light came from the door-way at her back, the brittle translucent light of the desert. Then the door closed, shutting out the sun, and she experienced a sudden sensation of falling, which came from the wordless certainty that she would never see daylight again.

She felt a hand close over her arm with a tender, affectionate squeeze. The Gryphon guided her forward, into the middle of the room, navigat-ing around obstacles she couldn't see. She heard him unshoulder the drawstring bag and deposit it heavily on something soft and yielding, perhaps a bed.

Metal clicked. A jet of flame sprang from the cigarette lighter in his hand. She watched, mo-tionless, still holding the two shopping bags from the trunk of the car, as he lit the candles scattered throughout the trailer's interior.

The narrow tunnellike space was a single room, forty feet long, eight feet wide, nine feet high. It was no more than a shell of steel, like a storage shed, with no bathroom or kitchen, no built-in amenities of any kind. Gray short-nap carpet covered the floor. Sheets of corkboard lined the walls and ceiling. Cork, Wendy knew, was often used for soundproofing. What went on within these walls that the Gryphon didn't want passersby to hear? Too many possibilities occurred to her, none good.

A futon was stretched along one wall. Near it stood a bookcase, the kind made of pressed wood with simulated grain, put together from a do-it-yourself kit. The shelves were stocked, not with books, but with boxes of Ritz crackers, bags of Doritos and Lay's potato chips, and bottles of soda pop and mineral water. Beyond the bookcase was a table piled high with picnic plates, Styrofoam cups, paper napkins, and plastic utensils, as well as more food: jars of Skippy peanut butter, bags of Oreo cookies, a loaf of Wonder Bread, and a litter of candy bars.

On another table, against the opposite wall, three boombox-style cassette players were displayed. The speakers had been detached; the speaker wires ran along the floor, crawled up the side of the large storage cabinet next to the table, and disappeared under the lumpy white sheet that draped the cabinet as if it were a body in a morgue.

Not far from where she stood, four metal folding chairs were arranged around a card table dressed in a red-and-white–checkered vinyl tablecloth. Two candles in silver holders flanked a plastic floral centerpiece. The Gryphon lit those candles last.

She looked around at the trailer that had become her prison. The candles' flickering glow rippled over the walls and ceiling like rain shadows.

"So what do you think?" the Gryphon asked.

"It's very nice. Very . . . homey."

"I know you're going to be happy here, Wendy."

Her name sounded obscene sliding out of his mouth, filthy and slimy, a pale mucid earthworm emerging from its hole.

She forced a smile. "I'm sure I will."

The twenty-five–minute drive from the gas station to the trailer, most of which had passed in silence, had given her time to think. She'd decided her best hope of survival was to agree with everything he said. If she could mollify him, humor him, go along with whatever he wanted, then maybe he wouldn't kill her. Maybe.

She was pretty sure he'd been serious when he claimed to feel something like love for her. Of course it wasn't love in any terms a normal person would understand. He seemed to regard her not as a human being but as a toy, a plaything, like . . . like one of those life-size inflatable dolls sold as masturbatory aids.

"Penny for your thoughts, Wendy."

She realized he was watching her face. "Oh, nothing," she answered lightly.

"No, no. When I say, 'Penny for your thoughts,' you have to tell me what you're thinking. It's a rule, see? A rule for lovers."

"I see. Well, I was just thinking that . . ." Make it good. "That, as nice as this hideaway of yours is, it sure could use a woman's touch."

"Which is precisely why you're here. To make my special place even more special." He grinned. "You can put those bags down now. Gently, please."

She'd forgotten she was holding them. She placed both shopping bags carefully on the floor near the card table.

When she looked up, she saw the Gryphon slip his sunglasses into his pocket, then put on an ordinary pair of glasses, which he hadn't worn before. Thick-lensed glasses with heavy black frames. They struck a chord of memory in her.

Gazing at him in the alley, she'd had the feeling his face was familiar; now she was certain of it. She'd seen this man before. And when she had, he'd been wearing those black-framed glasses—yes—glasses that had caught the amber glow of a computer terminal's display screen.

The clerk at Crane's. That was who he was.

"You," she whispered.

He smiled at her. "Recognition at last."

"You sold me the necklace."

"It wasn't much of a sales job. You wanted it quite badly. And it looked lovely on you too. I saw you wearing it when you came home last night." He made a tsk-tsk sound. "Shame you don't have it with you." His face brightened. "Hey, I'll tell you what. I'll buy you a new necklace, just like the old one. And a beautiful new dress too; we can't have you wearing that plain gray skirt in here. Not that there's anything wrong with your outfit, but I want you to look your very best for me. What's your size?"

"Four."

"I'll remember that. Tomorrow, when I'm in the department store, I'll buy you a gorgeous evening gown, and then when I come here after work, you can dress up for me. Won't that be fun?"

"I'm sure it will. I love getting new clothes."

"Women always do. They need to feel pretty and feminine. It's in their nature, the same way a man needs to feel strong."

Smiling happily, he shrugged off the brown coat and tossed it on the futon, next to the drawstring bag. Despite the uniform, he looked nothing like a policeman to her now. She wondered how she could ever have been fooled.

"In a moment I'll fix you something to eat. I'll bet you're hungry."

She had no appetite whatsoever. "Starved."

"First, however, I have a little chore to take care of. It won't take long."

He lifted one of the shopping bags off the floor and set it down on the card table. Holstering the Beretta, he turned his back to her and leaned over the bag.

She tensed.

He'd just made a mistake.

The pistol's checkered plastic grip shone in the candlelight. Almost within her reach.

"Unfortunately," he was saying, "lunch won't be anything fancy. You see, I've got no electricity here, no refrigerator or stove, so I'm limited in what I can prepare. I've been meaning to buy one of those portable generators, but I never seem to get around to it."

"I'm sure"—her voice was steady—"whatever you make for me will be fine."

She took a step toward him.

"Well, it won't be as tasty as what you're used to, I'll bet." He reached into the bag with both hands. "You must be a wonderful cook."

"Not really."

Another step.

The holstered automatic was inches away.

"Oh," he said pleasantly, "you're just being modest. I'm sure you can cook the pants off me.

Hey, that's a funny way of putting it, don't you think? Cook the *pants* off—"

She lunged for the gun. Her fingers closed over the handle. He spun to face her, and his hands flew free of the shopping bag and scrabbled at the holster—too late.

Wendy aimed the pistol at him from a foot away.

I did it, a voice in her mind exulted from a great distance. *I did it, did it, did it.*

"All right," she said tensely, "put your hands up." The words a legacy of every TV crime drama she'd ever watched.

He stared at her, his eyes almost comically wide, his mouth hanging open. Then he took a shambling step backward and thumped into the card table. The shopping bag fell over with a thud and whatever was inside rolled toward the edge.

"Come on, come on." She was losing patience. "Put them up in the air."

He went on staring, staring.

"Do it!" she screamed. "Do it, or I'll shoot!"

His eyes narrowed. A smile lifted the corners of his mouth. A calm, almost beatific smile.

"No, you won't, Wendy," he said with quiet certainty.

"Raise your hands." A tremor skipped lightly over the words. She noticed that the gun was shaking. "Goddammit, raise them right *now*."

He shook his head. "It's no use. I know you won't kill me. You can't. And do you know why? Because, deep down, you love me, just as I love you. Oh, you may not want to admit it yet, even to yourself. But your heart knows how you really feel." He reached out with one hand. "Now give me the gun, and let's quit all this foolishness."

She drew back the hammer with a sharp click. The sound was loud in the room.

He froze. She could read the bewilderment in his face, the hint of fear.

"Hey, Wendy, come on. Don't joke around."

She looked into his eyes.

"Hands up, you asshole," she whispered. "Or I'll blow a fucking hole in you. I swear to Christ I will."

He swallowed. She saw his adam's apple jerk once.

Slowly, very slowly, he began to lift his hands from his sides.

"Come on," she breathed. "Get them up there."

His hands were level with his shoulders.

"Over your head."

As she watched, he raised his hands higher, still higher.

Wendy was sure she had him now. Oh, yes. She'd done it, all right. She'd taken control of the situation. The only thing left to do was—

A sharp crack, like a handclap in the silence.

Automatically she glanced down. An object was rolling on the floor. Something large and round and horribly familiar, which had dropped from the shopping bag on the card table. It came to rest at Wendy's feet, staring up at her with green eyes. Jennifer's eyes.

Her head. Jennifer Kutzlow's *head*.

For one second Wendy was paralyzed by shock, and in that instant the Gryphon struck.

He grabbed the Beretta and jerked it sideways. Her finger squeezed the trigger reflexively. The gun went off like a bomb. She screamed. The recoil kicked her backward, loosening her grip, and the gun was ripped out of her hand. She stared into the black hole of the muzzle at point-blank range. The killer's face loomed behind it, twisted into an extremity of hatred.

"Bitch," he whispered. "Bitch. Bitch. Bitch."

He shoved her against a wall, then pressed the muzzle to her forehead, bearing down painfully hard, as if trying to push the gleaming blue-black barrel right through her skull.

Why didn't you shoot him when you had the chance? she was screaming to herself in helpless, hopeless terror. *Why, Wendy? Why?*

She waited for the gun to explode in her face. She could feel his index finger bearing down on the trigger. Could *feel* it.

Then, incredibly, the pressure on her forehead eased. Slowly he withdrew the pistol, then jerked his head in the direction of the card table.

"Sit down," he snapped.

Heart thumping, she sat in one of the folding chairs.

"Now I'm going to look at my trophy. The one that fell on the floor because of you and your . . . your irresponsible behavior. And if I find that it was damaged in any way, why, then I'll just have to find myself a substitute, won't I? Guess what that means, Wendy. Just guess."

She didn't have to guess.

Holstering the automatic once more, he knelt and examined Jennifer's head with a connoisseur's eye. Wendy stared at the head as he turned it over and over in his hands. It looked almost unreal, a wax replica, the smooth skin shiny in the candles' wavering glow. The long neck, severed at its base, was stiff and straight like the stem of a mushroom.

Finally he rose to his feet, cupping the head in both hands. She waited for his verdict.

"You're lucky," he breathed. "She's still fine. Still beautiful." A smile flashed, lizard-quick. "Of course, not as beautiful as you."

Wendy said nothing. She didn't trust herself to speak.

Gingerly he placed the head on the table. From the second shopping bag he removed another head. Wendy recognized the woman's face from TV news reports. Elizabeth Osborn, the Gryphon's third victim.

Then it occurred to her that she had carried those bags into the trailer, had felt their contents swinging lightly against her calves as she mounted the stairs. She shuddered.

The Gryphon opened the hinged doors of the storage cabinet and took out two large glass jars half-filled with a colorless liquid. He unscrewed the lids and dropped the heads in.

"Formaldehyde," he told her conversationally. The anger was gone from his voice. "Strictly speaking, formalin. Mixture of formaldehyde, water, and methyl alcohol. They use it to preserve biological specimens. You know, frogs and stuff."

And stuff, she thought numbly. *Yes. And stuff.*

He replaced the lids and left the jars on the table. Wendy shifted her gaze from one to the other, unable to stop looking at the pale dead things inside. With their floating strands of kelp-like hair and mushroom white flesh, the two pickled heads no longer looked human at all; they reminded her instead of some bizarre species of plant life cultivated in the darkness of this trailer like fungus in a basement.

The Gryphon admired his specimens for a long

moment, then turned to her. He was outwardly composed, though a little sad.

"You really were going to shoot me, weren't you?" He seemed astonished, as if he couldn't bring himself to fully accept the idea. "You were ready to pull the trigger."

"I . . . I'm sorry."

"Oh, don't say that, Wendy. Remember, love means never having to say you're sorry."

She tasted something bad at the back of her mouth. She kept silent.

"I'm not asking for an apology. I simply want to know why you chose to act the way you did. I've said I love you. Don't you believe me?"

"Yes."

"Then . . . why?"

"I'm afraid of you," she answered. She didn't know what else to say.

Her answer didn't seem to offend him. If anything, he looked vaguely pleased.

"I understand. They all are. They should be," he added, lowering his voice to inject a brief, stressed note of menace. "They. But not you. I won't hurt you, my darling."

She shivered, hearing those words from his mouth.

"I would never, ever hurt you," he said. "Unless . . ." He looked at her with less fondness than before, his glasses glinting in the candlelight. "Unless you make it necessary."

"I understand."

"Good. You're a fighter, Wendy, and I admire that, but even so, there *is* a limit to what I'll put up with."

"I don't blame you."

He sighed. "I wish I hadn't been so rough with

you a few minutes ago. But I had to get hold of
that gun before one of us got hurt."

"Of course."

"And I'm afraid I did lose my temper. I shouldn't
have called you . . . that word. Such an ugly
word. I didn't mean it. I was upset, that's all. But
I think you knew that. Didn't you?"

"Yes."

He reached out and ruffled her hair. She bit
back the urge to scream.

"Friends again?" he asked.

She tried to answer, nearly choked, finally got
the word out.

"Friends," she said. Somehow she managed a
smile.

"I'm glad." Then the sadness returned to his
face. "Even so, I'm afraid I just can't trust you,
Wendy. I can never tell when you might pull another one of your silly stunts." He shrugged
heavily. "It looks like you've given me no choice
but to do something I'd very much hoped to
avoid."

"What's that?" she whispered.

He ran his hand through her hair again, his
fingers crawling over her scalp like beetles.

"I'm going to make sure you give me no further
trouble, Wendy. No trouble at all."

He removed a roll of heavy black electrician's
tape from the drawstring bag.

"Put your hands behind your back, please."

She obeyed. A strip of tape was wound snugly
around her wrists, binding them.

"That's awfully tight." She tried to keep her
voice level, not to betray her mounting panic. "I
think it's cutting off my circulation."

"Well, I suppose that's what you get for being

such a bad girl. I don't take kindly to people using guns on me, Wendy. I don't take kindly to it at all." He pressed his mouth to her ear. "Better be glad I'm in love with you. Otherwise you could be in real trouble."

She made no reply.

"Now how about if I fix you that lunch I promised?" He thrust his fist in front of her face and worked his thumb like a mouth. "Sorright?"

She nodded weakly. "Sorright." The word came out like a cough.

Whistling, he busied himself with the preparations for their meal. Wendy sat in the chair and tugged uselessly at the tape, knowing there was no hope of working her hands free.

She'd been given one last chance, and she'd blown it.

No way out now. No escape.

29

Delgado drove fast, Lionel Robertson at his side. Hugging their tail was a second motor-pool sedan carrying Donna Wildman and Tom Gardner. Four black-and-whites loaded with eight patrol cops took up the rear.

The trip would be short; Rood's address was less than half a mile from the station.

"Right in our backyard," Delgado muttered as he steered the Caprice onto Nebraska Boulevard, heading west. "Right under our damn noses."

Robertson glanced at him. "You say something, Seb?"

"Never mind. Look, when we get there, I want you to cover the rear exit, if there is one. I'm going in through the front door with Wildman and Gardner."

"Right."

"Warrantless entry should be no problem, given the exigent circumstances. I thought about securing a Ramey warrant anyway—it would have taken ten minutes—but that's ten minutes more than I care to waste."

"Believe me, Seb, we're not going to have to kick this guy loose. You got him. You fucking *nailed* him."

"It's all circumstantial so far. We've established

a link between Rood and the four victims, but we've got no hard evidence."

"Just wait," Robertson said confidently.

They arrived at Rood's address. A group of teenage boys bouncing a basketball watched with mingled curiosity and suspicion as the eight uniformed cops and four plainclothes officers converged on the apartment complex. The U-shaped one-story building, its wood-shingle walls painted an unappealing shade of green, bracketed a courtyard of weed-tufted cement. In one of the units, a dog barked loudly and monotonously in a deep throaty voice.

According to Khouri, Rood lived in Apartment 2. It was not a corner unit. The occupant could escape only via the front or the rear.

Delgado sent Robertson and two patrol officers around to the back. A minute later his radio handset squawked with Robertson's transmission: "Glass sliding door opens onto a patio with a high brick wall. He could probably climb it."

"Stay there. I'll alert you just before we go in."

Delgado ordered the remaining six uniforms to fan out silently and position themselves on either side of Rood's front door. Then he drew his Beretta 9mm. Gardner and Wildman did the same.

"I hope you two have been logging some hours on the shooting range," he said, his mouth dry.

"That's why they call me Dead-Shot Donna," Wildman cracked. Nobody laughed.

Delgado keyed the transmit button on his radio. "Lionel. We're doing it."

"That's a roger."

He nodded to Gardner and Wildman. "Let's go."

Then he was moving up the front steps to the

door, throwing open the screen door, raising his foot to deliver a powerful kick to the lock—a second kick—the door popped open, and he was inside, Wildman and Gardner following, the three of them breathing in the smell of air freshener and disinfectant.

The apartment was dark, the windows curtained, but there was enough ambient light for Delgado to see that the living room was unoccupied.

They checked out the kitchen. Empty. Bathroom. Empty. Bedroom. Empty.

"Looks like nobody's home," Wildman whispered in a shaky voice.

Gardner swore.

Delgado was on the handset again. "Lionel, any activity out back?"

"Not a thing."

"Okay. The Gryphon has flown. Come around to the front."

He switched to the duplex setting and made a connection on Tac-4 with the West L.A. watch commander. Before leaving the station, he'd requested a Department of Motor Vehicles computer search to learn Rood's vehicle registration. The watch commander relayed the information, which Delgado jotted down. He was telescoping the handset's antenna when Robertson stepped into the living room.

"Lionel," Delgado said briskly, "I want you to take two officers and search the vicinity for a white sixty-three Ford Falcon." He recited the license number. "If it's around, you ought to find it within a radius of two blocks. There's no shortage of parking spaces in this neighborhood."

"Got you, Seb." Robertson hurried out.

Delgado looked at Wildman and Gardner. "The

three of us are going to toss this place. Quickly but thoroughly."

By unspoken agreement they checked out the kitchen first. Delgado tensed his body before opening the refrigerator door. He remembered Jeffrey Dahmer in Milwaukee, the things he had kept in the fridge among the leftovers and the jugs of milk.

But Franklin Rood was a different story, apparently. Delgado saw nothing unusual in either the refrigerator or the freezer compartment.

He told Gardner to explore the rest of the kitchen and sent Wildman to look at the bedroom. Then he set to work in the living room.

There was no dust anywhere, no dirt, no clutter. The place was immaculate, almost obsessively so.

Clay figurines were displayed around the room. Small, tidy sculptures of mythological subjects: centaurs, dragons, mermaids, unicorns, satyrs, the multiheaded Hydra, the cyclops Polyphemus, the Minotaur, the Roc, the Kraken. A clay menagerie.

No gryphons, though. Rood had found another use for them.

Near the TV was a stack of videotapes. Delgado loaded one into the machine and watched it for a few moments. A news report on the Gryphon. He saw himself delivering yesterday's statement to the press, and suddenly a picture came to him of Rood watching this tape, freezing the image, studying the face of his nemesis with hungry, hateful eyes. Delgado shut off the tape as a chill passed over him like a ghost's caress.

Nothing else in the living room was of interest. He entered the bedroom, passing under a chin-up bar screwed into the door frame, and found Wildman poring over a stack of bills and receipts.

"Found these in a desk drawer," she said. "Thought I could find some reference to another address, a second home. No luck."

On Rood's desk lay a chunk of red sandstone, presumably used as a paperweight. Delgado was reminded of the geode of agate on his own desk at work. The comparison disturbed him. He wanted nothing in common with the Gryphon.

He picked up the rock, wondering where Rood had gotten it. In the Mojave, most likely. Huge projections of sandstone could be seen out there, breaking the skin of the earth like the jagged spines of buried dinosaurs. Small pieces were constantly being chipped off by time or tools.

Wildman was searching the desk's bottom drawer. Delgado heard a sharp intake of breath. "Hey, Seb, look at this."

She pulled out a thick scrapbook and opened it. The book was crowded with newspaper and magazine clippings about the Gryphon's murder spree. But not the Gryphon alone; the earliest articles concerned miscellaneous murders and disappearances in Idaho, and later, in the L.A. area.

"Kathy Lutton," Delgado read aloud as Wildman flipped pages stiff with glue. "Georgia Grant. Lynn Peters. Stacy Brannon. Erin Thompson. Kelly Widmark. Carla Aguilar."

"He did all of them," Wildman muttered. "God *damn*."

The task force had suspected that the Gryphon had been responsible for some of those killings. Some, but not all.

"He's been a busy man," Delgado said softly.

His fists clenched briefly, then relaxed. No time for anger now. Later.

Beneath the scrapbook was a pile of papers. Wildman sifted through them. Photo spreads torn from magazines catering to those who enjoyed violent, sadistic pornography. Crude sketches of bound women subjected to elaborate tortures. A collage of photo cutouts—the heads of fashion models and actresses, neatly scissored at the base of the neck, glued to a sheet of black construction paper.

"Jesus Christ," she whispered, her shoulders hunching in an unconscious reaction.

Delgado let his gaze drift from the ugly images. Scanning the shelves of a bookcase, he saw titles on sculpture, criminology, and medieval torture. Among the books were copies of *Bulfinch's Mythology*, *The Golden Bough*, and *Alice's Adventures in Wonderland*. The Gryphon had been a character in *Alice*, hadn't he? Perhaps that was where Rood had gotten the idea.

The door of the bedroom closet had been yanked open during the initial search. Inside the closet Delgado found the mixing board Rood must have used to prepare the edited versions of the tapes. Stored with it was a collection of pop-music cassettes. Nothing else.

He left the bedroom and looked in the bathroom down the hall. The wastebasket under the sink contained evidence that Rood had bandaged his knife wound last night. That information was of no help to anyone now.

Finally Delgado found himself back in the living room with Gardner and Wildman.

"What have we learned?" he asked.

"That he's got another place," Wildman said immediately.

Gardner was skeptical. "How do we know that?"

"For one thing, the carpet doesn't match the fibers found at the crime scenes. Rood must have picked up those fibers someplace else. Someplace where he spends a lot of time."

"At work," Gardner said with a shrug.

Wildman shook her head. "No way. An upscale department store like Crane's wouldn't use cheap short-nap carpeting. It's more like something you'd find in a low-rent office—maybe someplace he's renting."

"And there's another thing," Delgado added before Gardner could reply. "Rood doesn't keep his trophies here. Since he's unlikely to throw them away, he must hide them at another location. A location that offers privacy—isolation or concealment."

"That could be anywhere," Gardner said.

Delgado sighed. "I'm afraid so."

A rap on the open door. Robertson was back. "No luck, Seb. Car's nowhere in sight."

That was no surprise. Delgado hadn't expected the Ford to be around. Presumably Rood had stored it in the alley near Sepulveda while using the stolen Dodge. Then he'd switched to the Falcon and driven Wendy to his hiding place.

He took a moment to gather his thoughts, then clapped his hands.

"All right, listen up. Donna, you're going to Crane's right now. Interview Mr. Khouri and all the employees who knew or worked with Franklin Rood. See if any of them ever heard Rood talk about a weekend getaway spot or a second home—anything that might give us some clue to where he's gone."

"I got you, Seb."

"Tom, go to that alley where the Dodge was found. Take two officers with you. Canvass the neighborhood, find out if anyone remembers seeing the Ford Falcon leave the area sometime after nine a.m. If we know what direction he was headed in, we may be able to narrow down the search."

Gardner nodded. "I'll check the locations near the freeway on-ramps too. Maybe somebody saw him get on."

"Do that. Lionel, it looks like you're off flower-shop duty for good. Now you're doing service-station duty. Make the rounds of the neighborhood gas stations and auto-repair shops. Ask the attendants and mechanics if they remember ever seeing the Ford. If any of them do, find out if the car has any identifiable features not found in the standard model—customized chrome or grillwork, dents, rust spots, special tires."

"Maybe the sucker's got steer horns on the hood and Old Glory flapping from the radio antenna," Robertson said. "I sure hope so."

"So do I."

Delgado left two uniforms to watch the apartment in case Rood returned, then walked back to his car, rubbing his head. Tired. He was so tired.

He tried to be an optimist. The '63 Falcon was a distinctive automobile, far easier to spot than one of the lookalike models produced by contemporary car manufacturers. The APB could yield results. Sure it could.

But he knew there was no substance to his hopes. L.A. was a city of cars, millions of them, crowding every street and freeway. The chances of finding any one vehicle, no matter how unusual, were remote.

In his fourteen years on the force, he had faced frustration many times; it went with the job. But he could not recall ever feeling this abjectly helpless.

Despite his best efforts, the Gryphon continued to elude him; and if Wendy was still alive, whatever time she might have left was rapidly slipping away.

30

In a corner of the trailer, the Gryphon was pouring Pepsi-Cola into two Styrofoam cups. He was still whistling cheerily. Wendy recognized the tune. It was that old Eagles song, the one that had been such a big hit for Linda Ronstadt. "Desperado."

Abruptly the whistling stopped. A moment later the Styrofoam cups were set down on the checkered tablecloth, followed by a handful of paper napkins and two picnic plates with sandwiches on them. Wendy tried not to look past the plates at the two jars, their contents lit by the candles' flickering glow.

The Gryphon settled into one of the folding chairs, facing her from across the table. Candlelight shimmered on his glasses. His eyes behind the lenses, flat and dead, reminded her oddly of the eyes of the two women in the jars.

"Lunch is served," he announced with a melodramatic flourish.

She gazed down at her sandwich. Two slices of white bread with some kind of brown goop overspilling the edges. Peanut butter, she realized. No jelly. Her eyes flicked to the cup of Pepsi. It had gone flat.

"Gee, this looks good," she said with whatever

conviction she could muster. Then she had an idea. Casually she added, "But, you know, I need my hands free in order to eat."

He merely smiled indulgently, the smile of a sage parent who has seen through a small child's pitifully obvious ploy.

"No, you don't, Wendy. I'll feed you myself." He picked up her sandwich and raised it to her mouth. "Open wide."

"Really, I don't think I—"

He wedged the sandwich between her jaws, silencing her. Reluctantly she took a bite. The peanut butter tasted like glue; the untoasted bread, slightly stale, had the texture and consistency of a sheaf of newsprint. The gluey, flavorless mixture turned to papier-mâché as she chewed.

"How about something to wash it down with?" he asked.

Without waiting for a reply, he lifted a cup and pressed it to her lips. Warm Pepsi flowed into her mouth. She tried to swallow, but the wet pulp of bread and peanut butter got in the way. She coughed, spitting soda on the floor.

"Can't," she gasped. "Can't do it."

He shook his head sadly. "I'm afraid you'll have to. That's what you get for being such a naughtykins. Now, come on, eat some more of your sandwich."

She looked at the jars again. The pale dead faces. The bloodless flesh.

"I guess I don't have much of an appetite right now," she said softly.

The Gryphon brushed aside the comment with an irritated wave of his hand. "Not long ago you told me you were starved. Anyway, I went to all the trouble of fixing you a nice lunch, and you

wouldn't want me to think of you as ungrateful.
Would you?"

"No." She sighed. "No, of course not."

"All right, then. So let's stop being stubborn
and eat our nice lunch. Here, I'll show you the
way." He lifted her sandwich. "This is the train."
With his other hand he gently pried her lips
apart. "And this is the tunnel." Slowly he guided
the sandwich toward her mouth. "Choo-choo.
Choo-choo."

Somehow she managed to consume the rest of
the sandwich. When she was done, the Gryphon
set to work on his own lunch. He ate quickly and
sloppily, smacking his lips, gulping when he
swallowed, draining his cup of Pepsi in a series
of slurps and gasps. Bread crumbs and droplets of
soda spotted the blue uniform. He didn't notice.

"You know," he said suddenly, speaking
through a last mouthful of Wonder Bread, "this
is nice, Wendy. It's a genuine pleasure sharing a
meal with a beautiful woman. I could get used to
it."

I couldn't, she thought. She said nothing.

"You've still got a little soda left. Want it?"

She didn't dare refuse. "Sure."

Again he tipped the cup to her mouth, but he
was clumsy this time; Pepsi spilled down her
chin, splashing the front of her blouse.

His tongue clucked. "Oh, dear."

He grabbed one of the paper napkins and
began mopping up the mess. His hand moved
over her chest, scrubbing briskly, then reached
her left breast and stopped there, motionless, like
some pale scorpion frozen in the instant before its
strike. Wendy sat rigid in her chair, watching as
his thick, meaty fingers slowly curled into a half-

fist. Through the blouse's thin fabric, he gripped the cup of her bra.

She felt a scream welling at the bottom of her throat. Her heart pounded in her ears, its beat so loud and insistent she was certain he could hear it too.

His fingers twitched. She thought of a corpse's hand, jolted by an electric shock. He began squeezing her breast with a slow, mechanical motion that was not a caress.

"I want you, Wendy," he breathed, his voice blurred.

The scream tugged at her vocal cords, fighting for release. She let out a long shuddering breath and tried to stay in control. Somehow she had to stay in control.

His hand went on contracting rhythmically, the fingers digging in, then relaxing, then digging in again. A farmer milking a cow.

"I told you we'd be lovers. Now we will be. And it will be good. So good."

Say something, she ordered herself. *Say something now, dammit, or else he's going to do it—oh, my God—he's really going to do it.*

When she spoke, her voice was flat and almost normal.

"Before we . . . go any further, don't you think we ought to . . . get to know each other better?"

"I already know everything I need to know about you."

"But I hardly know anything about you."

"There'll be time for that. Later."

The binding on her wrists seemed tighter than before. She couldn't feel her hands at all. Her head hummed. The sticky sweet residue of the peanut butter rose in her throat. She was going to be sick.

"But I wasn't expecting this to happen so soon," she said desperately. "You said . . . tonight."

"It's night somewhere in the world. I don't want to wait any longer, not another second. And deep down, neither do you."

She whimpered and tried not to lose her mind.

His hand released her breast. He gazed at her for a long moment, his expression blank and unreadable, and she looked back at him, past the two jars with their white staring faces.

Then slowly he smiled. An ugly humorless smile.

He rose from his chair and circled the table, closing in on her.

Help me, she thought. *Help me, somebody. Don't let him do this. I'd rather be dead. Oh, God, I'd rather be dead.*

He reached her side. His right hand snaked under her buttocks; his left hand crawled up her back, spider-quick. The chair dropped away as he lifted her in his arms.

She shut her eyes, not to see him leering down at her, breathing hard, his nostrils flaring, his tongue gliding over the tips of his teeth like an eel. But even in the darkness behind her closed eyelids, she could smell him, the cloying greasy smells of sweat and peanut butter.

He was walking. Carrying her across the trailer like a groom delivering his bride to their wedding-night bed. Above the roar of blood in her ears, she heard the thumps of his footsteps on the thin carpet, the staccato hiss of his breath. They were sounds that might be made by some large, antique machine, the kind with steam-driven pistons. Thump. Hiss. Thump. Hiss.

She felt herself descending, felt a soft foam pad yielding under her. The futon. He was putting her on the futon. Laying her supine with her bound hands pinned under her. Helpless. His toy to play with. His masturbatory fantasy, his life-size doll.

The scream rose a notch in her throat. She gritted her teeth and held it in.

When she opened her eyes, she saw him leaning over her, looking down from inches away. He wasn't smiling anymore. His face was grave, the muscles drawn taut with what might have been passion.

"I love you, Wendy." His voice was ash, was dust. "And you love me. I know you do."

Then his mouth was devouring hers. She tried to break free, could not. His tongue, so wet and soft and cold, probed her with the urgency of hunger. She tasted the gritty, food-flecked pickets of his teeth. Blasts of hot air from his nostrils singed her cheeks, her eyelashes.

The kiss went on and on. It was like drowning in stagnant water, like sinking into a quicksand pool, like going insane.

Hours later he released her mouth. He lowered his head and kissed her neck, his lips like leeches on her skin. Then he was tugging at her blouse, unbuttoning it with the clumsy eagerness of a child unwrapping a birthday present. The flaps parted, and the clay statue tumbled out of her pocket and fell to the floor. His hands fumbled with the strap of her bra, and then she lay half-naked before him, the small white cones of her breasts rising like snow hills against the looming backdrop of his face.

He planted moist sucking kisses on her cleavage, licking the smooth freckled skin, his tongue as rough and sandpapery as a dog's. He was making noises, gulping, gasping noises, feeding-animal sounds. His glasses slid down his sweat-slick nose. She squirmed beneath him, twisting her wrists, trying frantically to free her hands.

Then his mouth stretched wide and swallowed half her breast, and she flashed on a crazy moment of panic at the thought that his jaws would snap shut and rip the breast from her body like a chunk of butchered meat.

The last of her control deserted her. The scream she'd been struggling to contain surged forward, no longer to be denied; it climbed up her throat and escaped into the open, a long ululant wail of terror and protest. He didn't seem to hear it. He went on chewing, sucking, biting.

Finally his mouth pulled free. Her breast was streaked with saliva and measled with red tooth marks. It looked like something an animal had gnawed.

He raised his head. His face came into the light. With a small shock, Wendy saw the furious anger printed there. His teeth were grinding, the tendons of his jaws standing out like strands of piano wire. He knocked his glasses back into place with a swipe of his hand.

"Cut it out, Wendy," he said coldly. "Just cut it out right now."

She had no idea what he meant and no time to think about it. As she watched in trembling horror, his hand moved to his fly and unzipped it slowly.

Then she understood.

He had no erection. He was limp, flaccid. And he thought it was her fault.

"God damn you, cut it out!" he screamed.

She didn't answer. Couldn't.

He stroked himself, gently at first, then with increasing violence. One hand clutched her breast while the other pumped and jerked. Nothing happened. The pale rubbery thing in his fist did not respond.

Frustration made him still more savage. Snarling, he fell on her. His mouth fastened on her breast like a lamprey. He bit down painfully hard. She screamed, her head whipsawing wildly. He dug his teeth into the tender flesh, and this time she knew, she knew, she *knew* he really did want to tear the breast free and leave only a gushing cavity. She bucked and jackknifed under him, her legs bicycling uselessly.

She hated him. God, she hated him so much. She hoped somebody would hurt him this badly before he was through.

At last he released her breast. Blood streaked his teeth. Her blood. His glasses were hanging from his nose on a string of sweat. He flicked them off his face and tossed them aside.

"Fucking bitch," he whispered.

He got up. For a dizzy moment she hoped he might have given up for now. But no. He knelt on the floor beside the futon, then unbuckled his belt and tugged down his pants. His fist clutched her hair. He pulled her head roughly toward his crotch.

"Do it to me," he ordered.

She stared at his cock, still bloodless and empty. She imagined putting that gray lifeless thing inside her mouth. The thought made her gag.

"No," she whispered. "I won't."

He pushed her face into his groin. *"Do it!"*

She had no choice. If she didn't obey him, he would kill her. And even now, she wasn't ready to die. Even now.

Her lips parted. She accepted him. Though he had no erection, still he seemed huge to her, his manhood a grotesque slimy mass crowding her mouth like a second tongue. The hairy bush of his crotch, jammed against her face, reeked of stale sweat.

"Lick me."

She couldn't do it. She would vomit. Would die.

"Goddammit, I said *lick me!*"

Crying, she moved her tongue over him, hoping she was doing it right, having no way to know.

He remained limp and soft inside her. She knew now that nothing she did, nothing he could make her do, would bring him the sexual release he wanted.

He seemed to reach the same conclusion. Angrily he pulled free. She jerked her head away, coughing spit.

"What are you doing to me, you little whore?" he muttered. "What the hell are you doing?"

"Not . . . not doing anything."

"Liar!" He sprang upright, his pants sagging around his knees. "You think you can make me weak. Think you can steal my power. You're wrong, bitch. Very goddamned wrong."

He thrust his hands between her thighs and pulled her legs apart, then scrabbled at her underpants, shredding the thin fabric. She heard herself screaming. Then he was on top of her, mounting her, grinding his pelvis desperately, humping her like a dog. She felt him in her, the head of his cock tickling her sex, but still he wasn't swelling with the erection he needed. He would never reach a climax, never. And she was glad. No matter what he did to her afterward, no matter how awful his punishment might be, she was grateful that his semen would not bloom inside her body.

"Bitch!" he shouted again and again, as his legs pumped and his back arched and the silver shield on his shirt flashed in the candlelight. "Goddamned sexless *bitch!*"

Finally, in fury and shame and frustration, he withdrew. Wendy turned over on her side and retched dryly, tasting peanut butter and Pepsi and death.

When she looked up, she saw him standing over her, his belt buckled once more, his shirttail hanging out in disarray. He had retrieved his glasses and put them on. Rage colored his face.

"All right, Wendy. All right." He was nodding furiously, as if in agreement with something she'd said. "I guess it's *not* going to work out between us, after all. You can't say I didn't try. You can't say I didn't give you every possible chance to prove yourself worthy of me."

"I did . . . everything . . . you asked for. Everything."

His hand flew at her, and his knuckles cracked hard against her jaw.

"You did *nothing!*" He slapped her again. "You gave me *nothing!*" He planted his fist in her belly, and she doubled up in pain. "You *fucked* with me, you lying slut! You *fucked* with me! Playing your

evil tricks. Making me weak. Making me *weak*!"
He grabbed her hair and slammed her facedown
into the foam pad.

She waited for another blow. None came. Instead he backed away. Suddenly, inexplicably, his
voice was calm again. Calm and thoughtful and
almost sad.

"I guess I was wrong about you, wasn't I?" He
sighed. "You're not special. You're not my equal.
You're nothing but a dumb, frigid cunt, like all
the others. I've got no use for you now."

He looked at her, and she swallowed.

"Or at least," he whispered slowly, "I've got
no use for you . . . alive."

31

At eleven-thirty, half an hour after putting out an APB on Franklin Rood's 1963 Ford Falcon, Delgado received word of an almost definite sighting.

Patrol units had been advised to be particularly alert when cruising Sepulveda Boulevard, since Rood was believed to have switched cars in an alley near that street, one of the city's main north–south traffic corridors. When two Studio City patrol officers stopped in a Union 76 service station on Sepulveda to use the rest room, they asked the employees if any car resembling the Falcon had been seen there that morning. The answer was yes.

The attendant on duty at the full-service island said he'd filled the tank of a car matching the Falcon's description at approximately nine-thirty. Furthermore, he'd been told by the man in the passenger seat that the car was a 1963 model. Although he hadn't gotten a good look at the man, the attendant remembered the woman behind the wheel as attractive, blonde, and young-looking.

Five minutes after he'd heard the report, Delgado was speeding north on the San Diego Freeway. He wanted to interview the attendant personally in the hope of eliciting further details. More than that, he wanted—needed—to be in motion, to be active. It was the only way to combat the heavy, suffocating sense of helplessness that pressed down on him otherwise.

"I already told them everything," the young man in orange coveralls said with a shrug when Delgado got out of the car, flashing his badge.

"I know you did, sir, but if you don't mind, I'd like to go over it with you anyway."

Another shrug. "Sure. Okay. You must be awful interested in these people. They fugitives or bank robbers or something?"

Delgado led him into a corner of the lot, close to the rattle and roar of the service bay. "Not exactly. If the man in that car was who we think he was, then he kidnapped the woman you spoke with. It's possible he was holding her at gunpoint during your conversation."

"I didn't see any gun."

"He might have been concealing it. Did either he or the woman leave the car while they were here?"

"No. She paid me through the window. Never got out. Him neither." He brightened. "I get it. You figure he was keeping her inside, huh? With a gun in her back or something?"

"Possibly. Now, I'd like you to take a look at this photograph and tell me if this is the woman you saw."

Delgado removed a four-by-five black-and-white glossy from his pocket. The photo, taken from Jeffrey Pellman's house, showed Wendy smiling self-consciously, posed against a brick backdrop dappled with sun. Her hair was knotted in a bun, not loose as Delgado remembered it.

He waited while the attendant studied the

glossy. "Yeah," the young man said finally. "That's her."

"You're certain?"

"Sure am."

Delgado took back the photo. "Did you see which way the car went when it left the station?"

"I might have, but I can't remember now."

"But you think you did see it leave?"

"Yeah, but like I said, I don't remember for sure." A note of testiness crept into his voice. "We get a lot of business in here, man. Cars going in and out all day."

"All right." Delgado was not quite ready to drop that subject, but he decided to approach it from another angle. "What time did you service the car?"

"It was maybe nine-thirty. Little before, little after."

"Did you check the oil? The tires?"

"They didn't want me to. The lady just asked for a full tank. That's all."

"The bill was paid in cash. Correct?"

"Yes."

"And while you were making change, you talked briefly about the car, what year it had come out, what sort of condition it was in?"

"Uh-huh. I like old cars. They've got, you know, character."

"How would you describe the vehicle's condition?"

"Good. Real good, considering the model year."

"Anything wrong with it?"

"Some of the chrome had fallen off."

"Where?"

"On the sides."

"Rust? Dents?"

"No rust I could see. No dents either."

"Did you notice if the headlights or taillights worked?"

"He didn't have the headlights on. It was broad daylight. Taillights . . . um, yeah. I saw the brake lights flash when they pulled out."

Delgado was careful to show no reaction. "How about the turn signals? Did they work?"

"The right-hand one did. It was blinking."

"Where were you when you saw the turn signal?"

"Still at the pump."

"And the car was where? At that exit?" He pointed.

"No, the other one."

"So if the car used that exit and the right-hand signal flashed," Delgado said slowly, "then it must have turned north onto Sepulveda."

The attendant blinked. "Hey, I guess so. Jeez. I didn't even know I knew that."

"Well"—Delgado allowed himself a smile—"we both know it now."

He asked a few more questions but obtained no further information. After thanking the attendant, he returned to his car and radioed an update to Dispatch, informing them that Rood's vehicle, when last seen, had been heading north on Sepulveda near Magnolia Boulevard.

Then he left the service station, taking the same exit the Falcon had used, heading in the same direction.

As he drove, he scanned the wide thoroughfare. He knew there was no realistic possibility that he would see the Falcon parked at the curb or nosing into traffic from an intersecting street. He watched anyway, alert for any flash of chrome;

and as he did, he pondered the destination Franklin Rood might have had in mind.

He hadn't taken Wendy to his apartment. Why not? Presumably because the apartment offered too little privacy. Someone in the neighborhood might hear a woman's cries. He must have wanted to find a remote, secluded area, where he could do whatever he wished to his captive, with no chance of being seen or heard.

But then why had he gone to the San Fernando Valley, which was nearly as crowded as West L.A.? True, there were pocket parks scattered throughout the Valley, but on a sunny day they would be brightened with scampering children and their watchful parents. The Sepulveda Dam Recreation Area was large enough to provide places of concealment, but Rood had been within a few blocks of that park when he'd made Wendy pull into the service station. There was no reason to stop for gas, let alone to fill the tank, if he had only a short distance left to travel.

No, he must have had miles yet to cover. Miles of shapeless, urban sprawl—a grid of streets lined with shops, restaurants, office buildings, apartment complexes, and rows of stucco bungalows. Few isolated locations there.

But perhaps he had gone still farther north. Out of the Valley and . . . and into the desert.

Delgado remembered the sandstone paperweight in Rood's apartment. He tightened his grip on the steering wheel.

Rood must have picked up that rock in the Mojave.

Did he spend a lot of time out there? Was that where he kept his trophies?

He imagined the attraction a man like Rood

would feel for the desert—vast stretches of emptiness, of desolation and dust—no strangers' eyes watching him, no police cars patrolling the streets. A lonely place where he would be free to be himself.

It seemed right. Felt right.

The high Mojave was too big to survey by car. Fifty patrol units would not do the job fast enough. But an aerial surveillance was a different matter.

As he hooked left on Sherman Way and raced toward Van Nuys Airport, Delgado was already speaking into the microphone in his hand, requesting a helicopter.

32

Wendy lay on the futon for what seemed like many minutes while the Gryphon paced the trailer, talking to himself in a muttering undertone. She had no idea what he was saying and no desire to find out. She still struggled to free her hands, but the tape binding her wrists was thick and strong, and she couldn't work it loose.

Finally he approached her. She waited for him to begin whatever torture he had planned. But he merely stooped and picked up the statuette that had fallen from her pocket.

"The poor thing is chipped," he said sadly. "Broke one of its wings. That's a shame, isn't it, Wendy? A shame that such a beautiful thing could be damaged."

She watched as he carried the figurine to the card table and set it down gently. It lay there, recumbent, a tiny sphinx.

"Still," Rood whispered, "it's lost only a wing. Could be worse. Suppose its head had come off." His lips parted in a chilly, feral smile. "Wouldn't that have been a tragedy?"

He clapped his hands once.

"Get up."

She didn't move.

"You heard me," he said quietly.

"I'm not going to help you kill me."

"Sure you are. You're going to do exactly as I say." He tapped the butt of the holstered automatic. "Because if you don't, I'll shoot off your kneecaps. Bang. Bang. Then I'll still be free to do whatever I wish with you. So what will you have gained, besides unnecessary pain?"

"All right," she mumbled, defeated. With difficulty she climbed off the futon.

"Now come here."

She walked to the card table. Her unbuttoned blouse hung open, exposing her red raw breasts to his eyes.

The Gryphon turned one of the folding chairs sideways to face the shrouded cabinet. "Sit."

She obeyed.

"Very good. I've been considering how to do this, Wendy, and I've decided to put on a show for you. A very special show, one that means a great deal to me. I hope you enjoy it. It's the last entertainment you're ever going to have."

He tore a strip of cloth from his shirttail, then blindfolded her. She drew a sharp breath when the room disappeared from her view.

"Is that necessary?" she whispered.

"Humor me. I have a flair for the dramatic."

She heard him move away from the chair. Some stretch of time passed, filled with faint rustling sounds and circling footsteps and his low breathing. After that, silence. Silence and darkness.

Then from somewhere before her, a woman's voice, faint and whispery, rising in a trembling monotone like a furtive, frightened prayer.

"Please don't kill me. I don't . . . want to die. I'll do whatever you say . . ."

A second woman began to plead, joining the first.

"Of course I'm afraid of you. What kind of question is that? My God, who wouldn't be afraid?"

A third voice mingled with the others in an unreal chorus.

". . . never done anything to deserve this. It's not fair, not right, not right at all . . ."

Wendy felt the Gryphon's hands at the sides of her face. The blindfold was lifted. She gazed straight ahead.

The white sheet that had draped the cabinet was gone. In its place were four heads displayed in a neat row. Four pale staring faces, each in its own jar. One was Jennifer's, and one was Elizabeth Osborn's. The other two were new to her, but she knew them too; she'd seen their pictures in the newspaper after the Gryphon's first two kills. Julia Stern and . . . and Rebecca somebody. But those photographs had been of living women, young and vital and intelligent, women who bore only a passing resemblance to these surreal laboratory specimens, these freak-show exhibits with their bulging eyes and swollen tongues.

Every candle in the room had been extinguished, save two that had been placed on the cabinet. Their dim flickering glow trembled on the waxen features of the women in the jars.

But it was not the faces that held Wendy paralyzed with disbelieving horror. It was the voices.

Of the four women, Jennifer alone remained silent, speaking of her terror only with her wide staring eyes. The other three were pleading for mercy, whispering and moaning, their cries emanating—it seemed—directly from their open mouths.

". . . promised you'd let me go if I said those things." The words were spoken by Julia Stern, the first woman in line, a brunette with sharp, clear features that reflected the fear and indignation in her voice. "You *promised*. . . ."

"Reasons?" asked the redhead beside her, Rebecca somebody-or-other. Girlish freckles were scattered across her nose and cheeks. "Of course I have reasons to live." Dead Rebecca made a sound that might have been a laugh or a strangled sob. "For God's sake, I'm only thirty-one. . . ."

"And I want to get married again," Elizabeth Osborn said. "The first time didn't work out. I want to have a family before it's too late. What else? I want to travel. The Grand Canyon, the Rockies. There's so much out there, so much to see. . . ."

Speaking. They were speaking. Dead, but alive. Their spirits bottled along with their flesh.

Then Wendy's shock cleared, and she understood.

Behind the first three jars, nearly invisible in the dim wavering light, were pairs of detachable stereo speakers connected by long wires to the three cassette players on the nearest table.

Tape recordings. That was all the voices were. Recordings of the pleas and confessions the Gryphon had extorted from his victims before he'd pulled the circle of wire taut. Recordings that had been edited to remove the killer's own threats and lying promises, leaving only the voices of the dead.

". . . can't do this," Julia breathed. "You just *can't*."

Rebecca groaned. "I'm asking you . . . if you have any mercy . . . please . . ."

Elizabeth was sobbing. "I'll do anything, anything at all . . ."

He must have recorded what I said too, Wendy thought numbly. *When he has my head in a jar, he can make it talk. Can make me beg forever, beg and reveal my secret hopes. He'll sit here in this chair, and he'll listen to me babble about going to Santa Barbara and falling in love and wanting to live. And he'll laugh.*

A shudder rippled through her body and left her feeling ill and dizzy.

The voices grew louder and took on a tinny quality. She looked at the table where the cassette players were displayed. The Gryphon had moved over there. He was adjusting the volume controls and fiddling with the equalizers to boost the treble. Perhaps he fussed constantly with the knobs and levers, customizing each performance, raising the volume ever higher till the trailer rocked. No wonder he'd lined the walls with cork.

It occurred to her that she was hearing some of the same words for the second time. The tapes must have been spliced into loops. They would play forever, the agonies they preserved never to end.

". . . you're so powerful," Elizabeth whispered, "you're a god, more than a god, more than anything I've ever imagined . . ."

"Think of my baby," Julia moaned.

"You're going to kill me anyway," Rebecca said tonelessly. "I know you are."

Suddenly the Gryphon was laughing, a cheerless rasping sound. Wendy saw that he'd turned away from the cassette players and was watching her, thrilling at the horror that must be written on her face, drinking it in like blood.

"Well, what do you think, Wendy? Aren't they talented, my four beauties? Don't they put on a *wonderful* show?"

She looked at him, candlelight sparkling on the blank lenses of his glasses, and then at the pickled heads, gibbering and weeping, and suddenly she was shaking all over, shaking and wanting desperately to be anywhere but here, in this trailer in the desert, this den of death.

Desperately she twisted her wrists, still trying to loosen the tape that bound them. She lurched sideways in her chair, and her struggling hands banged the corner of the card table beside her. The table rattled. It was metal.

And the corner felt sharp.

"I do love to watch them, Wendy," the Gryphon said loudly, almost shouting to be heard over the keening voices. "Sometimes I come here at night and stay till dawn, when the batteries have drained and the tapes are playing at one-quarter speed. The happiest moments I've ever known have been spent here, in my special place, with my beautiful friends."

Carefully, hoping she would not be seen in the weak fluttery light, Wendy lifted the vinyl tablecloth and folded it back to expose the corner of the table. She touched it. Yes, it was sharp, all right. Sharp enough to cut through the tape binding her hands. If she had time.

She began to rub her wrists against the corner. Up and down. Up and down.

"Soon you'll join my friends, Wendy. You'll be one of them. I've got a jar all ready for you." The Gryphon went on laughing, laughing, while the dead women whimpered and groaned. "I'll put you in the place of honor. Just think of it, my dearest. Why, soon you'll be the star of the show!"

33

A Bell Jet Ranger helicopter, painted with the blue and white color scheme of the LAPD, swooped down on Van Nuys Airport less than three minutes after Delgado arrived. He was running toward it even before the skids touched the tarmac. Ducking under the overhead rotor, he climbed into the backseat behind the two Air Support Unit officers—pilot and observer—in the cockpit.

"Take me north!" he shouted over the engine roar. "To the Mojave!"

The pilot pulled up on the collective-pitch lever. Engine noise increased as the throttle opened. The airport shrank to a dark irregular stain, then glided away as the pilot's feet worked the yaw pedals to steer the chopper north.

"Follow the four-oh-five to the five," Delgado ordered, referring to the San Diego and Golden State freeways. "Give me all the speed you've got."

"Yes, sir."

Delgado looked out the side window, staring down at the wide white streak of the San Diego Freeway five hundred feet below. On either side of the freeway, the rooftops of shops and apartment buildings glided by, some darkened briefly by the copter's oblong shadow. Parking lots, open jewel cases at this height, glittered with shiny treasures that were cars. Lawns and public parks gleamed bright and fuzzy, squares of green velvet.

The chopper took less than ten minutes to reach city limits, where the Valley ended and the high desert began. Delgado spent the duration of the trip considering where best to look for Franklin Rood. The man might have gone anywhere, of course. Might have traveled fifty miles into the desert. Might still be driving, perhaps headed for Bakersfield or San Francisco—or the Canadian border, for that matter.

But Delgado didn't think so. If his assumptions were correct, Rood was going to a place already known to him, the place where he kept his trophies. Some secluded hideaway, close enough to be convenient, most likely on one of the back roads that snaked through the desert like trails traced by a restless finger in the dust.

He saw such a road running parallel to Route Five and decided to try it first.

"Fly over that route," he said, leaning into the cockpit and pointing. "At a lower altitude."

The pilot pulled the lever down, decreasing the pitch angle of the main rotor blades. The pale pink Mojave expanded as the helicopter began its descent.

Delgado accepted a pair of binoculars from the observer, then scanned the roadside, looking for a white car that resembled a Ford Falcon. He saw one old junker that intrigued him for a moment, but when the copter obligingly dipped still nearer to the ground, he shook his head.

Several other roads, some of them little better than dirt paths, branched off from the one they were following. At Delgado's order, the pilot showed him each in detail. The roads hugged the scalloped rims of canyons or meandered into the desert and dead-ended amid the cholla and bitterroot. Delgado saw nothing that looked like the car he sought.

"Let's try the Sierra Highway," he said. It was the next logical place to look.

There was little to see along the highway itself except a few isolated ranches and what appeared to be large sheds or cheap repair shops with metal roofs. The few vehicles parked here and there were all wrong.

Again Delgado tried the back roads. Scanning the first one that branched off the highway, he saw a horse ranch, a scatter of picnic tables at a campsite, and a young boy who gazed up at the helicopter, waving his arm in broad sweeps.

The chopper returned to the Sierra Highway and continued north. A second side road crawled into view like the dry tributary of a dead river. The pilot took it without the need for an order. Delgado peered down. He saw a graveyard of abandoned automobiles, a desolate ranch, and, not far ahead, the silvery shimmer of a trailer.

Near the trailer was a car. White. Not new.

Suddenly the back of his neck was warm.

"Lower," he said. The word came out so softly as to be nearly inaudible. He had to repeat it to make himself heard.

The copter descended.

"Don't hover. Pass by." He didn't want to make too much noise. Just in case.

The copter swept past the car. It was a Falcon. Delgado was sure of that.

But was it Franklin Rood's Falcon? He would have to read the license plate.

The observer glanced at him. "What now, Detective?"

"Set us down on the road about fifty yards from the trailer." Delgado touched the grip of his Beretta, simply to reassure himself that it was there. "I'm taking a closer look."

34

Wendy was sure the tape on her wrists was beginning to split. She needed only another minute or two, that was all, and she would be free. Then maybe somehow she could find a way to fight back. Maybe—

"I hope you've appreciated this wonderful performance, my dear." The Gryphon had turned away from the display on the cabinet and was smiling at her, smiling like a skull. "But now I think you've seen enough."

Oh, no, she thought with a chill of fear. *Not yet. Please, not yet.*

He crossed the room to the futon. Looking over her shoulder, she saw him kneel and reach into the drawstring bag, which had fallen on the floor during his ugly, pointless attempt at lovemaking.

From the bag he removed a hacksaw. The blade gleamed in the candlelight.

"Normally I wait until my victim is dead before taking my trophy." He circled around the card table with the hacksaw in his hands. "But not this time."

She tugged at the tape. It was partly worn through, but still it wouldn't yield.

"This time I intend to try a new technique. I'm

going to cut your head off while you're still alive."

He was coming toward her. Still smiling. His eyes dead.

"And I'm going to do it right now."

She had to free her hands or she was dead. She had to. Had to.

With a final desperate tug she ripped the tape apart, then sprang to her feet, facing him from a yard away. He stared at the torn black adhesive clinging to her wrists.

"You never quit, do you?" he breathed, the words almost swallowed in the confusion of voices from the stereo speakers. "Well, it makes no difference. I've got you now."

He advanced on her. She retreated. She backed into the cabinet. The two candles there, the only ones still lit, guttered fitfully. She grabbed the nearest one and thrust it at his face.

Blind him, a crazed inner voice was screaming, *burn out his damn dead eyes!*

But he was too quick. He dodged the flame, then swatted the candle from her hand. It hit the floor and went out.

She seized the one remaining candle and held it in front of her. Absurdly she thought of a movie heroine wielding a crucifix to ward off a vampire.

The Gryphon took another step toward her. He was laughing, enjoying her fear, savoring the pain he was soon to inflict. It was all a game to him, wasn't it? Torture, murder—a game. He'd used that very word in the alley. The women he killed were the unwilling contestants in that game, and their heads were the prizes he won.

Their heads . . .

Suddenly she saw a way to hurt him, really

hurt him, let him taste at least a hint of the suffering he'd caused.

With a sweep of her arm she sent the four jars sliding off the cabinet to shatter on the floor.

His laughter died in a hiccuping gasp. The sharp, biting odor of formaldehyde rose in the air. He stared aghast at the wreckage of his trophies, the pools of clear liquid soaking into the carpet, the four heads rolling amid the litter of glass shards.

"No," he whispered in disbelieving horror. The word trailed into a moan, then rose to a wail of pain that reminded her incongruously of a baby's cry.

His head jerked up. His eyes locked on hers. She stared at him past the leaping flame of the candle in her hand.

"You . . . you shit," he hissed. "You filthy, evil little *shit!*"

He tossed the hacksaw aside. Scrabbled at his holster. He would point and shoot. Couldn't miss at this range.

Unless he couldn't see.

With a puff of breath, she extinguished the candle.

Darkness.

She dropped to her knees, then crawled blindly, seeking a place to hide. The darkness was total, absolute. Even her own hands, groping inches from her face, were invisible.

The disembodied voices of the dead went on and on, still more eerie in the sudden unreal night.

". . . help me, somebody, please help, oh, God, please . . ."

"I'll do anything you say, anything . . ."

". . . want to live, that's all, don't you understand, *I want to live!*"

She kept crawling. Her breath came in ragged bursts. Could he locate her by the sound of her breathing? Maybe he already had. He might be right behind her. At any second she might feel his hand on her neck. Her body shivered with ghost sensations of his touch. She glanced around wildly and saw nothing but impenetrable blackness on all sides.

"I'll get you, Wendy," the Gryphon boomed from some indeterminate distance, not near, not far. "You can't escape."

He was right. He could flick his lighter and find her, or hunt her in the dark if he preferred.

She crawled faster, then collided with something—him—his legs—no, no, only the futon, that was all, keep calm now, try to stay in control.

Her hands scurried along the edge of the futon and discovered a lumpy, shapeless object lying near it. The drawstring bag. There might be a weapon inside. She rummaged in the bag, feeling its contents. A square of metal the size and thinness of a credit card. A wire hook. A plastic cylinder, perhaps four inches long, which she couldn't identify. She fumbled with it, and a beam snapped on, shining in her face, blinding her—a flashlight—some sort of lightweight, miniature flashlight—it was revealing her position—turn it off, Jesus, *turn it off!*

She twisted the top of the cylinder counterclockwise, and the beam winked out, and then three shots exploded, blue muzzle flashes cutting the darkness, and she was screaming.

35

Delgado jumped out of the helicopter even before it had set down on the road. He sprinted toward the Falcon. A yard away he stopped, read the license plate, and almost smiled.

Rood's car.

Drawing his Beretta, he approached the trailer. He wanted to make sure the door visible from this angle was the only exit before he went in. The two Air Support Unit officers would have to cover him. Like all flight officers, they were armed, and they would have been required to log time on street patrol.

As Delgado drew nearer, he became aware of faint, muffled sounds from inside the trailer. Voices? Perhaps.

A sudden loud pop, like a firecracker. Another. Another.

Gunshots.

A woman's scream, abruptly cut off.

Wendy's scream. He knew it. Rood was killing her. Killing her right now.

Then he was racing for the trailer door, his jacket flapping around him, shoes kicking up desert dust.

*　　*　　*

Rood knew exactly what had happened. Wendy had found his Tekna Micro-Lite in the canvas bag and turned it on without realizing what it was. That was why her face had appeared briefly in the gloom, a white circle lit by the beam. Then the light had vanished, and he'd aimed and fired three times in the direction of the blue image fast fading on his retinas.

He was fairly sure he'd hit her. He'd heard her sudden cry, a cry of either pain or fear. She was silent now. Dead, perhaps, or unconscious. Or, just possibly, unhurt and hiding.

He needed to see. Needed light. But how? He'd already checked his pockets and discovered that his cigarette lighter was missing. He must have put it down absent-mindedly on one of the tables. He couldn't find it now.

The door, then. Of course.

He would open the door and let in the sun.

Swiftly Rood moved toward the door, feeling his way. He hoped Wendy wasn't dead. He hoped he'd only wounded her. He wanted to take more time with the killing, wanted her to suffer, wanted to watch her eyes grow huge as he pressed the hacksaw's blade to her throat and began to stroke. That would be fun, such fun. Then, when she was dead, he would take her headless body and make it his. Yes, and take her head too. His manhood, swollen and empurpled, would slide into her screaming mouth and find release.

Let her try to rob him of his power then. Rood chuckled. Just let her try.

His questing hand slapped the door. He groped for the lever that controlled the dead bolt, found it, and retracted the bolt with a click. He turned the knob. The door swung open and daylight flooded in like water cascading through a burst dam, and a man was there.

He stood in the doorway, his tall figure outlined in an aureole of sun. Rood took a step back, staring at his face, at the jet-black hair swept back from his high forehead, at the sharp, hawklike nose, at the angry mouth bracketed by chiseled grooves.

He knew that face. He'd studied it in newspaper photos and on television newscasts. He'd memorized every detail.

"You," Rood said, his voice hushed.

Detective Sebastián Delgado nodded once. "Me."

Delgado had been poised to shoot off the locks securing the trailer door when suddenly the door opened from inside and he found himself facing a man in a police officer's uniform—a man with a gun held loosely in his hand, pointing down—a man who was, of course, Franklin Rood.

Shock held Rood paralyzed. He muttered one word, signifying recognition, and Delgado answered, confirming it, and then before Rood could react, before he had time to raise the gun hanging uselessly at his side, Delgado struck.

He lashed out with his pistol and whickered it across Rood's face, breaking off one stem of his glasses, then seized Rood's gun hand and twisted hard. Rood's fingers splayed, and the Beretta dropped from his grasp. Delgado spun him around, put him in a choke hold, and hauled him out of the trailer onto the landing of the iron staircase. Rood drove his elbow into Delgado's abdomen. Delgado took the blow without flinching, then shoved Rood head first down the stairs. He hit the ground on his side and tried to rise, but already Delgado was on top of him, slamming his face into the dirt again and again, then yanking Rood's hands roughly behind his back and pinning them there.

He fished a pair of handcuffs from his jacket pocket, snapped them on, and rolled Rood onto his back, hands manacled behind him. Rood gazed up at him, breathing hard. His eyes, half-concealed behind the glasses askew on his face, were small and gray and lifeless. They caught the sunlight, glittering colorlessly like flecks of pond scum.

A moment passed while the two men studied each other. Then slowly Rood smiled.

"The Gryphon claimed another victim, Detective," he whispered. "The loveliest one of all."

Delgado stiffened.

"Go in and see." It was the same taunting voice he'd heard on the tapes, the voice that had defied him to catch the Gryphon. "Go on."

Delgado raised his service pistol and tried to remind himself of all the reasons why he couldn't pull the trigger.

Then the Air Support Unit officers ran up, their weapons drawn.

"Cover him," Delgado snapped.

He turned and rushed up the stairs.

The voices he'd heard faintly from outside greeted him as he entered the trailer. He recognized them now. The voices of Julia Stern and Rebecca Morris and Elizabeth Osborn, which had spoken to him so many times, first on tape, then in the depths of dreams.

The interior of the trailer was a long narrow

space, dimly illuminated by the sun through the doorway. There was no other light. Delgado scanned the room and saw four round objects on the floor perhaps twenty feet from where he stood. Sudden fear clutched his stomach as he realized what they were.

Heads.

But Rood couldn't have taken Wendy's head, not if he'd shot her just moments ago. Unless he hadn't been shooting at her. The shots might have signified something else entirely.

There was only one way to know.

Tensely Delgado moved closer. He identified the heads one by one. Julia Stern, Rebecca Morris, Elizabeth Osborn. The fourth was turned face-down, her hair blondish in the uncertain light.

With the toe of his shoe he turned the head over, then relaxed slightly. The face was one he didn't recognize. Jennifer Kutzlow's face, perhaps.

"Wendy?" he called.

No answer.

He crept past the cabinet, avoiding the heads haloed in chemical puddles. On a small folding table, he saw three cassette players, their red diodes glowing to indicate that the power was on. He switched them off, and the voices fell silent. All but one, whimpering softly.

That voice was not on tape.

"Wendy?" he said again, hope and apprehension mingled in the word.

The sound was coming from the rear of the trailer, far from the sun. He moved through the deepening gloom, squinting. Then he saw her.

She was huddled behind a bookcase. She must have pulled it away from the wall to make a hiding place. Curled up in a tight fetal ball, her arms locked around her knees, she was shivering and crying. She didn't seem to know he was there.

"Wendy, it's all right now. We've got him."

She gave no reply.

He knelt by her and looked her over. He saw no blood, no sign that she'd been knifed or shot. If Rood had fired at her, he'd missed.

"Wendy. Talk to me."

Blinking, she looked up at him through a skein of hair. He saw that her blouse was open and her breasts had been badly bruised.

"Hello, Detective," she said with a note of surprise.

"Call me Sebastián."

"Yes. Yes, I'll do that."

She became aware of the tears streaking her face and wiped them away self-consciously.

"I was strong," she told him, as if in explanation or apology. "Really. Right up to the end. But I guess I . . . I just don't like the dark."

Delgado smiled. "Well, you're out of the dark now. Out of it for good."

36

"Franklin. Hey, Franklin. You ever fuck your mama?"

"Yeah, she suck you off, weirdo?"

"Bet you fucked her like you fucked them dead girls."

"Your mama ain't here to help you now, asshole."

"Nobody's here to help you, Gryphon."

"You're gonna have yourself a serious accident."

"Gonna die, Franklin. Baby-killer gonna die."

"Baby-killer gonna die!"

"Baby-killer gonna die!"

Scum. Rabble. Filth.

Rood sat on the cot in his cell, staring straight ahead, trying not to hear the voices of the caged animals around him, the chattering monkeys in this human zoo. He'd always despised the gutter garbage of humanity, the street trash, and now he was penned up with them, surrounded by their foul smells and coarse jokes and ugly, evil threats.

At first he couldn't understand why he'd been chosen as the focus of their collective hatred. Then gradually he'd come to realize that there was a kind of social hierarchy among prisoners. Rapists were very low on the scale, but lower still were murderers of women. And lowest of all, at the very bottom, were killers of pregnant women.

Mrs. Julia Stern had been pregnant.

"Franklin . . . Oh, Franklin . . ."

The big black convict in the adjacent cell always called him by his first name, pronouncing it in a girlish falsetto that contrasted sharply with the deep baritone of his normal speaking voice. It had taken Rood several days to realize that by saying the word in this way, the man was insinuating that Rood was a homosexual.

"You got yourself a real pretty set of choppers there, Franklin. But I figure to do a little dental work on you."

"*Es dentista!*" screeched one of the Hispanics farther down the row, laughing wildly.

"Gonna knock out all your damn teeth," the man went on, his voice slowing, deepening, as thick and dark as river mud. "So you ain't got nothing but gums. See?"

"*Ningunos dientes!*"

"And you know why, Franklin? I say, you know why, motherfucker?" He paused for dramatic effect. " 'Cause I like my pussy . . . smooth."

Rood gripped the edge of his bunk with both hands and tried not to be here. Not to know how close those animals were to him, and how powerless he felt, and how dirty this place was, how disgustingly unclean.

He had never really believed he would be imprisoned. Oh, he'd known that it was a possibility, but the thought had always seemed unreal and faintly absurd. And even if he had believed it, he never could have imagined that jail would be so much like . . . like school. Yet here he was, reliving the horrible nightmare of his childhood. Once again he was weak and helpless, abused by bullies and thugs, laughed at and insulted and scorned, his manhood questioned, his safety threatened. It was like being back in the locker room. His life had come full circle, a snake swallowing itself, and he'd returned to his beginnings, having accomplished nothing. Nothing.

Don't think like that, he told himself. *You're the Gryphon. You've got power. You've traveled a great distance, and you have much farther yet to go.*

Brave words. Brave, empty words.

Rood stared morosely at the bars of his private cell, the same bars he'd been studying for eleven days, ever since his incarceration on B row, the section of the Los Angeles County Jail reserved for the most dangerous or notorious offenders.

At first he'd found it terribly unjust that he would be held prisoner. It was a violation of his Constitutional rights, he'd been sure. After all, there had been no trial yet, not even a preliminary hearing—only an arraignment where he'd been summarily denied bail. He'd had no chance to defend himself, to tell his side of the story. It was all so outrageously unfair.

For several days he'd mused ruefully that it had been bad luck to call himself the Gryphon. That beast appeared in *Alice in Wonderland*; and now he seemed to have fallen down a rabbit hole himself, into some topsy-turvy world where the legal system functioned in accordance with the Queen of Hearts' nonsensical pronouncement: "Sentence first—verdict afterwards."

Then gradually he'd come to understand that his anger and indignation were wasted. It didn't matter when the preliminary hearing and trial were held. They would be only formalities in this

case. The verdict was a certainty. There was no
way out for him this time.

That was when he'd dismissed the court-
appointed attorney. No lawyer could blow a
smokescreen dense enough to cover the evidence
in his trailer or the testimony of the bitch.

The bitch. Yes. That was what she was, and
that was all she was. He no longer thought of her
as Wendy, let alone as Miss Alden. She was the
bitch. Period.

He still wanted her to die. He yearned for the
chance to kill her, to erase her from existence. He
dreamed of her death, fantasized it, obsessed on
it. Nothing else mattered to him, not food, not
freedom, not even his life. If he could kill her, he
would redeem himself. He would not have failed
after all. He would have won the game.

After what he'd heard this morning on the
radio, he craved revenge more than ever.

Many of the cells on the row, although not
Rood's, had radios. Rap, heavy metal, and maria-
chi competed with one another all day long like
blasts of gunfire. Rood hated all that noise. How
he longed for the pleasant pop music he used to
play in his car.

Occasional news updates interrupted the bar-
rage of unmelodious sounds. Many of the reports
were about him; the Gryphon, he sometimes
thought with a nostalgic touch of pride, was still
the city's major story.

A few hours earlier he'd overheard one such
report on a radio in an adjacent cell. The an-
nouncer recited some meaningless lines about the
preliminary hearing tomorrow and about Detective Delgado's continuing work on the case, then
added, "Delgado is rumored to have become ro-

mantically involved with Wendy Alden, the alleged serial killer's last intended victim."

Rood had felt hot, then cold, then hot again.

Romantically involved.

He was fucking her. That smug, smiling bastard. Fucking the bitch.

He pictured the two of them in bed together, gasping after the orgasm they'd shared. He saw the bitch comparing Detective Sebastián Delgado's mighty cock with Franklin Rood's puny, shriveled manhood. Heard her whispering that Rood had been unable to achieve even the beginnings of an erection with her. Heard them laughing, laughing at his impotence.

He had to stop that laughter. Had to. Had to.

But how?

"I love you, Franklin. You got such nice soft tits. I'm gonna marry you in the showers, man. We're gonna have a real nice wedding. And an even better honeymoon."

"Luna del miel!"

"You're gonna like that, ain't you, queerbait?"

Rood took off his glasses and wearily rubbed his eyes. The glasses had been badly damaged when Detective Delgado smacked him in the face. Fortunately both lenses, though scratched, were still intact; but the hinge that had attached the right temple to the front of the frame had broken off. Before Rood had posed for his mug shots, the photographer had inexpertly secured the temple with adhesive tape; but since then, the tape had kept coming loose.

"Yo, faggot! Answer the man!"

"What's the matter with you, Franklin? You deaf or something?"

"Shit, I don't think he even hears us."

At least, Rood thought, the temple itself hadn't cracked. It struck him as odd that the thin plastic would hold up better than the metal hinge.

"He's a nutcase, all right."

"Dead meat, what he is."

Mildly curious, he raised the glasses to the light. The black plastic, backlit, became translucent.

Suddenly his heart was beating fast. His old sense of power, of control, had returned.

"Look at that sucker. He's smiling, man! Like he's got a frigging hard-on or something!"

"Bet you he's thinking about them women he wasted."

"Nah, he's thinking about that little baby he snuffed."

"Too bad the baby-killer gonna die."

"Baby-killer gonna *die*!"

"*Baby-killer gonna die!*"

The chant continued. It was far away. Unimportant now.

Rood slipped his glasses back on.

37

Wendy gazed out the restaurant window at the daisy chains of spangles bobbing on the waters of the bay. Proud sloops and ketches, their white sails gleaming in the afternoon sun, glided behind shimmering curtains of sea gulls. Far in the distance, the misty humps of the Channel Islands broke the blue line of the horizon.

Santa Barbara, she thought in dreamy contentment. *It really is beautiful.*

Then, turning from the window to face the man seated across the table, she asked the question that had been nibbling at the corners of her mind all day.

"Sebastián, how did you know I'd always wanted to come here?"

Delgado didn't answer at once. With the meticulous care that seemed typical of him, he cut another piece of his swordfish steak, chewed it slowly, and washed it down with a sip of Dos Equis. Only then did he speak.

"When the Scientific Investigation Division searched Rood's apartment, they found an audiocassette—a homemade recording hidden in a stack of ordinary pop-music tapes. The recording he made when he ambushed you for the first time."

Slowly her hand rose to the tender white line on her throat that still marked the garrote's kiss. She remembered the voice of the Gryphon in her ear, demanding that she reveal her reasons for living. Her first response had been that she wanted to see Santa Barbara.

"Oh," she whispered. "I see."

She wished she hadn't asked. Less than two weeks had passed since the nightmare in the trailer, and the memories were still as sharp as glass. Although she'd returned to work, her concentration was poor. She ate little and found it difficult to read or even to watch television. She had trouble sleeping and often woke in the night to find herself slick with sweat, shivering all over.

The funerals hadn't helped, of course. There had been four of them in the week after her rescue. Jennifer, Jeffrey, Sanchez, and Porter had been returned to the earth as she watched.

Her phone rang incessantly with demands for interviews and offers of book deals, all of which she'd turned down. She and Delgado had become celebrities; even in Santa Barbara, ninety miles from L.A., they'd caught curious stares from shoppers and passersby.

But the worst legacy of her experience was her fear of the man sharing the table with her. She knew that Sebastián Delgado would not hurt her, that he was the opposite of Franklin Rood in every respect; yet she was irrationally afraid of his touch, of his body, of any reminder of the humiliation she'd suffered at Rood's hands. But Delgado was gentle and patient, and he seemed to understand. He was giving her time.

Today she hadn't thought of Rood at all until now. Everything had been perfect: the scenic drive up the coast—the hours spent exploring the quaint shopping plazas in Santa Barbara's downtown—the stroll through the Presidio Gardens—the climb to the top of the courthouse's clock tower, which offered a panoramic view of the city, a checkerboard of red tile roofs extending to the Santa Ynez Mountains, the palm-lined beaches, and the glittering bay.

It had been nearly three o'clock when they drove down State Street to Stearns Wharf and found a restaurant. Wendy hadn't even noticed she was hungry. She was too excited for hunger—excited, yet at the same time relaxed. She supposed that was what happiness felt like.

And now, in the middle of lunch, she'd had to raise the subject of the Gryphon and risk spoiling it all.

Delgado was watching her with his gray compassionate eyes. "I had to hear that tape, Wendy," he said softly. "Believe me, I didn't want to. I've heard more than enough recordings like it. But I had no choice."

"Of course." She managed a shrug. With effort she dug her fork into the shrimp salad before her. The fork, she noticed, was trembling. "I understand. It's evidence." A new thought struck her. "Will they have to play the tape at the trial?"

"Yes. If there is a trial. Perhaps he'll plead guilty and save us the trouble."

"You don't believe that."

"No."

"The hearing is tomorrow morning, isn't it?"

He nodded. "At ten-thirty."

"I'm glad I don't have to be there."

"You won't be in the same room with him again until you give your testimony."

"I hope they put him away for life."

"I'm sure they will."

She nodded. She could change the subject now. Part of her wanted to. But another part wanted to keep talking about Franklin Rood, as if conversation could exorcise the fears within her.

Franklin Rood, she thought with a touch of disbelief. She still couldn't get used to that name. So ordinary, so meaningless. Not the right name at all. To her, the killer would always be the Gryphon.

"What else did they find out about the . . . about Rood, when they searched his place?" she asked.

"Not too much. He videotaped all the TV reports about the murders, and he kept a scrapbook full of newspaper clippings. His neighbors described him as quiet and polite. That's what they always say."

"So you haven't learned anything new?"

Delgado took another sip of the dark foamy beer. "On the contrary. I've learned a great deal, but not from the things in his apartment."

"Tell me," she said quietly.

"Are you sure you want to hear it?"

She smiled. "No. But tell me anyway."

"All right."

It was Delgado's turn to gaze out the window. She watched his face in profile, his sharp features outlined in the shifting sun reflected off the water.

"Franklin Rood grew up in Idaho, in a small town near Twin Falls. He was not a product of poverty; as the only child of comfortably middle-class parents, he was raised in a nice home in a quiet, safe neighborhood. The Idaho authorities have located his parents, some of his teachers, and various other people who knew him through the years. From their statements, we've been able to piece together his past. He has no prior arrests, you know, no criminal record at all. But that doesn't mean he stayed out of trouble.

"He was physically weak throughout his childhood. At least Franklin himself seemed to believe that the problem was physical; no doctor ever found anything wrong with him other than a generalized malaise. His supposed infirmity made him the target of abuse from the other kids. He was bullied a lot. I don't have the impression that his parents or teachers understood what he was going through, or that they offered him much support. It must have been rough for the kid, I'll admit that. But no matter how difficult his childhood was, there was no excuse for the way he chose to strike back at the world around him.

"The first time Franklin killed anything, so far as anyone knows, was when he was nine years old. He took the family dog into the woods and tortured the animal till it died. His parents went looking for the dog and found its remains, horribly cut up. They had no idea their own son was responsible; only years later, in hindsight, did they realize the truth.

"Other pets disappeared from the neighborhood and were never found. It seems that Franklin was butchering animals on a regular basis. For a while the neighborhood was in a panic; people thought there was a maniac on the loose. And they were right; but they never suspected that the maniac in question was still in grade school, or that the first pet he'd killed was his own.

"At age eleven, Franklin invented a new game. He stole a can of gasoline from the garage and a book of matches from his father's bureau, then set fire to a neighbor's house."

"Jesus." Wendy gulped ice water from a frosted glass.

"The house sustained only minor damage, so a few days later Franklin tried again. That time he was caught in the act. His parents took him to a psychiatrist, but the boy was hostile and uncooperative, and therapy accomplished nothing. He didn't want to be helped. He saw nothing wrong in what he'd done. He'd felt like burning down somebody's house, and his feeling, his desire, was all that mattered. His only regret was that he'd failed.

"For a couple of years after that, he managed to avoid further trouble. His parents persuaded themselves that he'd overcome whatever impulses had plagued him. He had no friends, but he was a model student, earning excellent grades. In his spare time he read a great deal. Reading, it seems safe to say, provided him with a temporary escape from a world he found intolerable, a world he wanted only to wound and shock and, if possible, destroy.

"Then, when Franklin was in the tenth grade, his parents discovered a secret cache of women's underwear in his bedroom closet. They knew he must have stolen the stuff, probably by breaking into houses around town. When they confronted him with the evidence, he denied everything and became violent. They didn't pursue the matter. They were afraid of him. Afraid of what he might do."

"What did he want with the clothes?" Wendy asked.

"I think they were, in a sense, totems. Precursors of the so-called trophies or souvenirs he collected later—the ones in his trailer.

"After his high-school graduation, he continued living with his parents. He made no attempt to start college or find a job. He remained in that house, holed up in the room he'd grown up in, till he was twenty-two. That was when they finally threw him out."

"They got tired of supporting him, I suppose."

"There was more to it than that." Delgado hesitated. "Franklin's father was cleaning out the attic one day when he discovered a collection of specimen jars containing pieces of dead animals. Dogs, cats, squirrels, other things. Franklin had no job, but it seemed he did have a hobby. A hobby he'd purused in secret since he was nine years old.

"A few weeks after his parents cut him loose, their house mysteriously caught fire. Fortunately the flames were put out before any great harm was done. Arson was suspected, and everyone knew who was responsible, but there was no proof. Anyway, Franklin's parents couldn't stomach the thought of taking their own son to court. But for months afterward, they lived in fear of further retaliation. They were lucky; Franklin didn't bother them again. In fact, they heard nothing more about him until the news of his arrest in Los Angeles.

"The rest of the story is less clear, but the Idaho authorities have found a few people who remember a young man named Franklin Rood.

"Deprived of his parents' financial support, Rood took a variety of odd jobs, drifting from town to town, traversing the state of Idaho several times. Exactly what he was up to during that period may never be known. There are several murders or mysterious disappearances he may very well have had something to do with. He pasted clippings about them in his scrapbook, but he's admitted to nothing. I've attempted to interview him twice, and three other detectives have tried as well. He just sits and stares."

Wendy remembered those dull flat eyes, shark's eyes. She shivered. To dispel the image, she asked, "When did he move to L.A.?"

"A little more than two years ago, when he turned thirty."

"Why?"

"I don't know. Perhaps for the same reason so many people go to Hollywood: to become a star. L.A. is a media town, where any killer with a gimmick and a catchy name is guaranteed nationwide coverage. Clearly Rood craved publicity. He loved the news reports, the headlines, the panic his murder spree inspired. And L.A. is a big city, easy to get lost in. He may have felt he had less chance of being caught there than in a small town.

"Before he left Idaho, he appears to have come into some money—enough to permit the purchase of that storage trailer and the parcel of desert land. Our best guess as to the source of his sudden windfall is a rash of burglaries in the Pocatello area that occurred around that time. Rood, you remember, had experience in breaking and entering from his teenage years.

"With money in his pocket, he bought the Ford Falcon, drove to Los Angeles, and took an apartment on the Westside. He got a job at Crane's with the help of some false references that were never checked. Not long afterward he started making his clay sculptures. Then he became the Gryphon."

"In a strange way," Wendy said softly, "I can almost sympathize with him. I didn't have the greatest childhood either. And for a long time I thought I could never change, never grow, and I hated myself for that. I guess I hated the world too. Of course," she added, "I didn't take out my problems on other people."

Delgado nodded. "That's the difference. Nobody's blaming Rood for whatever private pain he suffered, only for the pain he caused. But we must blame him for that. We must not shrink from passing moral judgments. Not in a case like this. If we do, we only encourage more mayhem, more rampant violence, more Franklin Roods."

"And there will be more like him," Wendy whispered. "Many more. Won't there?"

Delgado sighed. "Yes. I'm afraid there will."

The two of them lingered in the restaurant over coffee and dessert. When they left at five-fifteen, the sun was sinking low in the sky. They strolled along West Beach to the yacht harbor and stood looking at the rows of pleasure craft tinted orange in the surreal light of late afternoon. The wind teased Wendy's hair and cast it streaming behind her, long and loose and unclipped, the way she always wore it now.

They said nothing for a long time. At last Wendy broke the silence.

"With the hearing tomorrow and so much else to do, I'm surprised you can take the time to"— *to be with me*, she was thinking—"to get away like this."

Delgado smiled, as if he'd heard the words she hadn't spoken.

"A couple of years ago," he said in a faraway voice, "there was a woman in my life. Her name was Karen. She loved me, but I never made time for her. My work always came first. And so I lost her." He looked at Wendy and smiled. "I've decided not to make the same mistake twice."

She felt the heat of blood in her cheeks and knew she was blushing. She wanted to turn her head, avoid his eyes, but she couldn't. His gaze held her.

Slowly, tentatively, he reached out and drew her close. An image flashed in her mind—Rood's face—and she almost pulled away, but then Delgado's lips were pressed lightly against hers, and the memory of Rood receded like a bad dream.

She let him kiss her. She felt no fear. She felt nothing but a sudden bouyant lightness, the wordless sense that she could float free of the earth like a helium balloon and fly and fly and fly.

And then she knew that she was healing, and that everything really would be all right.

38

Rood had no wristwatch—it had been taken from him along with all other personal items except his glasses—so he had no idea what time it was when the door of his cell opened on Monday morning. Two guards entered. At their command, he faced the rear wall and put his hands behind his back. He felt a pair of handcuffs snap into place. Click. Click.

When he turned to face the guards, one of them noticed that his glasses were now secured by only a single stem. The right temple, the one with the broken hinge, was missing.

"Hey, what happened to you, four-eyes?" a guard asked.

Rood just stared at him.

"Fuck that," the other guard said. "Let's get moving."

They hustled him out of the cell, then along the corridor to the elevator. Rood's heart was beating hard, but not with fear—never with fear. With energy. With power.

On the ground floor the guards transferred him to the custody of three deputies, stern square-shouldered men who wore gun belts and riot batons. They led him to a Department of Corrections cruiser parked in the underground garage.

The Los Angeles County Jail was located at 441
Bauchet Street in downtown L.A. The Criminal
Courts Building, where the hearing was to be
held, was several blocks away, on Temple Street,
between Spring Street and Broadway. The drive
would take at least five minutes.

Five seconds was all he would need.

He climbed into the rear of the cruiser. One of
the deputies slid in beside him. The other two sat
up front. A wire-mesh prisoner screen divided the
front and back seats.

The car left the garage through a gated exit. As
it crawled along Bauchet to Vignes Street, Rood
twisted slightly in his seat so that his manacled
hands were no longer within view of the deputy
beside him.

With his right hand, he reached underneath his
left sleeve.

His plan had formed whole in his mind yesterday afternoon, in the moment when he held his
glasses up to the light and saw the vein of flat-
tened steel running through the plastic temple.
The plastic had been molded around a thin blade
of metal for added sturdiness. It was this metal
stem, in fact, to which the broken hinge was
soldered.

Last night, once the lights were out and the
other convicts were snoring and muttering under
their blankets, he cracked open the plastic temple
in his powerful hands, then extricated the steel
blade. He scraped off clinging crumbs of plastic
with the heel of one of his black prison-issue
shoes, then carefully wedged the tip of the metal
stem under the heel and pulled up on the longer
end until it was bent at a ninety-degree angle.

For the rest of the night, he turned the metal

tool over and over in his hands, admiring it in
the dark. He was sure it would work. From his
readings on the art of locksmithing, he knew that
a handcuff lock was remarkably easy to pick. A
common locksmith's tool called a button hook
would do the job. And a button hook—crude but,
he believed, entirely adequate for his needs—was
what he'd just made.

As the cruiser continued west on Vignes, Rood's
questing fingers found the strip of adhesive tape,
formerly used to mend his glasses, which now
affixed the button hook to his left forearm. He
peeled off the tape and removed the tool.

Carefully, doing his best to betray no hint of
the subtle manipulations behind his back, he inserted the short end of the steel stem into the
keyhole of the left handcuff, then turned it.

Click.

The cuff was opened.

He was free.

The cruiser cut south onto a narrow side street
empty of traffic and people. A stop sign was just
ahead. Rood felt the car decelerate as the driver
eased his foot down on the brake.

Now.

He whipped his hands out from behind his
back. The handcuff on his right wrist was still
locked, the chain and the left cuff swinging with
it. The deputy beside him barely had time to pivot
in his seat before Rood smashed the empty handcuff into his face. The man's nose burst like a
snail. Rood grabbed at the gun in his holster, but
the deputy jerked away, shouting to his partners,
his own hand on the gun butt. The two men up
front were turning, drawing their revolvers.

Rood wrapped his arms around the deputy and

twisted the man roughly in front of his own body to shield himself. For a second time he swatted the cop hard in the face with the steel manacle. The deputy groaned and released his grip on the gun. Rood jerked it free.

The driver squeezed off a round, firing through the prisoner screen. The bullet impacted on the back of the seat inches from Rood's head. Rood lurched sideways, cocked the deputy's revolver, and jammed the muzzle up against the wire screen. He fired four times. The windshield was sprayed with red.

The deputy sharing the backseat with him moaned softly as Rood put the gun to his head and squeezed the trigger.

Then it was done. All three of them were dead.

Panting hard, Rood grabbed for a door handle, found none. The rear doors of the car could be opened only from the outside. He smashed the side window with the butt of the revolver, then reached through and fumbled the door open.

Swiftly he climbed out of the cruiser. The street was still empty. Someone might be watching from a window, but even so, it would take the cops awhile to piece together what had happened. Quite possibly nobody in the neighborhood had heard anything more than the repeated backfiring of a balky car; the cruiser's rolled-up windows would have muffled the gunshots.

Rood slipped behind the wheel, shoving the driver onto the lap of the dead man in the passenger seat. He laid his foot on the gas pedal, and the cruiser rocketed forward.

He heard himself laughing as he wiped blood off the windshield with the sleeve of his shirt.

It occurred to him that he could do whatever

he liked now. He could switch cars and drive to the Mexican border. Once on the other side, he could create a new identity for himself and start a new life. In time he could resume killing. There were many attractive young women in Mexico.

On the other hand, if he went through with the plan he had in mind, there would be no possibility of escape. He was certain to die.

But the bitch would die first.

Which mattered more to him? Ending her life—or preserving his own?

He considered the question carefully, and then, with full understanding of the consequences, he made his choice.

Parking at a curb, Rood unlocked the other handcuff, then ran to a pay phone, feeling terribly conspicuous in his blue overalls and prison grays. He leafed hurriedly through the directory hanging by the wire cord from the sheet-metal shelf. It took him less than thirty seconds to find the listing in the White Pages.

He smiled as he remembered driving the bitch down Santa Monica Boulevard in the stolen Dodge he'd passed off as an unmarked police car. As the towers of Century City glided by, she'd remarked, "I work there." He'd asked what sort of work she did. "I write informational booklets for an actuarial firm," she'd answered, then added helpfully, "Iver and Barnes."

He studied the company's address and memorized it.

A block away he pulled into an alley. He dumped the deputies' bodies on the pavement, then opened the trunk of the car. Inside, among the blankets and spare coats, he found a shotgun.

He hefted the gun. It was a Remington 870, a

12-gauge pump-action job fitted with a shoulder sling and pistol grip instead of a full buttstock. The magazine held five shells. Rood searched the interior of the trunk till he found two boxes of additional shells, twenty-five in each. The shells, he was pleased to see, were three-inch Magnums loaded with 00 buckshot. Powerful artillery, perfect for hunting deer or other large game.

He shrugged on a long raincoat from the trunk, stuffed the boxes of ammo in the deep pockets, and carried the shotgun with him as he slid back into the driver's seat. He sped off, heading toward Century City and the offices of Iver & Barnes.

Along the way he stopped at an art store in Hollywood. He pumped the Remington's action and released a spray of buckshot, laughing as the clerk and his customers dived to the floor. They gave him no trouble as he searched the shop and took a box of modeling clay.

He returned to the car and drove west, gripping the wheel with one hand, while with the other he wrested a hunk of clay from the package and shaped it with his quick, dexterous fingers. There was no time to put in detail or to get the proportions exactly right. Still, the object in his hand took form. Four stumps for legs, twin bulges for wings, a tapering projection for a head.

The clay was moist and soft; air would not harden it for hours, long after the bitch was dead. That was all right. The figure would stiffen as she did, the clay becoming rigid while rigor mortis crept through her body on a tray in the morgue.

Grinning, Rood placed the statue in his pocket. A last gift for his love.

At ten-forty-five by the cruiser's dashboard

clock, he turned onto the Avenue of the Stars and parked in a red zone directly outside the office building.

He took a deep breath and smiled. He knew he would die soon, but he was unafraid. He would play his last and greatest game, win against all odds, then perish in a firestorm of glory.

"And so," he whispered, "let the game begin."

Next he was running up the concrete staircase, taking the steps two at a time, then streaking across the wide concourse to the lobby doors. He threw open the doors and entered shooting. Two men in business suits went down in a duet of moans. The security guard at the desk danced. In the bank adjacent to the lobby somebody was screaming.

Rood scanned the lighted directory. The offices of Iver & Barnes were on the eighth floor. He leaned his fist on the elevator call button till he heard the chime. The double doors parted, and a small crowd of people stood there staring at him with sheep's eyes. He waved the shotgun at them, and they scattered, bleating in terror.

Boarding the elevator, he pressed the button marked 8. As he ascended, he was singing softly to himself. The song was "Desperado."

He had power. He was in control.

On the eighth floor the doors slid apart. He strode down the gray-carpeted corridor under tubes of fluorescent light, loading more shells into the magazine to replace those he'd expended in the lobby. The reception area of Iver & Barnes Consultants, Inc., was framed behind a wall of glass. Rood pushed open the door and pointed the shotgun directly at the woman behind the curved mahogany desk.

"Wendy Alden," he said quietly. "She in today?"

The woman's eyes were wide and unblinking. A voice buzzed from the receiver of the telephone clutched forgotten in her hand. "Yes."

"Where?"

"Communications."

"Where is that?"

She pointed feebly at a rear doorway. "End of the hall. On the left."

"Thank you very much," Rood said politely as he pulled the trigger once.

He left the reception area and entered the suite of offices, marching swiftly down the hall.

Wendy was at her desk working on a booklet for a chain of convenience stores when her telephone rang.

"Communications."

"Wendy"—the voice was Delgado's—"there may be a problem."

Cold. She was cold.

"Problem?" she echoed blankly.

"I'm at the courthouse. Rood hasn't shown up for the hearing. The jail can't establish contact with the deputies assigned to him. It's possible he got away somehow."

The chair under her was suddenly unsteady. She leaned her free hand on the desk to keep from falling.

"Wendy? Do you hear me?"

From down the hall, a sharp crack.

"Oh, Jesus," she whispered.

Another echoing report. Another.

Then . . . screams.

"He's here," she breathed into the receiver. "He's here, oh, my God, *he's here!*"

*   *   *

Rood strode briskly down the corridor, firing
into rooms at random. He hosed an empty office
and blew out the ceiling-to-floor windows in a
tinkling rain of glass. In the office next door he
found an executive in a three-piece suit screaming
hysterically into the telephone; a cloud of buckshot cut him in half.

His glasses, secured by only one stem, kept
threatening to ski off his nose. Impatiently he
knocked them back with a swipe of his knuckles.
He fished more shells out of his pocket and
thumbed them into the magazine, his movements
precise, controlled, efficient. He felt he could do
anything. He was flying.

From behind him came the report of a handgun.

He spun, sinking to a half-crouch. At the other
end of the hall, near the doorway to the reception
area, a security guard stood with legs splayed in
the classic firing stance, a .38 revolver in both
hands.

The guard fired again, the bullet kicking up a
spray of splinters from the doorframe near Rood's
head. Coolly Rood stared down the Remington's
twenty-inch barrel, fixing the guard in the front
and rear beads. One shot, and the guard's shirt
bloomed red. An abdominal wound, messy but
not fatal. Before Rood could fire again, the guard
took cover in an office, shooting wildly, bullets
flying in all directions. Finally his revolver clicked,
empty.

Rood sprinted for the office while the guard,
kneeling as if in prayer, his pants soaked scarlet,
frantically swung open the cylinder and dumped
the empty cartridge cases, then reached into the
ammo pouch of his gun belt. He was trying to

reload with shaking hands when Rood finished him with a shot to the head.

Easy.

Turning from the office doorway where the guard lay motionless in a burgundy pool, Rood jogged down the hall toward the door marked COMMUNICATIONS.

Delgado's voice was still buzzing on the line, but Wendy barely heard him. She dropped the phone and left her cubicle at a run.

The other writers were looking around in confusion. She had to get them out of the office. The only exit that didn't lead to the hall was the door to the stairwell.

"Everybody!" Her scream cut through the babble of voices. "The stairs. *Take the stairs!*"

She hustled them toward the red Exit sign. The gunshots were closer now.

"What's going on out there?" Monica was asking. Her black bangs flapped wildly. "Why are they screaming?"

"It's him, isn't it?" Kirsten shouted. "The Gryphon?"

Wendy nodded once and heard Monica moan.

They reached the stairwell and streamed through the doorway as Wendy hurried them along. Kirsten was last in line. She looked at Wendy, standing outside the door, making no move to follow.

"Come on!" Kirsten shouted.

Wendy shook her head. "It's me he's after. If I go with you, I'll get you all killed. And . . ." Another gunshot racketed down the hall. "And enough people have died for me already."

"Wendy—"

"*Go!*"

Kirsten went. The door banged shut behind her.

Then Wendy was alone in the room under the grid of fluorescent panels, with the deep, guttural coughs of gunfire closing in on her like the throaty growls of a hungry animal.

She ran toward the cubicles, thinking vaguely that she could hide in that maze of compartments, knowing her plan was hopeless, and then Franklin Rood rushed in through the open door, and his gaze swept the room and came to rest on her.

For a moment they both stood paralyzed, facing each other across a distance of thirty feet. Then Rood made a sound that might have been laughter.

"Got something for you, Wendy! Got a present for you!"

The shotgun bucked in his hands. She dived to the carpet, and the spray of shot whipped past her, cutting the windows at her back into a litter of jigsaw pieces. She snap-rolled behind the row of cubicles. Half-stumbling, half-crawling, she tried to outpace the hail of buckspot punching holes in the compartments' thin particleboard walls. The hinged units swayed and fell like card houses. Computers exploded in showers of pinwheeling sparks.

The gunfire grew louder, nearer. Rood was circling around to the rear of the cubicles, chasing her down. At any second he would turn the corner and have her in his sights.

She reached a narrow aisle between two rows of partitions and cut through it to the front of the room. The doorway to the hall was unguarded for the moment. She ran for it, gasping.

Then she was racing down the corridor toward

the reception area a million miles away. She wouldn't make it. Couldn't. Once Rood realized she'd eluded him, he would be after her again. He needed only one clear shot.

A blurred shape came up fast and nearly tripped her. She looked down and saw the body of a security guard sprawled in an office doorway. A revolver lay beside him, its cylinder open, a scatter of .38 cartridges near his outstretched fingers.

She stooped, grabbed the revolver and a handful of cartridges, and then gunfire boomed behind her.

She vaulted the guard's body and landed on one knee inside the office. She twisted to her feet and looked around. The office was small and empty save for a dead man in a business suit slumped over his desk, facedown on a blotter soaking up Rorschach patterns of blood. She recognized him—he was named Brady, and he'd had something to do with client relations—but she had no time to think about that now.

There was no way out other than the door to the hall. She would have to make her stand here. At least she had a gun, but, oh, God, such a little gun, no match for that cannon of Rood's. She looked at the cartridges in her hand. Three. That was all she'd had time to snatch. She tamped the rounds into the chambers, leaving three of the charge holes empty, and snapped the cylinder shut.

To have any hope of fighting back, she would have to ambush Rood somehow. She looked around and saw nowhere to hide except the obvious places. Inside the closet. Behind the desk. She looked up at the flourescent lights, the checker-board of acoustic ceiling panels.

Then she knew what she had to do.

Jamming the revolver into the waistband of her skirt, she climbed onto the desk.

Rood stopped a few yards from the office door-way. The bitch had a gun; he'd seen her grab it. He had to be cautious, very cautious. It would hardly be fair if he lost the game now.

He fed more shells into the magazine, worked the slide handle once, then crept toward the open door. Hugged the doorframe. Listened. Heard nothing, nothing anywhere, except some anony-mous victim's distant, dying moans.

With a high, warbling yell he pivoted into the doorway, straddling the dead guard, and opened fire.

The office window vanished in a haze of spar-kling dust. A geyser of glass and mineral water erupted from what had been a water cooler. Rood blasted the desk, hoping the bitch was concealed behind it. The dead man was thrown upright as if shocked awake. His swivel chair spun gaily, and his necktie flapped like a dog's lolling tongue.

Rood fired till the gun was empty, then stepped back and reloaded. Warily he entered the office, turning in a full circle. He saw a closet door and punched a gaping hole in it with another burst of buckshot. Then he kicked in the door and peered inside. The bitch wasn't there.

Behind the desk, then. That was where she'd hidden.

He circled the desk, booting the swivel chair out of his way.

She wasn't there either.

But it didn't make sense. He'd seen her take cover in this room, and he hadn't seen her leave. She had to be here someplace, dammit, simply had to be.

It had taken Wendy only a few seconds to push one of the large two-by-three ceiling panels out of its frame, then grab hold of the wooden beam behind it and hoist herself off the desk. There was a bad moment when she was sure she couldn't do it, couldn't pull her body all the way up. Then a fresh jolt of adrenaline recharged her muscles. Grunting with strain, she hauled herself onto the beam and lay flat on her stomach. She slid the panel back into place, leaving a narrow aperture to see through.

Seconds later Rood was demolishing the room. Glass and noise everywhere. She tugged the gun free of her waistband and held it in two shaking hands, the hammer cocked, muzzle pointing through the slot. She wanted to fire, but she didn't trust her aim; she had to wait till he was closer.

Finally he seemed satisfied that he'd killed her. He looked first in the closet, then behind the desk. He shook his head slowly.

As she watched, he moved to the front of the desk, still glancing around, his head tilted quizzically.

He was almost directly beneath her. She would never have a better opportunity.

Do it, she ordered.

She took a breath, gritted her teeth, and squeezed the trigger.

Click.

The gun hadn't fired.

An empty chamber—*oh, Jesus*—she'd hit one of the empty chambers.

Rood heard the faint metallic click and whirled. He stared up at the gap between two of the ceiling panels and saw the gun barrel poking out, the suggestion of a pale face behind it.

She was above him, the bitch, the fucking *bitch*. He raised the shotgun.

Wendy saw the shotgun come up fast. She pumped the trigger a second time.

Click.

Come on, *come on*!

She had time for one more try.

Her index finger flexed once.

The shock of recoil nearly threw her off the beam. The gunshot rang in her ears like an explosion. Rood staggered, blood blossoming on his chest.

She fired again. Another bullet slammed into Rood's chest and sent him reeling back. He collapsed on the floor, the shotgun flying from his grasp to boomerang into a corner, and then he just lay there, his glasses canted at a ridiculous angle, groaning and rolling his head from side to side like a child in the throes of a nightmare.

His raincoat fell open. Tucked in an inside pocket was a small clay gryphon.

Rood lay on his back, breathing hard. He tried to rise, couldn't. The bitch had won this game, God damn her, and now there was nothing in his private universe but pain, and he found he didn't like pain very much when it was his own.

The ceiling panel was kicked loose, and a moment later Wendy dropped down onto the desk. She hopped off and stood looming over him. The wind from the shattered window tossed her hair.

She aimed the revolver at him with both hands. The hammer snapped back.

"No," Rood whispered, forcing speech like paste through frozen lips. "Don't."

"Why not?" Her voice was ice. "Give me one reason."

He could think of no reasons, none at all, except that he couldn't die this way, as the loser of the contest, as a failure. A failure.

"Please," he moaned, hating to beg but afraid not to.

"I'll tell you what." She was smiling now, a smile like knives. "I may not shoot you again. I may let you live . . . if you'll say some words for me. Some very special words. Will you?"

Fury seized him. This was his game she was playing. His ritual, not hers.

He almost refused. Almost told the bitch to go to hell.

Then dimly he became aware of sirens blaring in the distance. And he knew he had to go along, because if he could hold her off a little longer, the police would be here, and she couldn't kill him then.

"All right," he croaked.

"You're most cooperative, Mr. Rood. I like that. Your chances of surviving this rendezvous are improving all the time. Now repeat after me: I have no power."

"I have"—he winced as something tightened up inside him—"no power."

"I'm not a god."

"I'm not . . . not . . ." The words were hard to say. His tongue wouldn't work right. He swallowed and tried again, tasting copper at the back of his mouth. "Not a . . . god."

"I'm nothing. Nothing at all."

A spasm rippled through his body. He coughed. Blood bubbled down his chin.

"I . . . I'm . . ."

His head reeled. The floor seemed strangely spongy, and he was sinking into it while the ceiling receded, the walls moving apart, everything turning white with an unreal shine. He closed his eyes, going away, not wanting to be here, not wanting to recite any more of these lies. If they were lies. Of course they were. They had to be. Had to be . . .

Abruptly something cold was pressed to his forehead. The gun, its muzzle chilly against his skin. Blinking alert, he saw the bitch leaning close to him, her face horrible to see, lips skinned back in a feral smile, eyes bright with fever.

"Say it," she commanded.

With a last trembling effort, he obeyed.

"I'm . . . nothing. Nothing. Nothing."

Life and strength and energy drained out of him. He was weak, so weak. Weak and helpless. And he was . . . He was . . .

"Nothing," he said again, but he barely heard his own voice over the rising hum in his brain.

A moment later he no longer heard even that.

Wendy watched Rood's chest rise and fall once more, and then his breath stopped and his wide, glassy eyes were staring not at her but at whatever it is the dead see.

His autopsy, she knew, would conclude that the cause of death had been two gunshots to the upper body. But the autopsy would be wrong.

Saying those words had killed the Gryphon.

Epilogue

A cold wind kicked up a swirl of snow, misting the windshield, as Wendy steered her car through the wrought-iron gates of the cemetery.

It had taken her all of yesterday and most of today to drive here, to this graveyard on the outskirts of a small town in Idaho. Delgado had offered to go with her, but she'd felt the need to make this pilgrimage alone. He had seemed to understand; and that was strange, because she wasn't sure she understood it herself.

Franklin Rood was dead. She knew that. She had shot him and watched him die. She had seen his body zipped into a plastic bag and wheeled away on a gurney. And yet at times she'd found herself wondering if his last spree of violence had been merely a vivid fantasy. There were nights when she woke up short of breath, having been chased through corridors of dreams by a man with a knife or a shotgun, a man whose glasses flashed with amber light. And whenever a prison break or a manhunt was reported on the news, she would think: *He's loose, he got out of jail, he's after me again.*

Many times in the seven months since Rood's death, she had visited the graves of his victims, often laying flowers there. But she had never stood before Rood's grave. And gradually she had come to realize that she would be free of him only once she had seen where he lay buried.

Early yesterday morning she had started out from L.A., heading northeast on Interstate 15. She had made good time racing through the desolate stretches of the Mojave and the sagebrush desert of Nevada. Then last night, as she slept in a motel outside Cedar City, Utah, a blizzard had hit, the first of the winter, icing the roads. The rough driving conditions had slowed her progress today, delaying her arrival until evening. As she guided her Honda along the narrow lane winding like a dry streambed among rows of marble headstones and bronze markers, the last of the sun was vanishing behind the bare skeletons of trees, leaving the bleached earth brighter than the sky.

From newspaper accounts of the funeral, Wendy knew where to find Rood's burial plot. It lay far from the other grave sites, on a lonely hill unsheltered by trees and unshielded from the wind.

She parked at the foot of the hill, got out of the car, and trudged up the whitened slope, trailing plumes of frosty breath. She came up short before the grave marker half-hidden in the snow.

Crisp letters were carved in the polished marble, spelling out two words: FRANKLIN ROOD.

Wendy looked at that name for a long time. Then slowly she stripped off her gloves, reached into the pocket of her coat, and removed the last clay gryphon.

She had taken the statuette from Rood's body, the clay still soft and pliant, and hidden it on her person only moments before the police arrived. At the time she hadn't known quite why she wanted it, except that, after all, it had been meant for her.

Thoughtfully she turned the model between her fingers, studying the crude suggestions of beak, wings, and claws. The clay was hard and brittle now, dusty and dry, reminding her of old bone.

Wendy brought her hands together, pressing the statue between her palms. She twisted her wrists in a slow grinding motion, crushing the gryphon to powder, to dust. She thought of Jeffrey, of Jennifer, of Sanchez and Porter, of Elizabeth Osborn and Rebecca Morris and Julia Stern. She thought of Kathy Lutton, a waitress in Twin Falls who had been Rood's first victim, and of the other women he had killed before he became the Gryphon. She thought of the deputies, the security guards, the random office workers—all the people whose lives had ended in his final, pointless rampage. She mourned for them, for every one of his victims.

Opening her hands, she let the dry flakes of the crumbled statue settle like ashes on the grave.

"It's done now," she whispered. "It's finished."

As she walked down the hill to her car, she knew Rood would not haunt her any longer.

At the gates she parked and got out to take a last look at the cemetery. Even from a distance the solitary headstone was visible, high on the hillside in the drifted snow, alone in the gathering darkness.

She gazed at the small monument that stood over Franklin Rood's grave, the grave to which his every choice had led him. She went on looking at it until the twilight had deepened and the stone was lost to sight.

Then she climbed back into her car, pulled

through the gates, and retraced the route she'd traveled, gliding past frozen fields and leafless trees under the cold, friendless stars. The dark back roads were poorly marked, the signposts hidden in shadows, and as she searched for the highway that would take her home, Wendy got lost several times.

It was late, but not too late, when she finally found her way.